DREAMJUMPER

BY GREG GRUNBERG & LUCAS TURNBLOOM

COLOR BY GUY MAJOR

BOOK ONE
NIGHTMARE ESCAPE

graphix

An Imprint of

SCHOLASTIC

Love and more love to my amazing wife, Elizabeth, and my three awesome
sons, whose little nightmares over the years inspired all of this.
—Greg

For my loving wife, Suzanne, for her encouragement
and patience. My two little boys, for their inspiration. And my
parents, brother, and sister for their support.
—Lucas

Text copyright © 2016 by Greg Grunberg and Lucas Turnbloom
Illustrations copyright © 2016 by Lucas Turnbloom

All rights reserved. Published by Graphix, an imprint of Scholastic Inc.,
Publishers since 1920. SCHOLASTIC, GRAPHIX, and associated logos are
trademarks and/or registered trademarks of Scholastic Inc.

Library of Congress Control Number: 2016931133

ISBN 978-0-545-82603-7 (hardcover)
ISBN 978-0-545-82604-4 (paperback)

10 9 8 7 6 5 4 3 2 1   16 17 18 19 20

Printed in China   62
First edition, July 2016
Edited by Adam Rau
Book design by Phil Falco
Creative Director: David Saylor

Dreams are a daily miracle.

We are all transported, as soon as we drift off to sleep, to somewhere else. A place we don't choose to go, with confrontations we can't predict. We may live in a technologically advanced age, but exactly how dreams work, why they happen, and what they mean, no one really knows.

A dream may enlighten, amuse, confuse, or terrify. And while some experience dreams more vividly, or recall them with more detail than others, we are all vulnerable to the whims of our subconscious.

Where will our dreams take us tonight? How will we handle it? And what if we can't? Dreams, after all, can become nightmares.

In this imaginative and exciting book, Greg Grunberg and Lucas Turnbloom explore the possibilities of this daily miracle, and in doing so create a new hero: the Dream Jumper. I don't want to ruin anything—the fact that you're holding this book right now gives me a pretty good idea that you intend to read it—but I will say that it's a great ride. One I'm especially excited about because I've known Greg for a long time. Longer than I'd care to admit. Long enough that I remember being in first grade with him and ordering Scholastic books together. So now he's worked on one of his own, and I'm happy for him and for Lucas. And for you, because you're about to dive into a world of adventure and discovery, where, like dreams themselves, anything is possible.

Enjoy!

J. J. Abrams is the director of *Star Wars: The Force Awakens*. He is also a director, producer, and writer known for the TV show *Lost* as well as the movies *Mission: Impossible III* and the most recent Star Trek series.

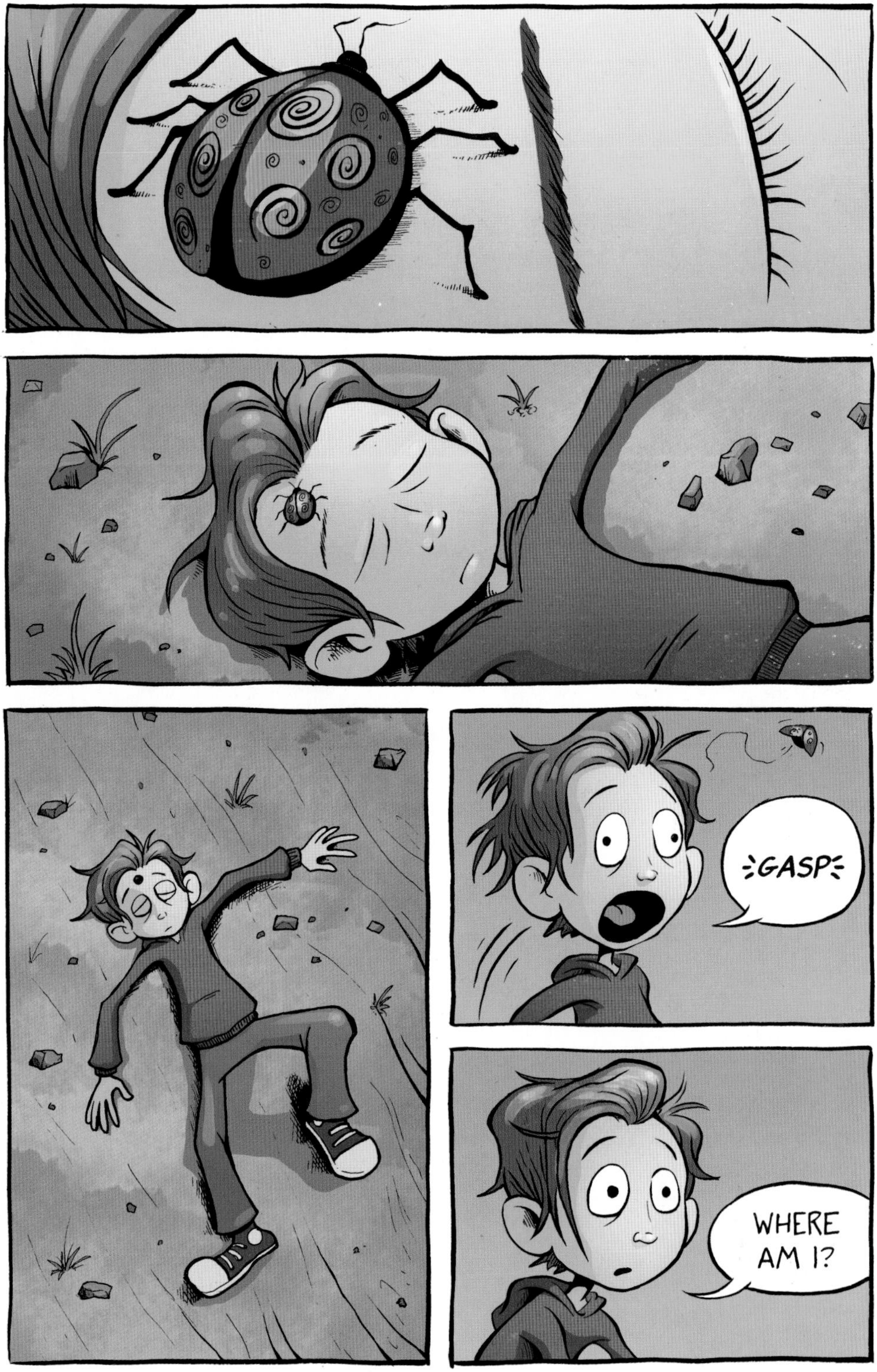
GASP
WHERE AM I?

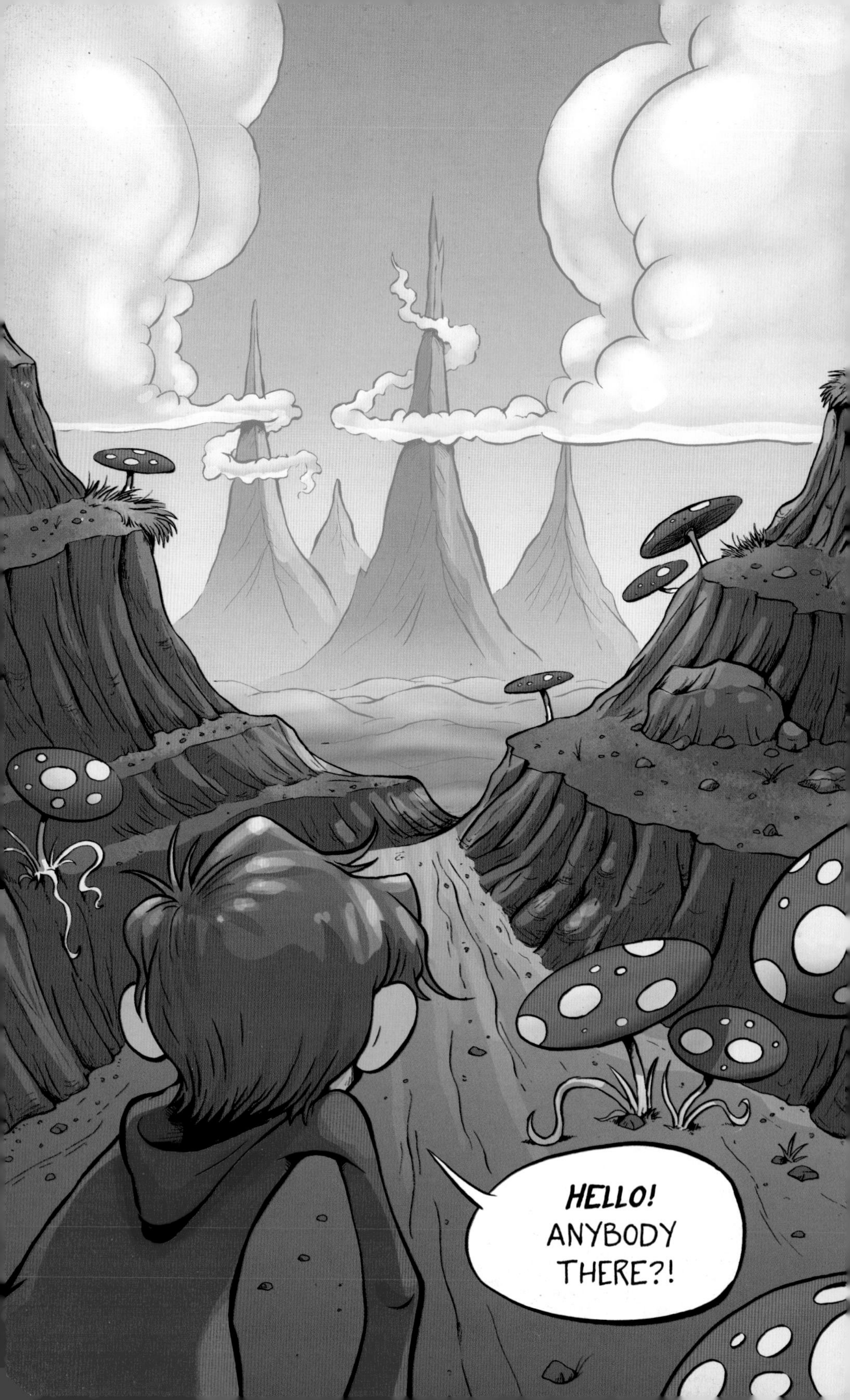
HELLO! ANYBODY THERE?!

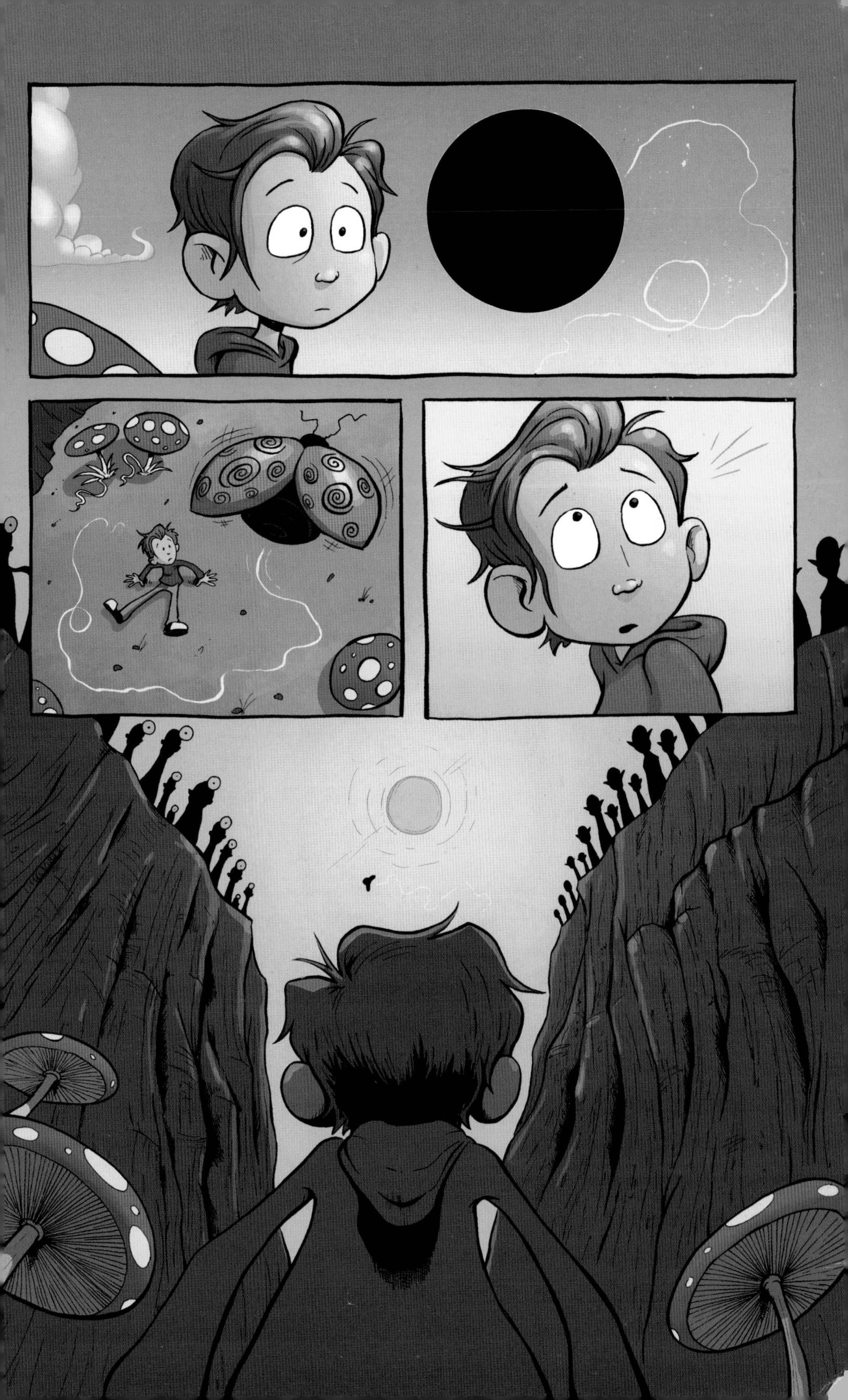

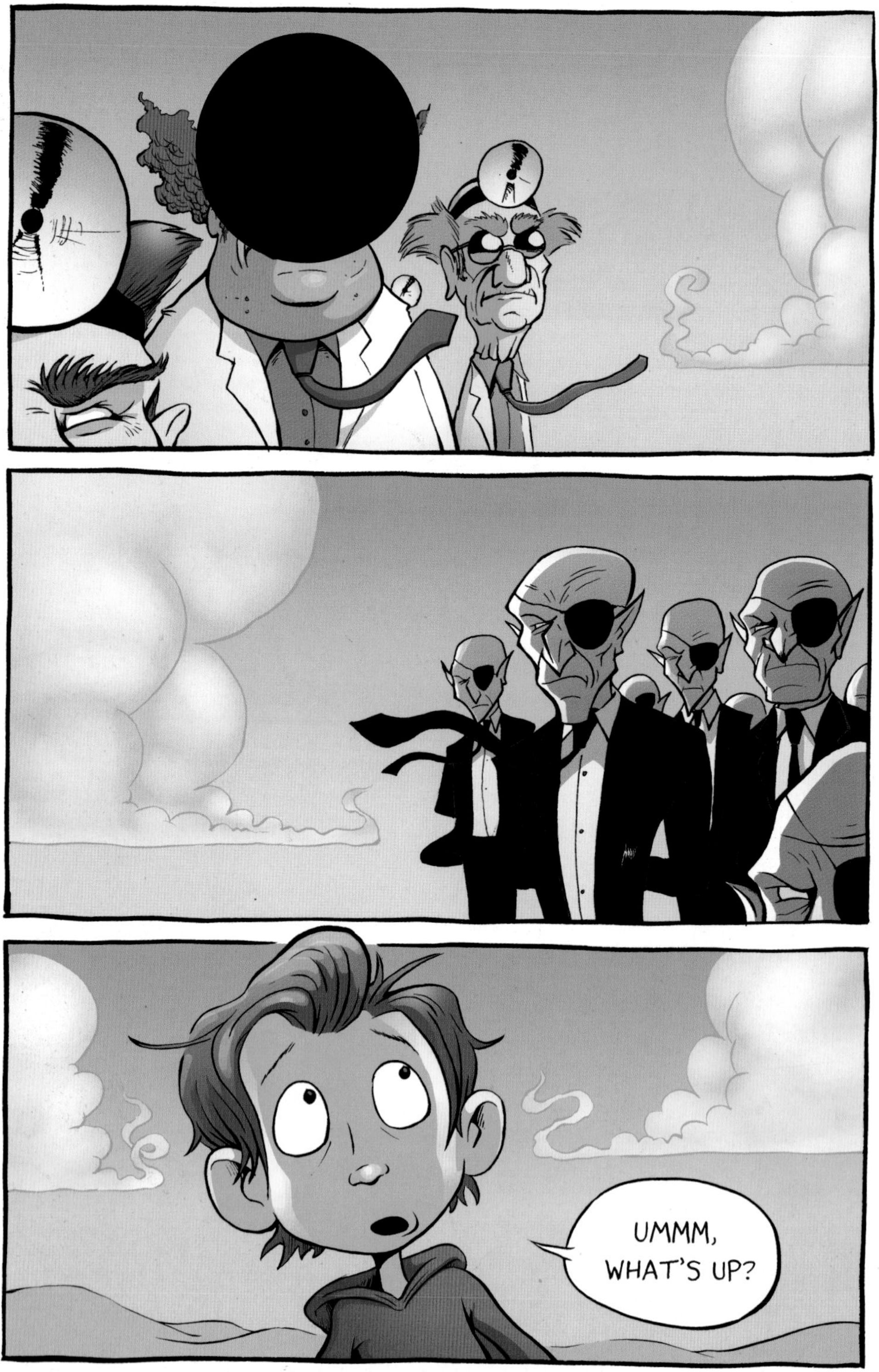
UMMM,
WHAT'S UP?

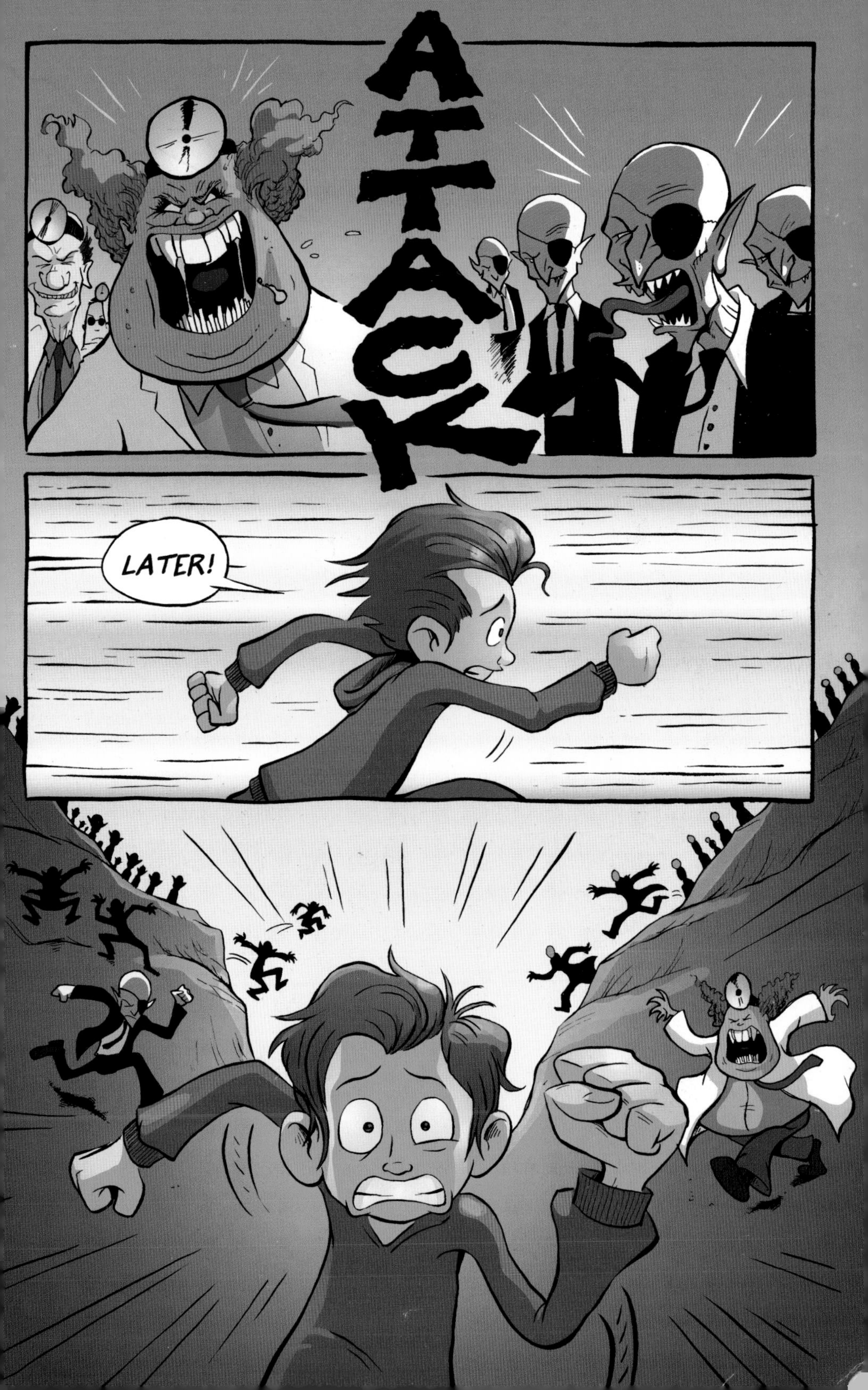
ATTACK
LATER!

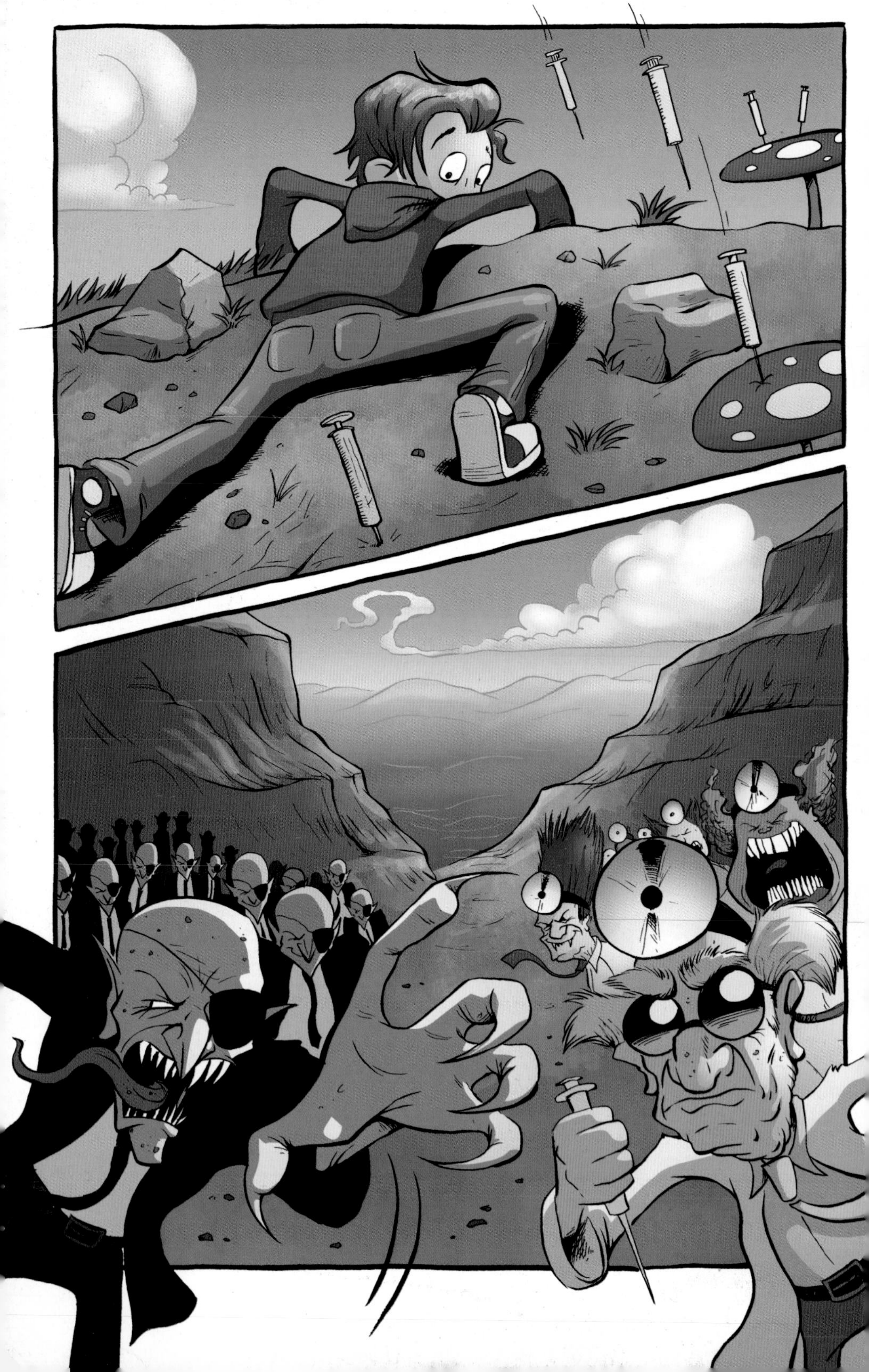

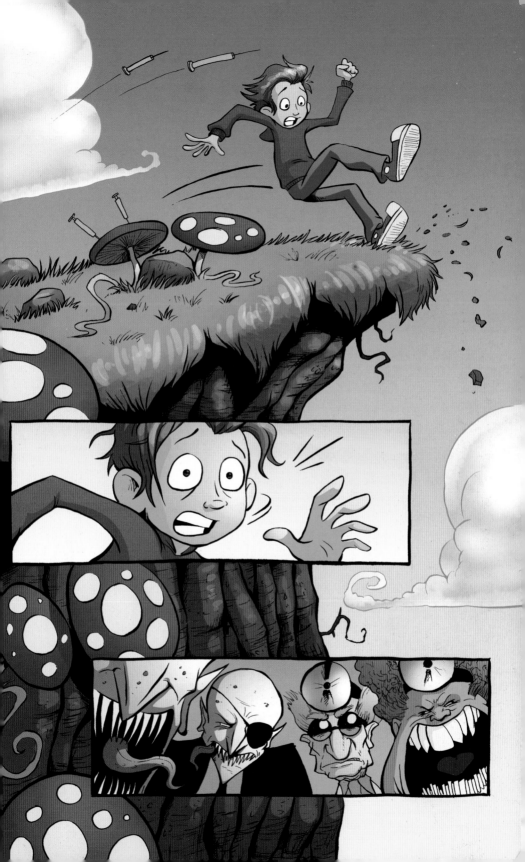

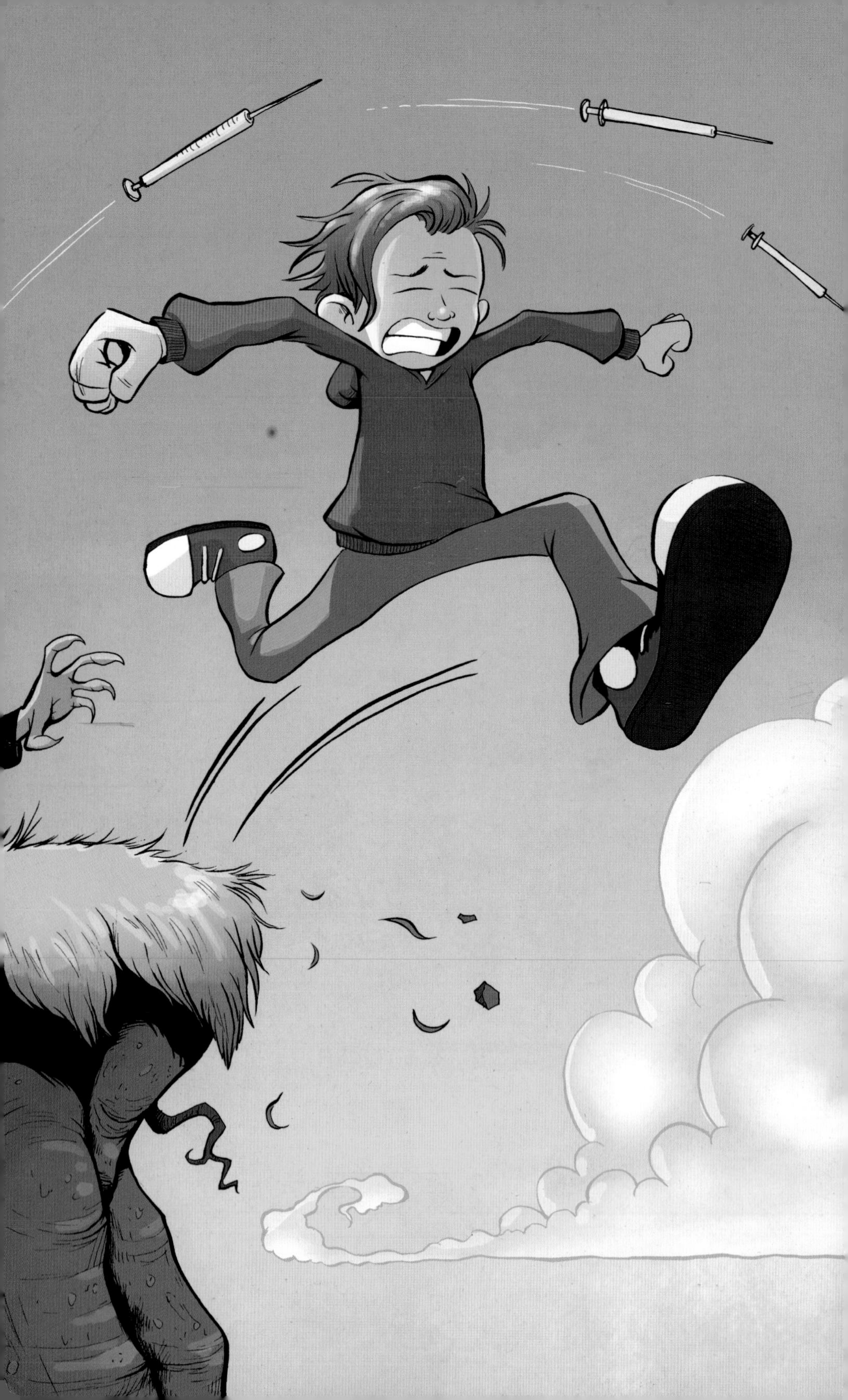

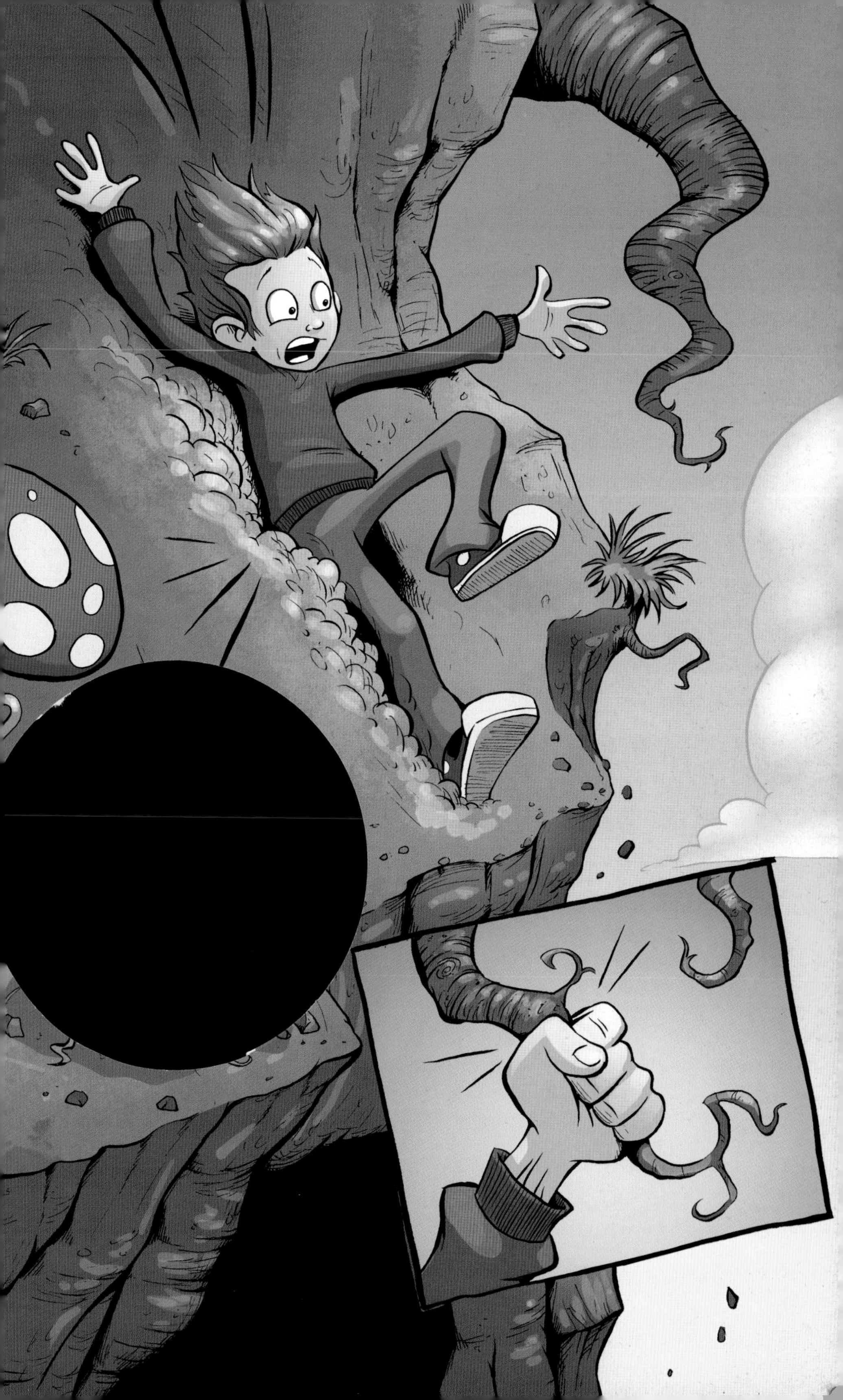

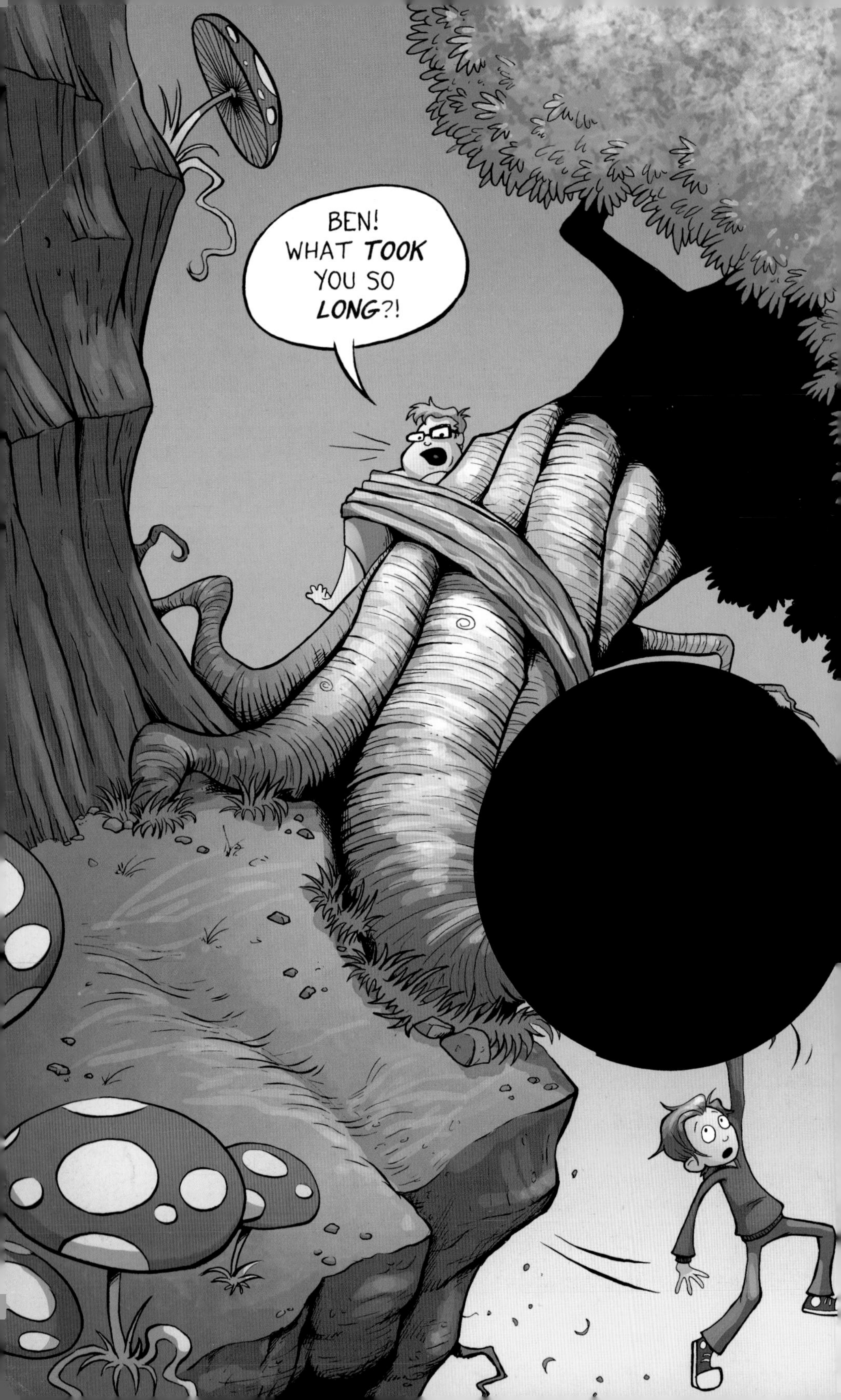
BEN! WHAT **TOOK** YOU SO ***LONG***?!

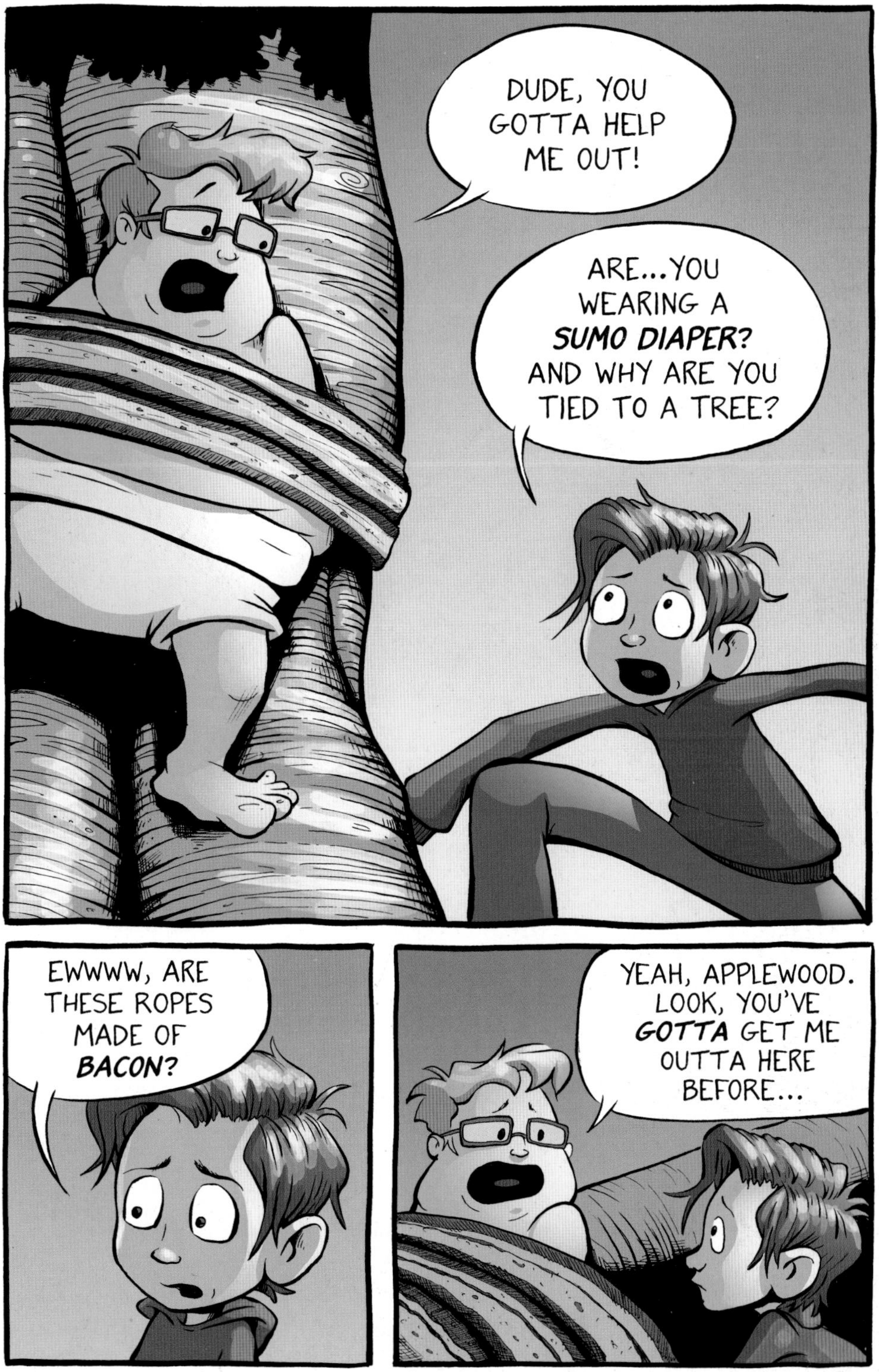
DUDE, YOU GOTTA HELP ME OUT!
ARE...YOU WEARING A **SUMO DIAPER?** AND WHY ARE YOU TIED TO A TREE?
EWWWW, ARE THESE ROPES MADE OF **BACON?**
YEAH, APPLEWOOD. LOOK, YOU'VE **GOTTA** GET ME OUTTA HERE BEFORE...

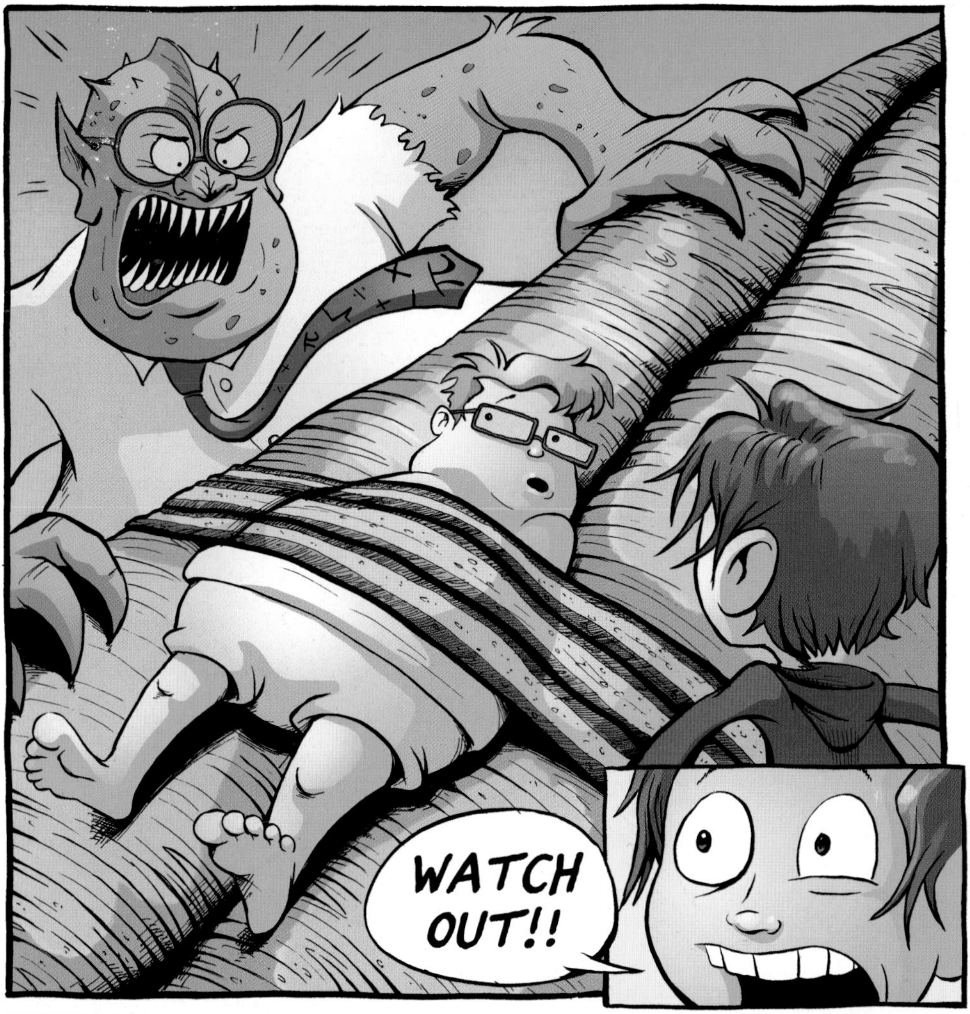
WATCH OUT!!

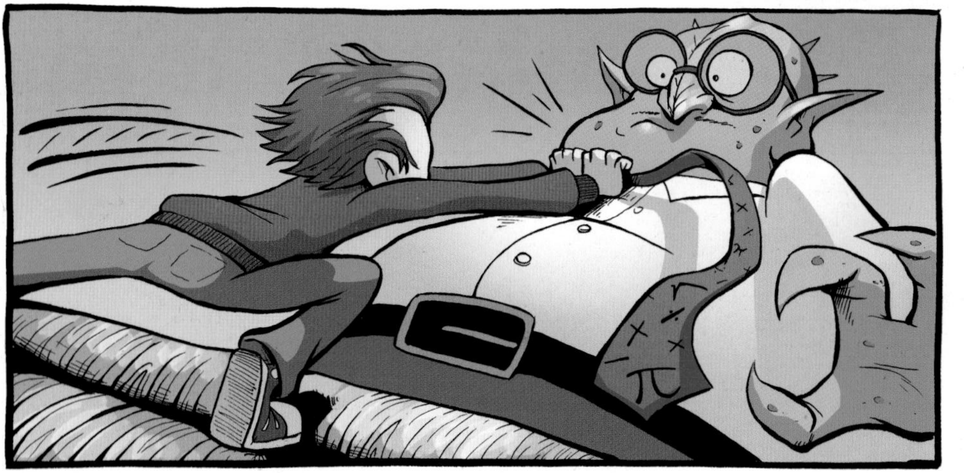

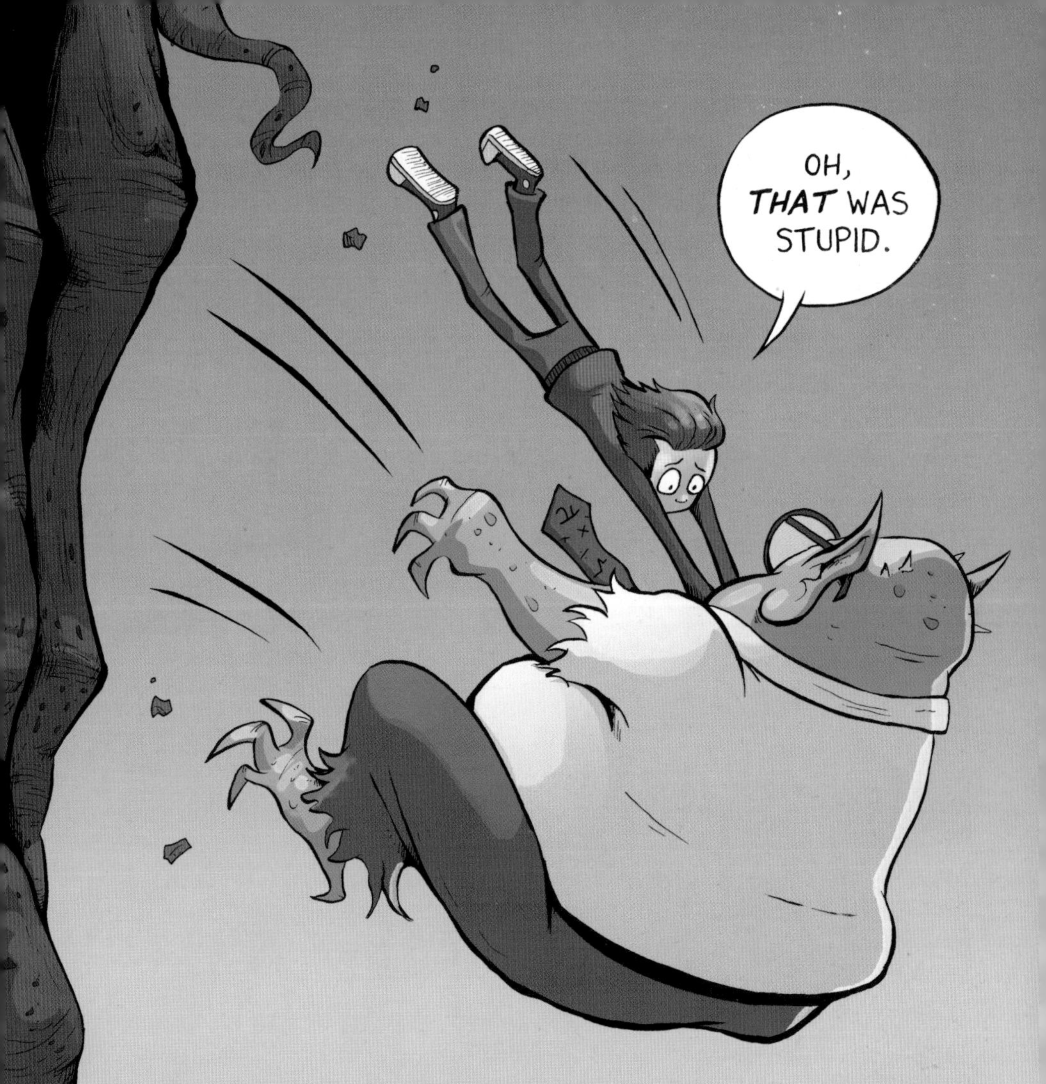
OH, *THAT* WAS STUPID.

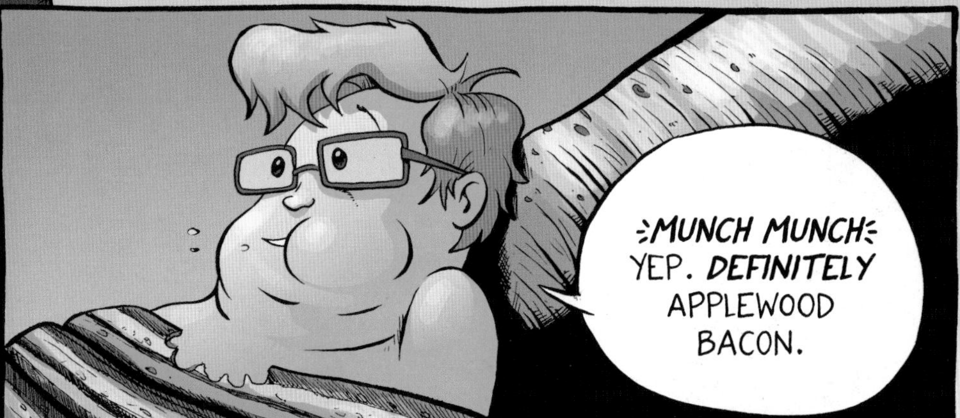
MUNCH MUNCH
YEP. **DEFINITELY** APPLEWOOD BACON.

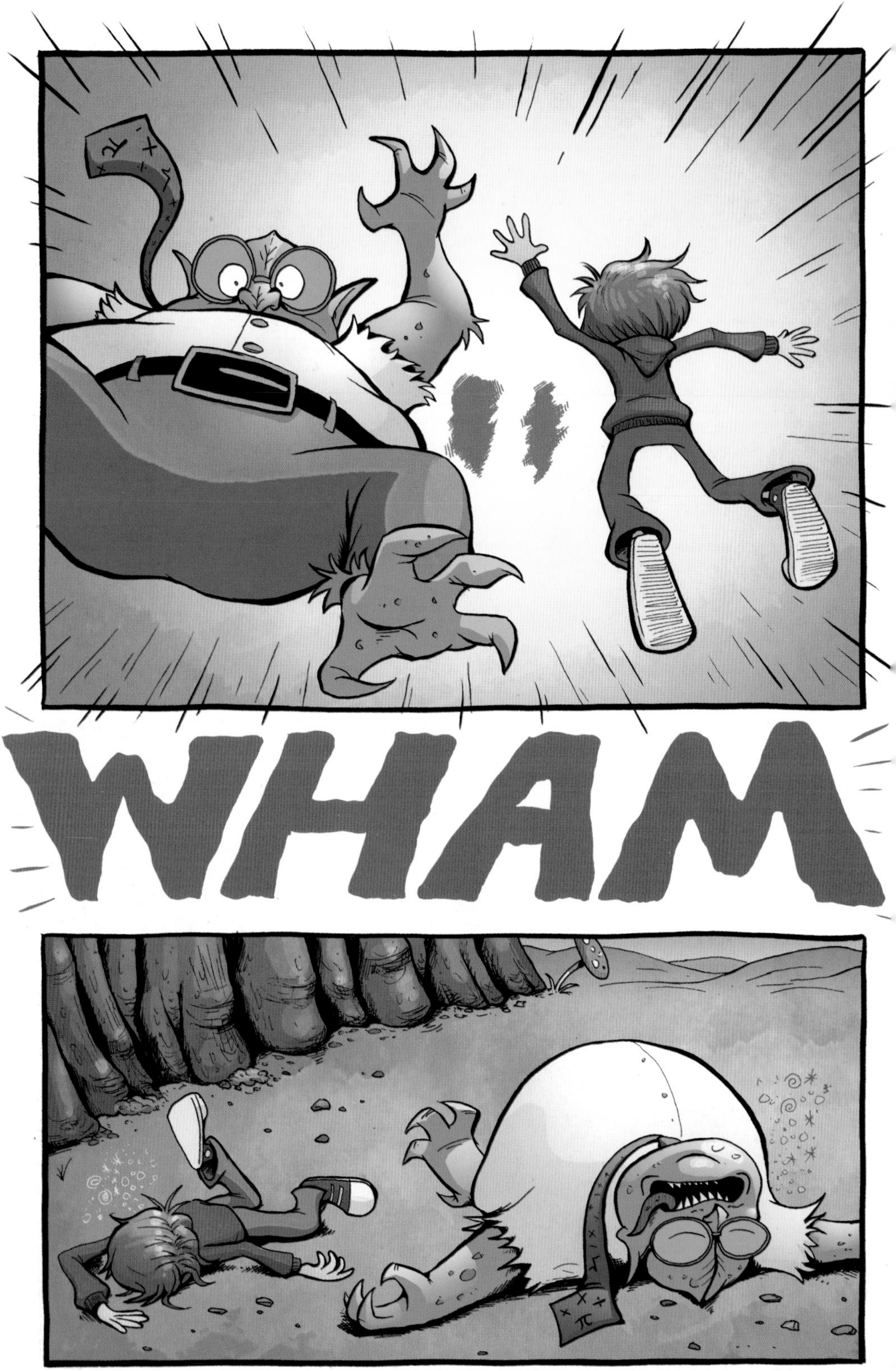
WHAM

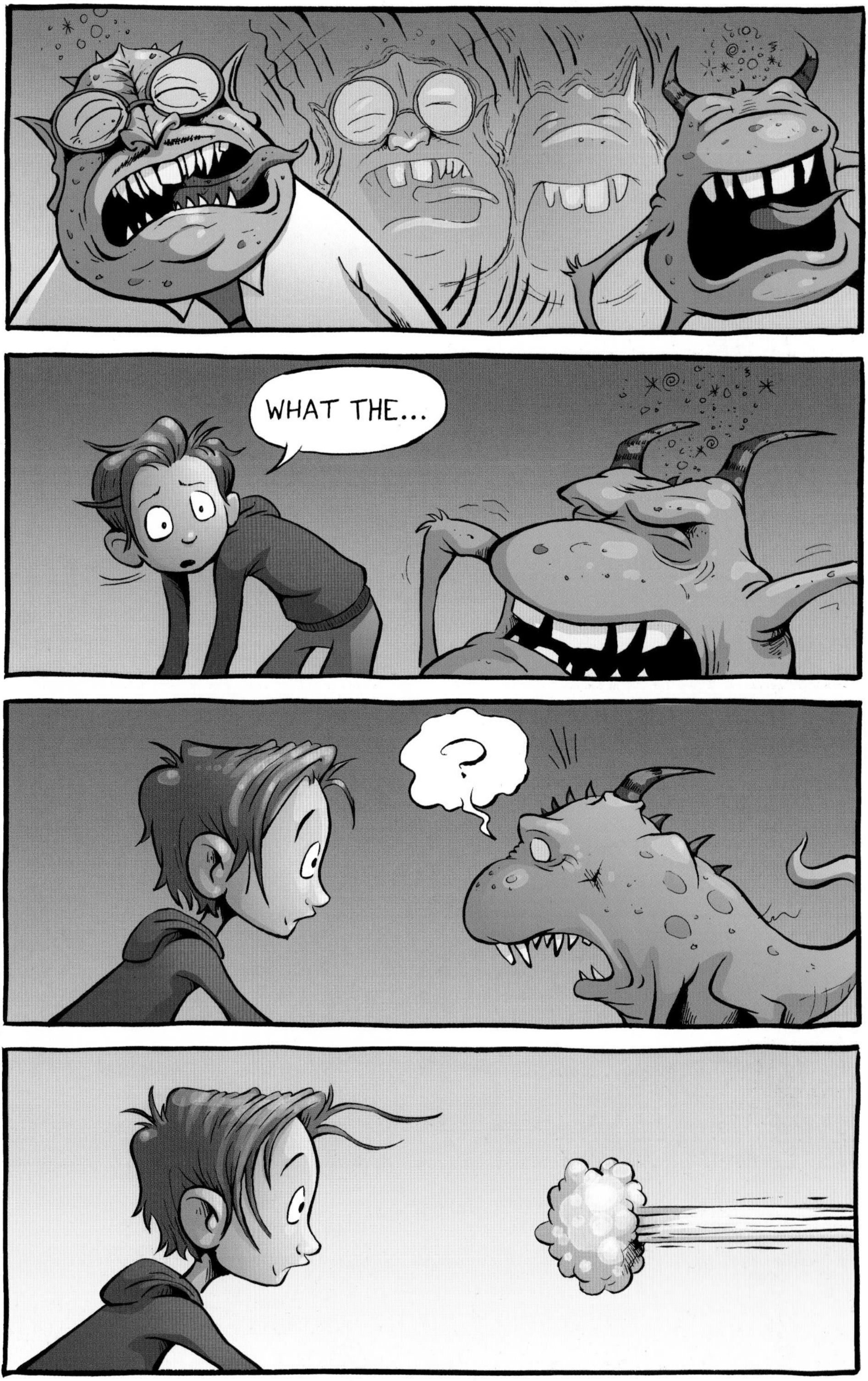
WHAT THE...
?

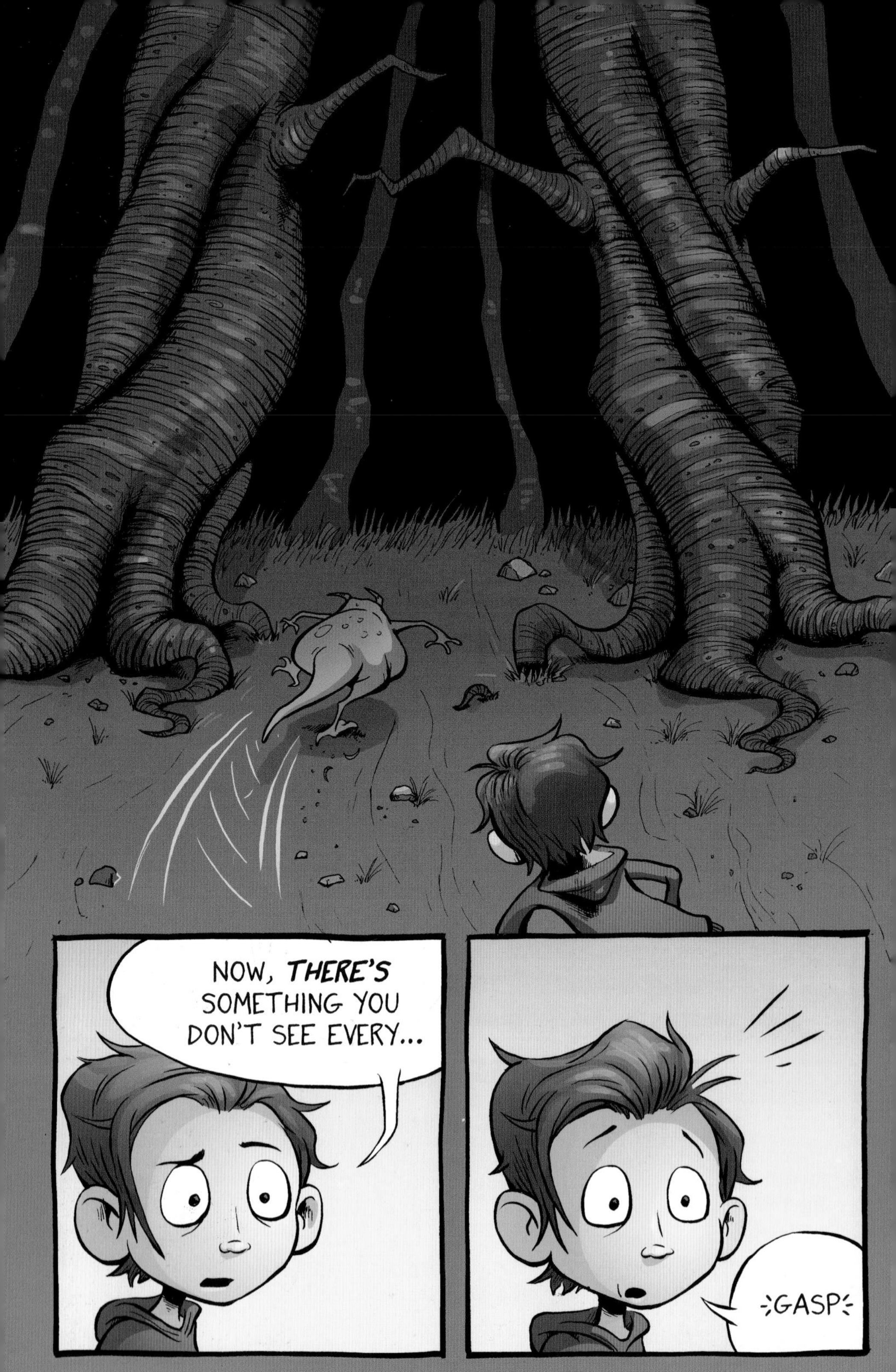
NOW, **THERE'S** SOMETHING YOU DON'T SEE EVERY...
GASP

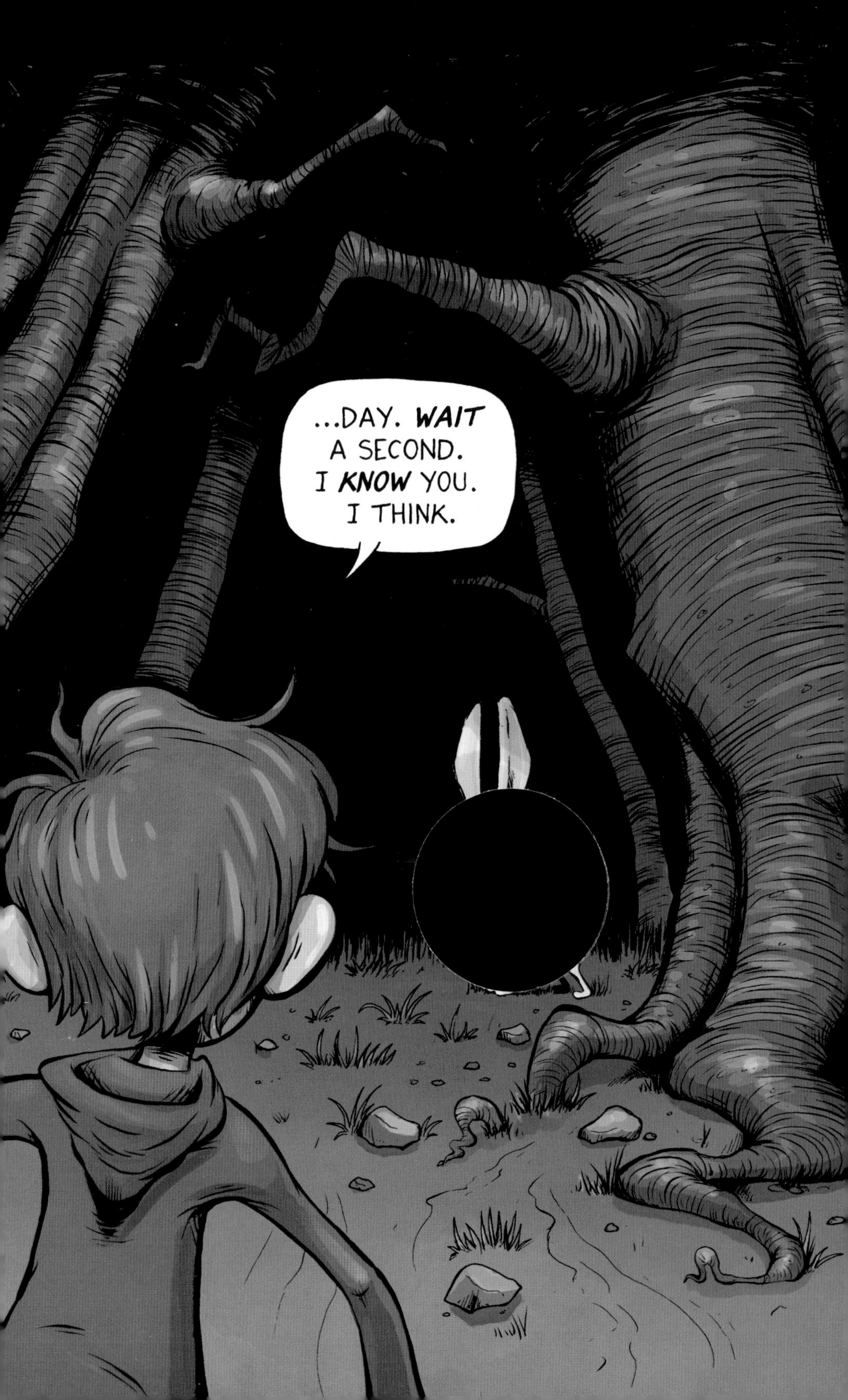
...DAY. WAIT A SECOND. I KNOW YOU. I THINK.

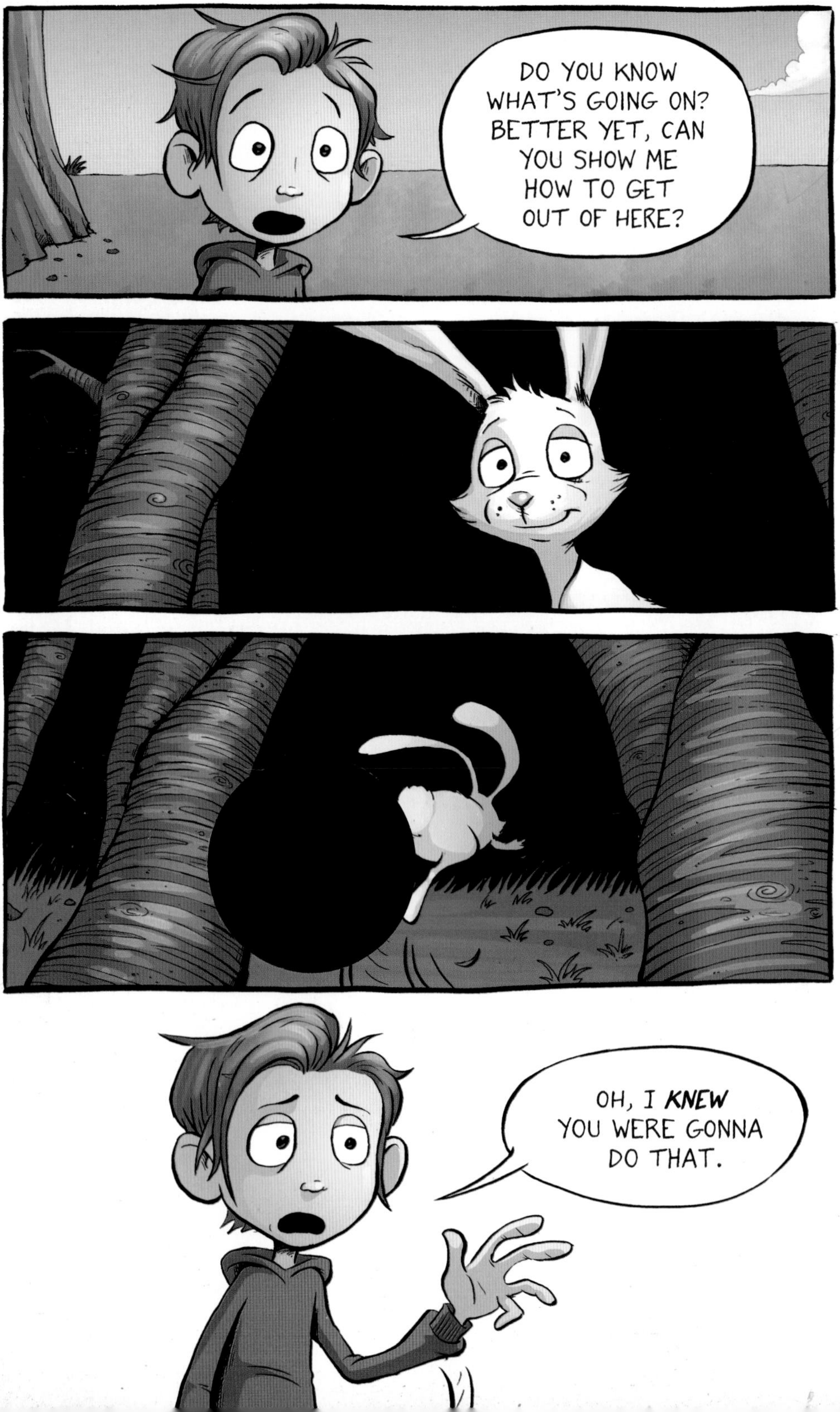
DO YOU KNOW WHAT'S GOING ON? BETTER YET, CAN YOU SHOW ME HOW TO GET OUT OF HERE?
OH, I **KNEW** YOU WERE GONNA DO THAT.

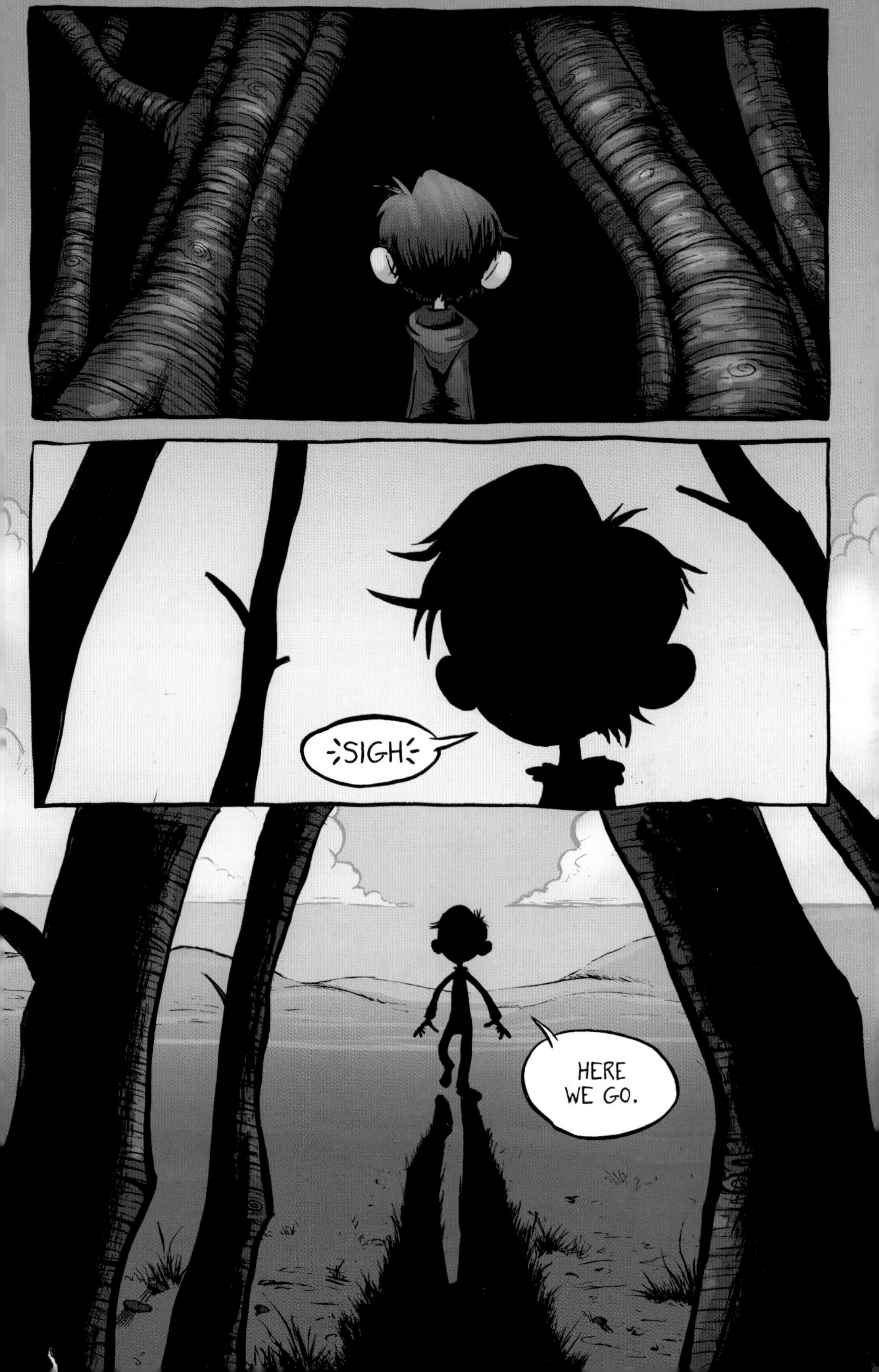
SIGH
HERE WE GO.

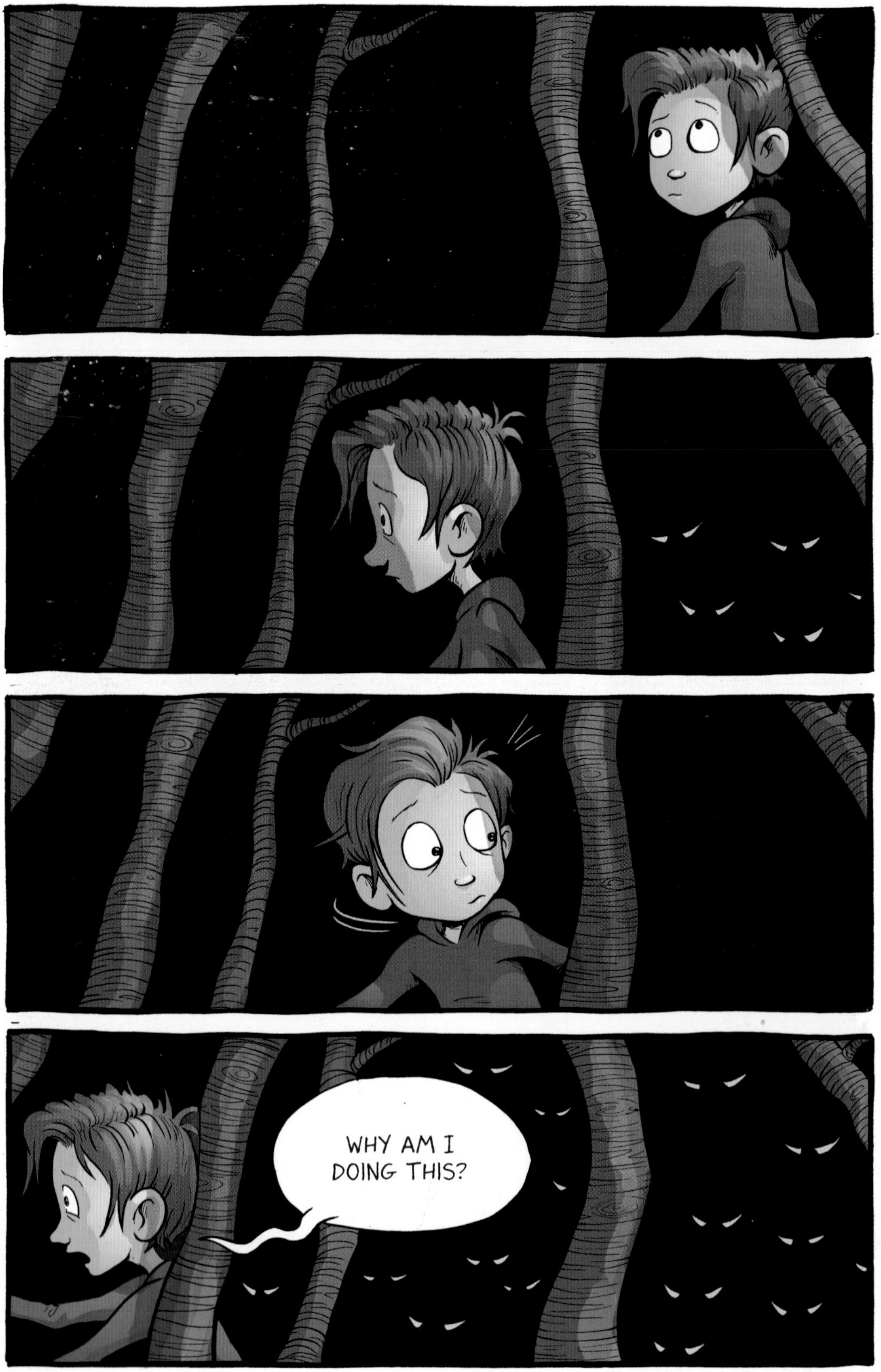
WHY AM I DOING THIS?

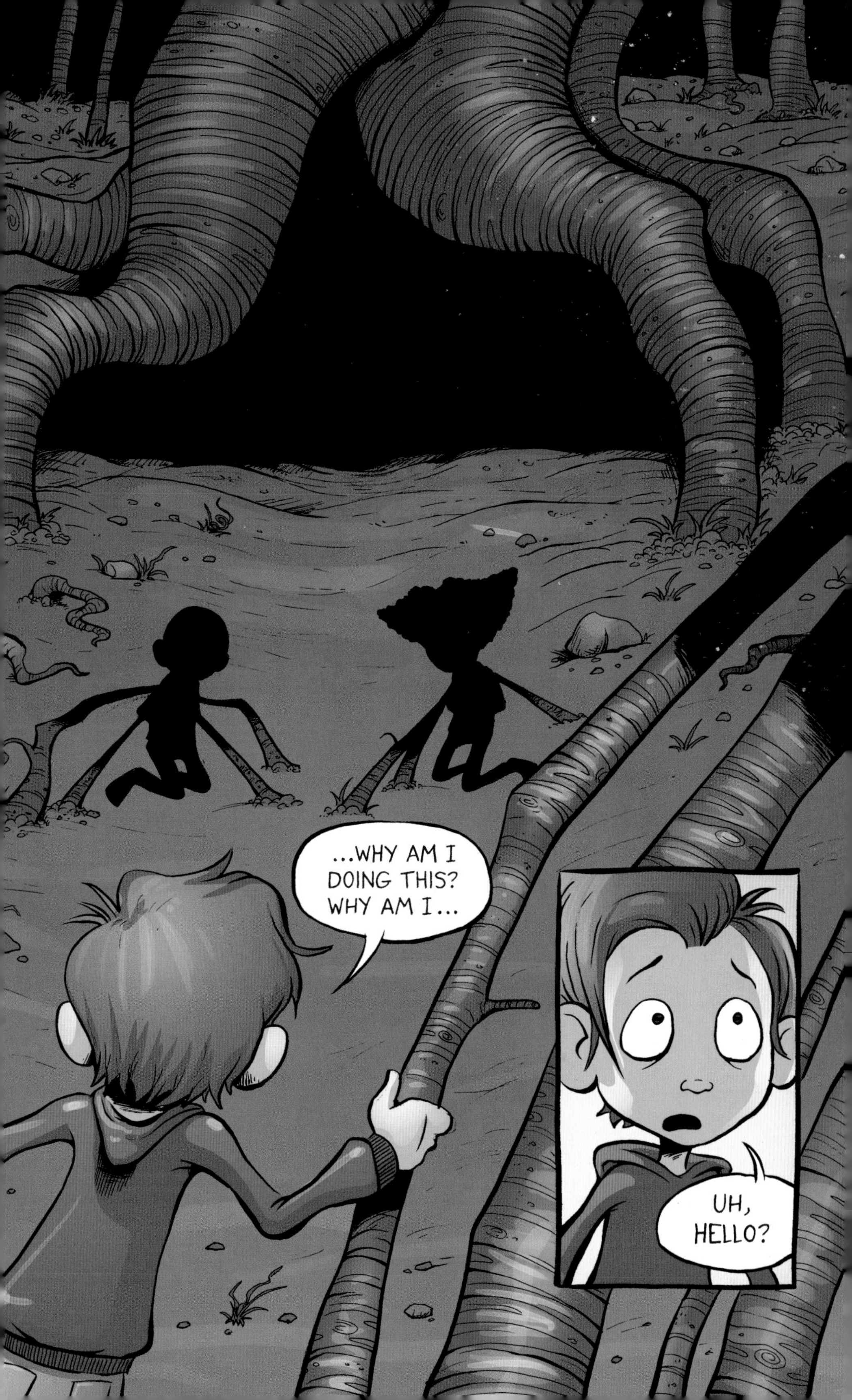
...WHY AM I DOING THIS? WHY AM I...
UH, HELLO?

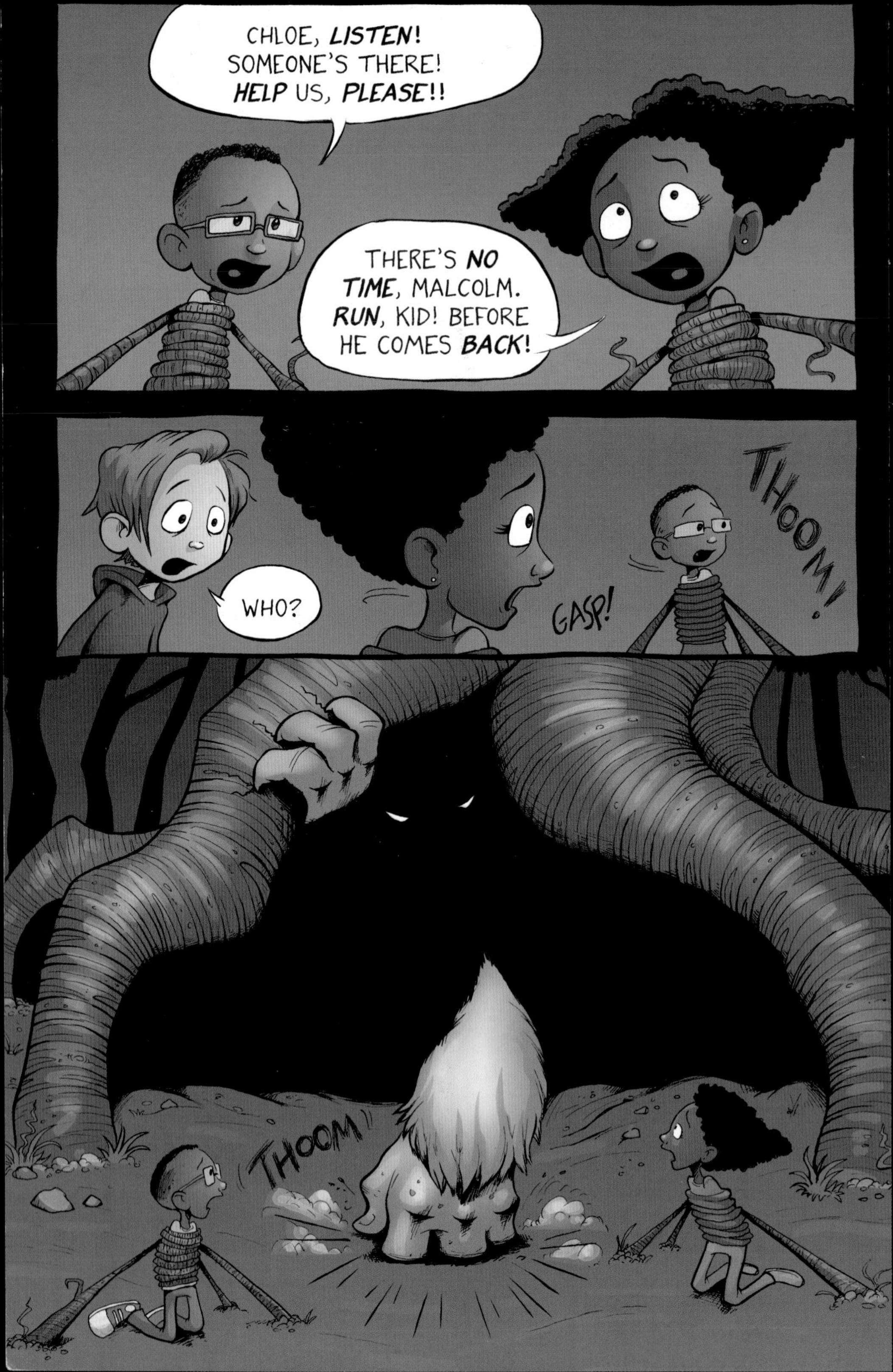
CHLOE, **LISTEN**! SOMEONE'S THERE! **HELP** US, **PLEASE**!!
THERE'S **NO TIME**, MALCOLM. **RUN**, KID! BEFORE HE COMES **BACK**!
THOOM!
WHO?
GASP!
THOOM

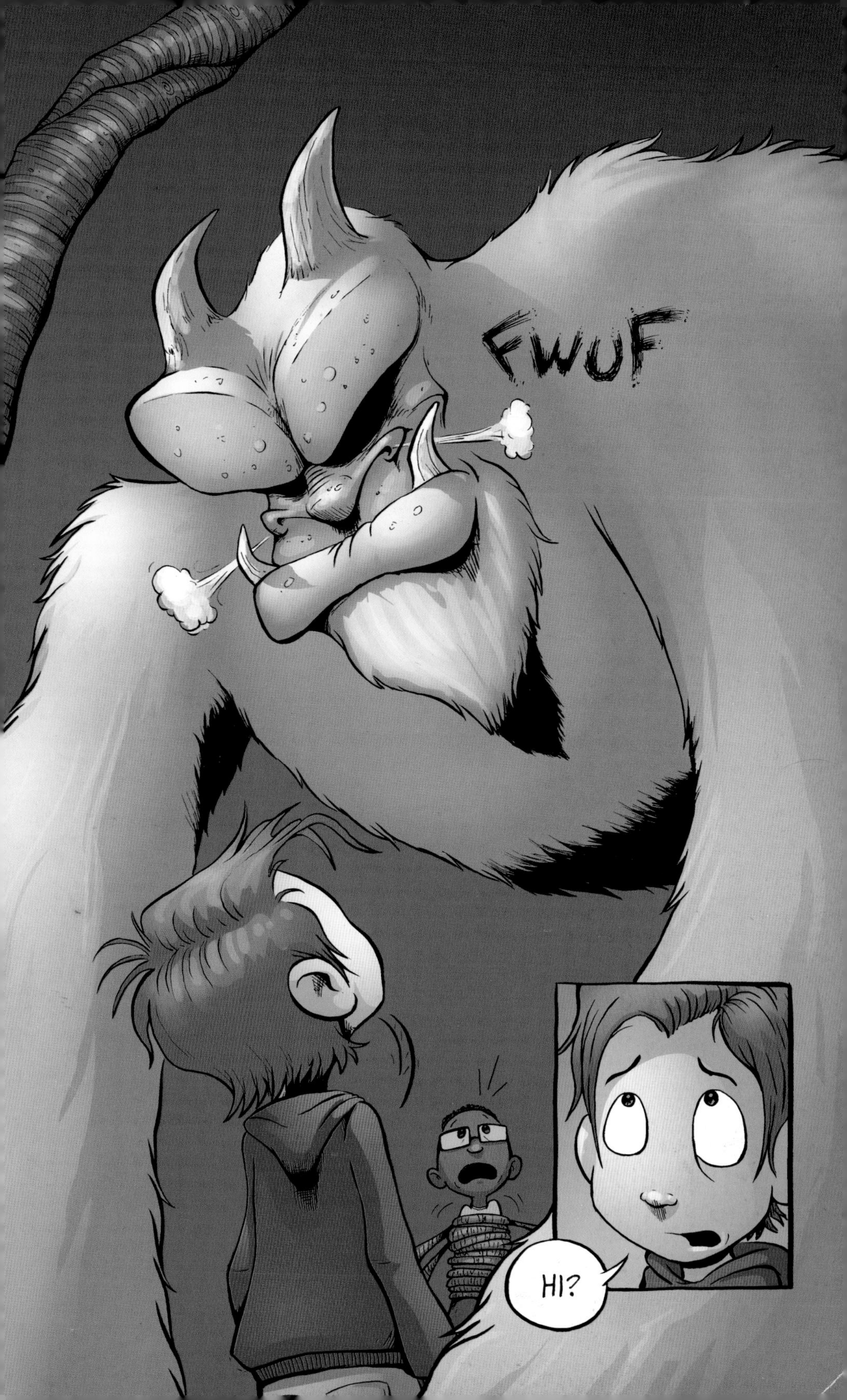
FWUF
HI?

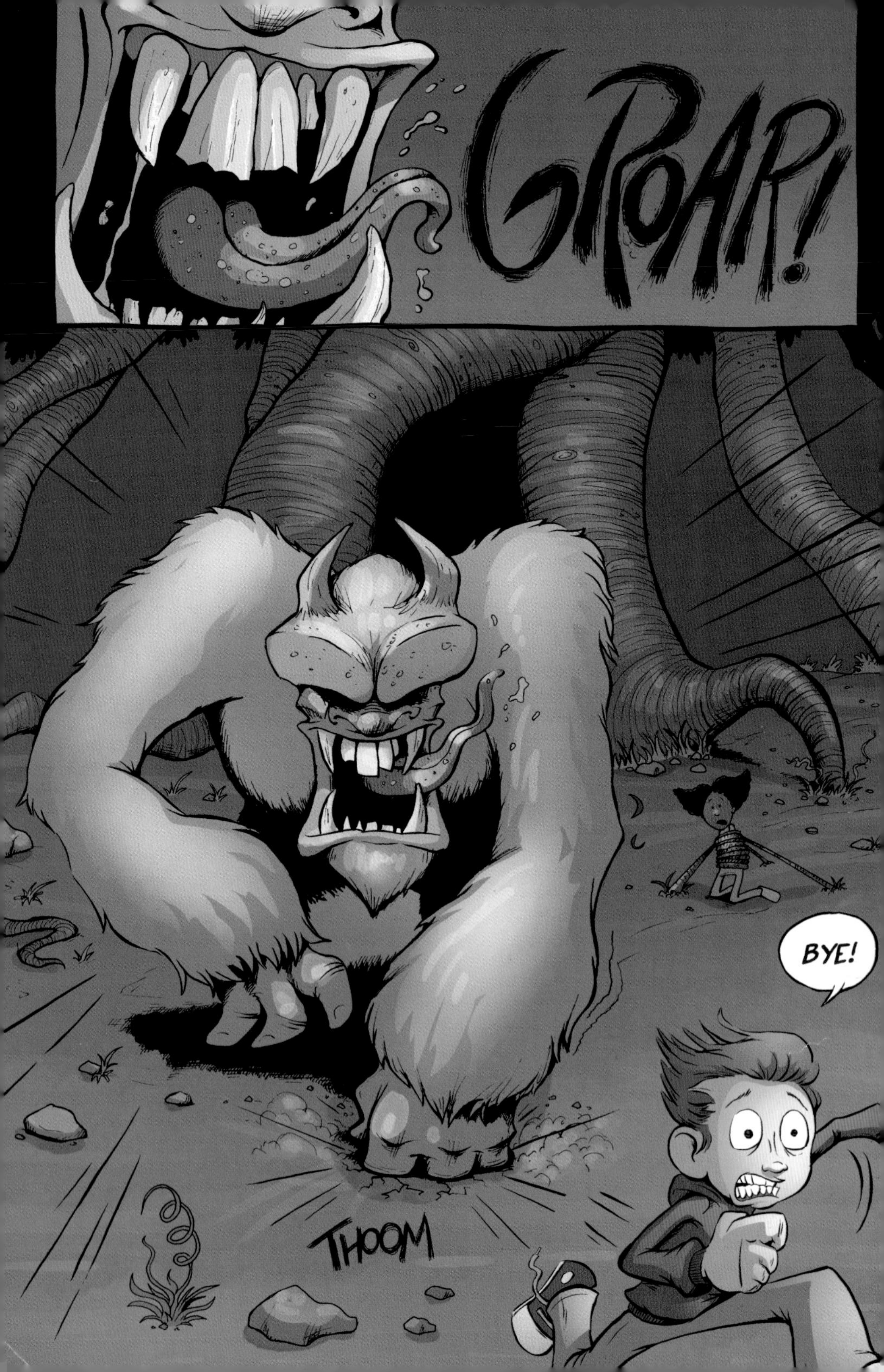
GROAR!
BYE!
THOOM

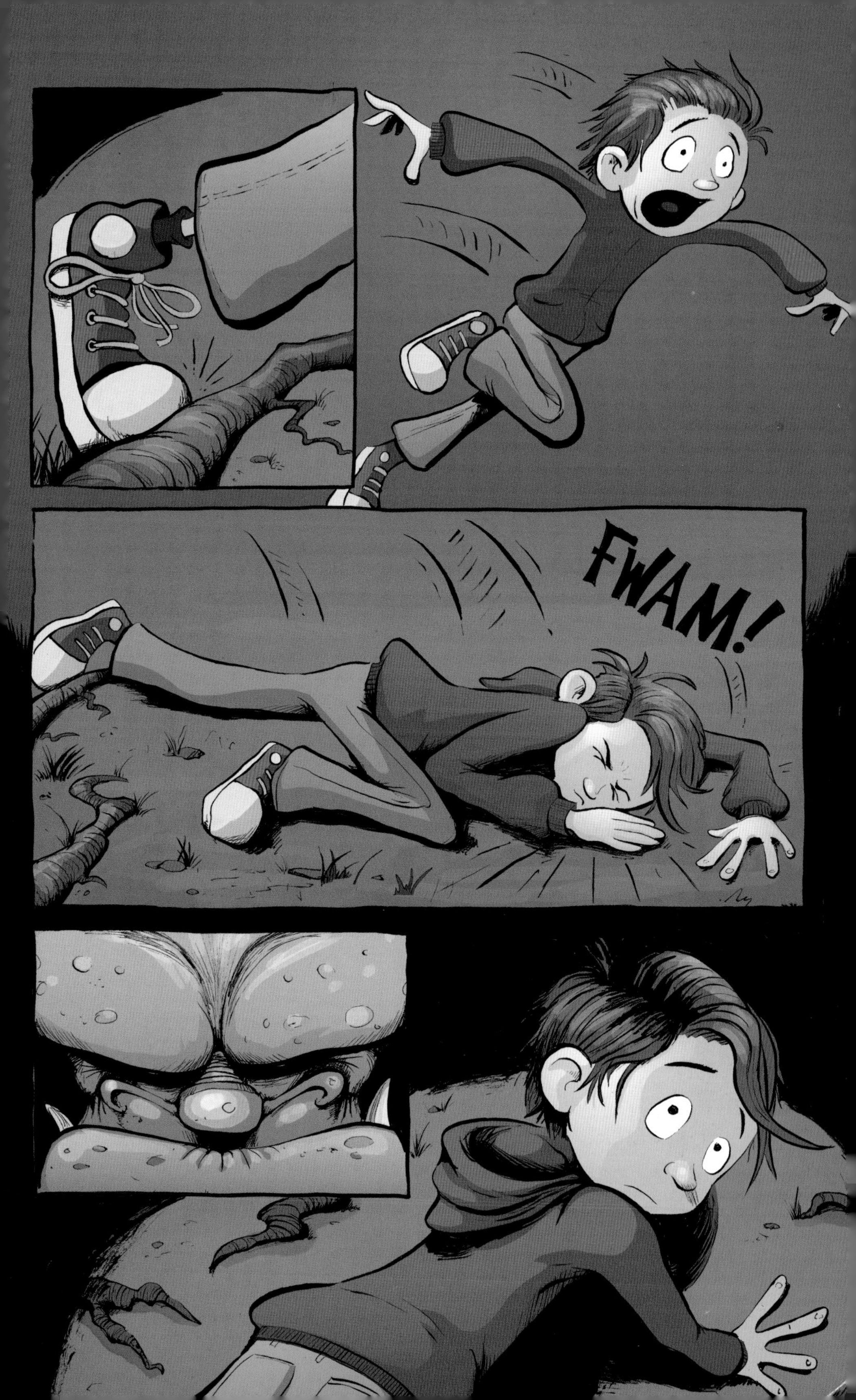
FWAM!

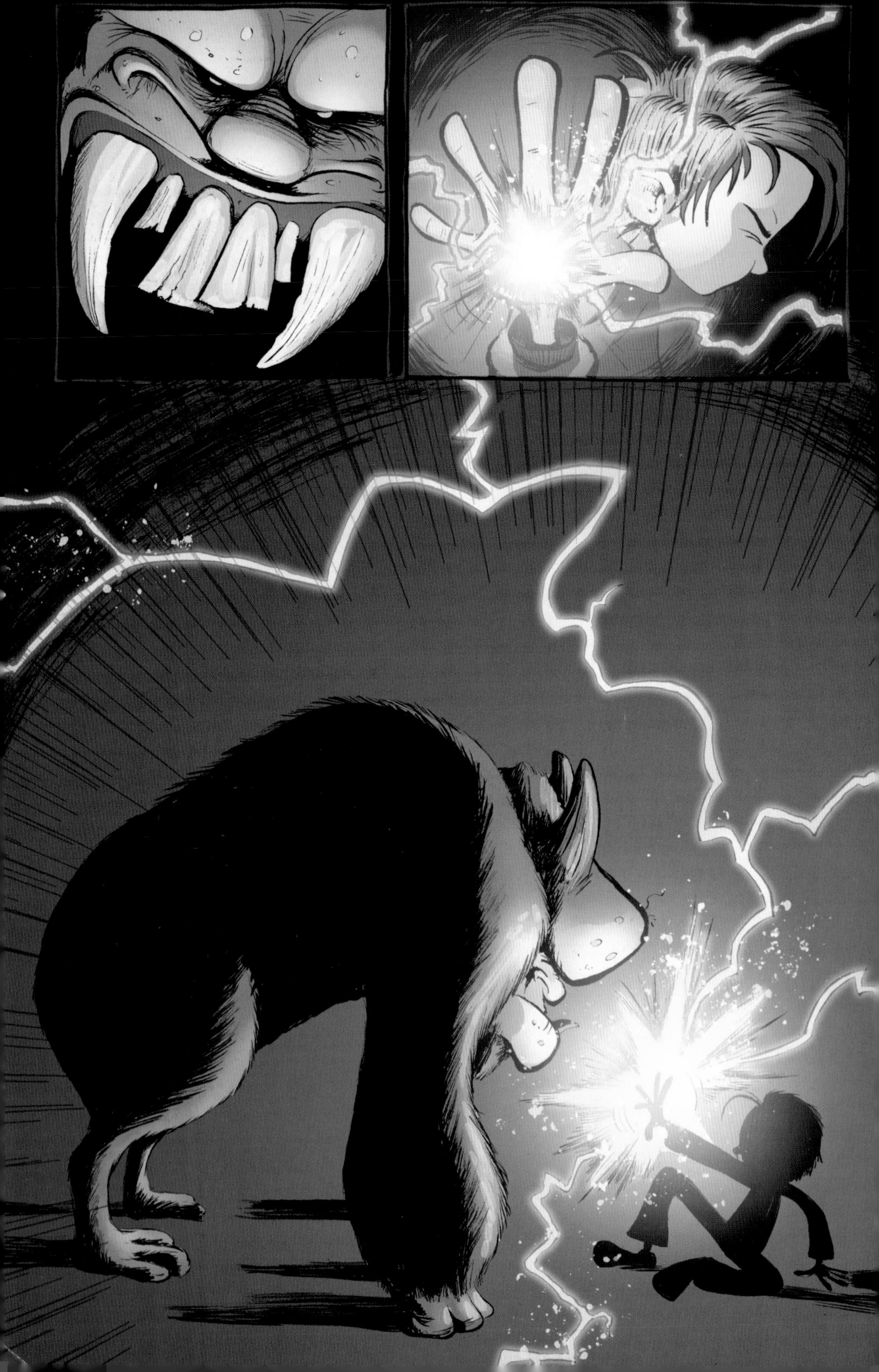

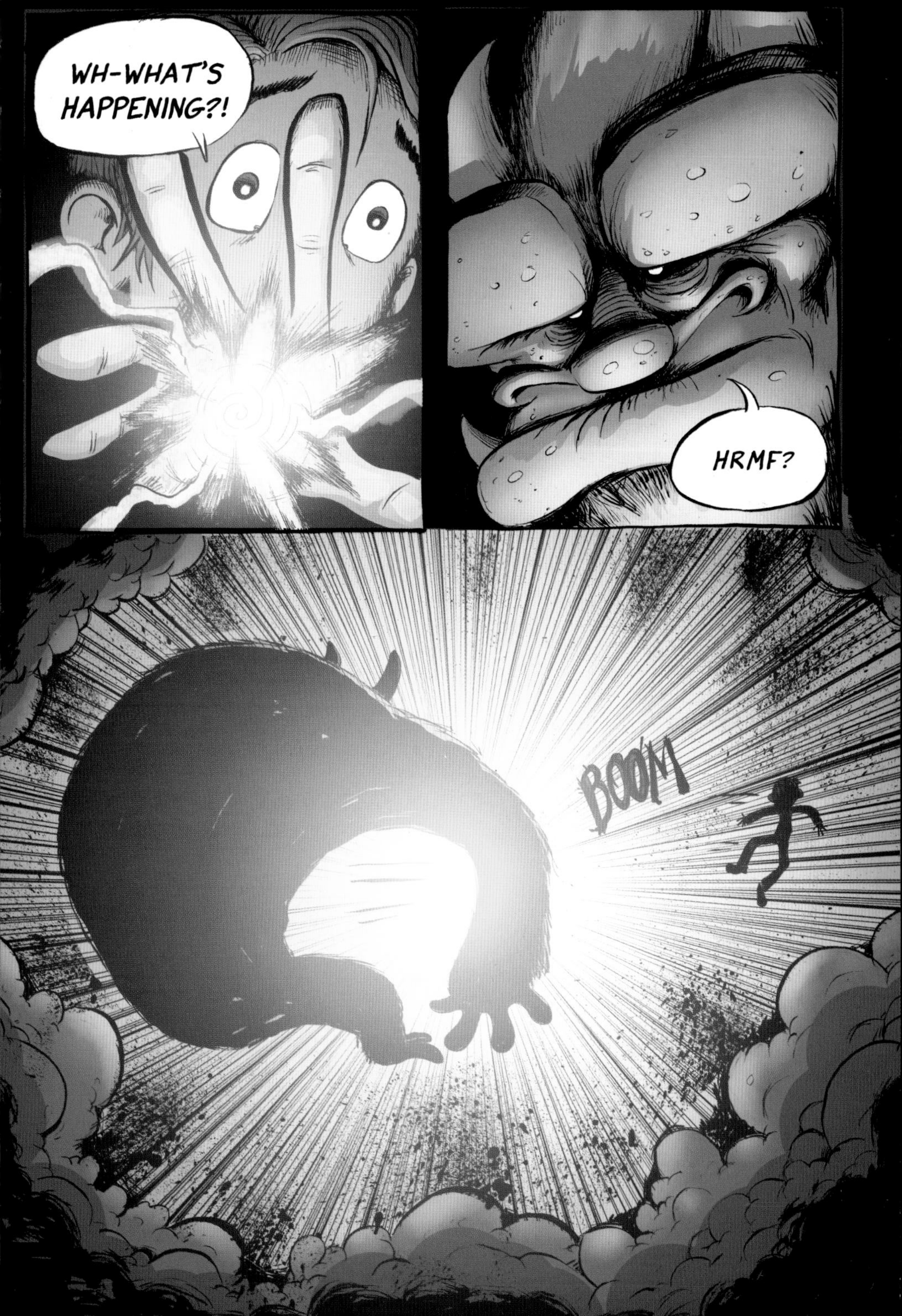
WH-WHAT'S HAPPENING?!
HRMF?
BOOM

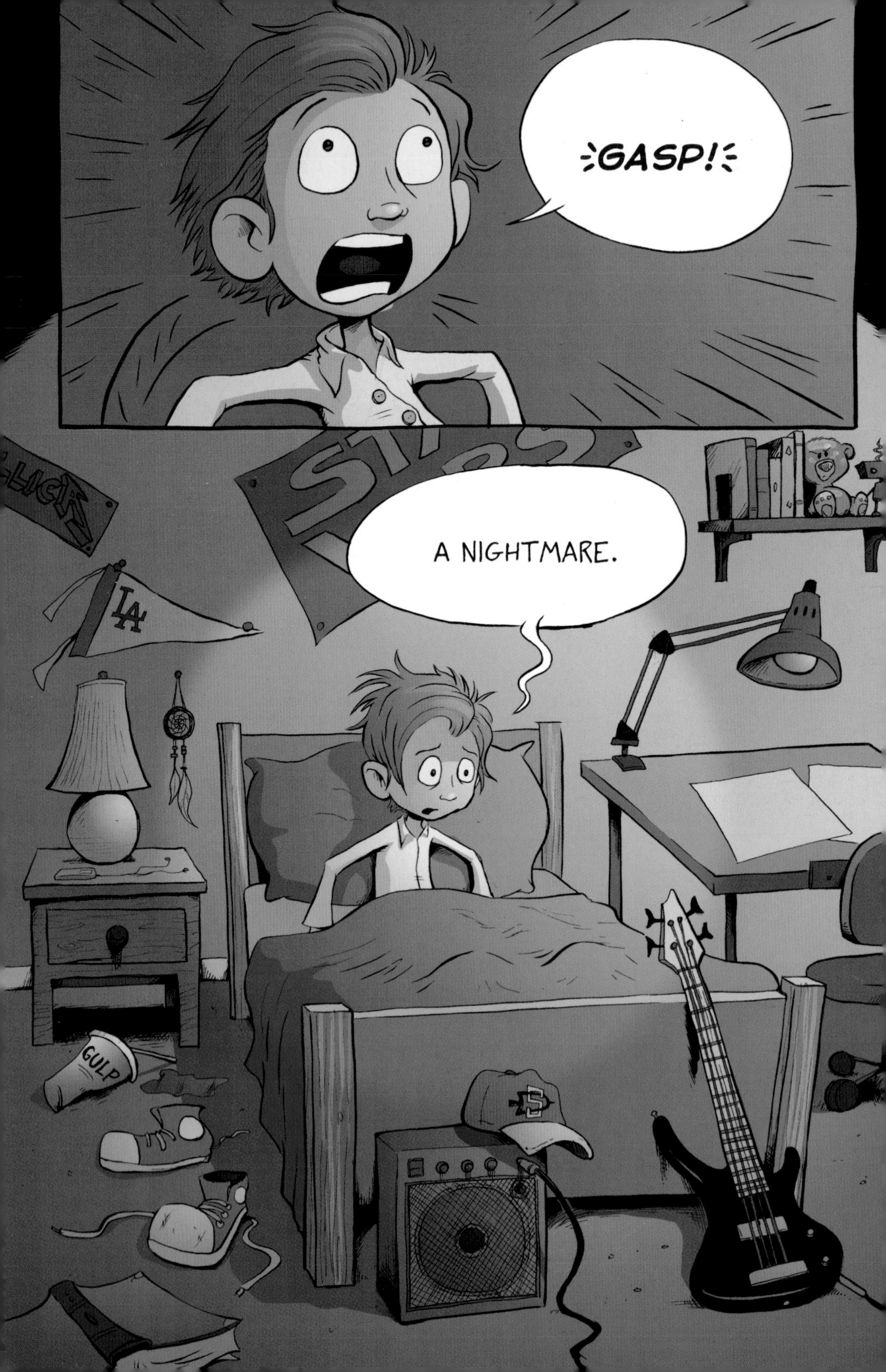
GASP!
A NIGHTMARE.
LA
GULP

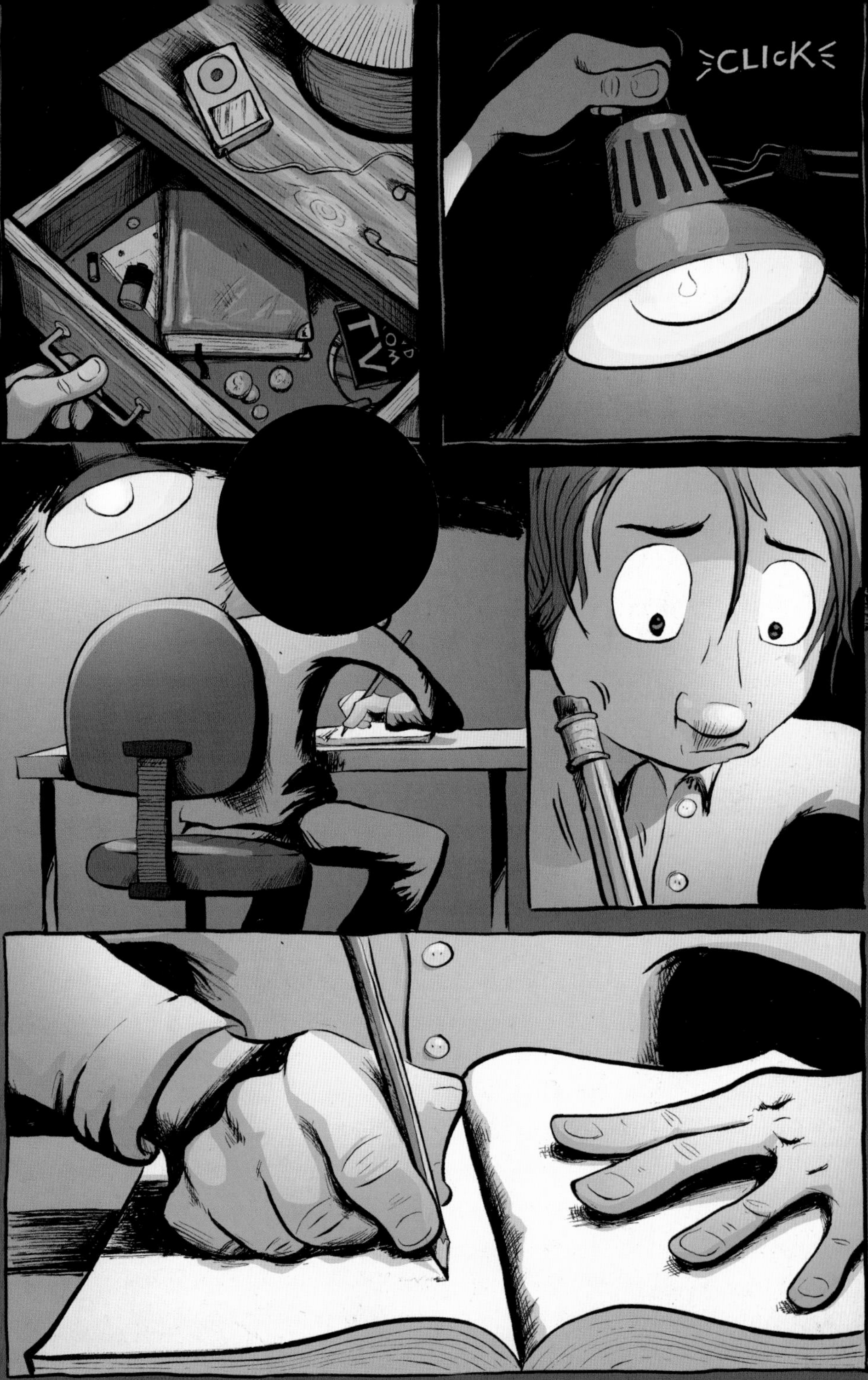
CLICK

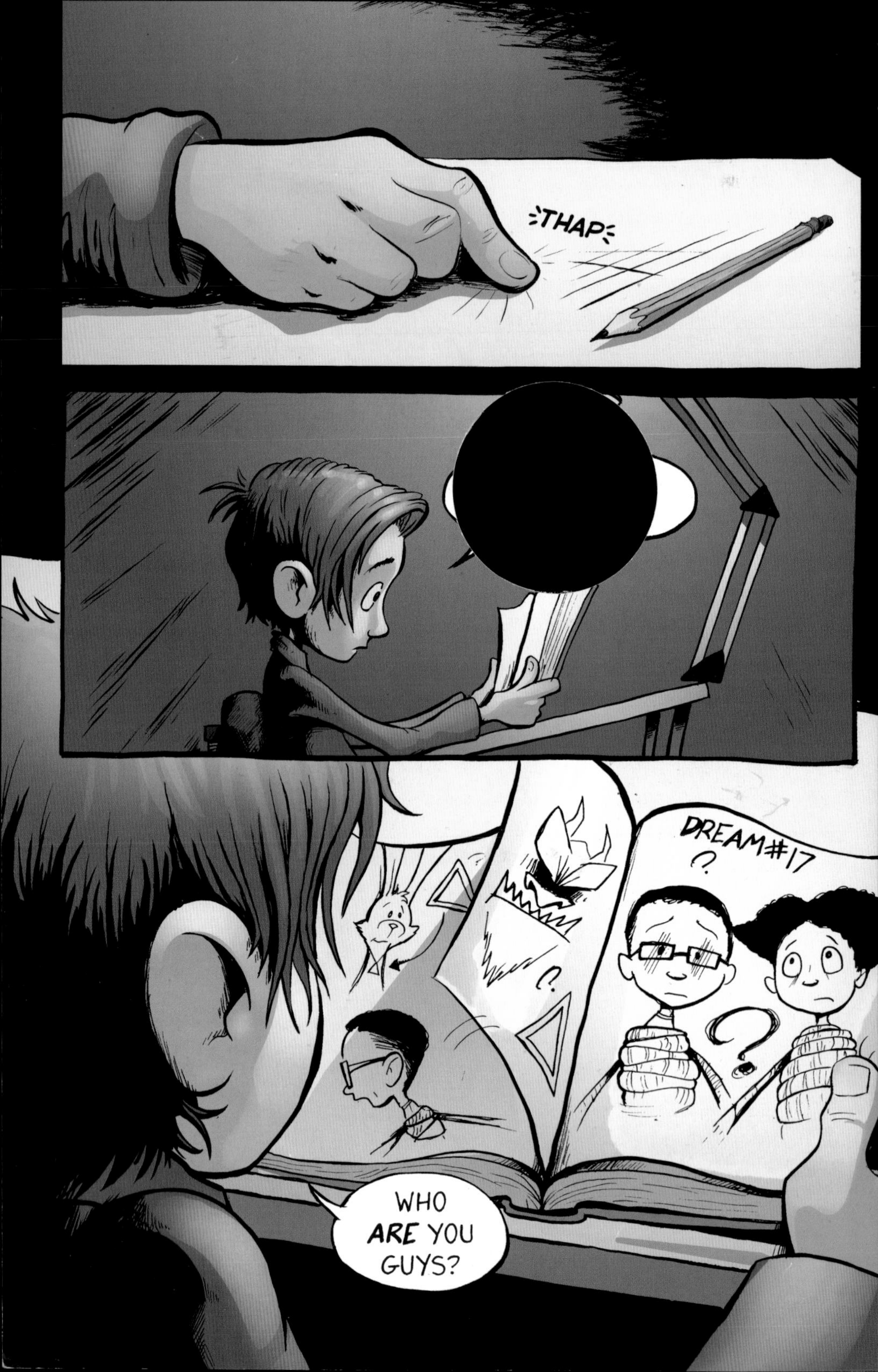
THAP
[redacted]
DREAM#17
WHO **ARE** YOU GUYS?

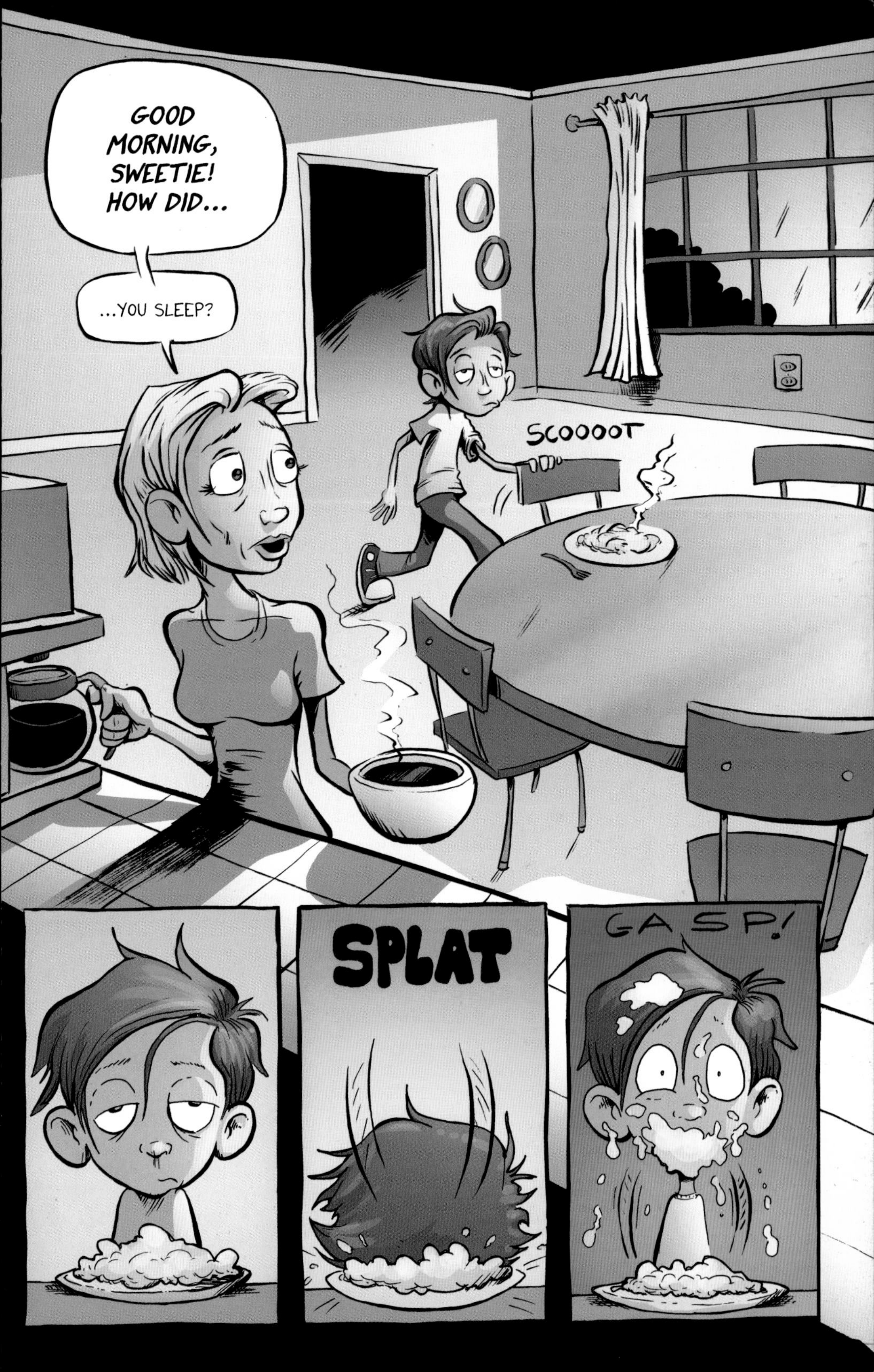
GOOD MORNING, SWEETIE! HOW DID...
...YOU SLEEP?
SCOOOOT
SPLAT
GASP!

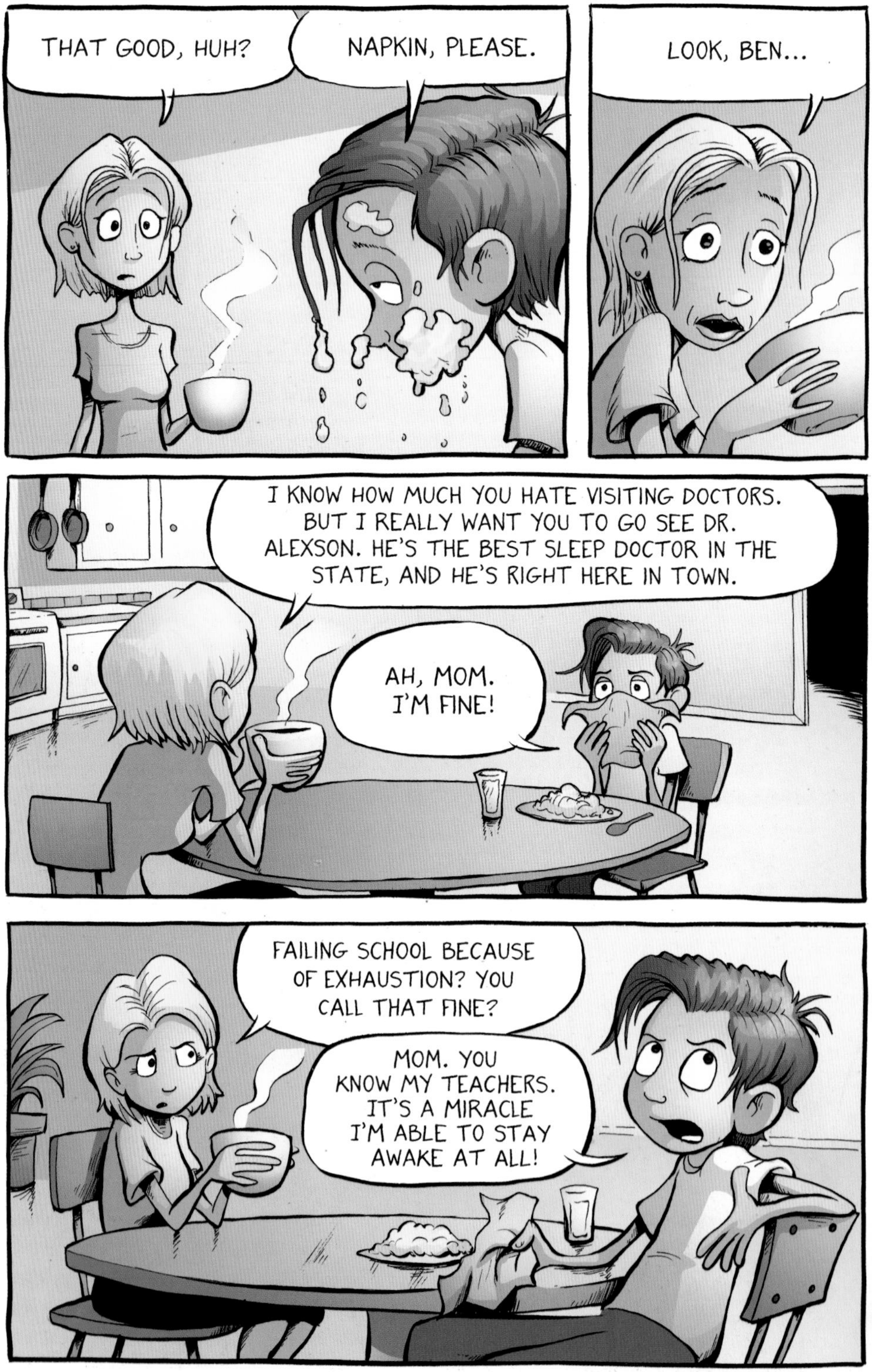
THAT GOOD, HUH?
NAPKIN, PLEASE.
LOOK, BEN...
I KNOW HOW MUCH YOU HATE VISITING DOCTORS. BUT I REALLY WANT YOU TO GO SEE DR. ALEXSON. HE'S THE BEST SLEEP DOCTOR IN THE STATE, AND HE'S RIGHT HERE IN TOWN.
AH, MOM. I'M FINE!
FAILING SCHOOL BECAUSE OF EXHAUSTION? YOU CALL THAT FINE?
MOM. YOU KNOW MY TEACHERS. IT'S A MIRACLE I'M ABLE TO STAY AWAKE AT ALL!

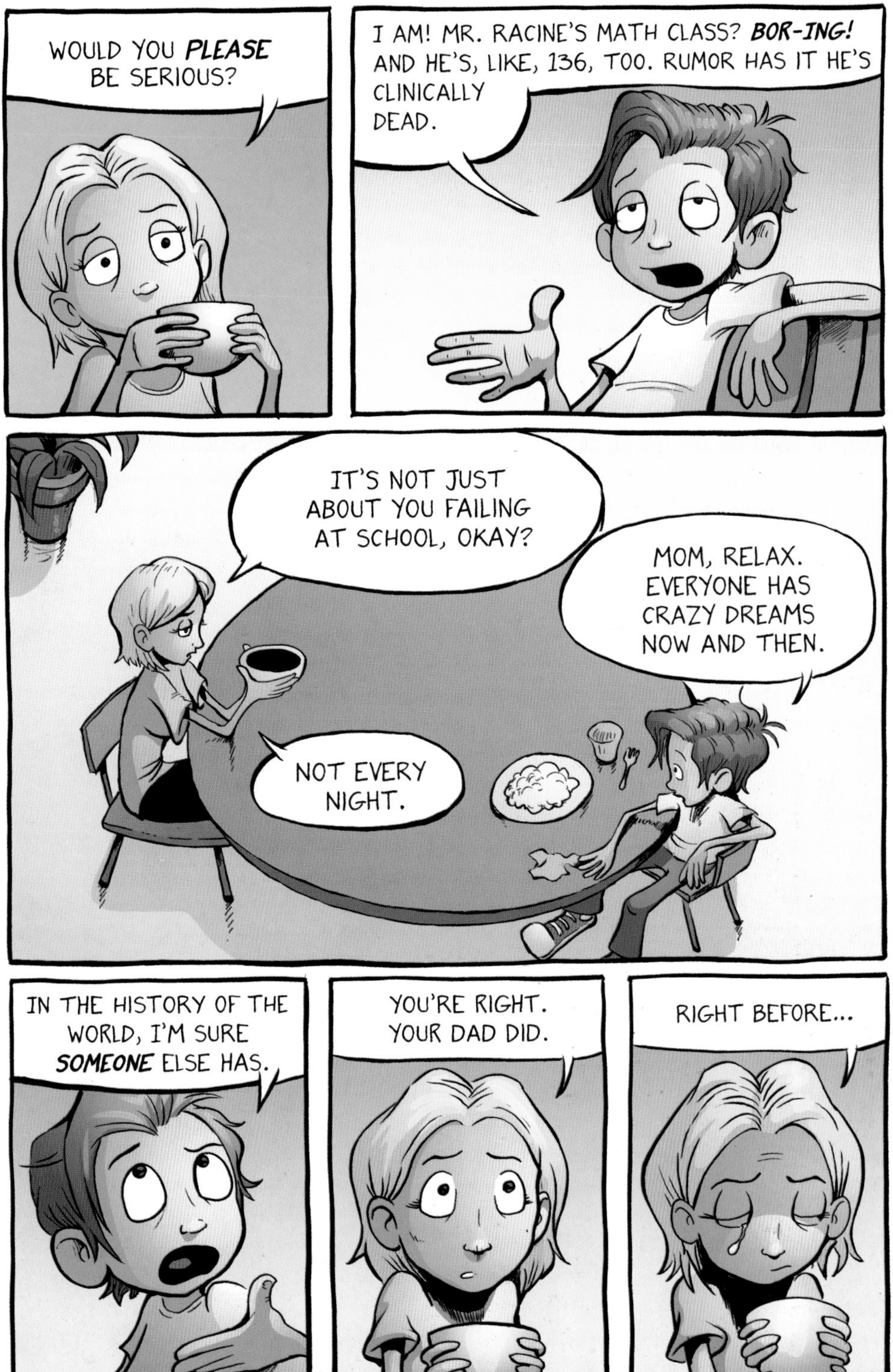
WOULD YOU **PLEASE** BE SERIOUS?
I AM! MR. RACINE'S MATH CLASS? **BOR-ING!** AND HE'S, LIKE, 136, TOO. RUMOR HAS IT HE'S CLINICALLY DEAD.
IT'S NOT JUST ABOUT YOU FAILING AT SCHOOL, OKAY?
MOM, RELAX. EVERYONE HAS CRAZY DREAMS NOW AND THEN.
NOT EVERY NIGHT.
IN THE HISTORY OF THE WORLD, I'M SURE **SOMEONE** ELSE HAS.
YOU'RE RIGHT. YOUR DAD DID.
RIGHT BEFORE...

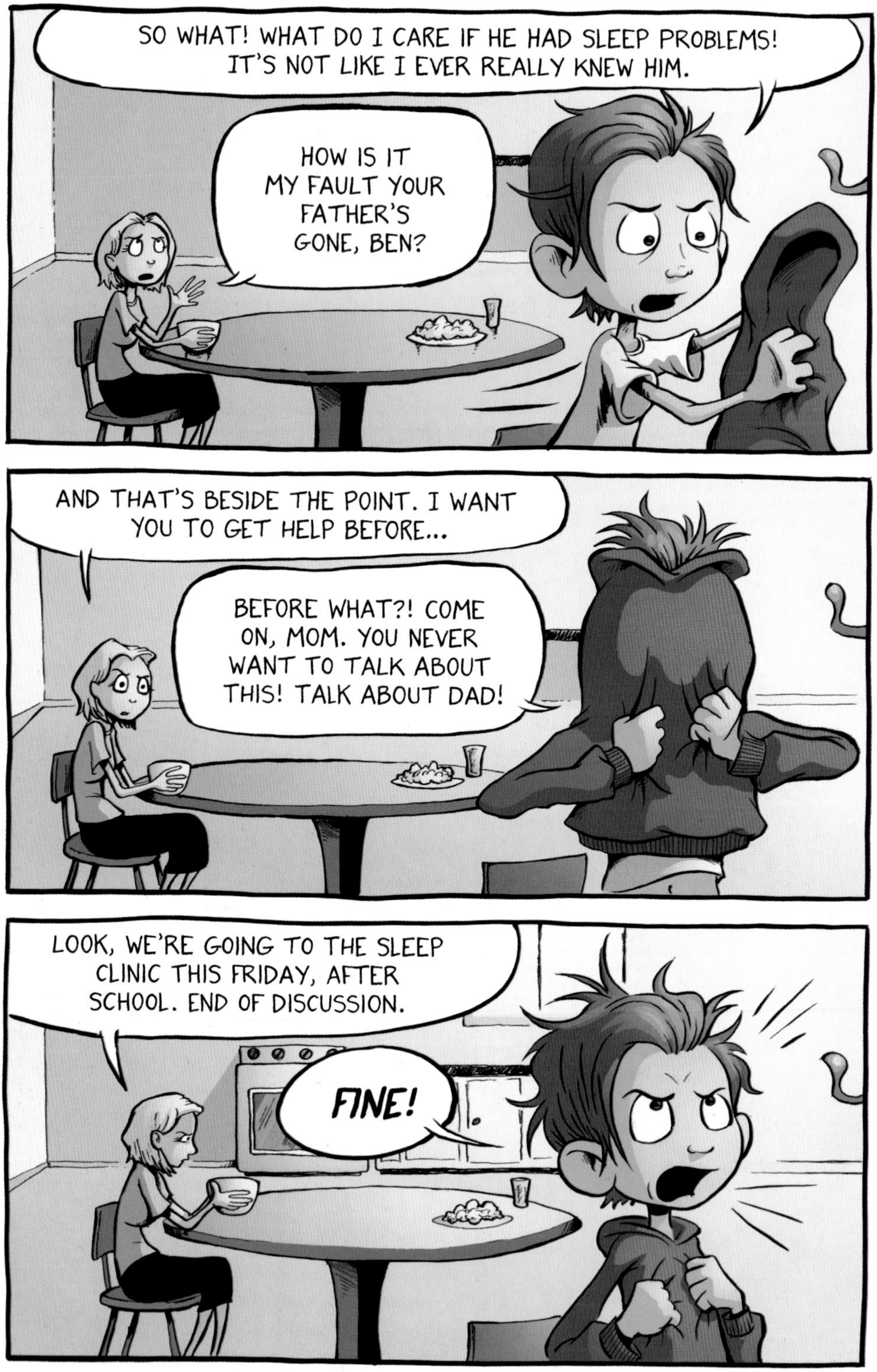
SO WHAT! WHAT DO I CARE IF HE HAD SLEEP PROBLEMS! IT'S NOT LIKE I EVER REALLY KNEW HIM.
HOW IS IT MY FAULT YOUR FATHER'S GONE, BEN?
AND THAT'S BESIDE THE POINT. I WANT YOU TO GET HELP BEFORE...
BEFORE WHAT?! COME ON, MOM. YOU NEVER WANT TO TALK ABOUT THIS! TALK ABOUT DAD!
LOOK, WE'RE GOING TO THE SLEEP CLINIC THIS FRIDAY, AFTER SCHOOL. END OF DISCUSSION.
FINE!

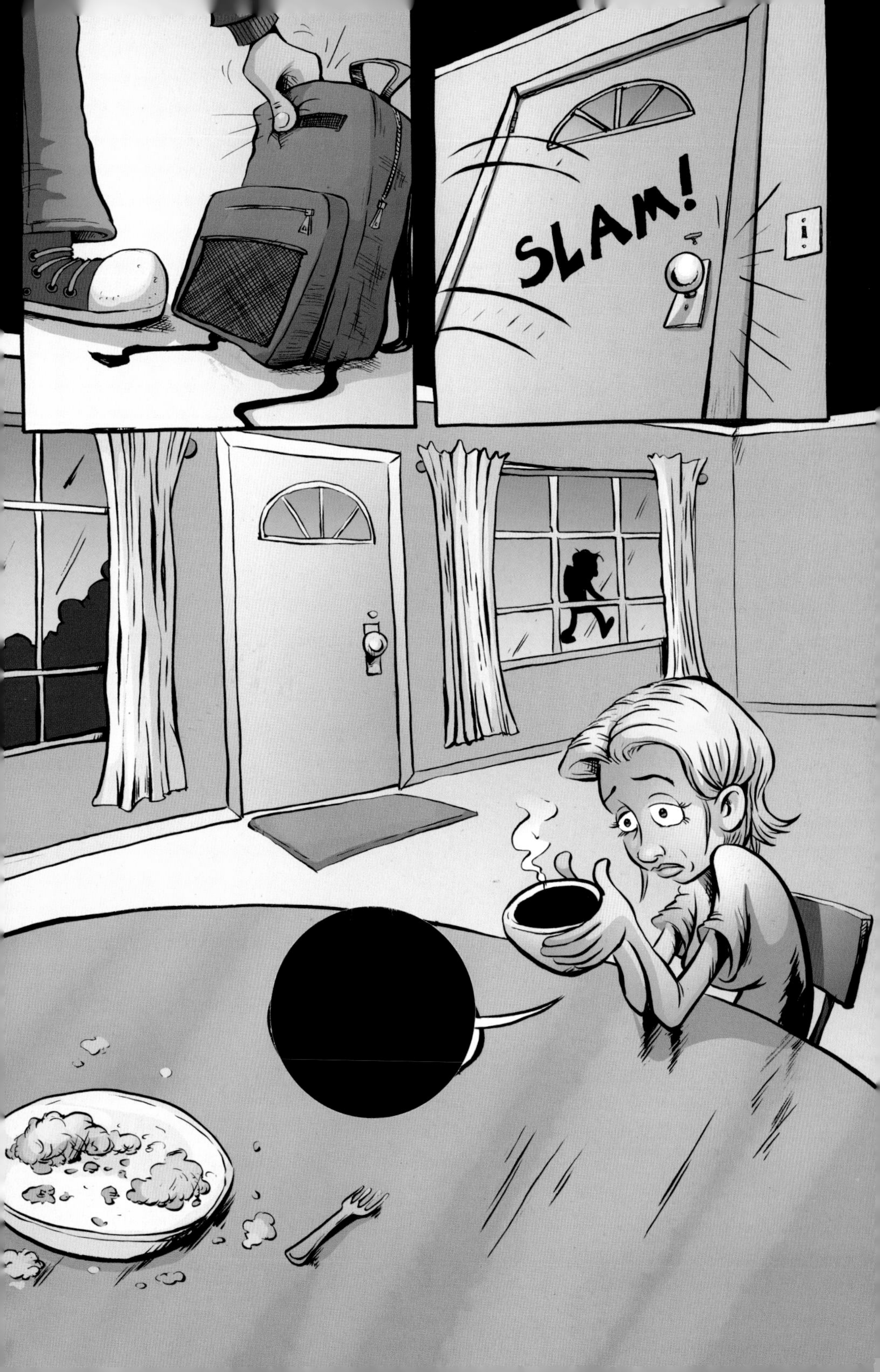
SLAM!
[redacted]

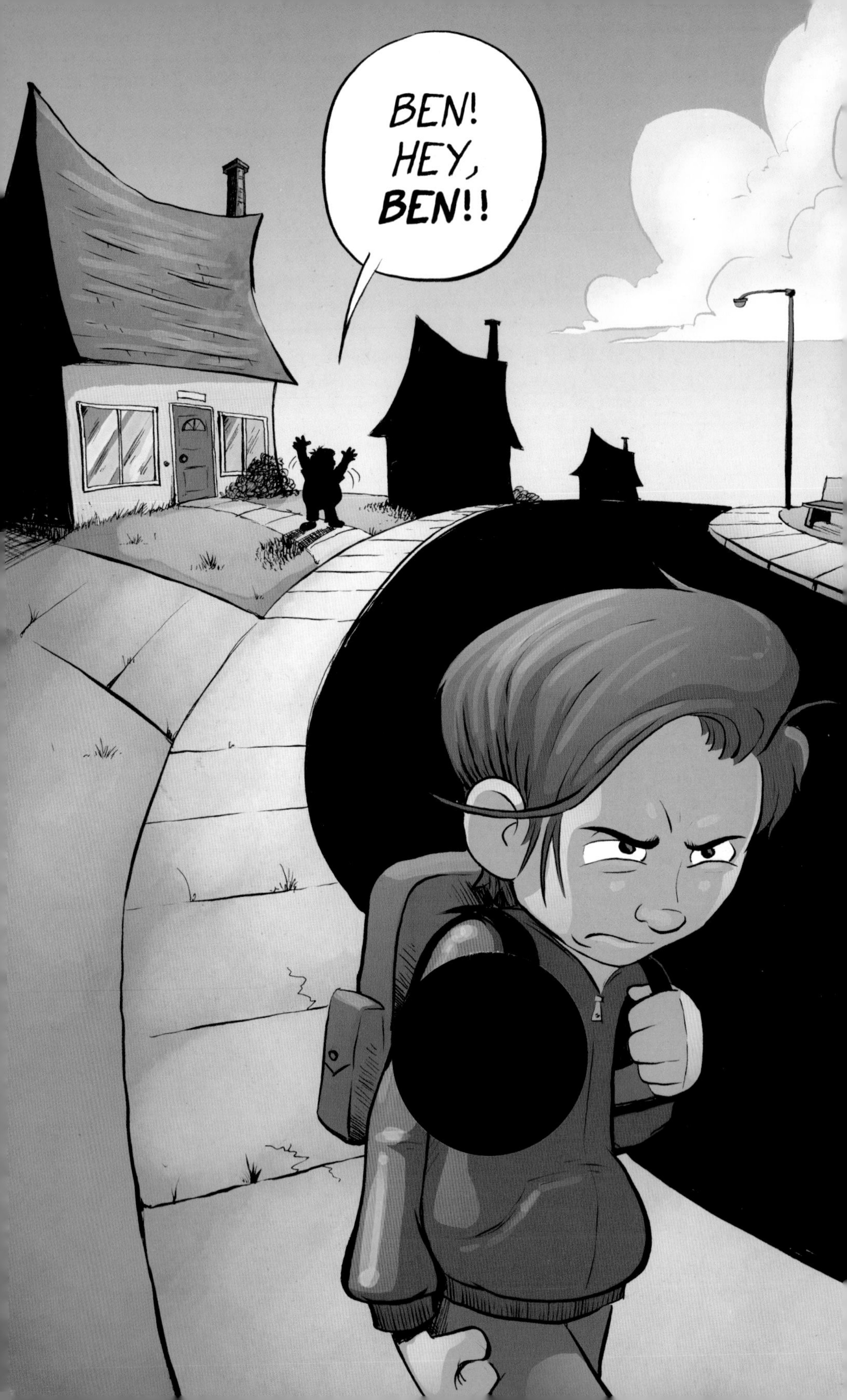
BEN! HEY, BEN!!

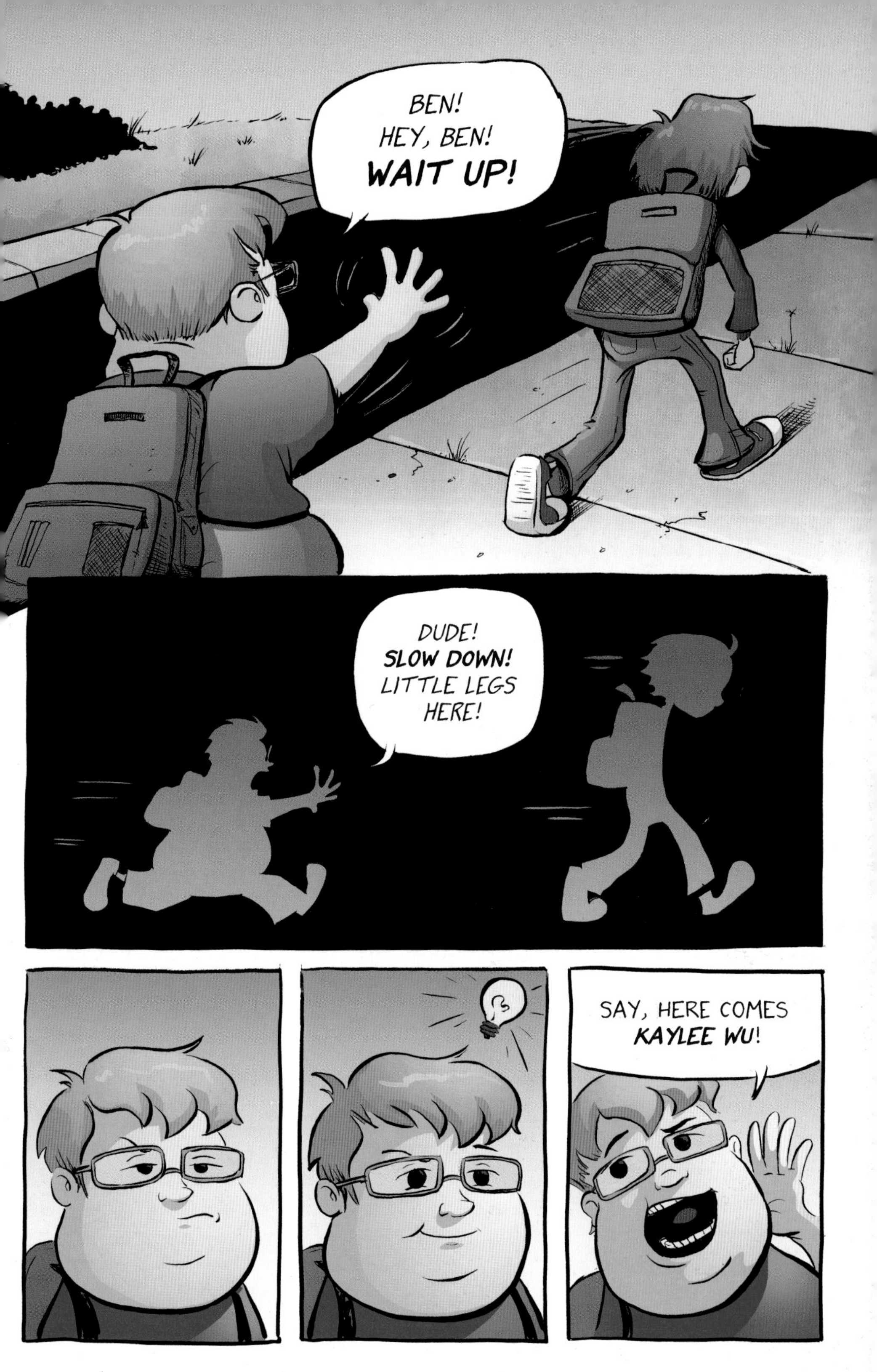
BEN!
HEY, BEN!
WAIT UP!
DUDE!
SLOW DOWN!
LITTLE LEGS
HERE!
SAY, HERE COMES
KAYLEE WU!

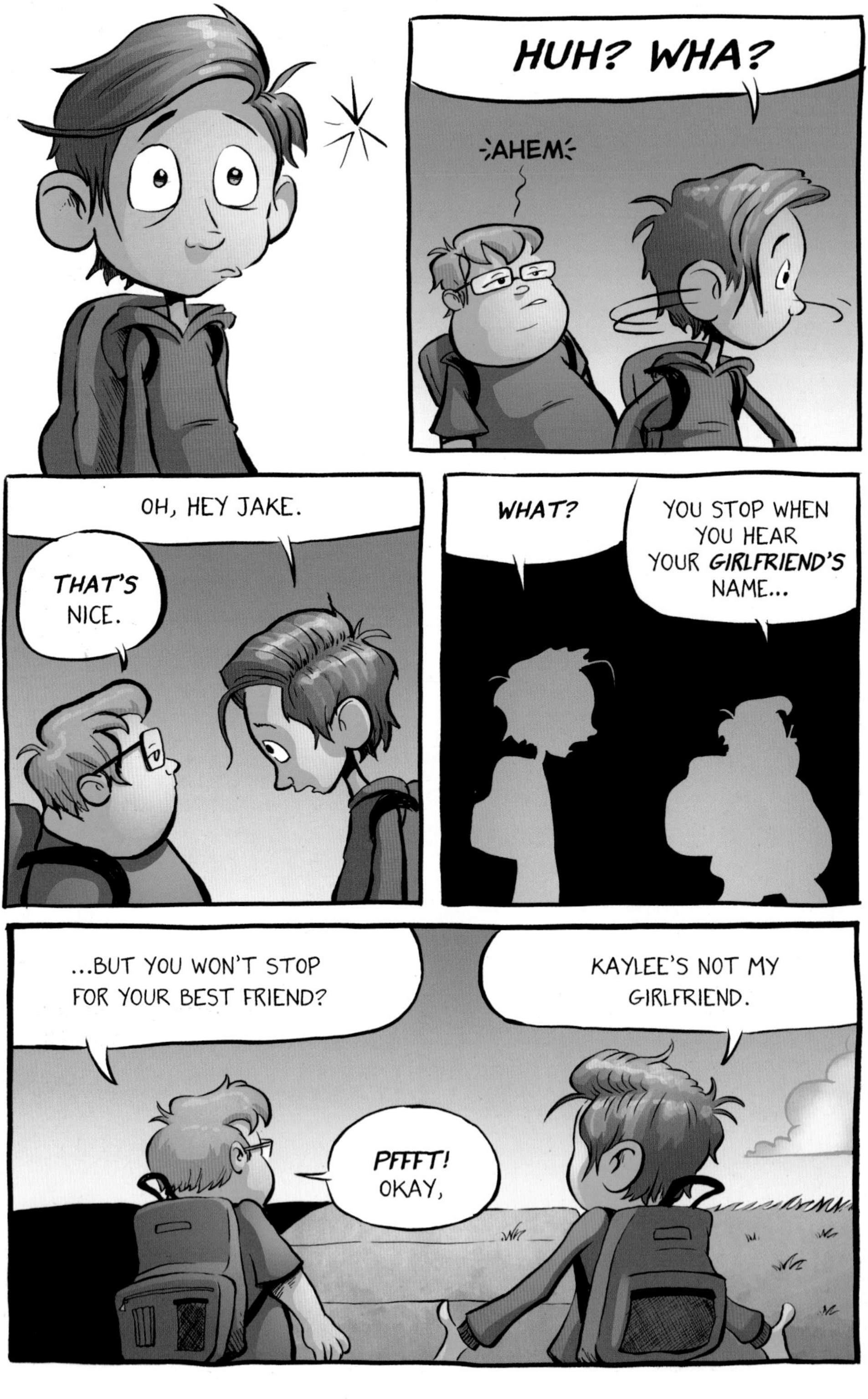
HUH? WHA?
AHEM
OH, HEY JAKE.
THAT'S NICE.
WHAT?
YOU STOP WHEN YOU HEAR YOUR GIRLFRIEND'S NAME...
...BUT YOU WON'T STOP FOR YOUR BEST FRIEND?
KAYLEE'S NOT MY GIRLFRIEND.
PFFFT! OKAY,

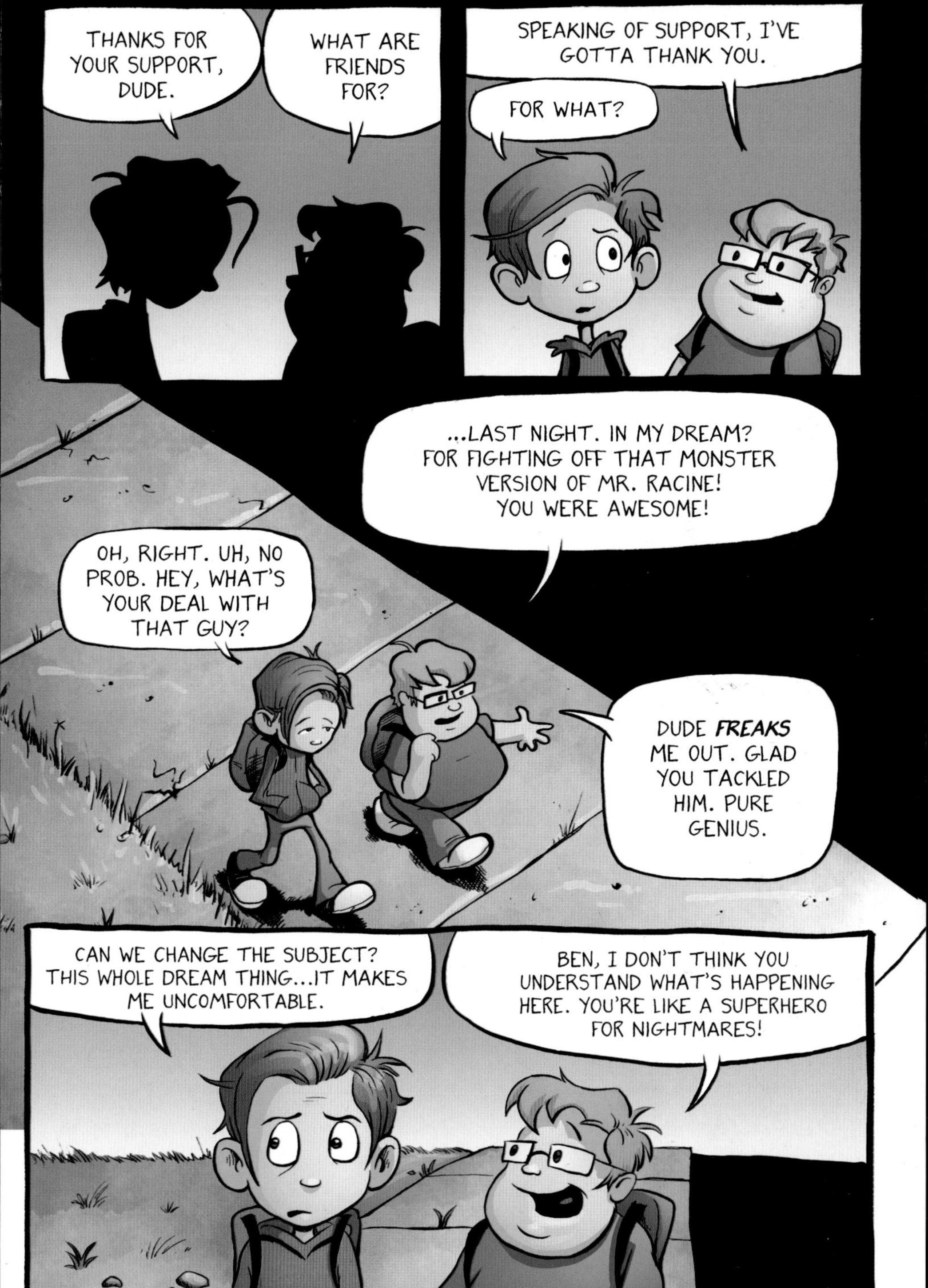
THANKS FOR YOUR SUPPORT, DUDE.
WHAT ARE FRIENDS FOR?
SPEAKING OF SUPPORT, I'VE GOTTA THANK YOU.
FOR WHAT?
...LAST NIGHT. IN MY DREAM? FOR FIGHTING OFF THAT MONSTER VERSION OF MR. RACINE! YOU WERE AWESOME!
OH, RIGHT. UH, NO PROB. HEY, WHAT'S YOUR DEAL WITH THAT GUY?
DUDE ***FREAKS*** ME OUT. GLAD YOU TACKLED HIM. PURE GENIUS.
CAN WE CHANGE THE SUBJECT? THIS WHOLE DREAM THING...IT MAKES ME UNCOMFORTABLE.
BEN, I DON'T THINK YOU UNDERSTAND WHAT'S HAPPENING HERE. YOU'RE LIKE A SUPERHERO FOR NIGHTMARES!

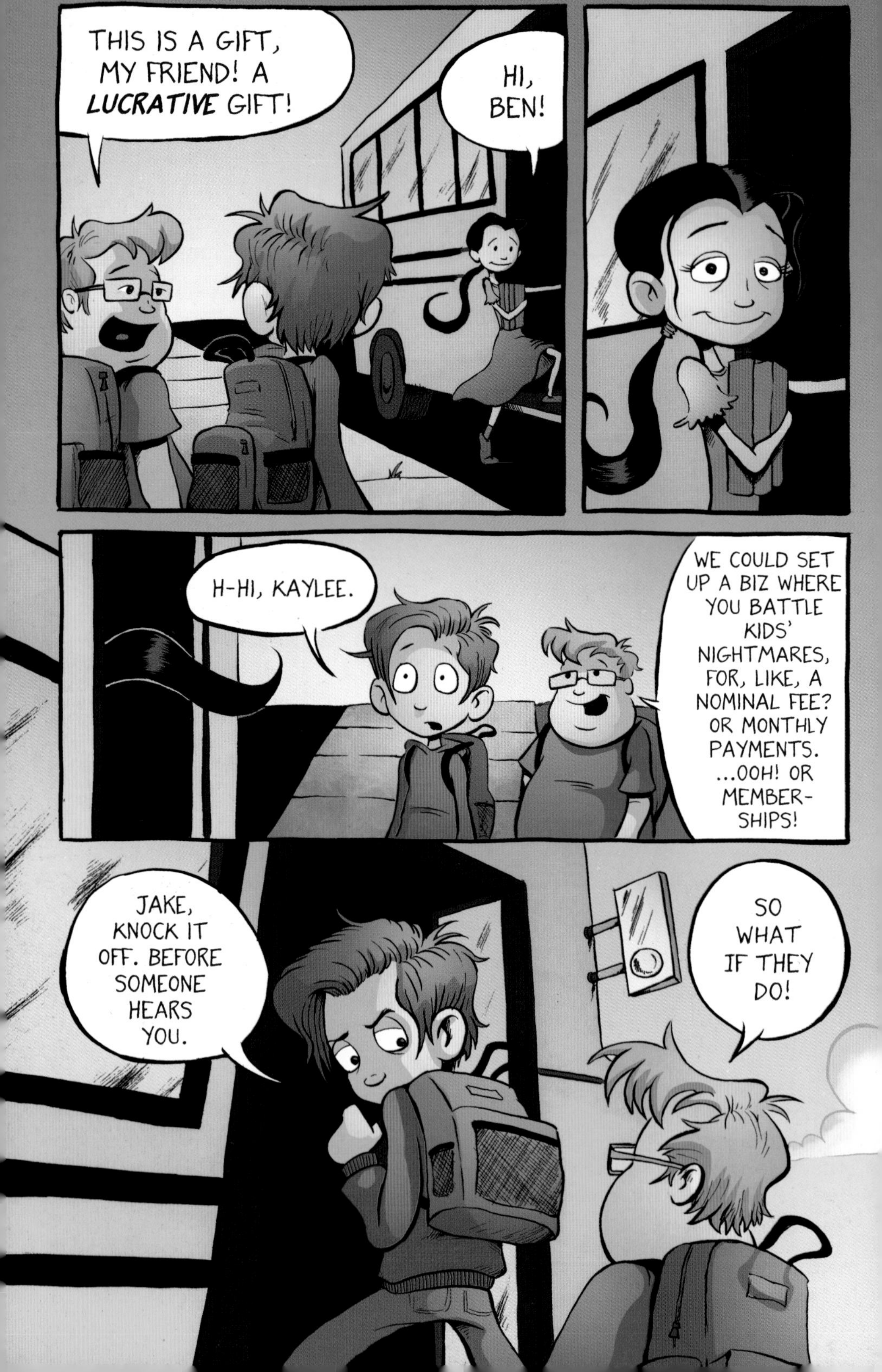
THIS IS A GIFT, MY FRIEND! A *LUCRATIVE* GIFT!
HI, BEN!
H-HI, KAYLEE.
WE COULD SET UP A BIZ WHERE YOU BATTLE KIDS' NIGHTMARES, FOR, LIKE, A NOMINAL FEE? OR MONTHLY PAYMENTS. ...OOH! OR MEMBER-SHIPS!
JAKE, KNOCK IT OFF. BEFORE SOMEONE HEARS YOU.
SO WHAT IF THEY DO!

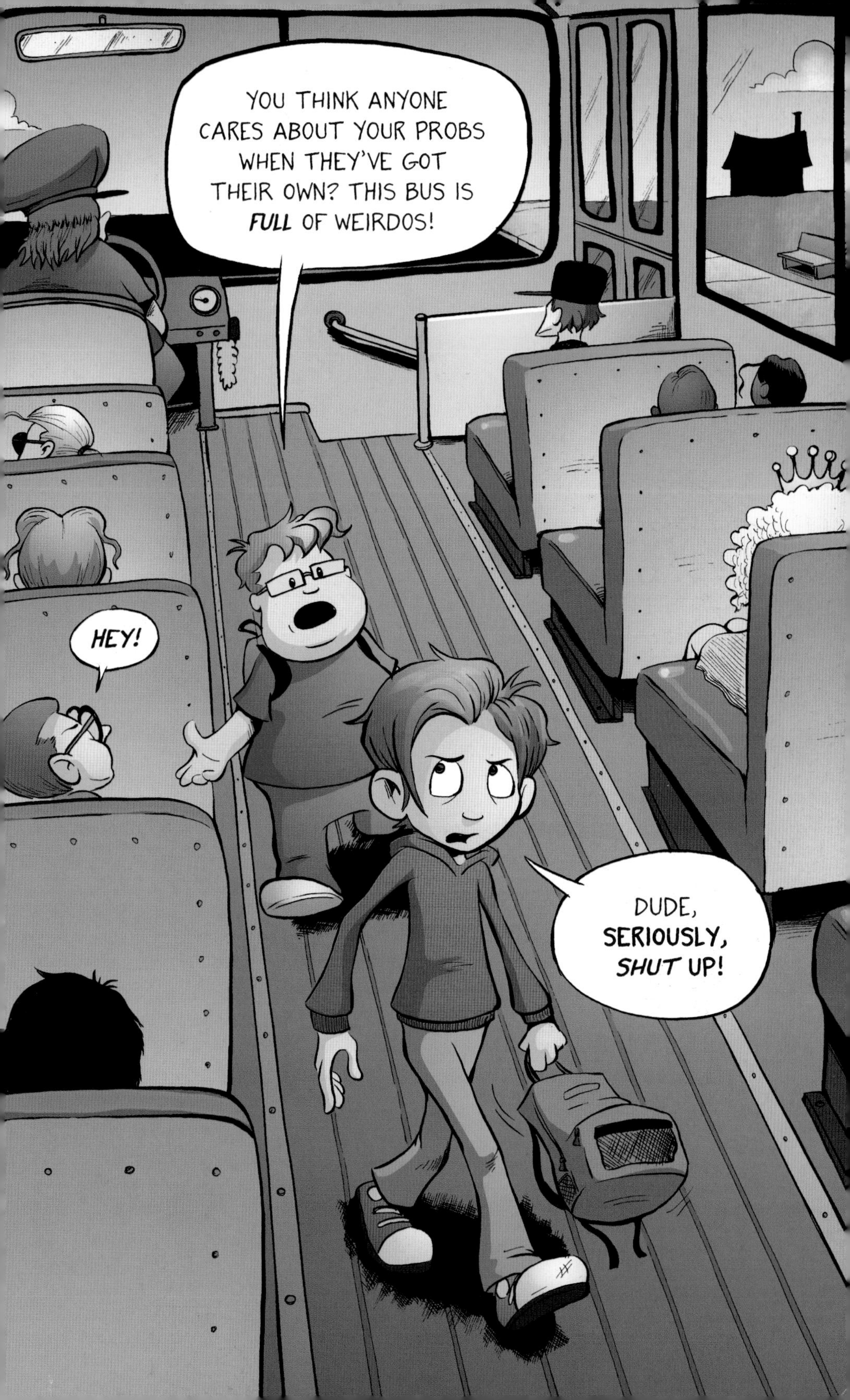
YOU THINK ANYONE CARES ABOUT YOUR PROBS WHEN THEY'VE GOT THEIR OWN? THIS BUS IS *FULL* OF WEIRDOS!
HEY!
DUDE, **SERIOUSLY,** ***SHUT*** UP!

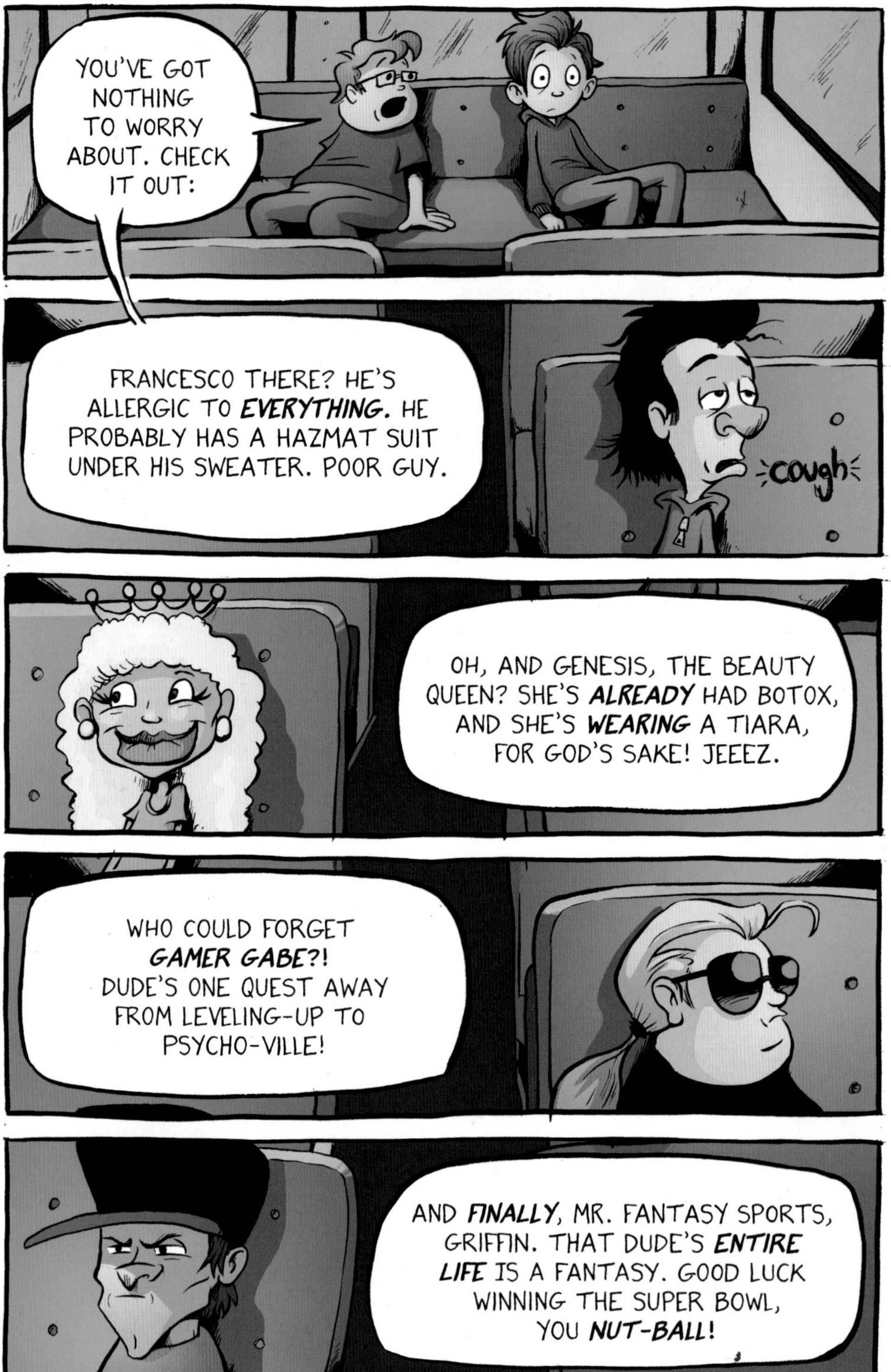
YOU'VE GOT NOTHING TO WORRY ABOUT. CHECK IT OUT:
FRANCESCO THERE? HE'S ALLERGIC TO EVERYTHING. HE PROBABLY HAS A HAZMAT SUIT UNDER HIS SWEATER. POOR GUY.
cough
OH, AND GENESIS, THE BEAUTY QUEEN? SHE'S ALREADY HAD BOTOX, AND SHE'S WEARING A TIARA, FOR GOD'S SAKE! JEEEZ.
WHO COULD FORGET GAMER GABE?! DUDE'S ONE QUEST AWAY FROM LEVELING-UP TO PSYCHO-VILLE!
AND FINALLY, MR. FANTASY SPORTS, GRIFFIN. THAT DUDE'S ENTIRE LIFE IS A FANTASY. GOOD LUCK WINNING THE SUPER BOWL, YOU NUT-BALL!

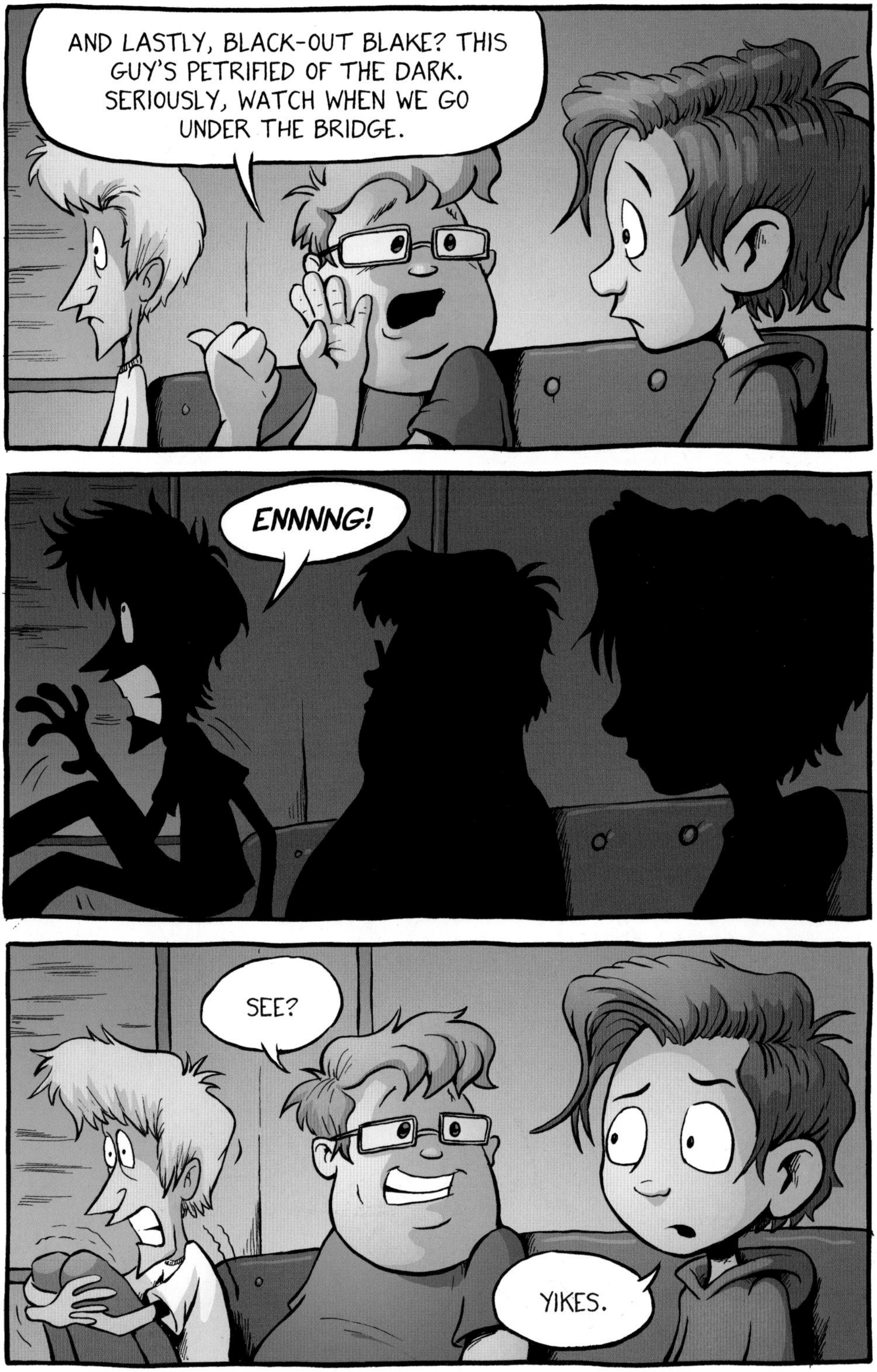
AND LASTLY, BLACK-OUT BLAKE? THIS GUY'S PETRIFIED OF THE DARK. SERIOUSLY, WATCH WHEN WE GO UNDER THE BRIDGE.
ENNNNG!
SEE?
YIKES.

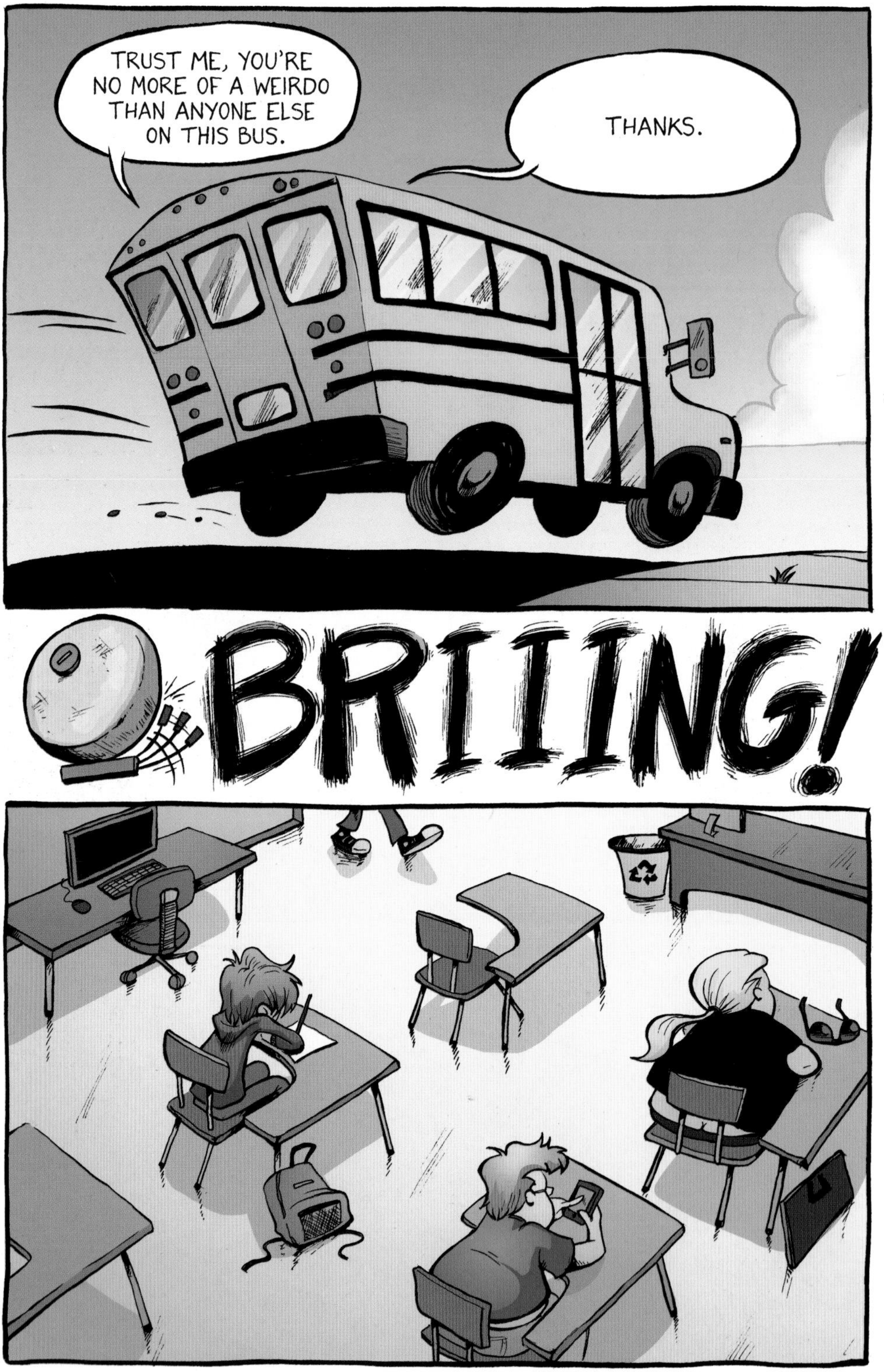
TRUST ME, YOU'RE NO MORE OF A WEIRDO THAN ANYONE ELSE ON THIS BUS.
THANKS.
BRIIING!

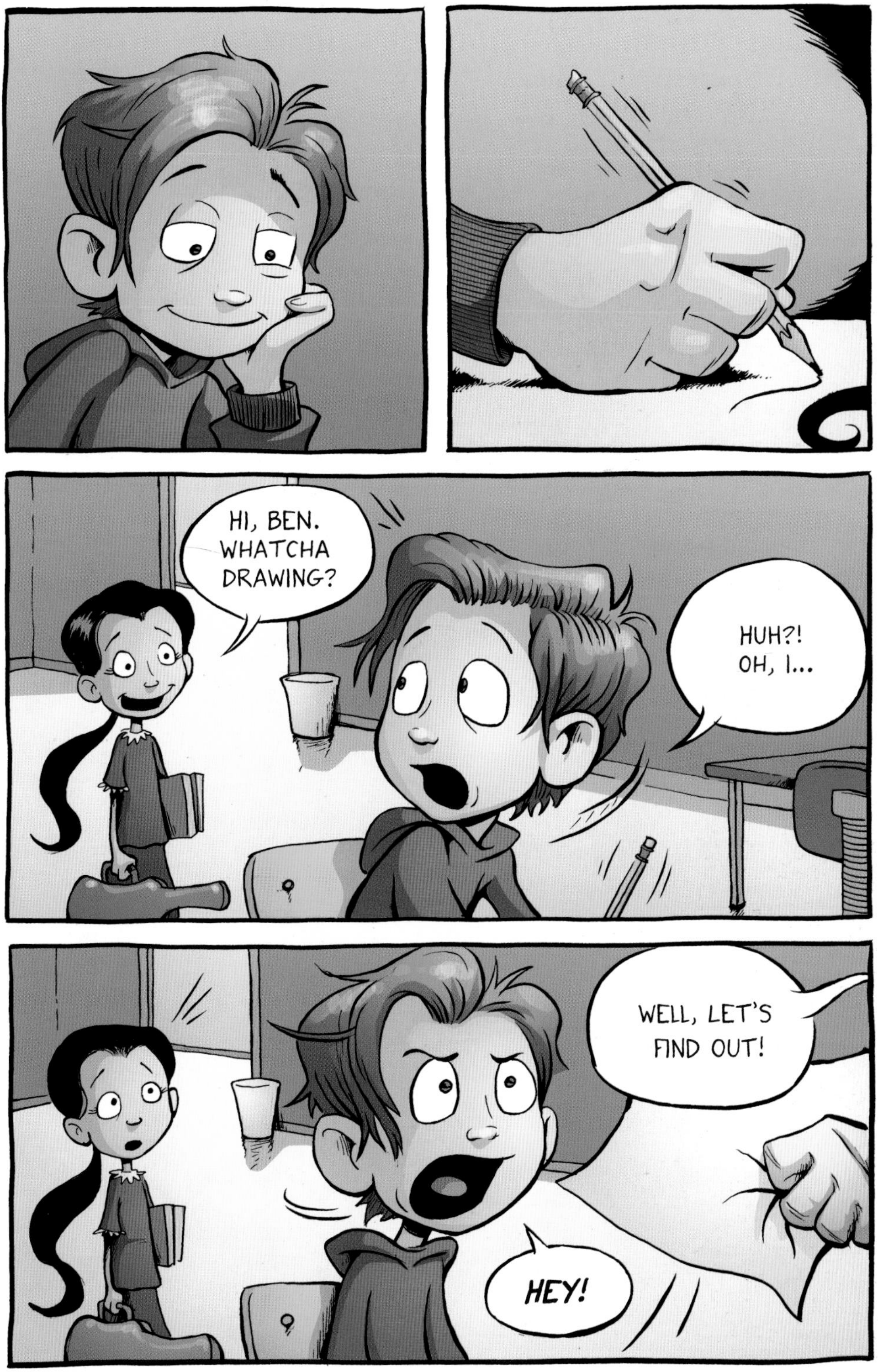
HI, BEN. WHATCHA DRAWING?
HUH?! OH, I...
WELL, LET'S FIND OUT!
HEY!

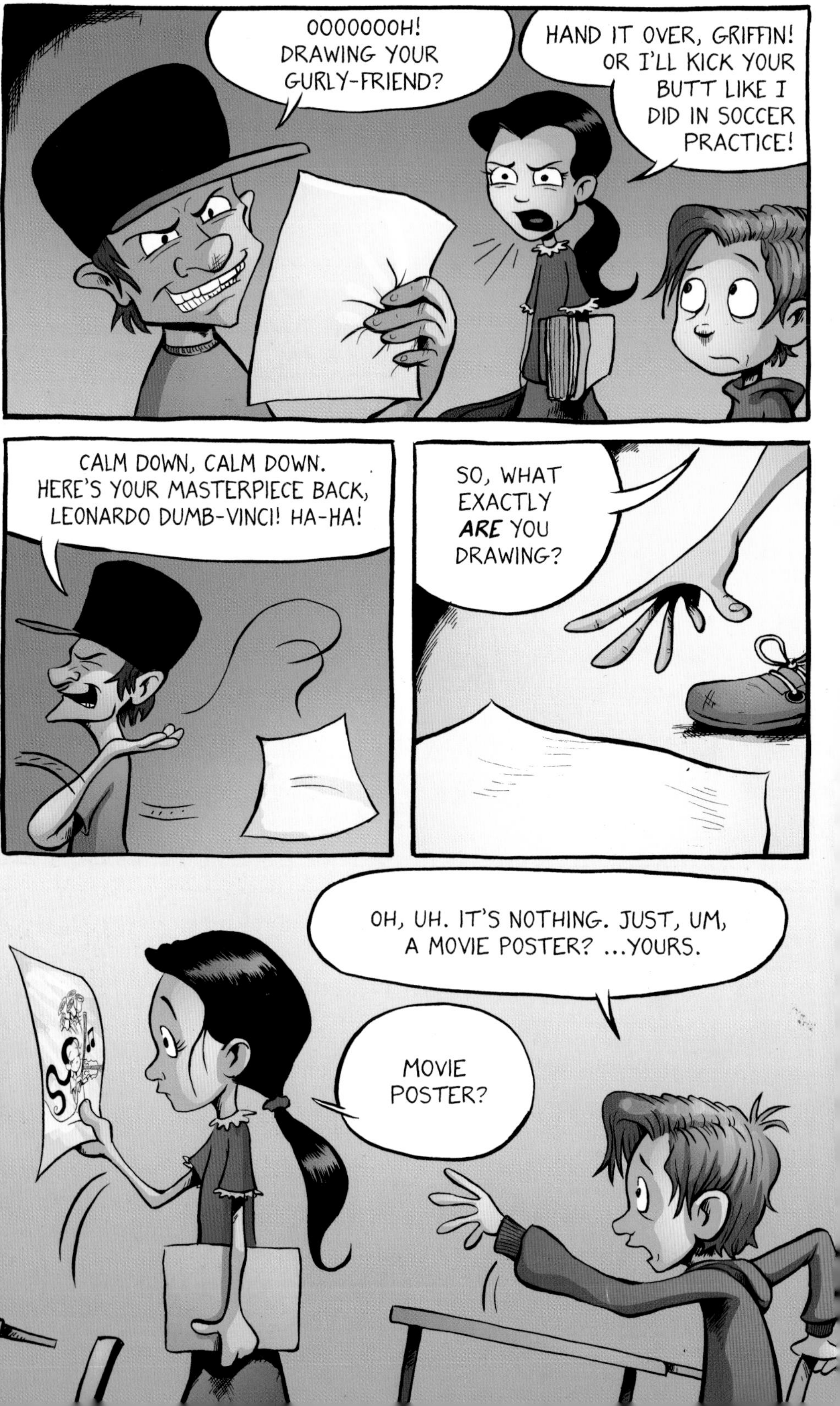

OOOOOOOH! DRAWING YOUR GURLY-FRIEND?
HAND IT OVER, GRIFFIN! OR I'LL KICK YOUR BUTT LIKE I DID IN SOCCER PRACTICE!
CALM DOWN, CALM DOWN. HERE'S YOUR MASTERPIECE BACK, LEONARDO DUMB-VINCI! HA-HA!
SO, WHAT EXACTLY **ARE** YOU DRAWING?
OH, UH. IT'S NOTHING. JUST, UM, A MOVIE POSTER? ...YOURS.
MOVIE POSTER?

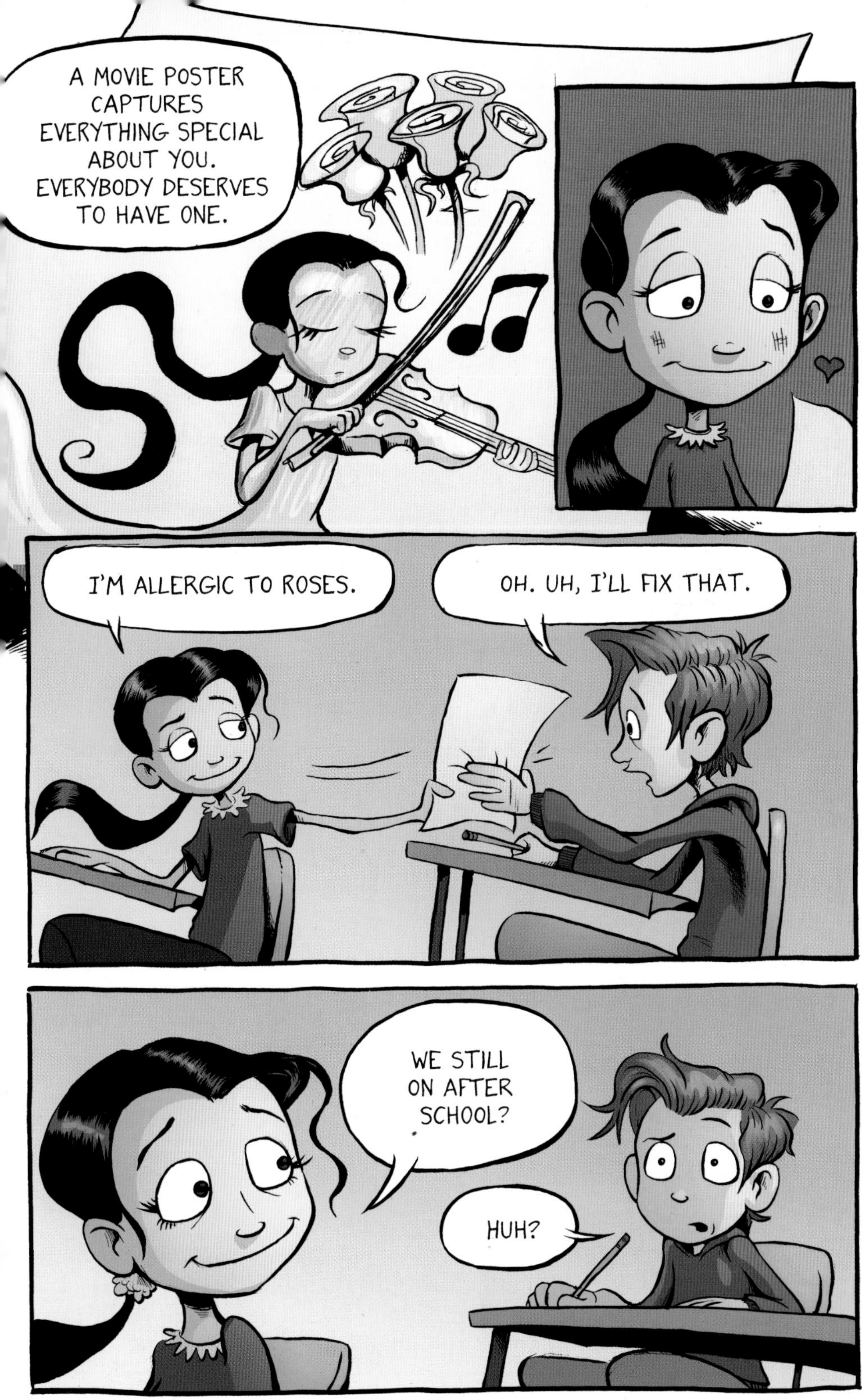
A MOVIE POSTER CAPTURES EVERYTHING SPECIAL ABOUT YOU. EVERYBODY DESERVES TO HAVE ONE.
I'M ALLERGIC TO ROSES.
OH. UH, I'LL FIX THAT.
WE STILL ON AFTER SCHOOL?
HUH?

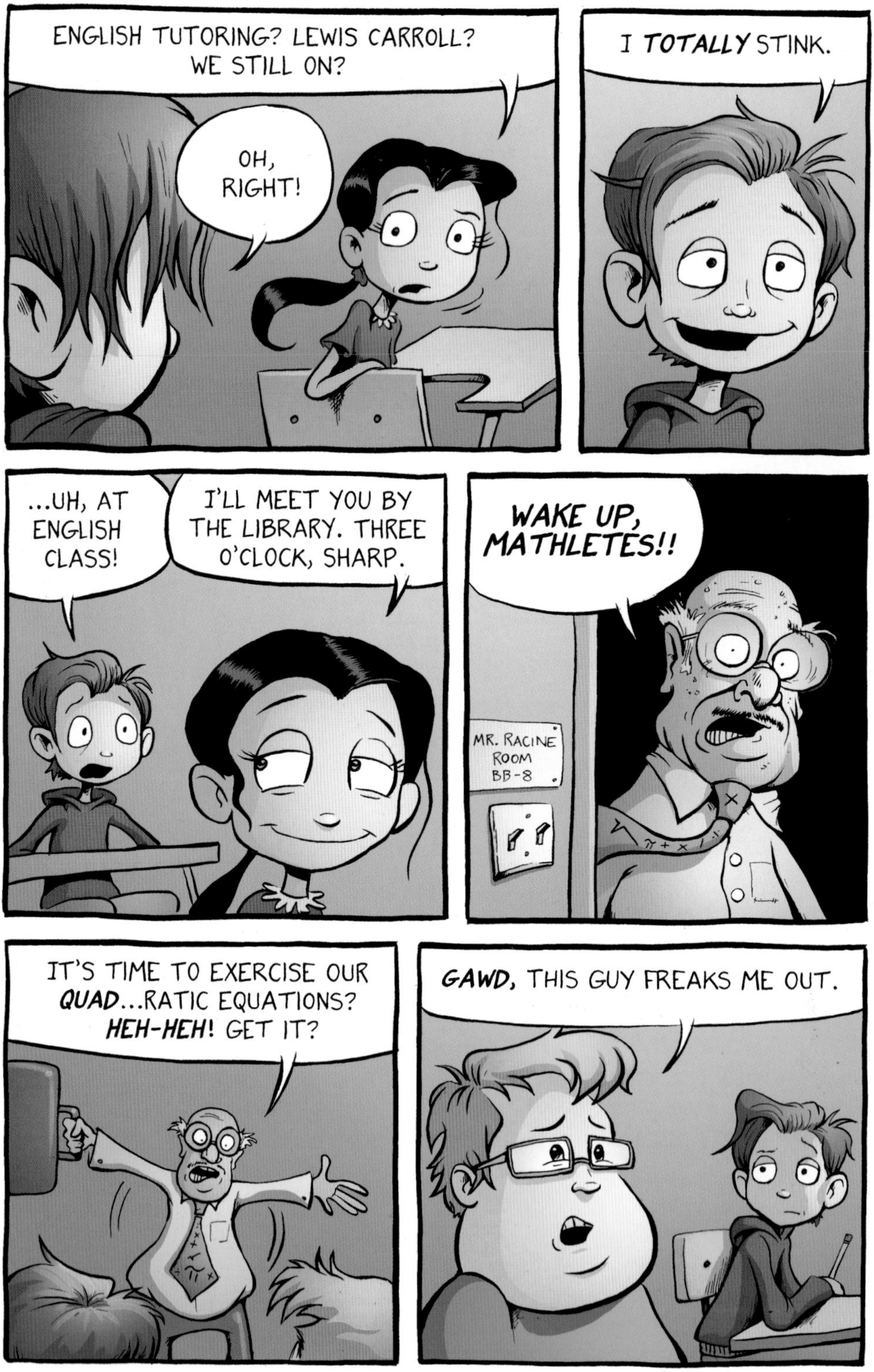
ENGLISH TUTORING? LEWIS CARROLL? WE STILL ON?
OH, RIGHT!
I TOTALLY STINK.
...UH, AT ENGLISH CLASS!
I'LL MEET YOU BY THE LIBRARY. THREE O'CLOCK, SHARP.
WAKE UP, MATHLETES!!
MR. RACINE ROOM BB-8
IT'S TIME TO EXERCISE OUR QUAD...RATIC EQUATIONS? HEH-HEH! GET IT?
GAWD, THIS GUY FREAKS ME OUT.

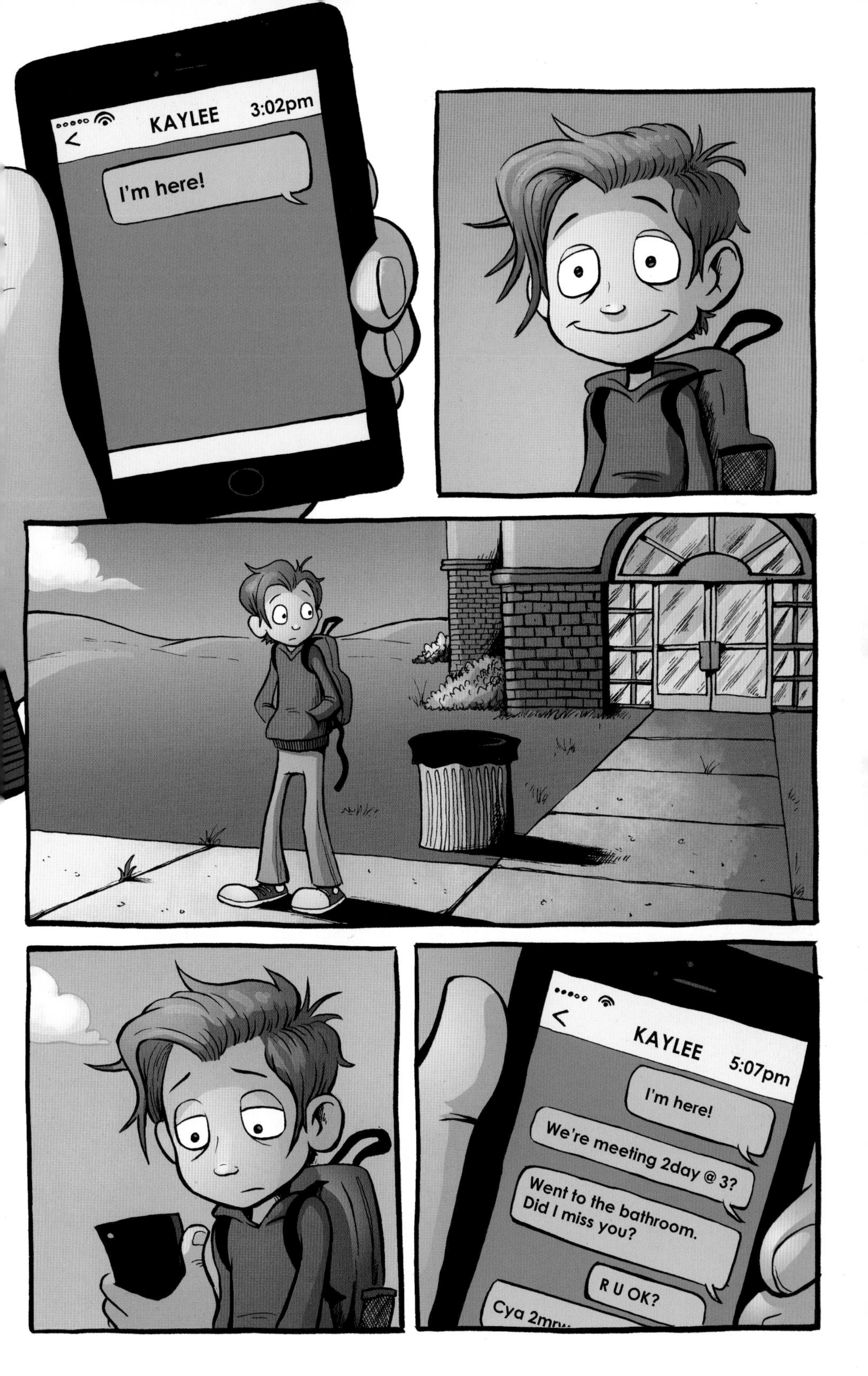
KAYLEE
3:02pm
I'm here!
KAYLEE
5:07pm
I'm here!
We're meeting 2day @ 3?
Went to the bathroom. Did I miss you?
R U OK?

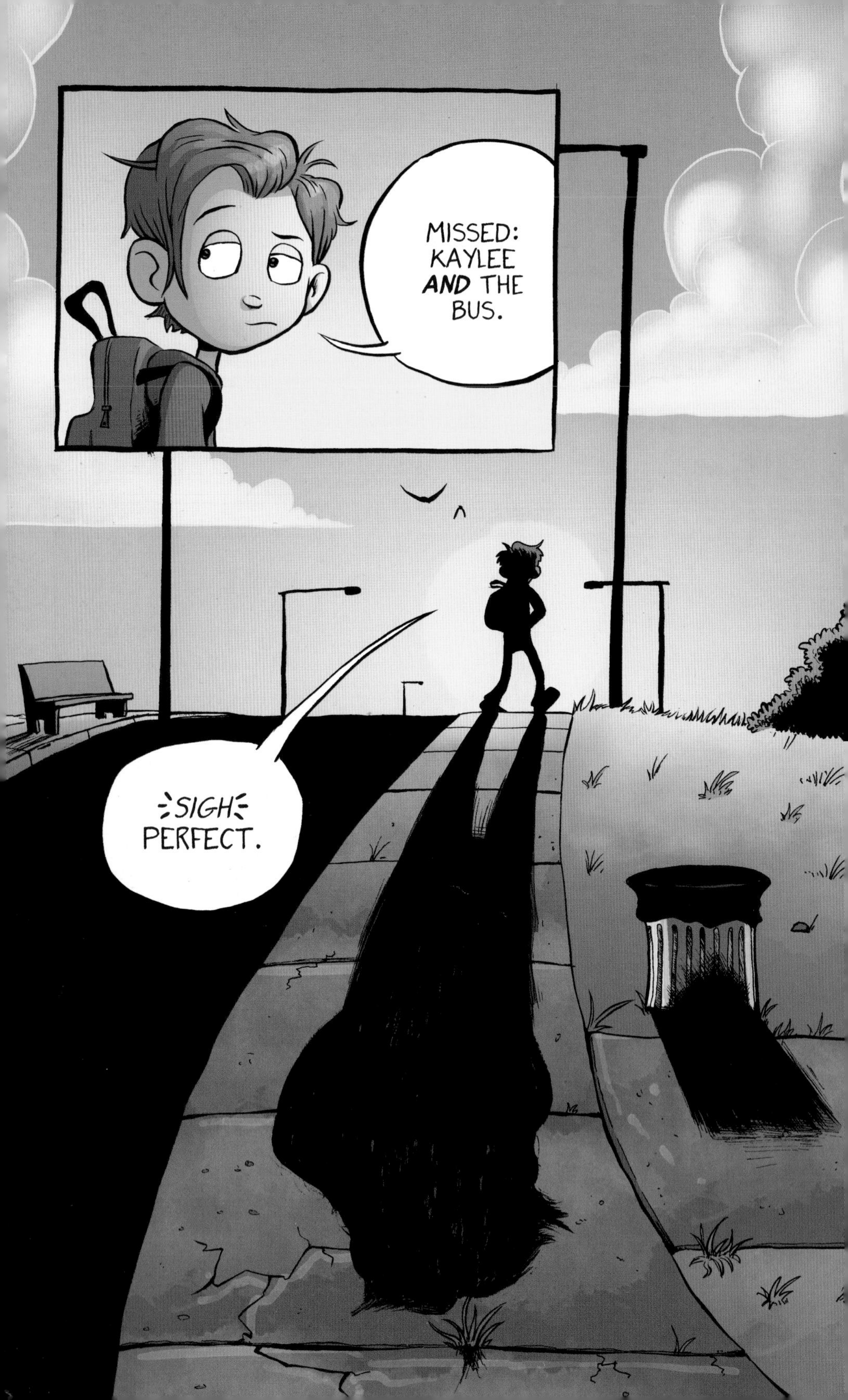
MISSED: KAYLEE AND THE BUS.
SIGH
PERFECT.

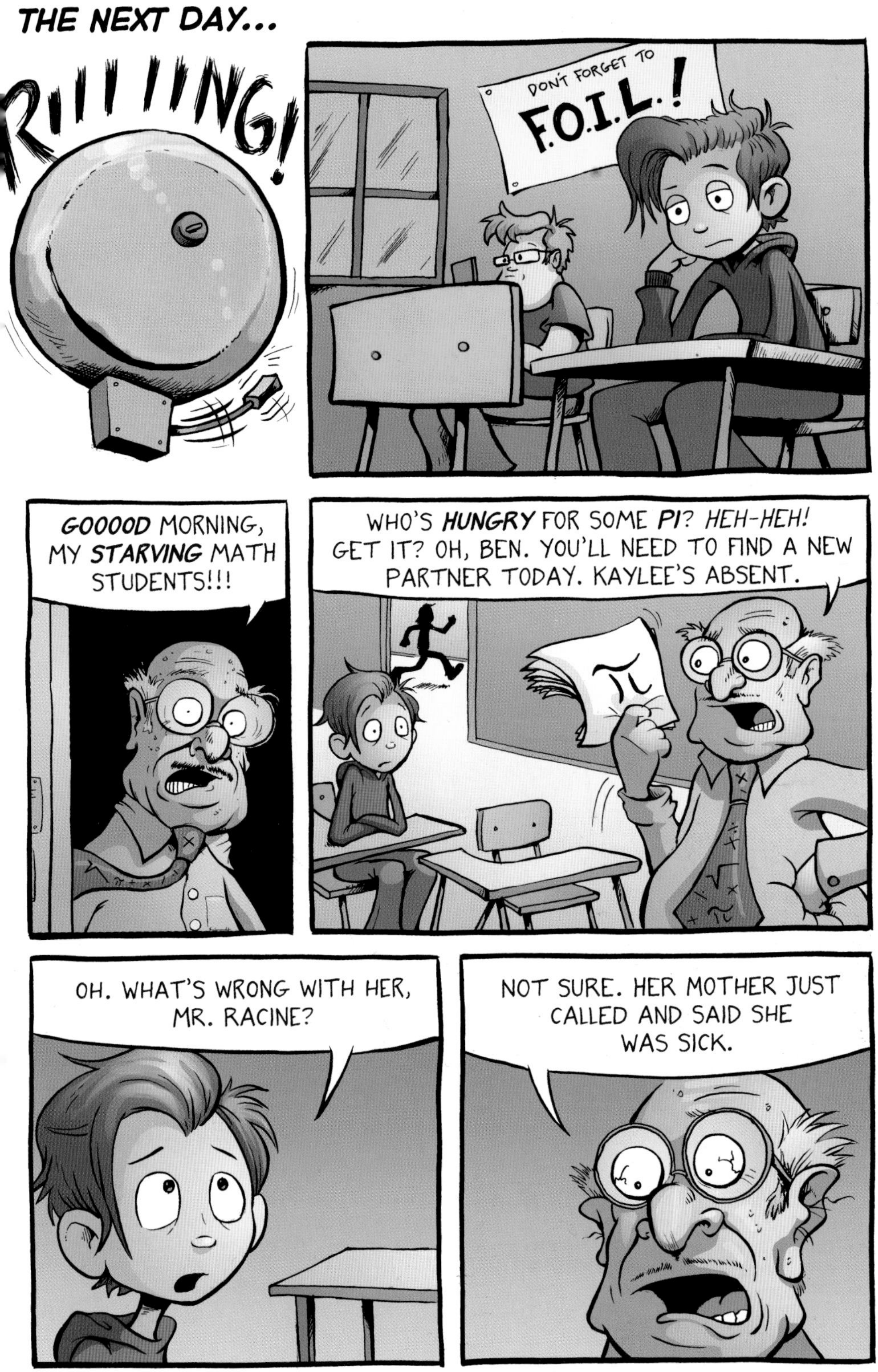
THE NEXT DAY...
RIIIIING!
DON'T FORGET TO F.O.I.L.!
GOOOOD MORNING, MY STARVING MATH STUDENTS!!!
WHO'S HUNGRY FOR SOME PI? HEH-HEH! GET IT? OH, BEN. YOU'LL NEED TO FIND A NEW PARTNER TODAY. KAYLEE'S ABSENT.
OH. WHAT'S WRONG WITH HER, MR. RACINE?
NOT SURE. HER MOTHER JUST CALLED AND SAID SHE WAS SICK.

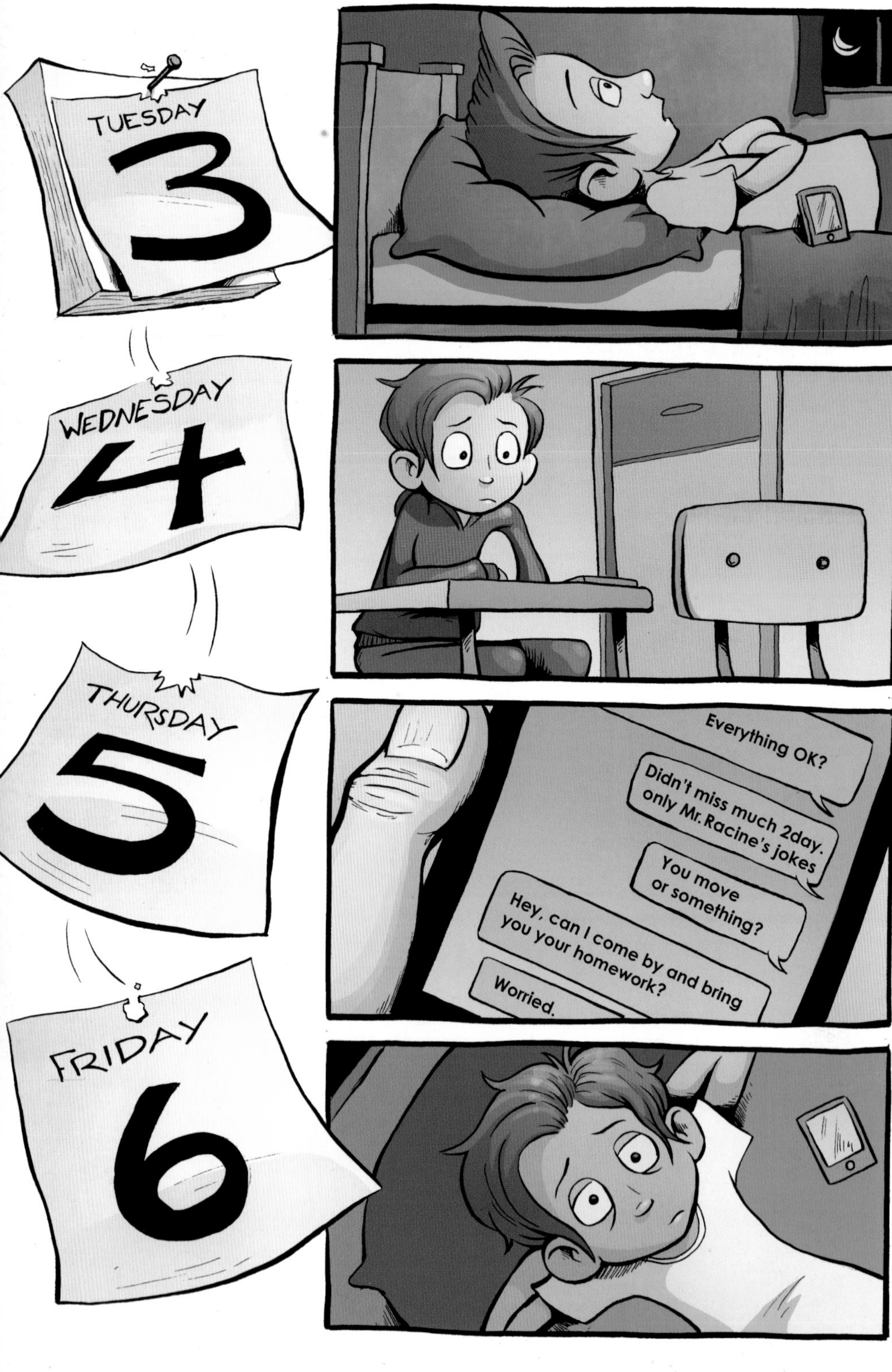
TUESDAY
3
WEDNESDAY
4
THURSDAY
5
Everything OK?
Didn't miss much 2day. only Mr. Racine's jokes
You move or something?
Hey, can I come by and bring you your homework?
Worried.
FRIDAY
6

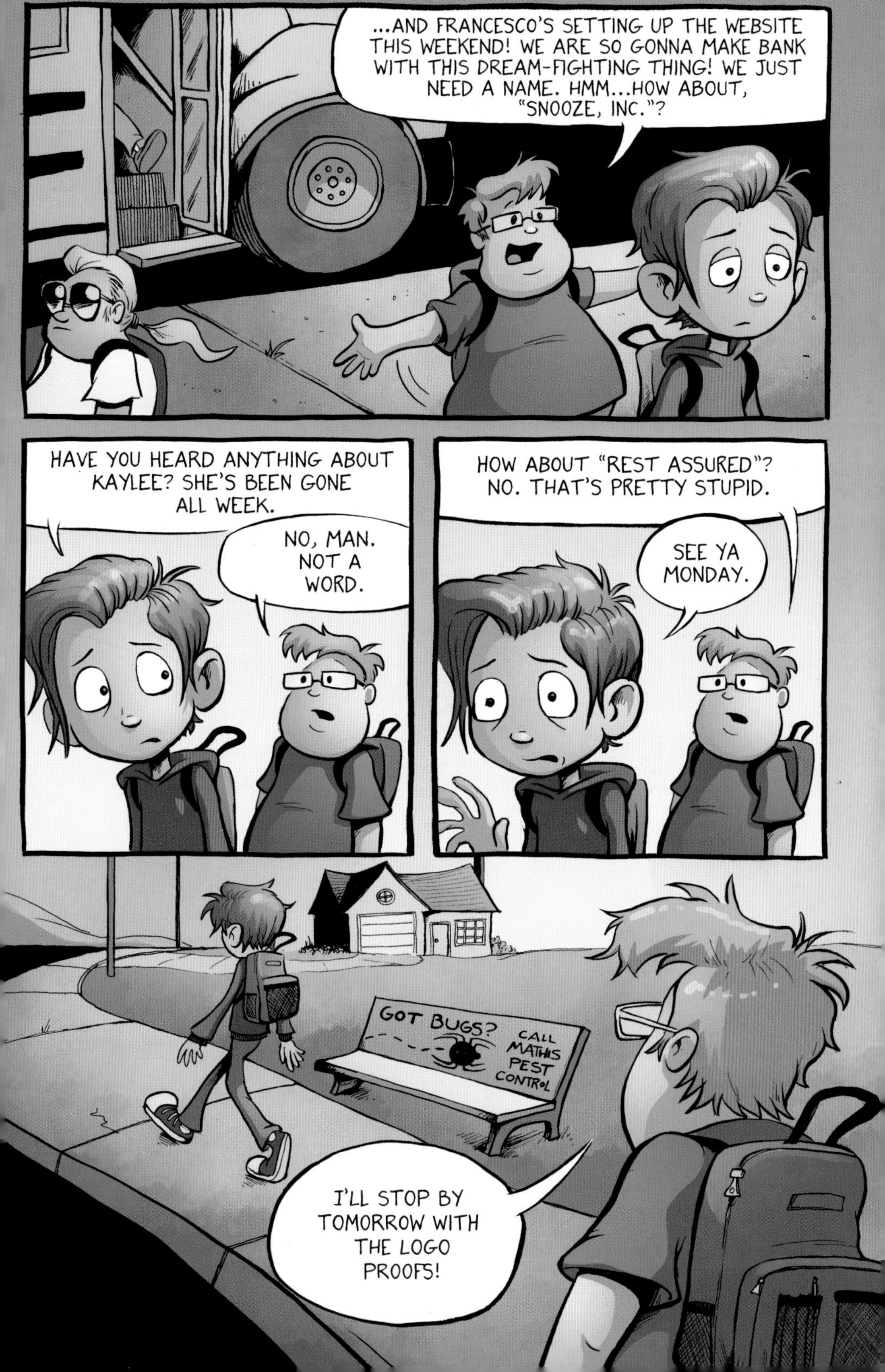
...AND FRANCESCO'S SETTING UP THE WEBSITE THIS WEEKEND! WE ARE SO GONNA MAKE BANK WITH THIS DREAM-FIGHTING THING! WE JUST NEED A NAME. HMM...HOW ABOUT, "SNOOZE, INC."?
HAVE YOU HEARD ANYTHING ABOUT KAYLEE? SHE'S BEEN GONE ALL WEEK.
NO, MAN. NOT A WORD.
HOW ABOUT "REST ASSURED"? NO. THAT'S PRETTY STUPID.
SEE YA MONDAY.
GOT BUGS?
CALL MATHIS PEST CONTROL
I'LL STOP BY TOMORROW WITH THE LOGO PROOFS!

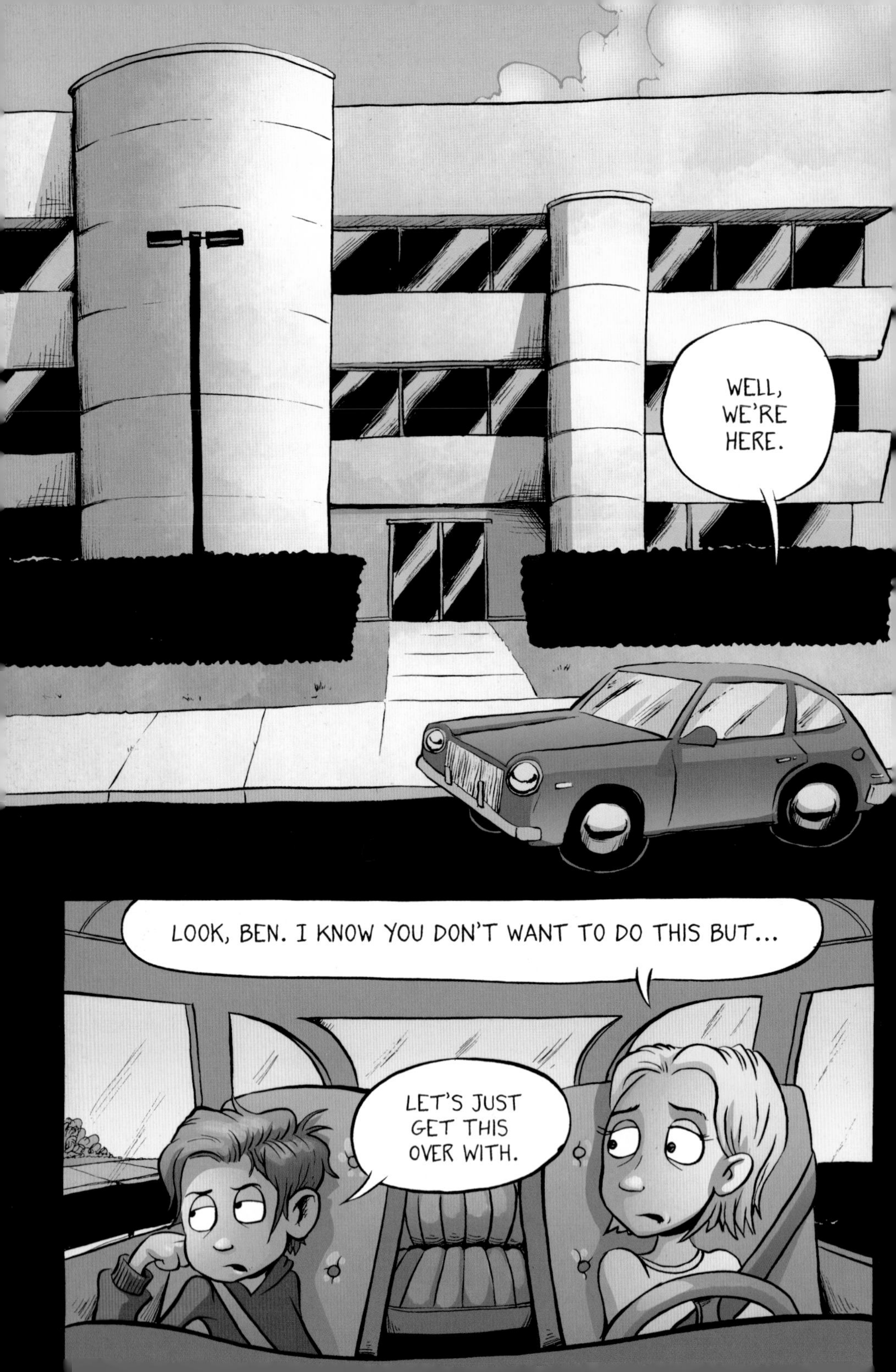
WELL, WE'RE HERE.
LOOK, BEN. I KNOW YOU DON'T WANT TO DO THIS BUT...
LET'S JUST GET THIS OVER WITH.

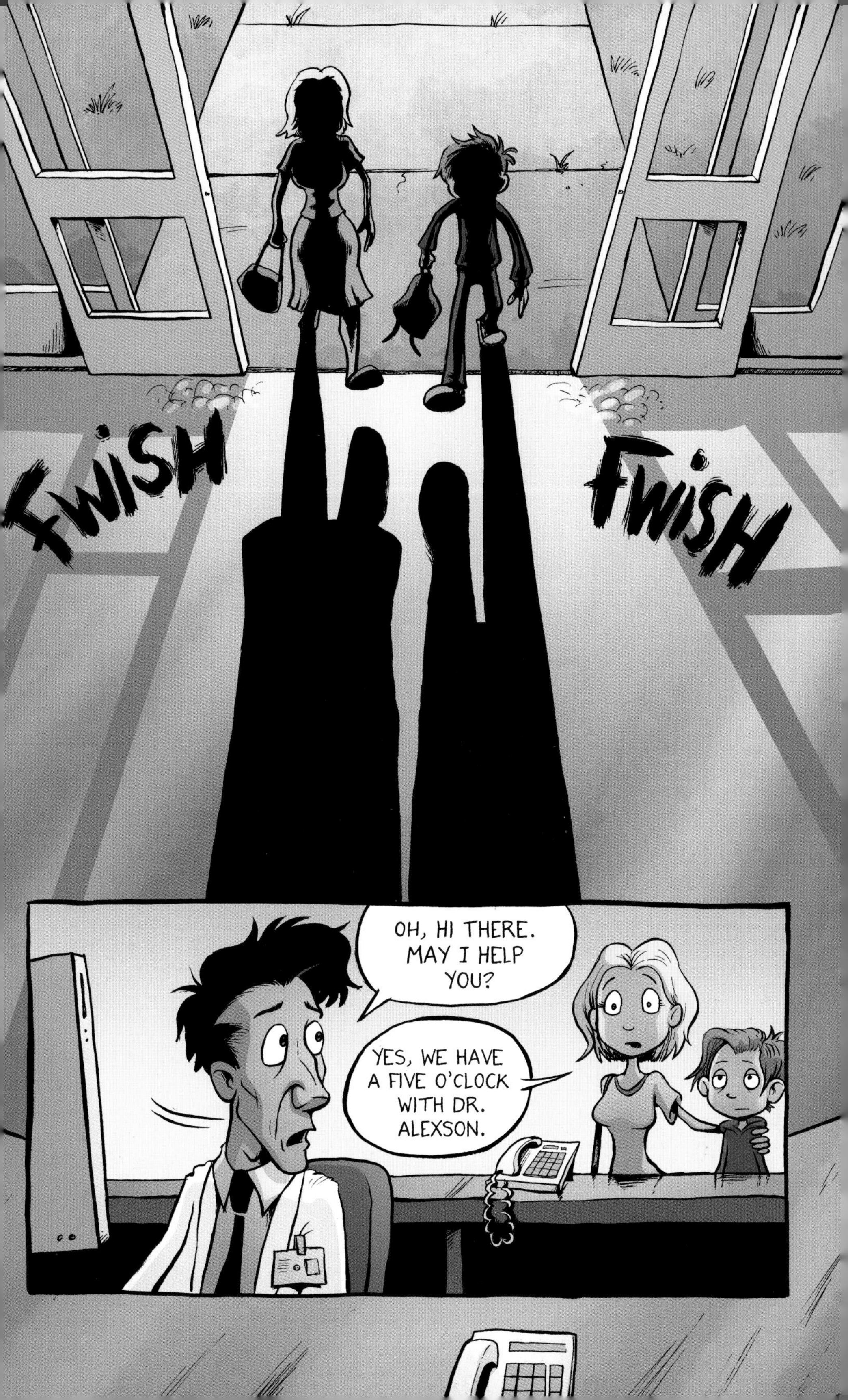
FWISH
FWISH
OH, HI THERE. MAY I HELP YOU?
YES, WE HAVE A FIVE O'CLOCK WITH DR. ALEXSON.

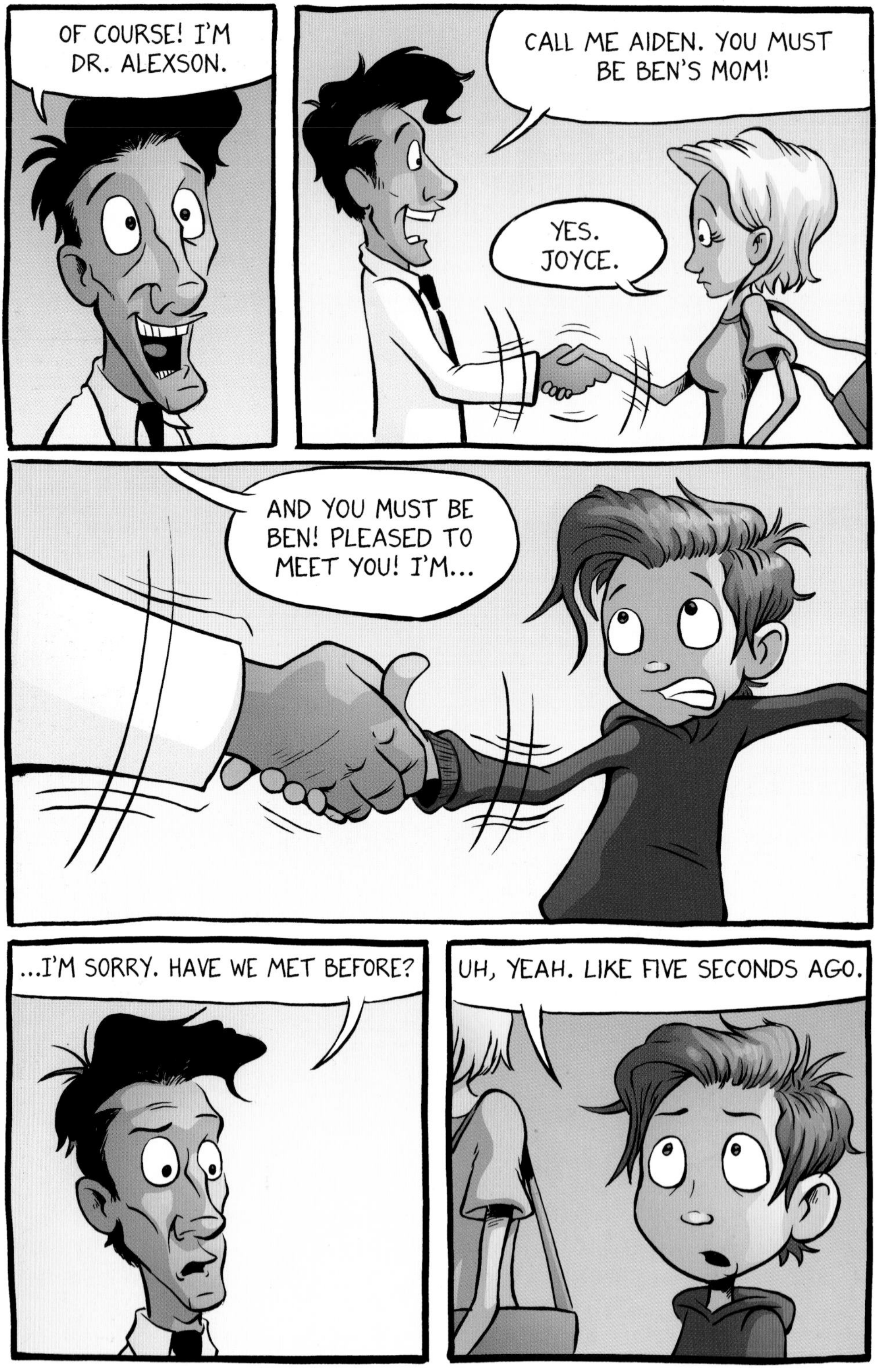
OF COURSE! I'M DR. ALEXSON.
CALL ME AIDEN. YOU MUST BE BEN'S MOM!
YES. JOYCE.
AND YOU MUST BE BEN! PLEASED TO MEET YOU! I'M...
...I'M SORRY. HAVE WE MET BEFORE?
UH, YEAH. LIKE FIVE SECONDS AGO.

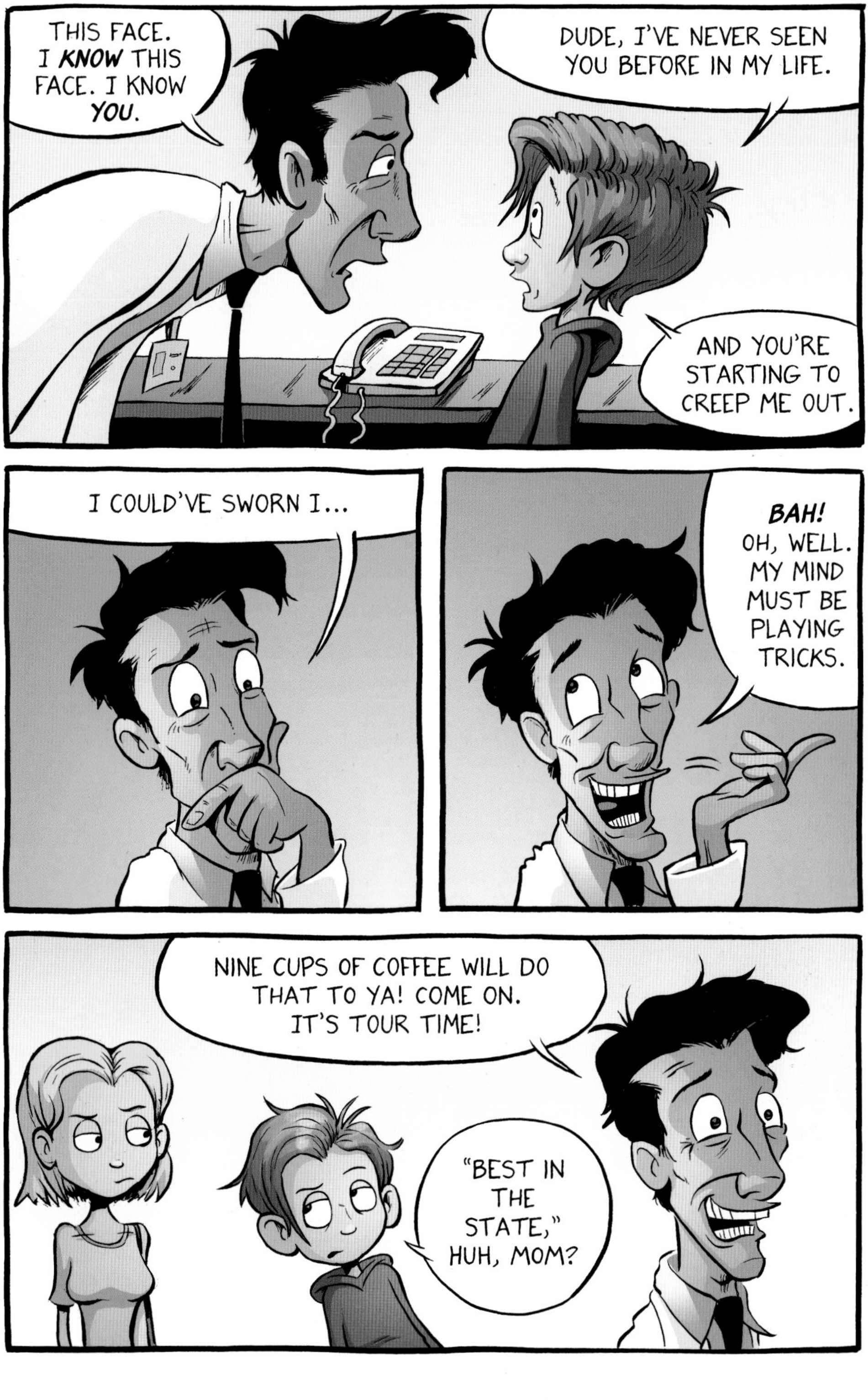
THIS FACE. I **KNOW** THIS FACE. I KNOW **YOU**.
DUDE, I'VE NEVER SEEN YOU BEFORE IN MY LIFE.
AND YOU'RE STARTING TO CREEP ME OUT.
I COULD'VE SWORN I...
BAH! OH, WELL. MY MIND MUST BE PLAYING TRICKS.
NINE CUPS OF COFFEE WILL DO THAT TO YA! COME ON. IT'S TOUR TIME!
"BEST IN THE STATE," HUH, MOM?

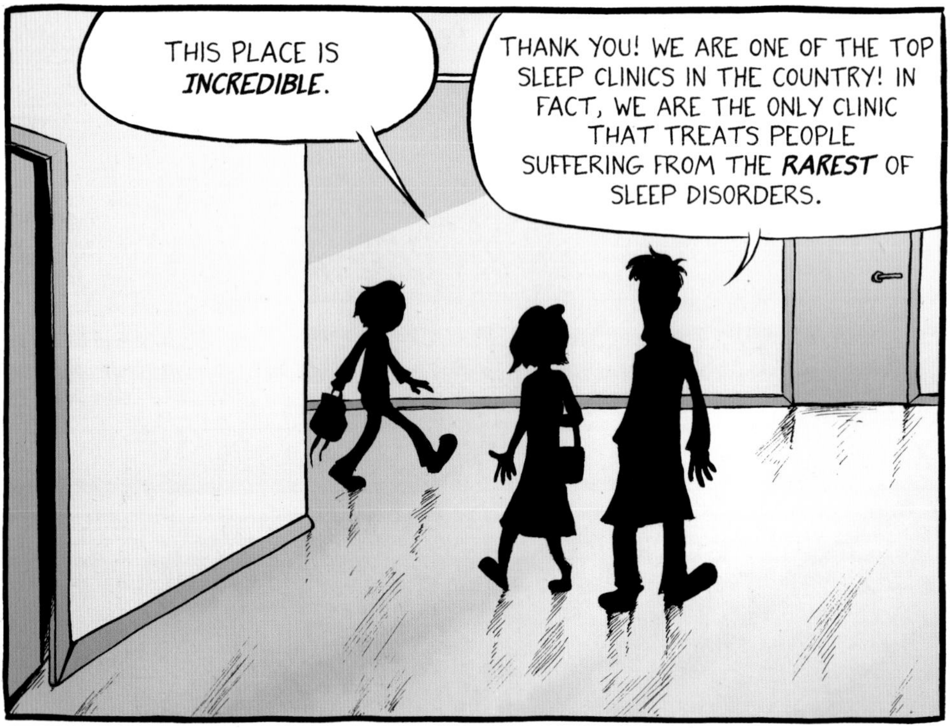
THIS PLACE IS INCREDIBLE.
THANK YOU! WE ARE ONE OF THE TOP SLEEP CLINICS IN THE COUNTRY! IN FACT, WE ARE THE ONLY CLINIC THAT TREATS PEOPLE SUFFERING FROM THE RAREST OF SLEEP DISORDERS.

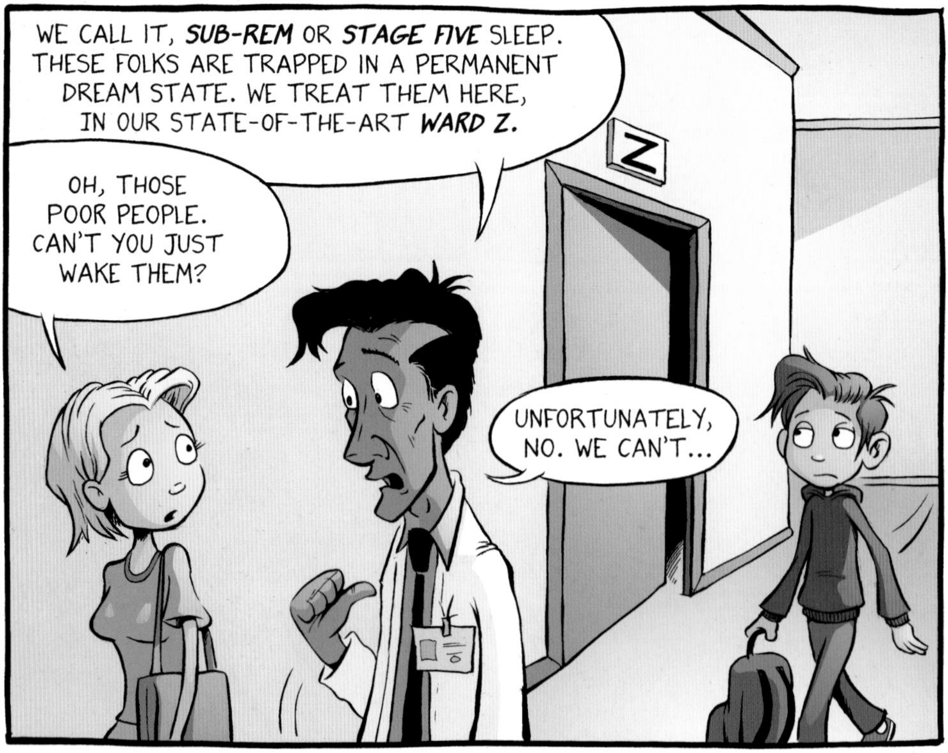
WE CALL IT, SUB-REM OR STAGE FIVE SLEEP. THESE FOLKS ARE TRAPPED IN A PERMANENT DREAM STATE. WE TREAT THEM HERE, IN OUR STATE-OF-THE-ART WARD Z.
Z
OH, THOSE POOR PEOPLE. CAN'T YOU JUST WAKE THEM?
UNFORTUNATELY, NO. WE CAN'T...

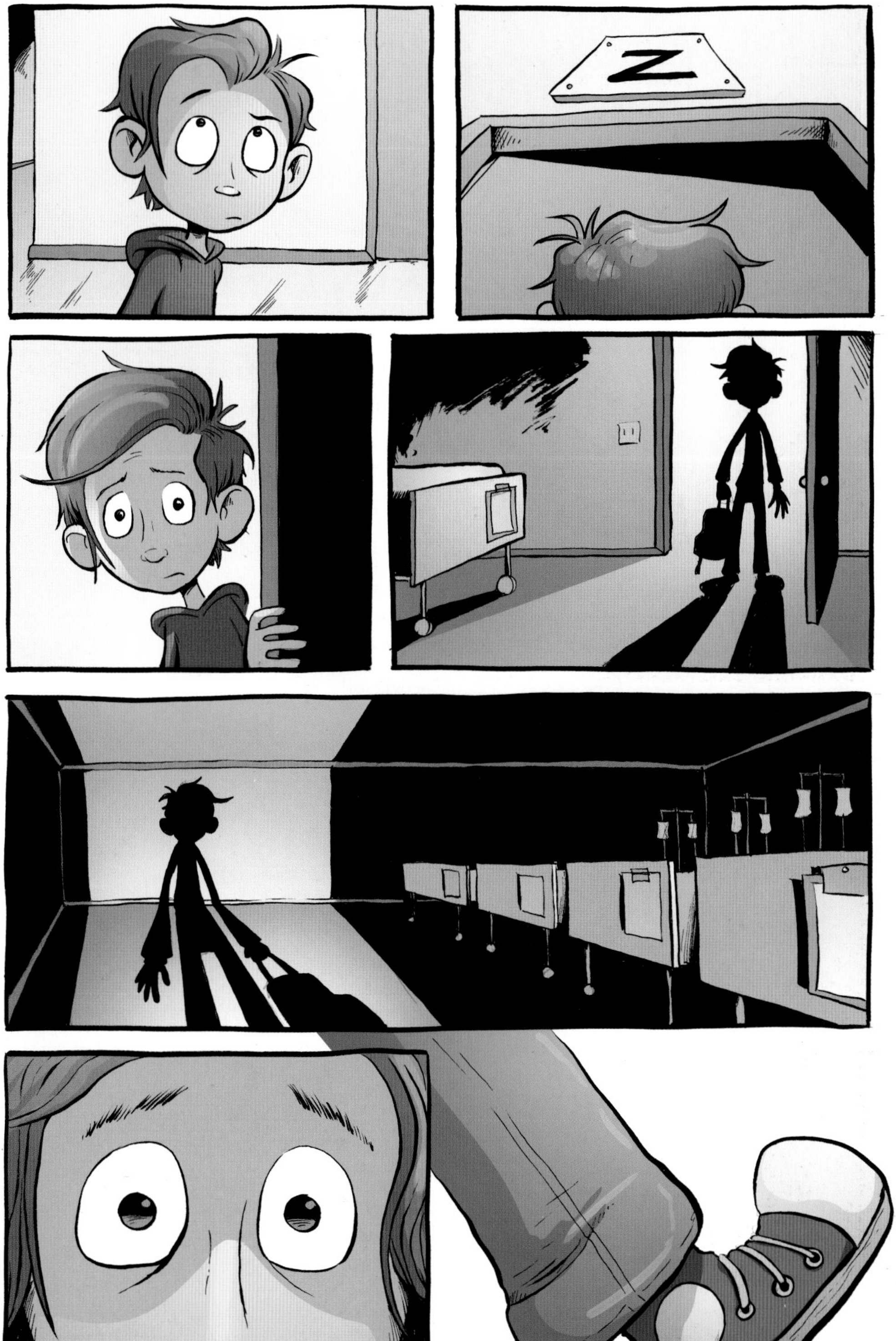
Z

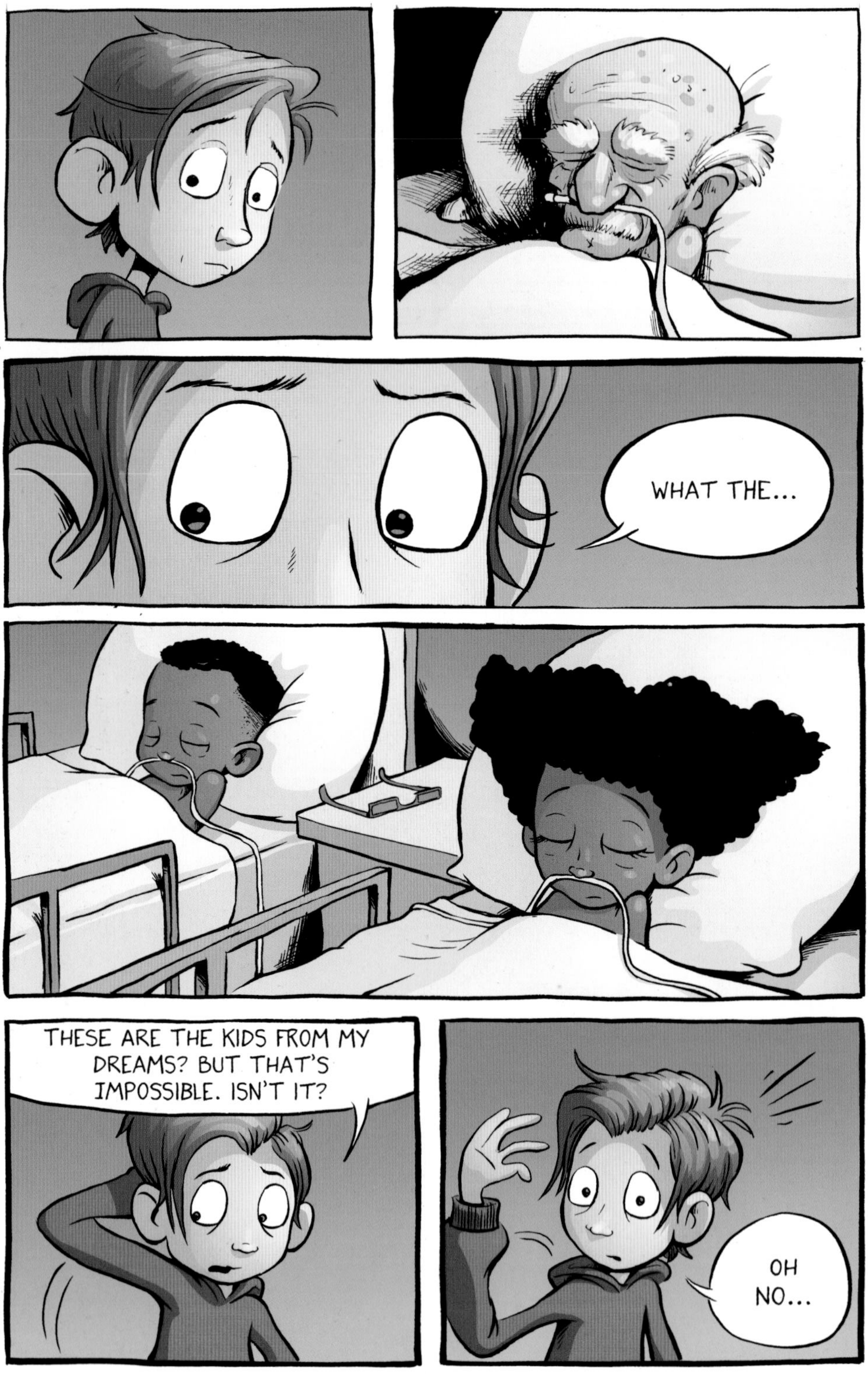
WHAT THE...
THESE ARE THE KIDS FROM MY DREAMS? BUT THAT'S IMPOSSIBLE. ISN'T IT?
OH NO...

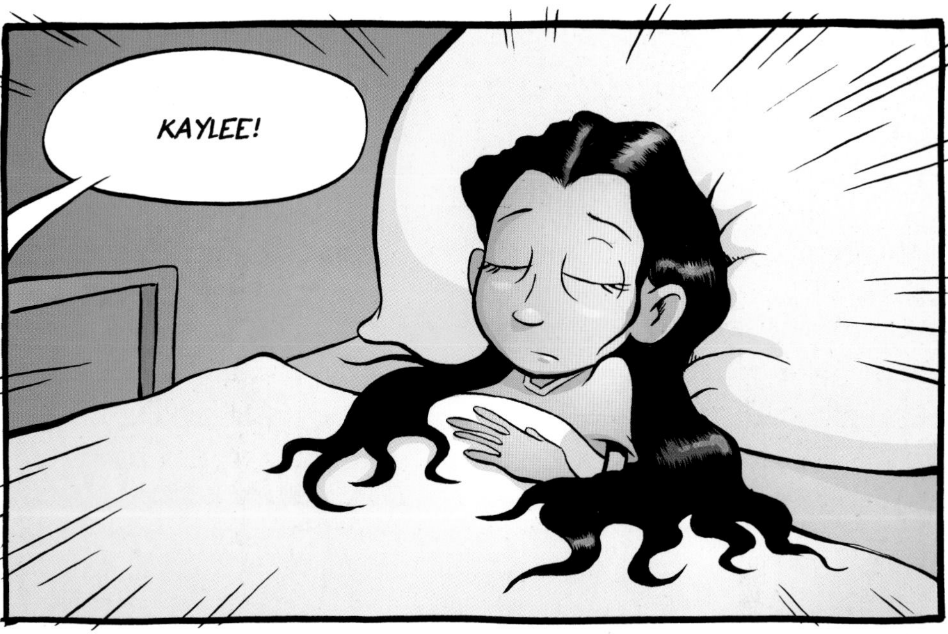
KAYLEE!

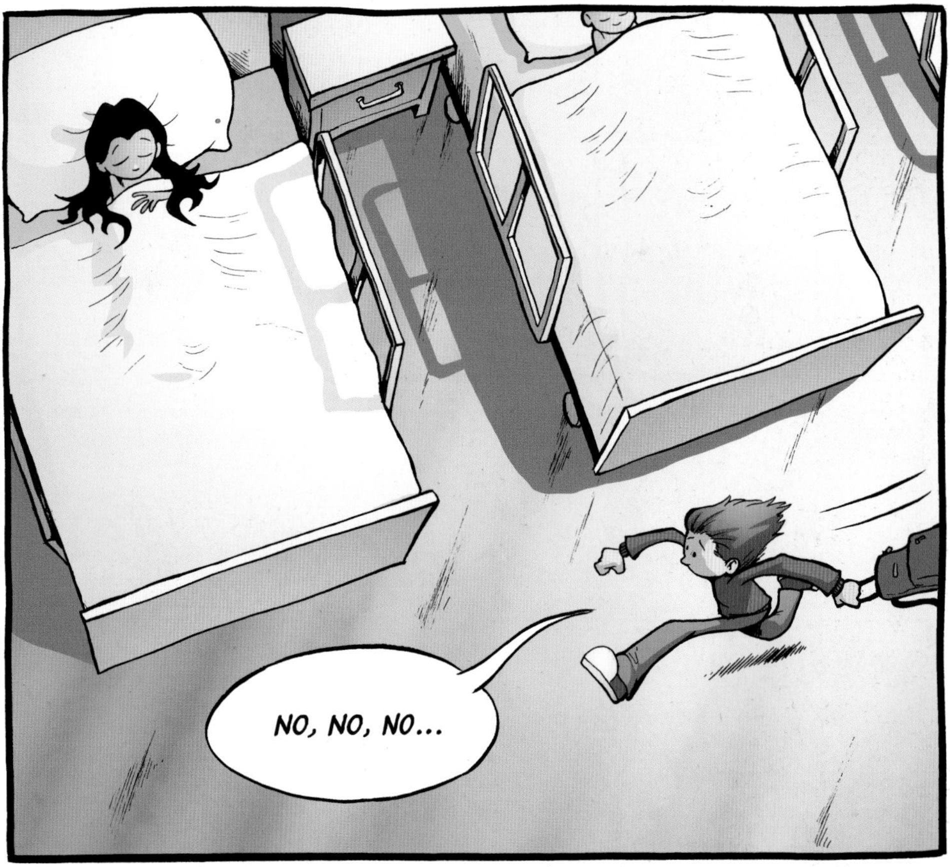
NO, NO, NO...

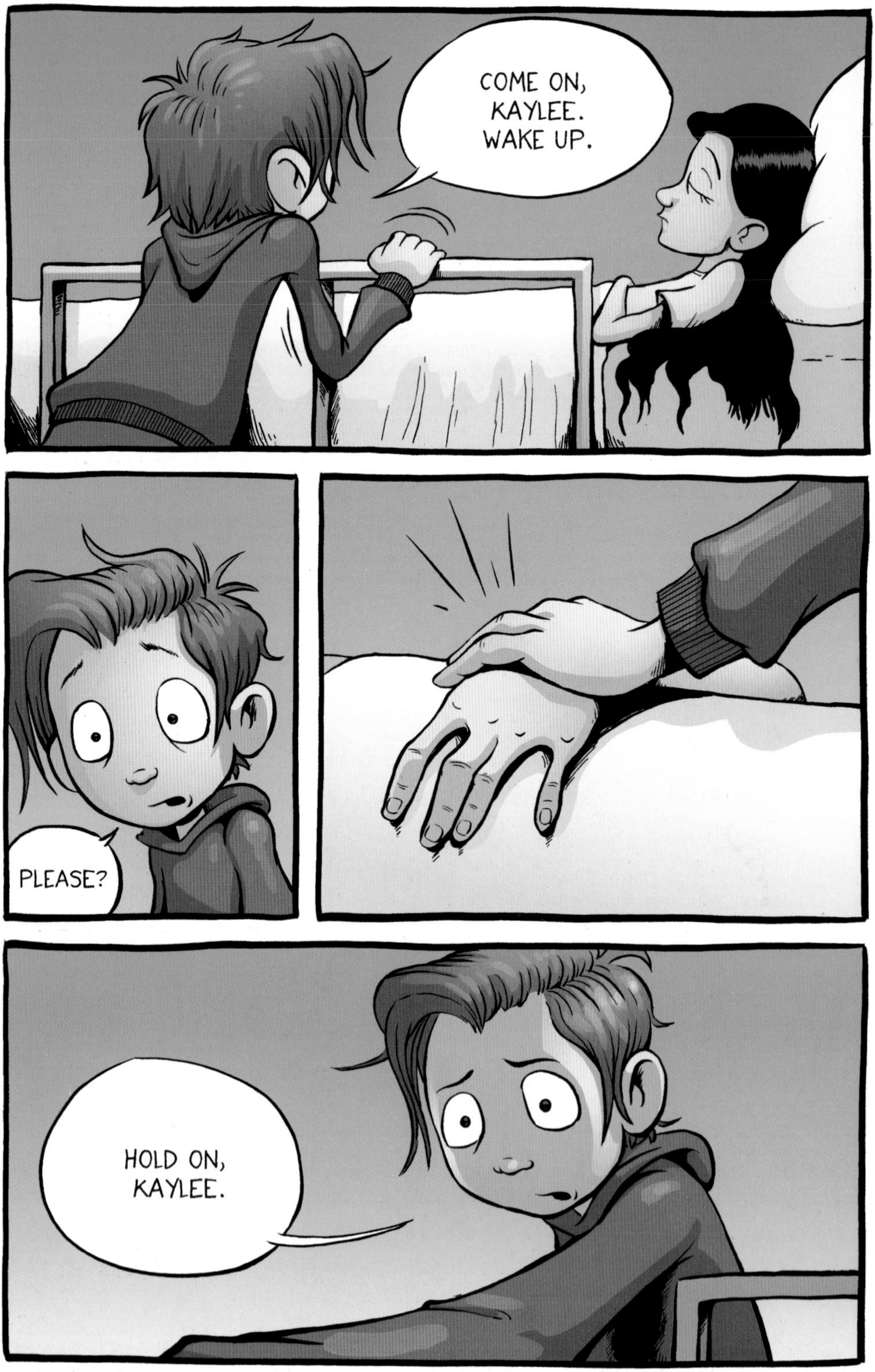
COME ON, KAYLEE. WAKE UP.
PLEASE?
HOLD ON, KAYLEE.

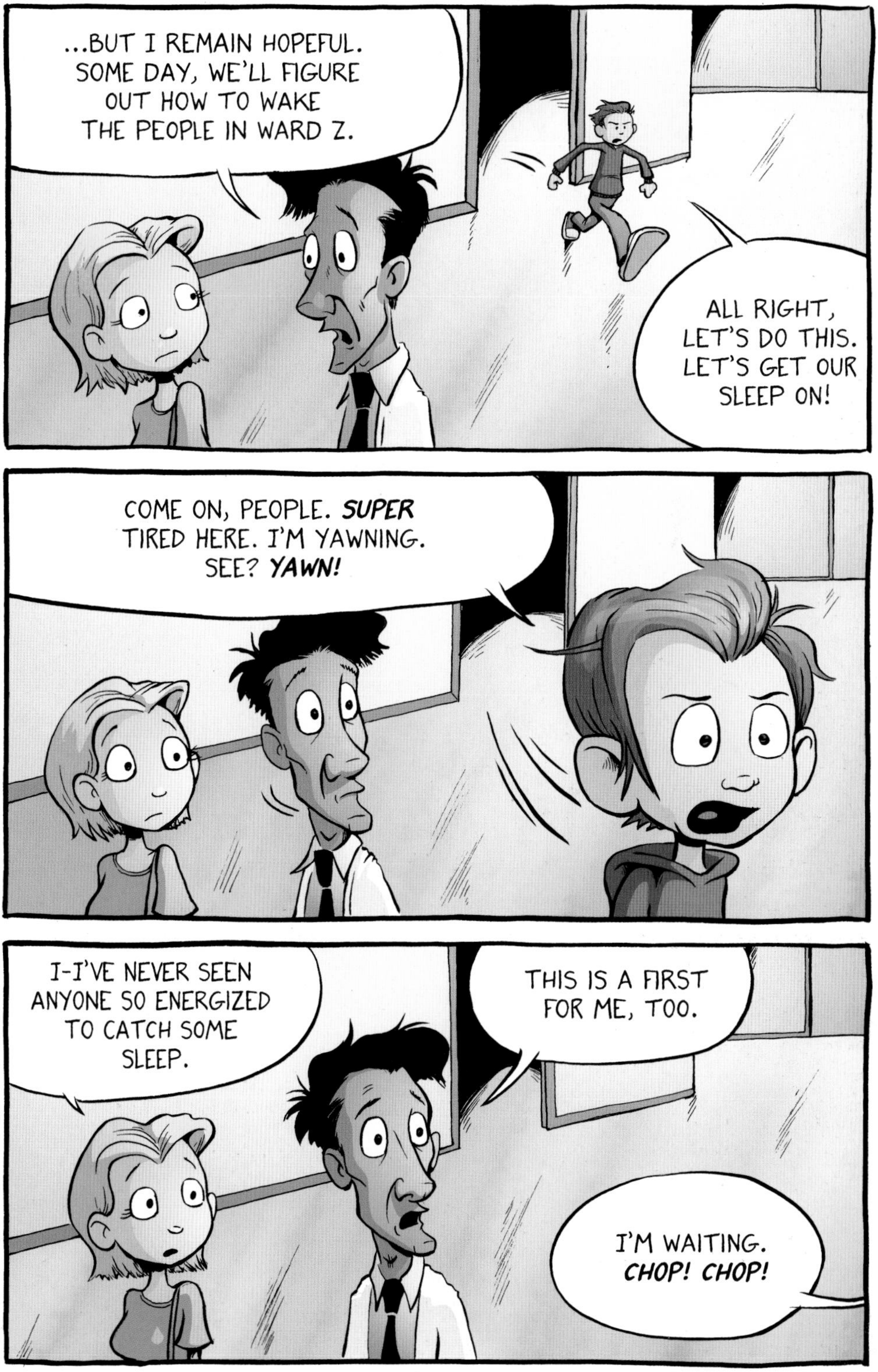
...BUT I REMAIN HOPEFUL. SOME DAY, WE'LL FIGURE OUT HOW TO WAKE THE PEOPLE IN WARD Z.
ALL RIGHT, LET'S DO THIS. LET'S GET OUR SLEEP ON!
COME ON, PEOPLE. **SUPER** TIRED HERE. I'M YAWNING. SEE? **YAWN!**
I-I'VE NEVER SEEN ANYONE SO ENERGIZED TO CATCH SOME SLEEP.
THIS IS A FIRST FOR ME, TOO.
I'M WAITING. **CHOP! CHOP!**

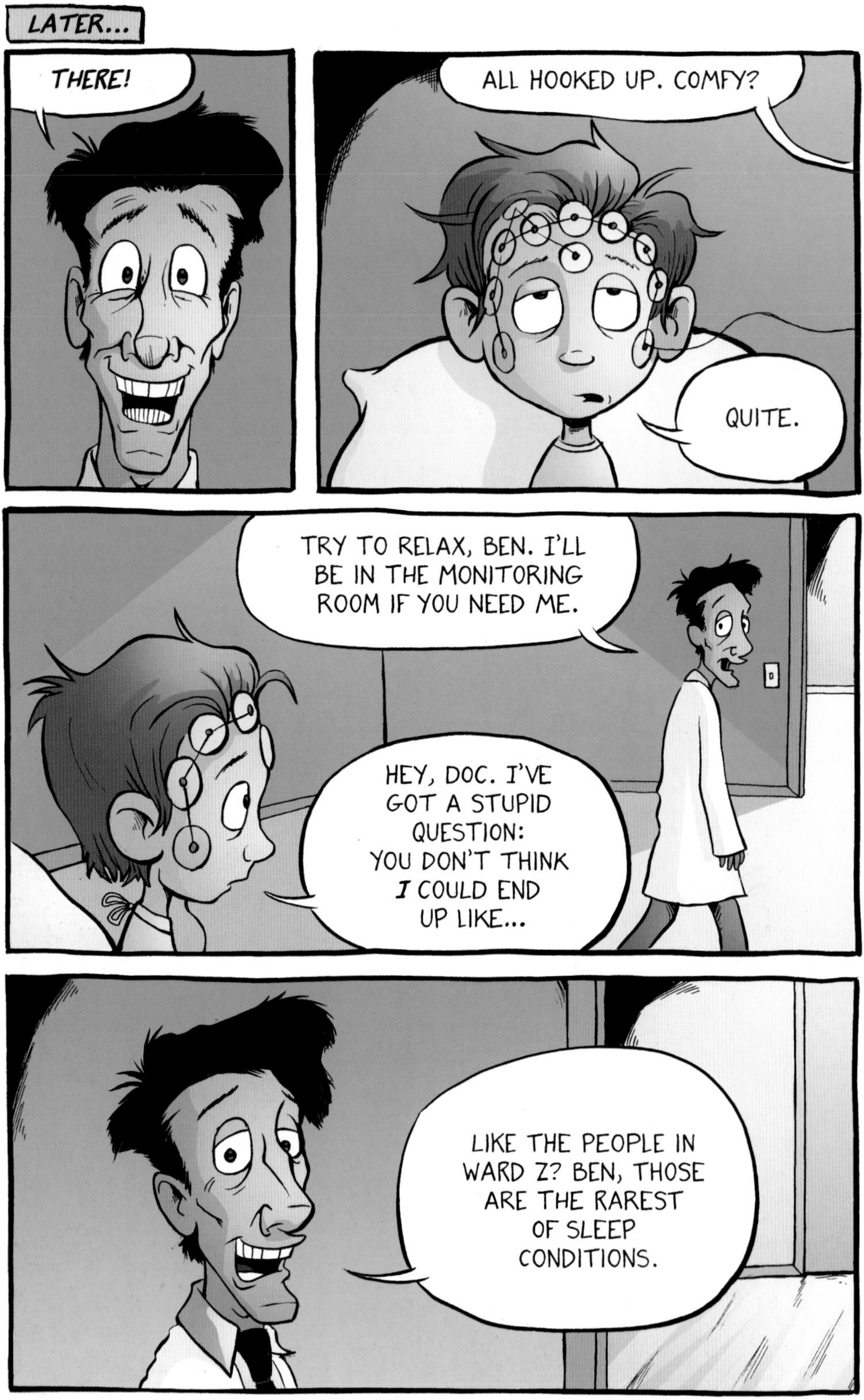
LATER...
THERE!
ALL HOOKED UP. COMFY?
QUITE.
TRY TO RELAX, BEN. I'LL BE IN THE MONITORING ROOM IF YOU NEED ME.
HEY, DOC. I'VE GOT A STUPID QUESTION: YOU DON'T THINK *I* COULD END UP LIKE...
LIKE THE PEOPLE IN WARD Z? BEN, THOSE ARE THE RAREST OF SLEEP CONDITIONS.

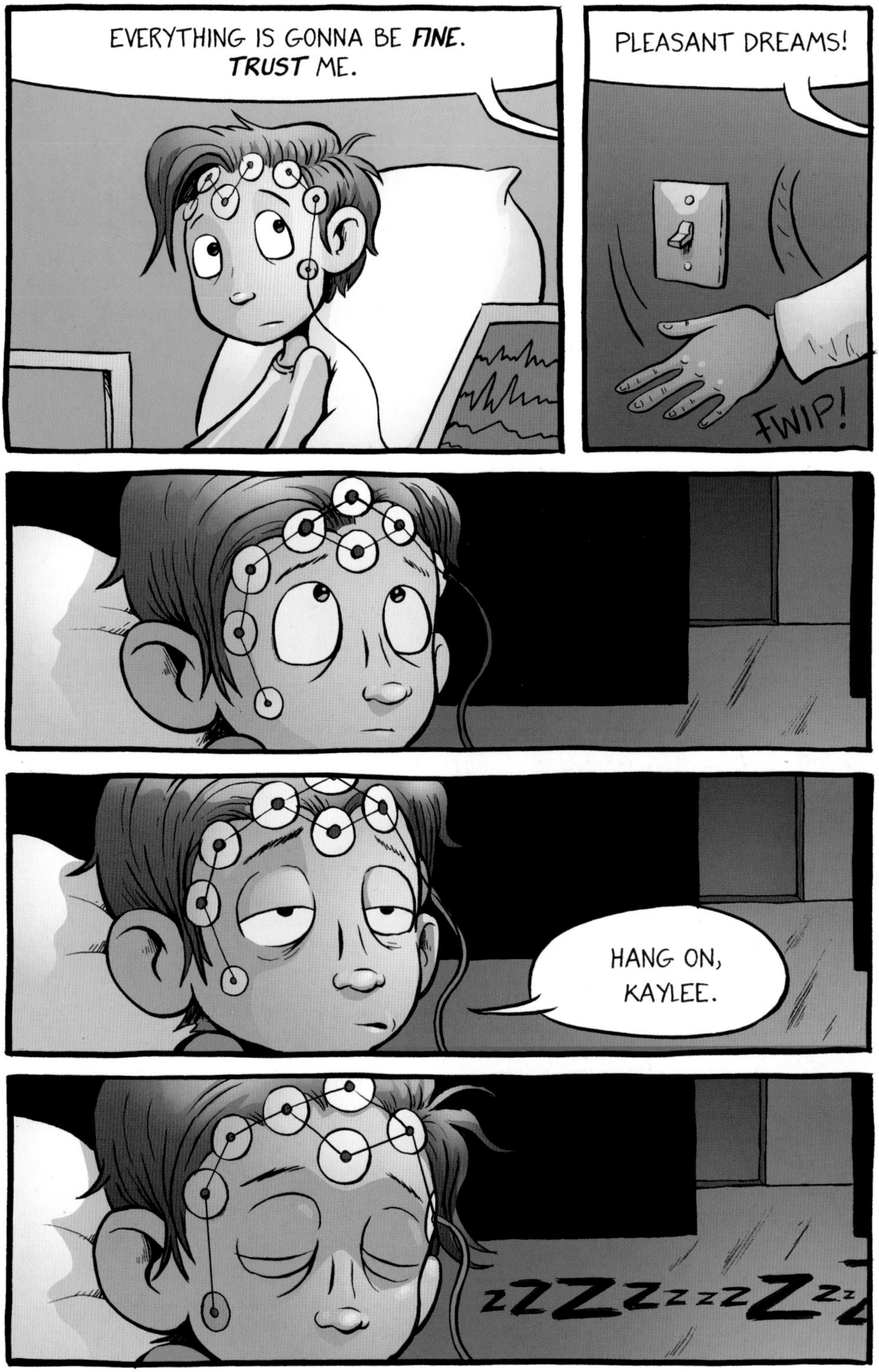
EVERYTHING IS GONNA BE FINE. TRUST ME.
PLEASANT DREAMS!
FWIP!
HANG ON, KAYLEE.
zZZZzzzzzZZz

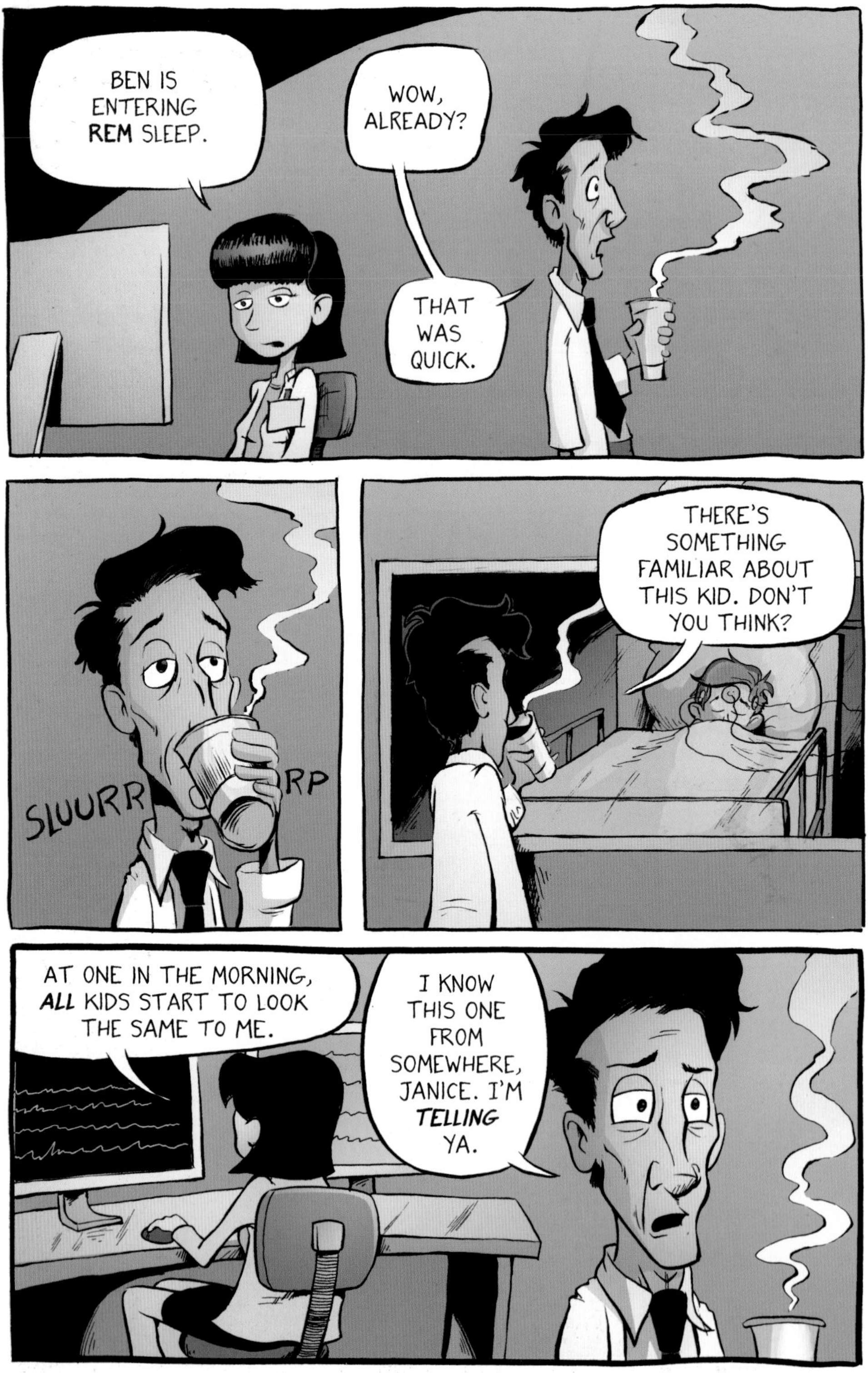
BEN IS ENTERING REM SLEEP.
WOW, ALREADY?
THAT WAS QUICK.
SLUURRRP
THERE'S SOMETHING FAMILIAR ABOUT THIS KID. DON'T YOU THINK?
AT ONE IN THE MORNING, ALL KIDS START TO LOOK THE SAME TO ME.
I KNOW THIS ONE FROM SOMEWHERE, JANICE. I'M TELLING YA.

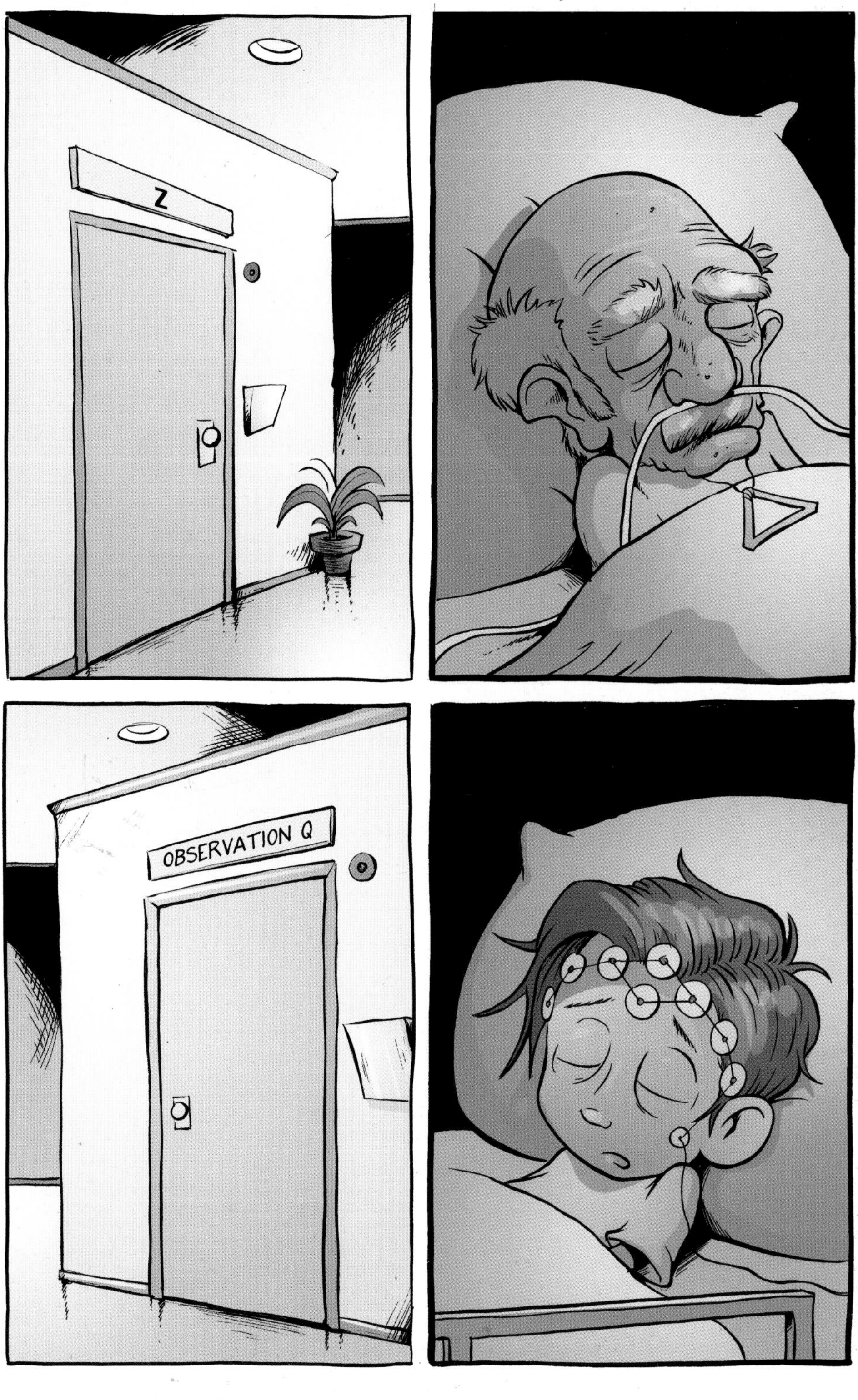
Z
OBSERVATION Q

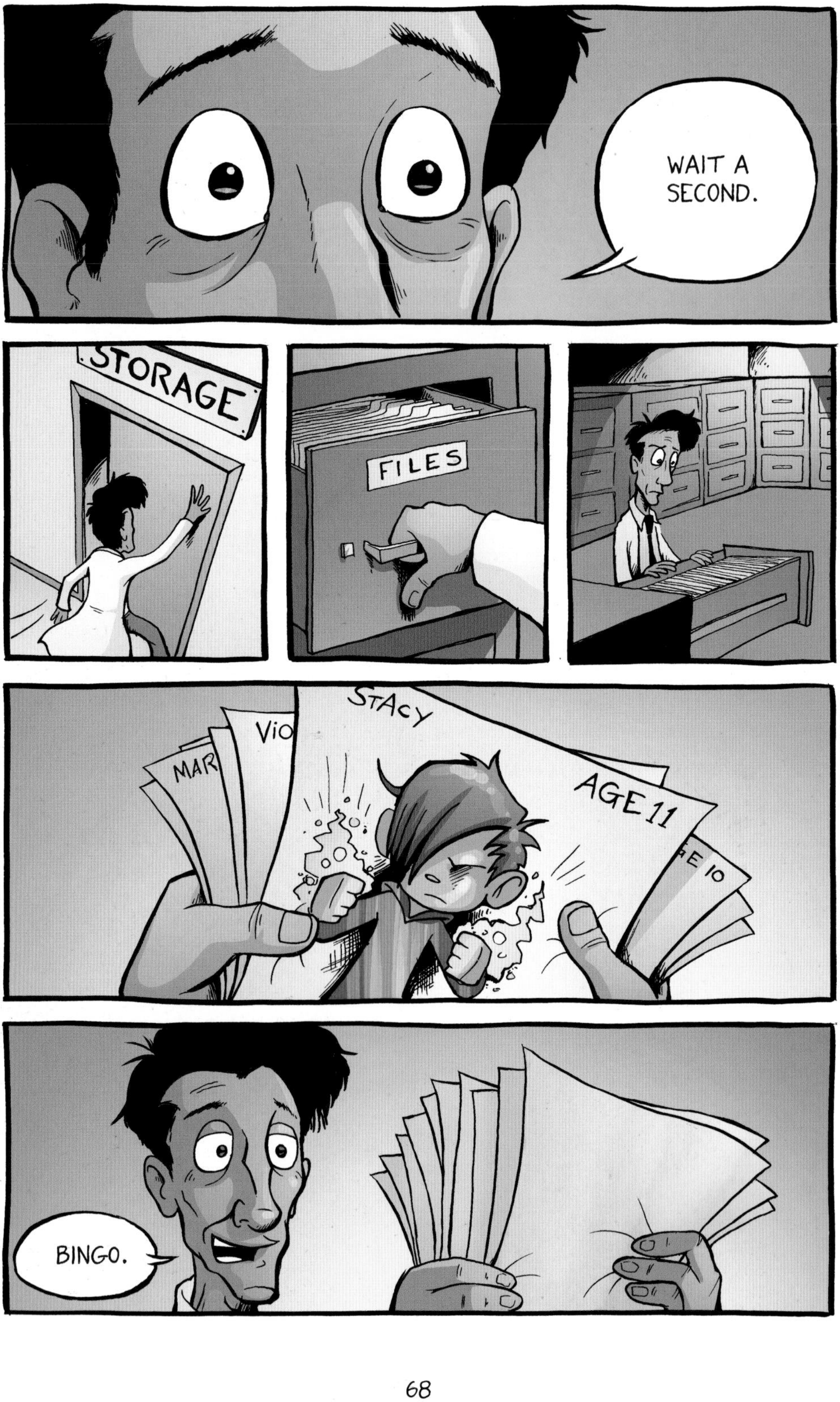
WAIT A SECOND.
STORAGE
FILES
STACY
AGE 11
BINGO.

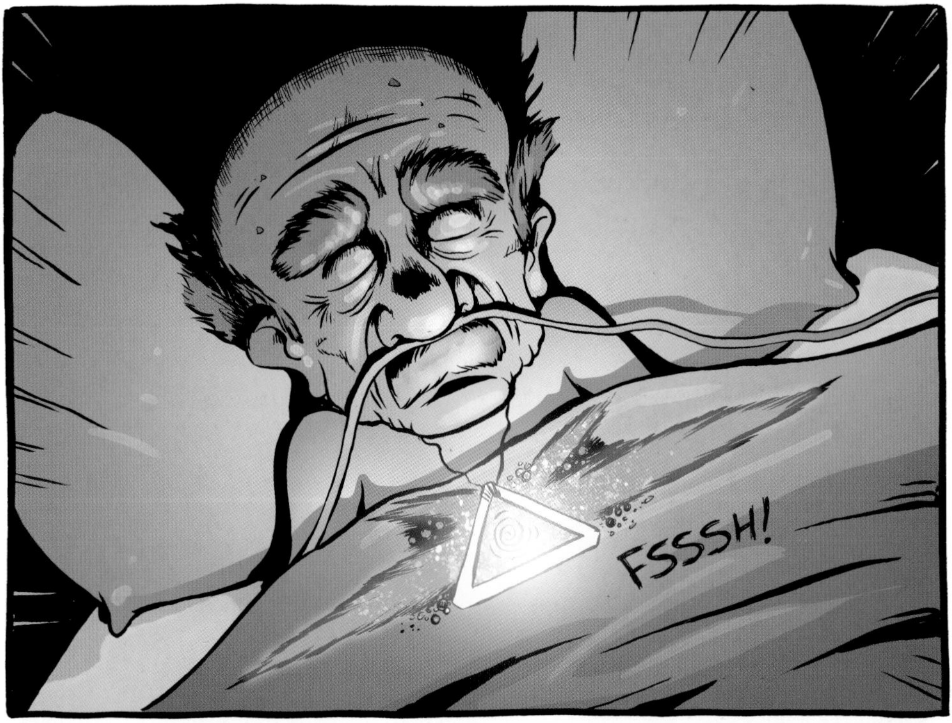
FSSSH!

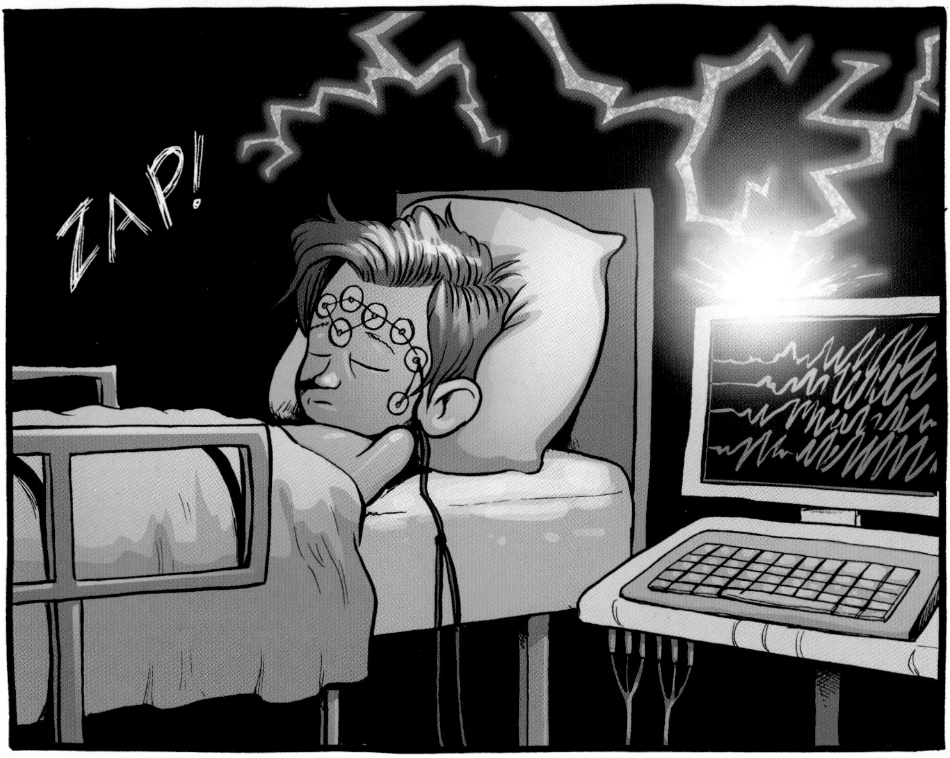
ZAP!

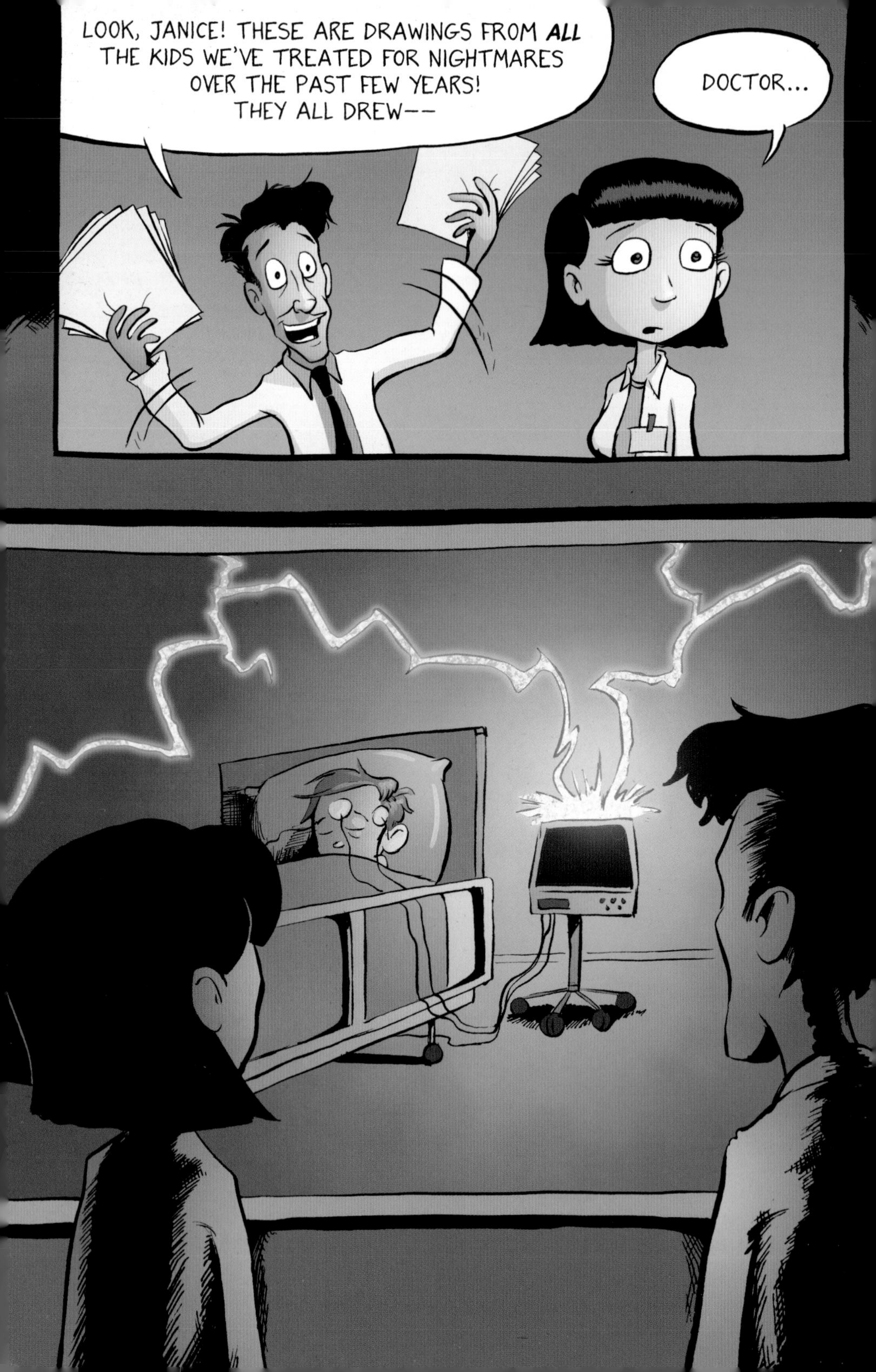
LOOK, JANICE! THESE ARE DRAWINGS FROM **ALL** THE KIDS WE'VE TREATED FOR NIGHTMARES OVER THE PAST FEW YEARS! THEY ALL DREW--
DOCTOR...

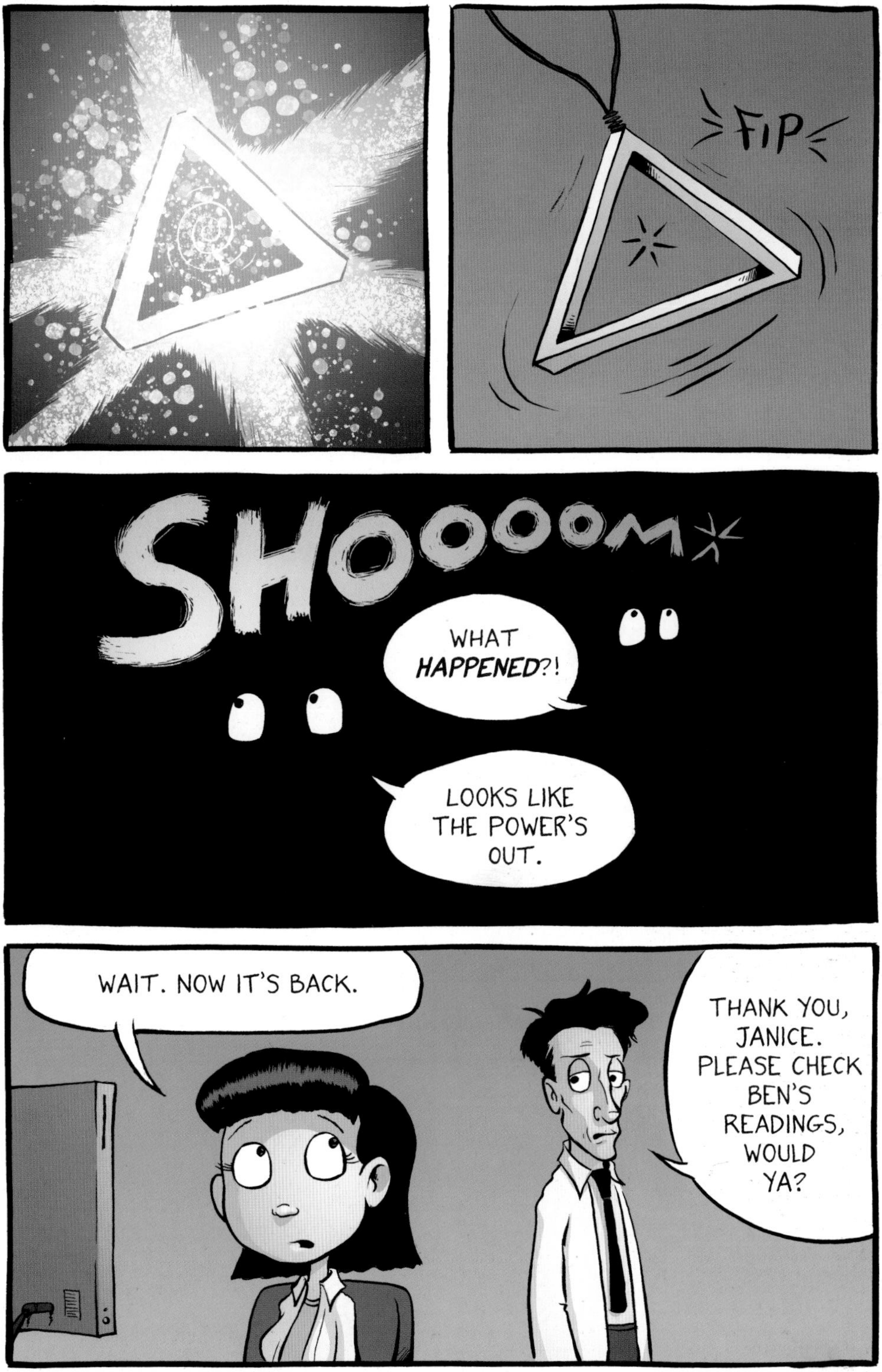
FIP
SHOOOOM
WHAT HAPPENED?!
LOOKS LIKE THE POWER'S OUT.
WAIT. NOW IT'S BACK.
THANK YOU, JANICE. PLEASE CHECK BEN'S READINGS, WOULD YA?

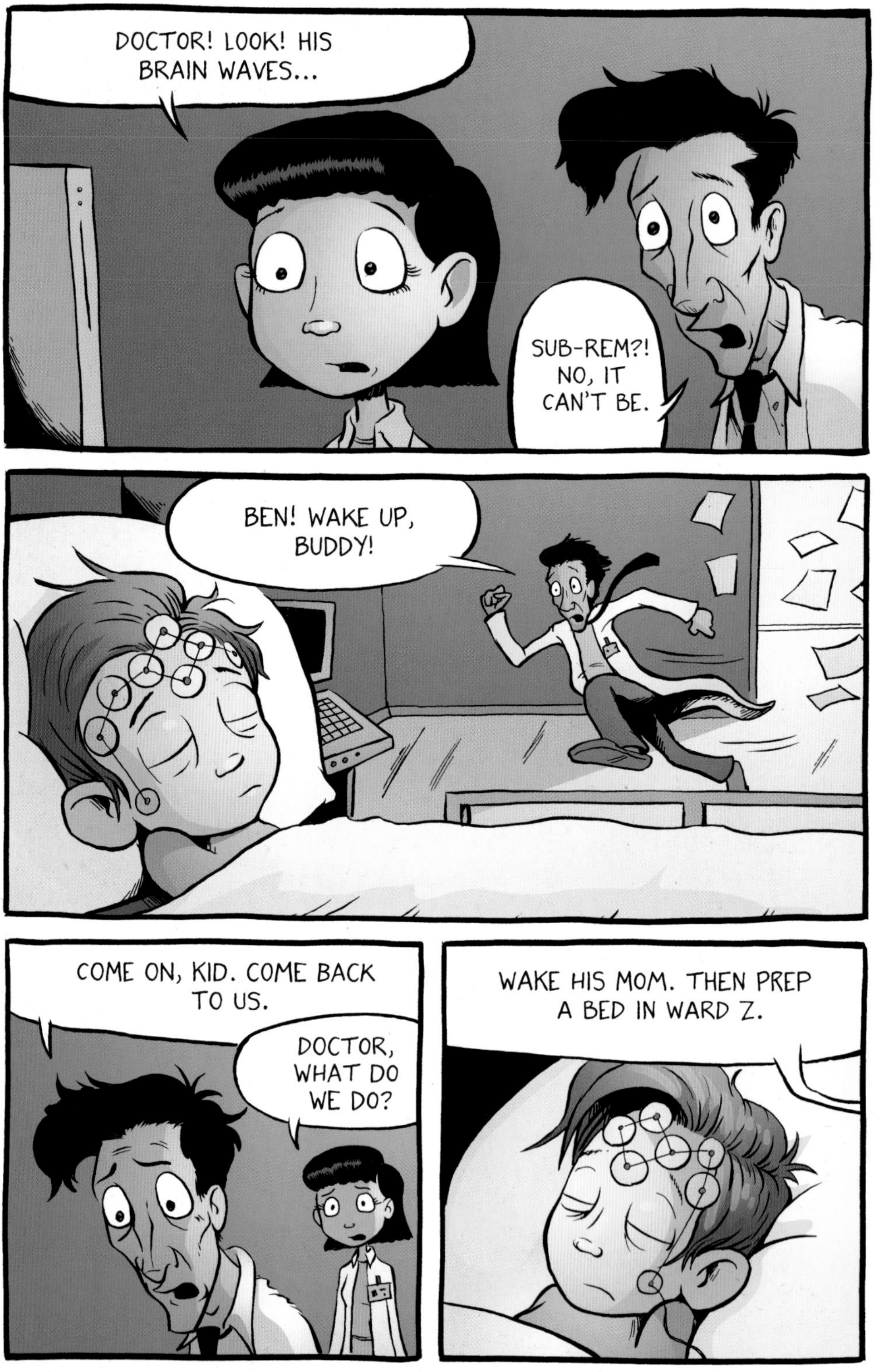
DOCTOR! LOOK! HIS BRAIN WAVES...
SUB-REM?! NO, IT CAN'T BE.
BEN! WAKE UP, BUDDY!
COME ON, KID. COME BACK TO US.
DOCTOR, WHAT DO WE DO?
WAKE HIS MOM. THEN PREP A BED IN WARD Z.

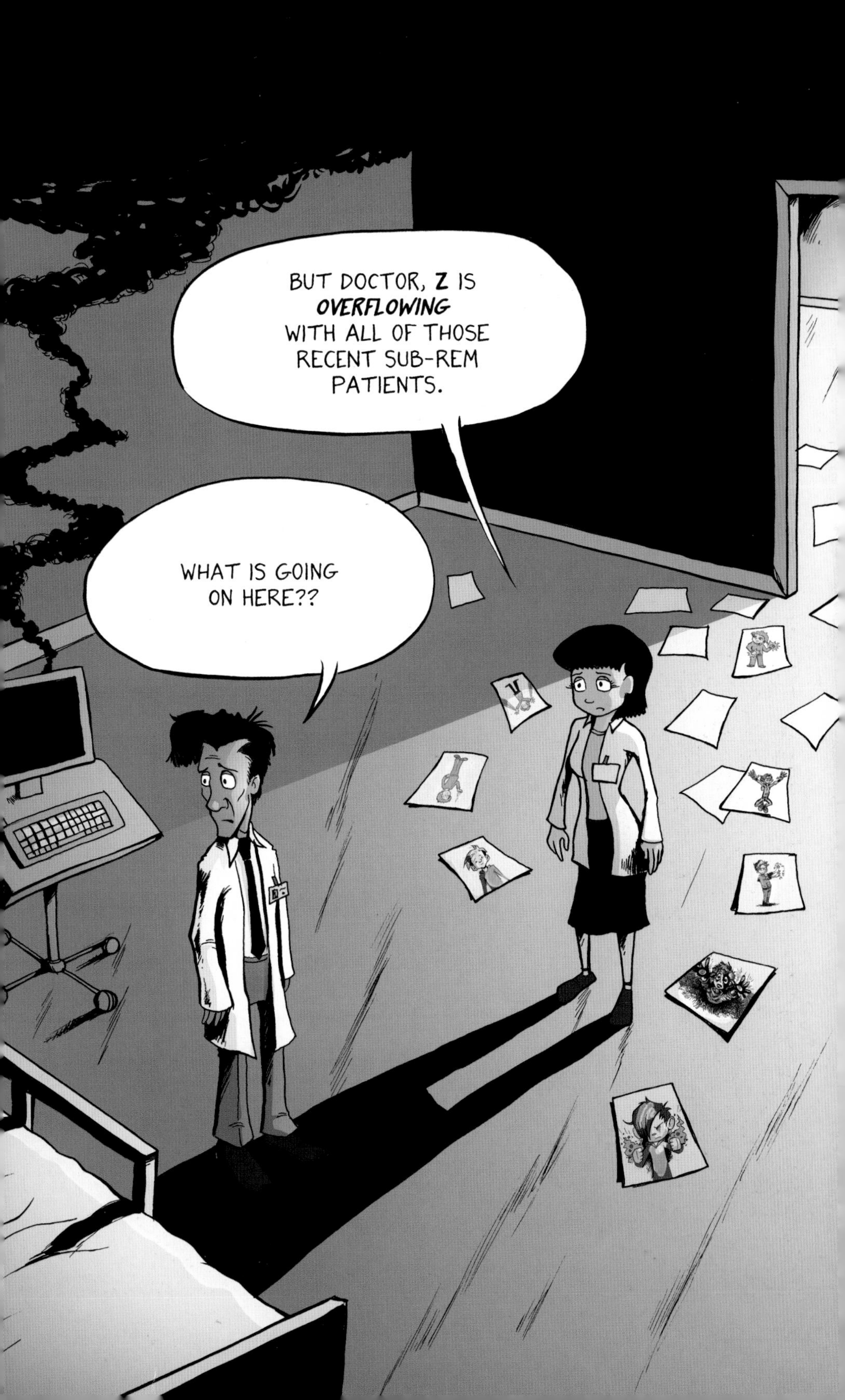
BUT DOCTOR, **Z** IS ***OVERFLOWING*** WITH ALL OF THOSE RECENT SUB-REM PATIENTS.
WHAT IS GOING ON HERE??

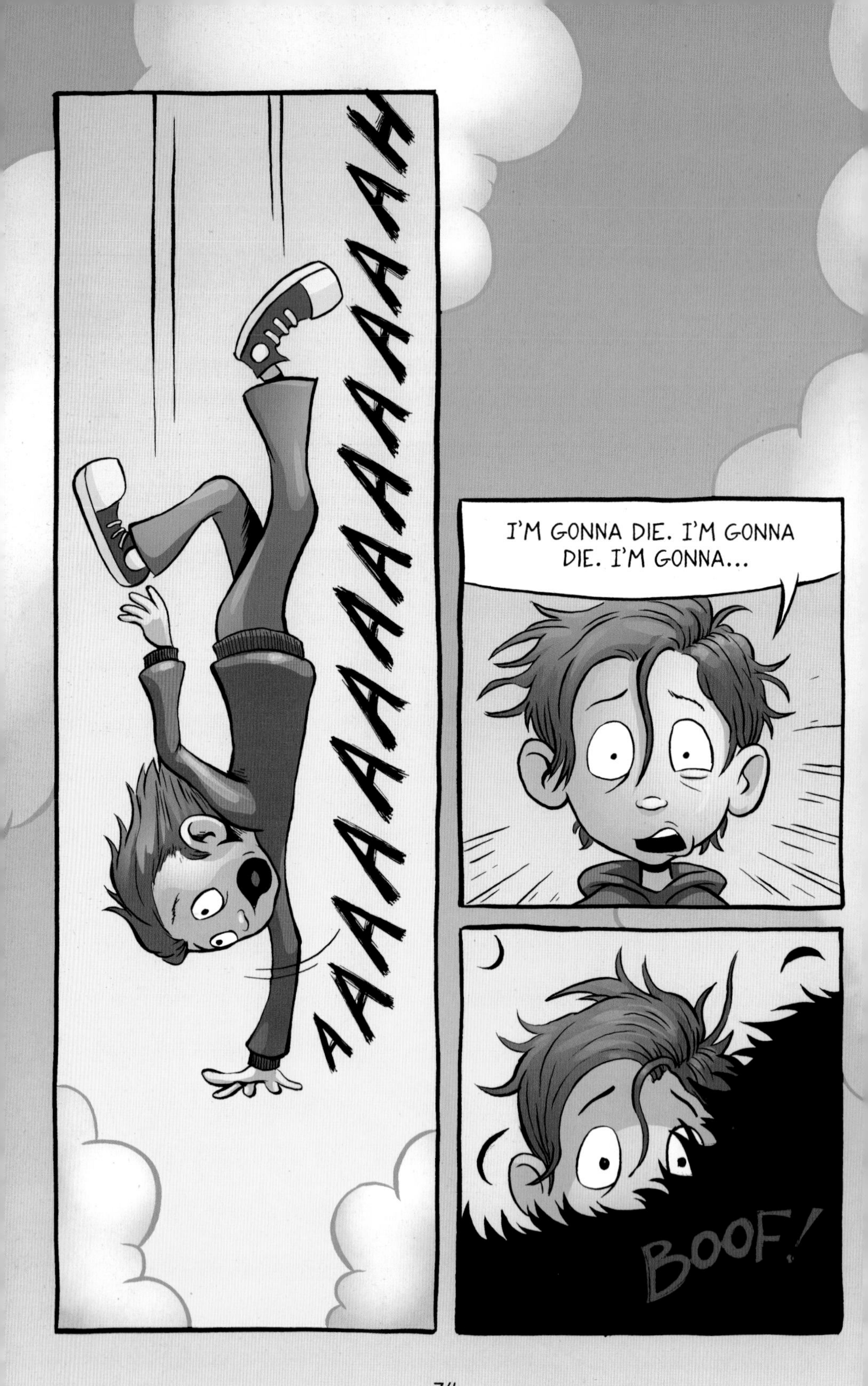
AAAAAAAAAAAAAH
I'M GONNA DIE. I'M GONNA DIE. I'M GONNA...
BOOF!

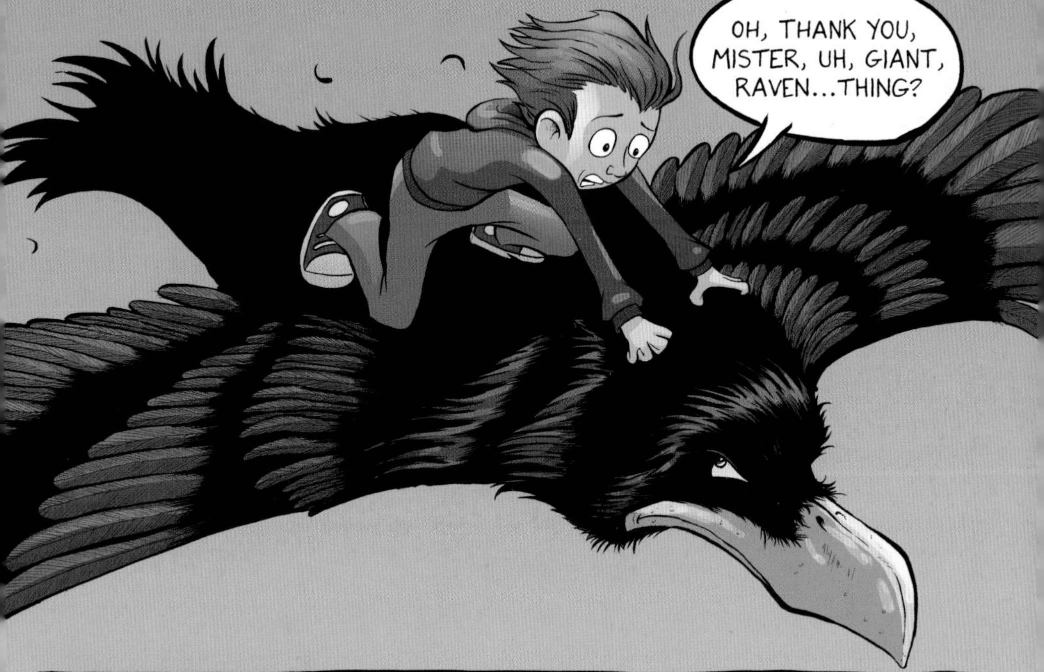
OH, THANK YOU, MISTER, UH, GIANT, RAVEN...THING?

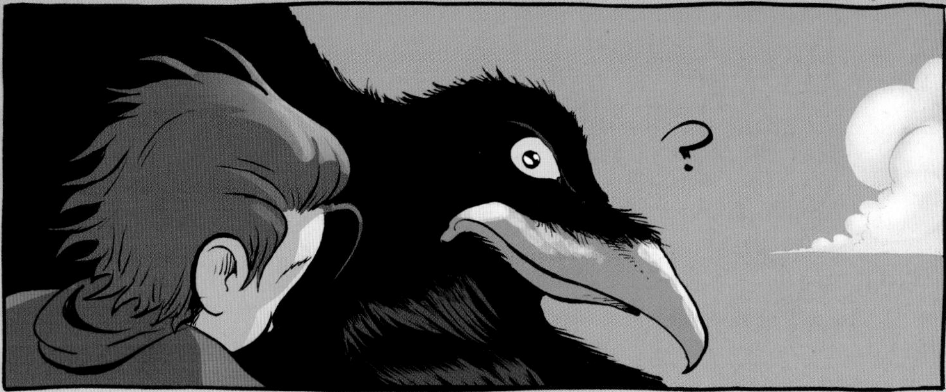
?

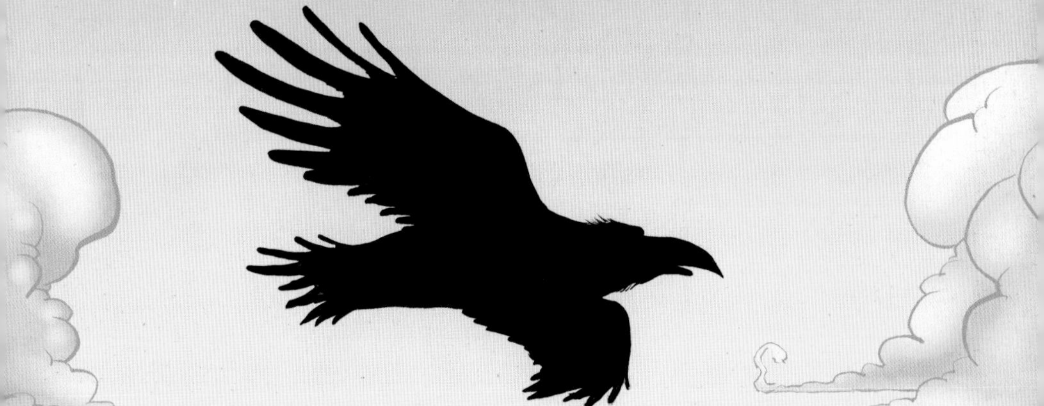

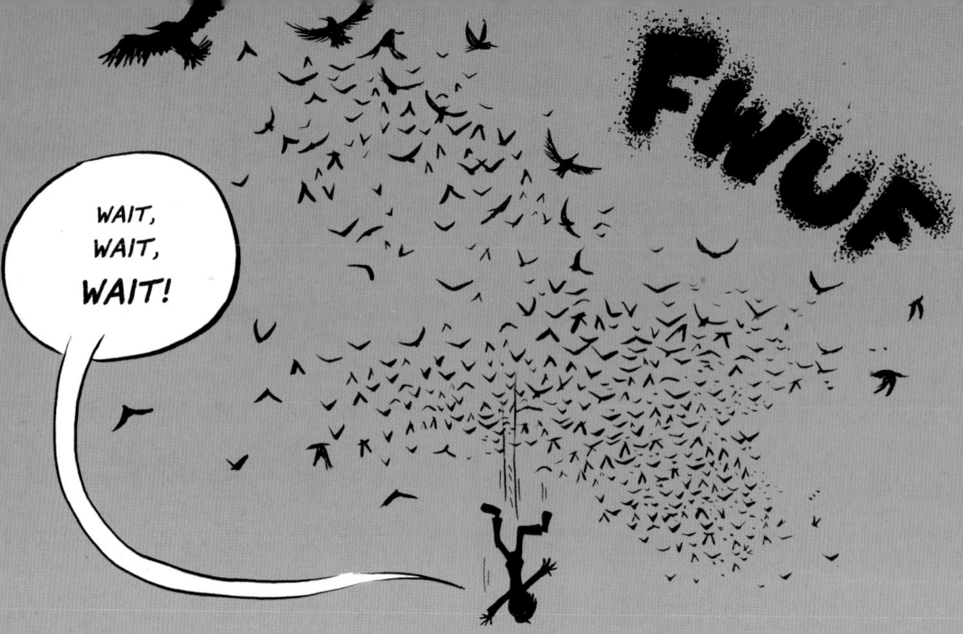
WAIT,
WAIT,
WAIT!
FWUF

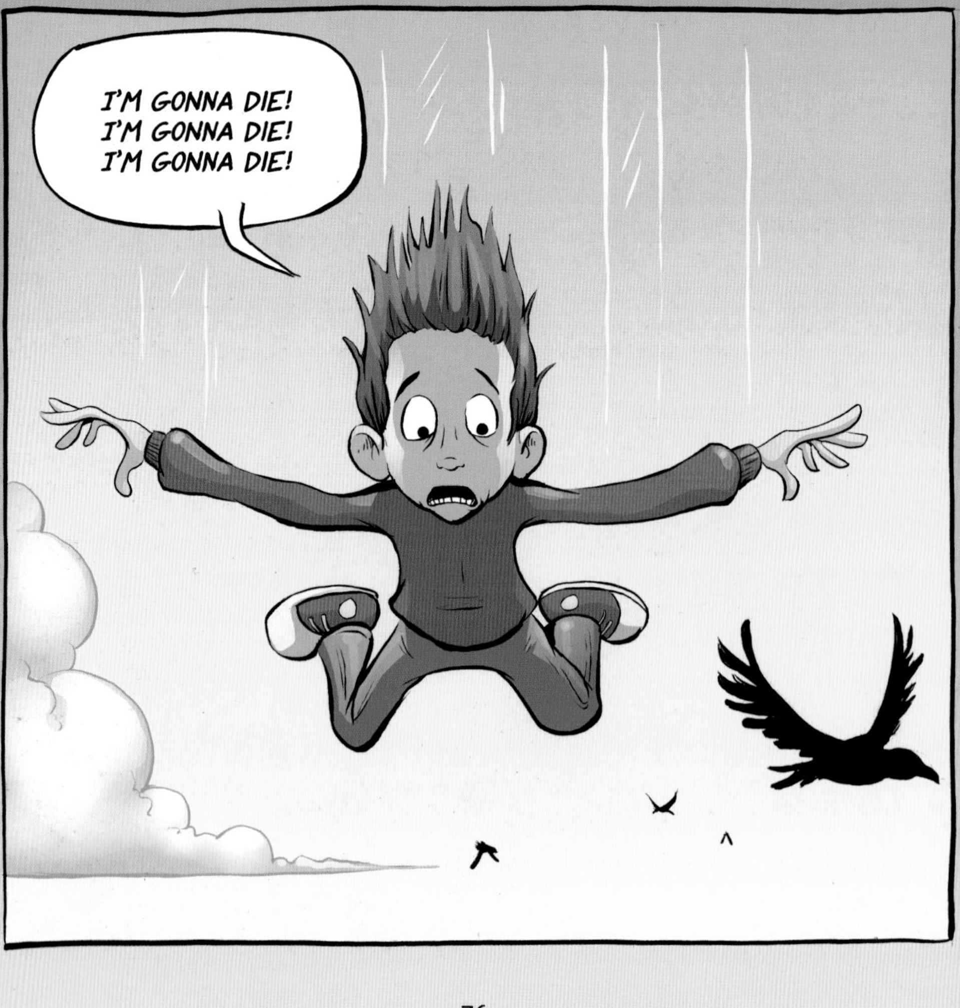
I'M GONNA DIE!
I'M GONNA DIE!
I'M GONNA DIE!

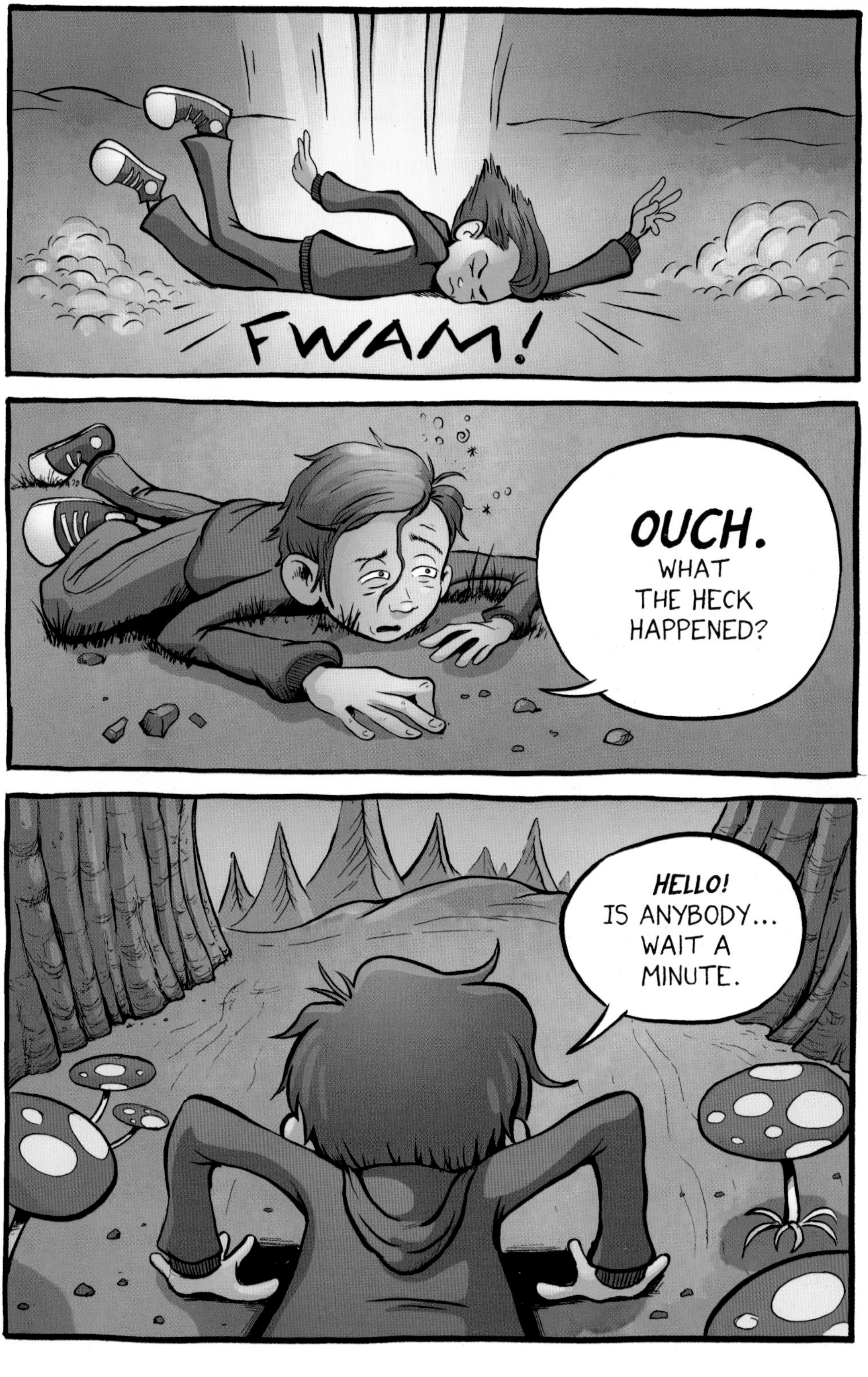
FWAM!
OUCH. WHAT THE HECK HAPPENED?
HELLO! IS ANYBODY... WAIT A MINUTE.

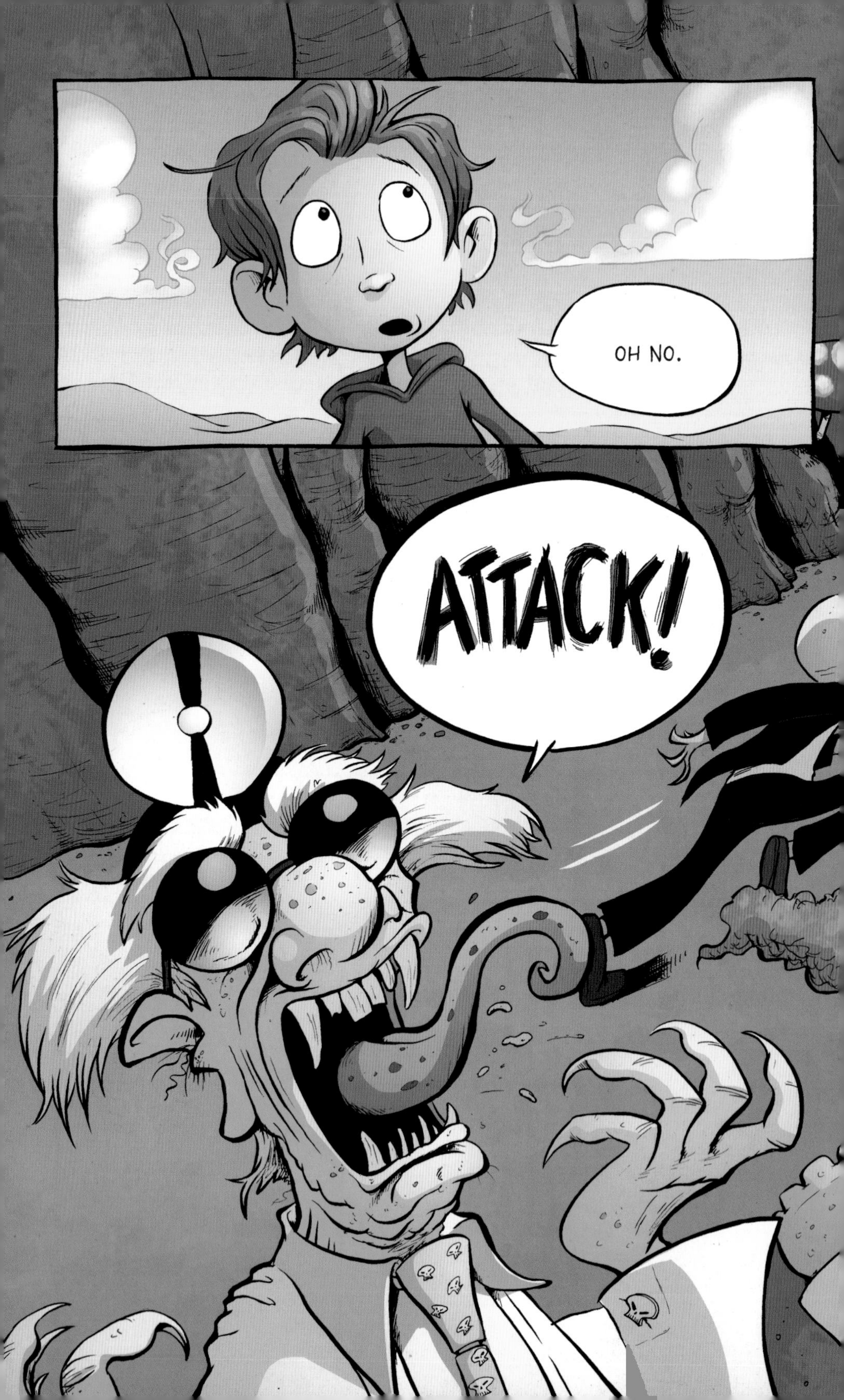
OH NO.
ATTACK!

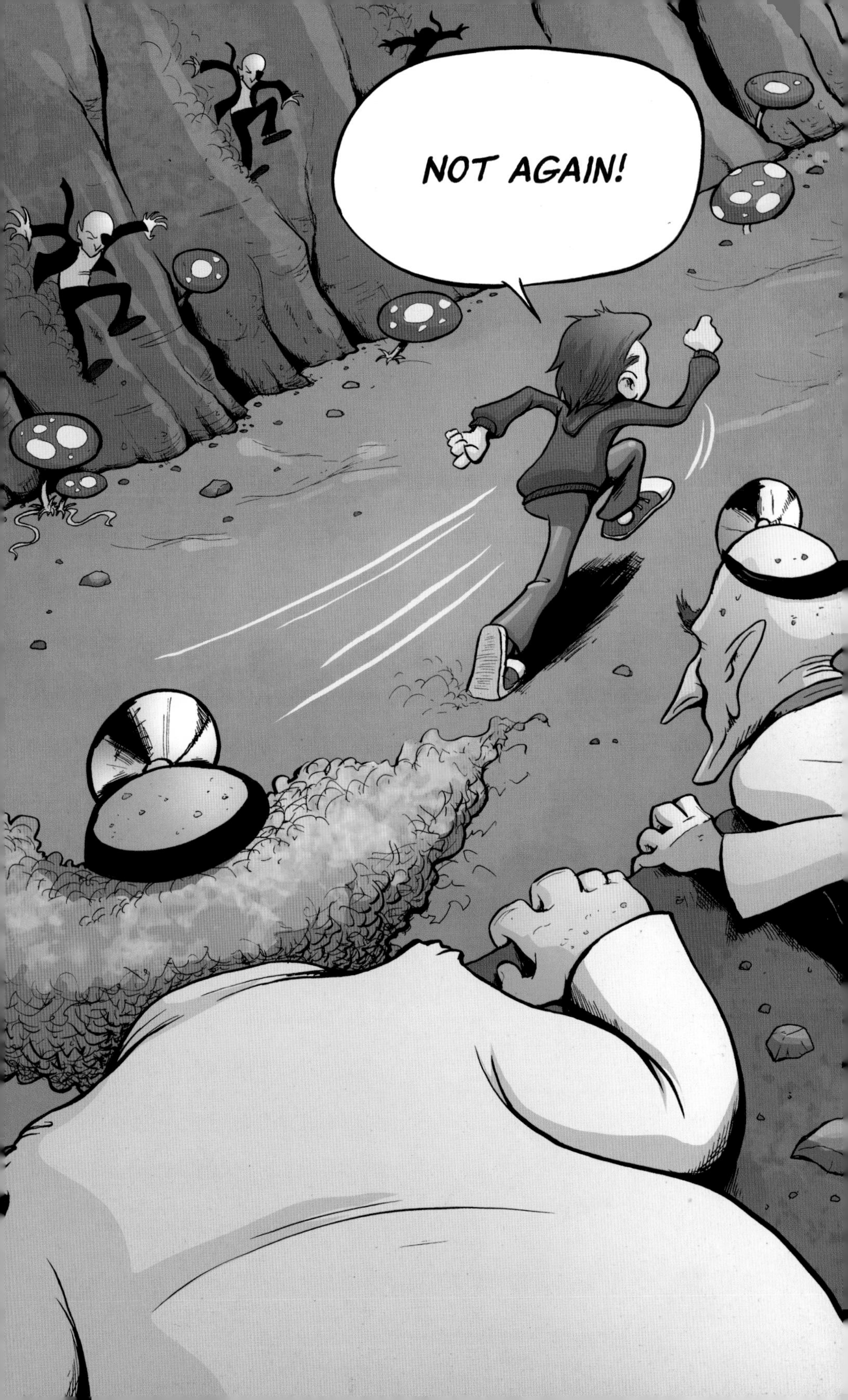
NOT AGAIN!

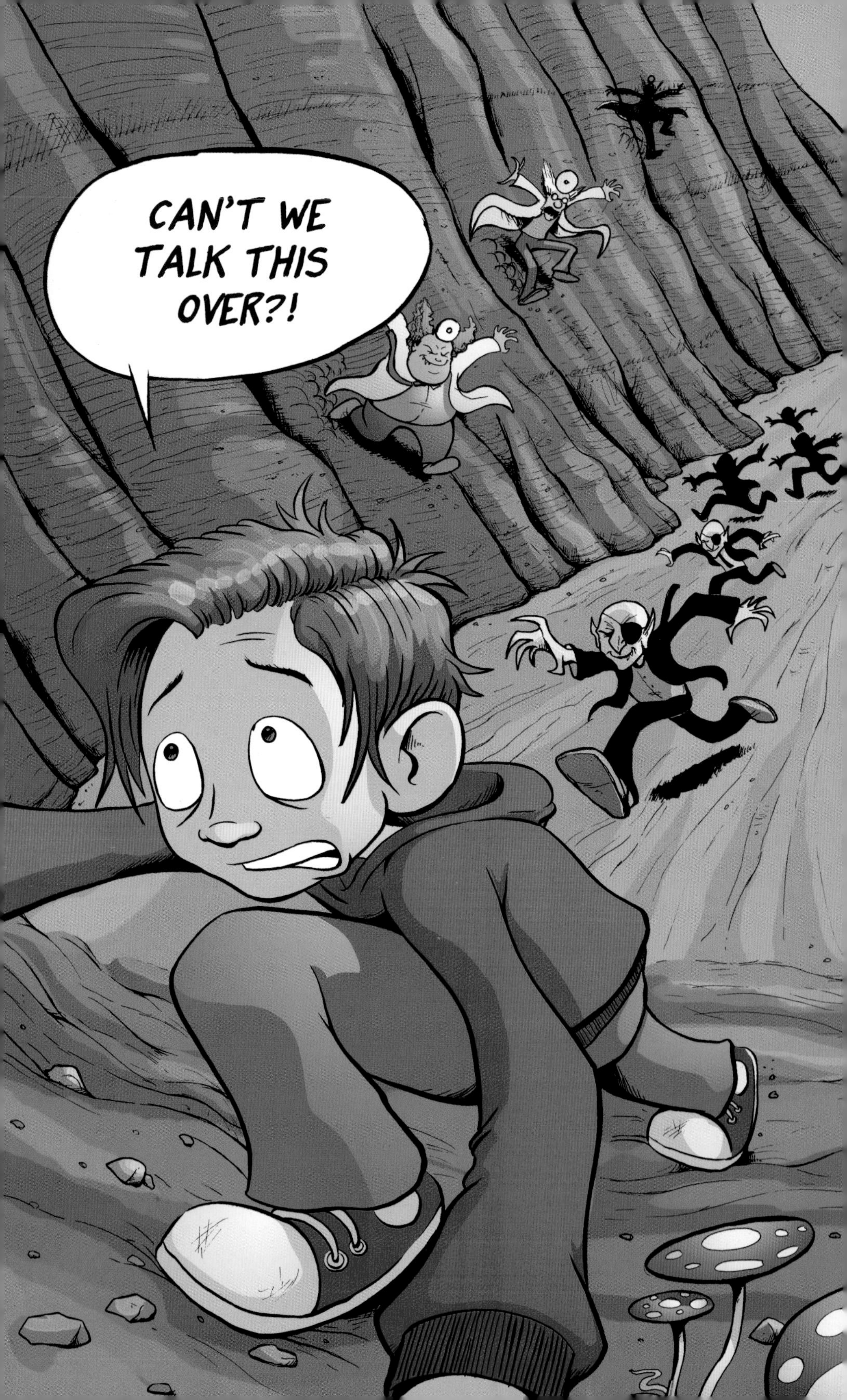
CAN'T WE TALK THIS OVER?!

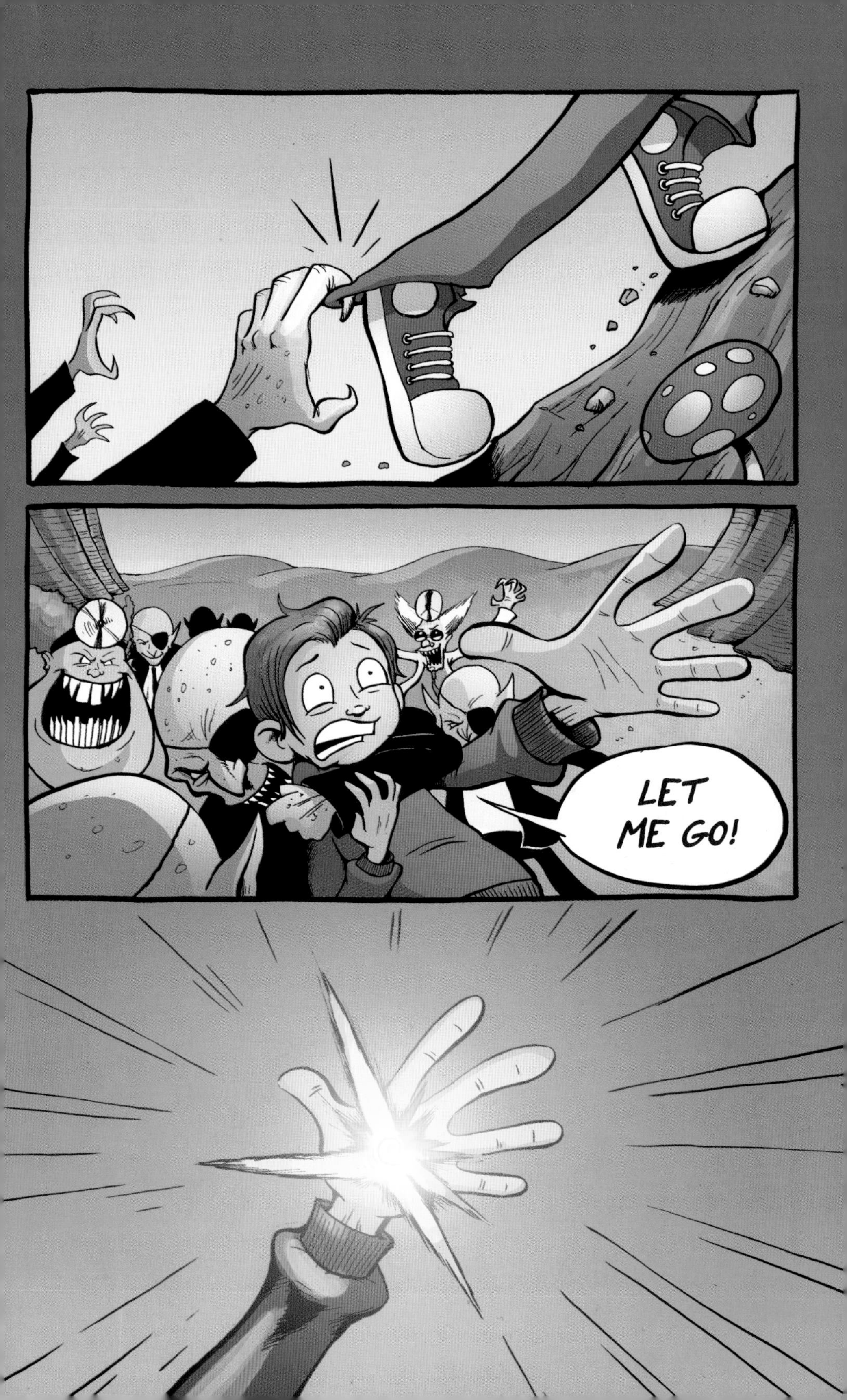
LET ME GO!

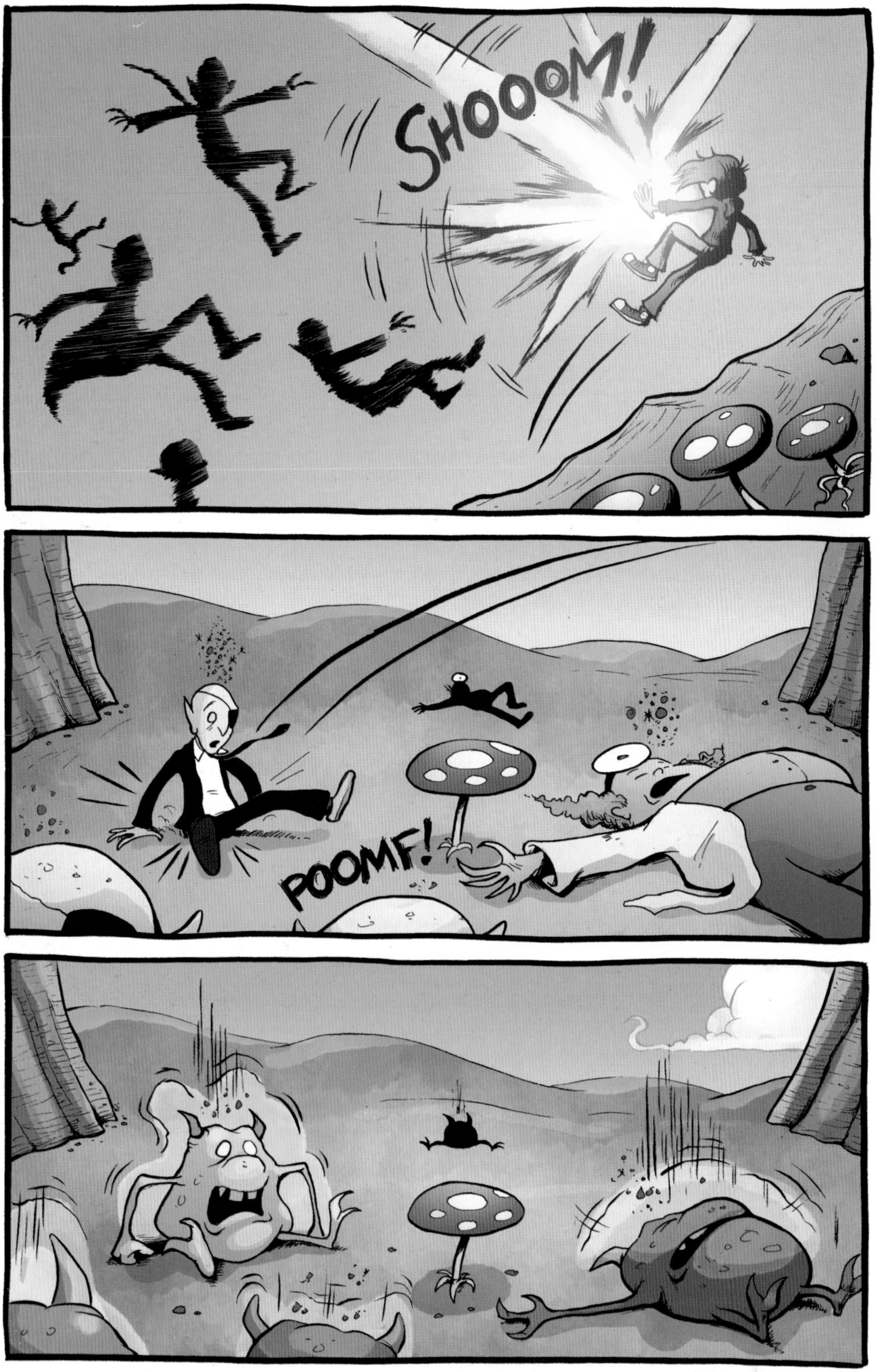
SHOOOM!
POOMF!

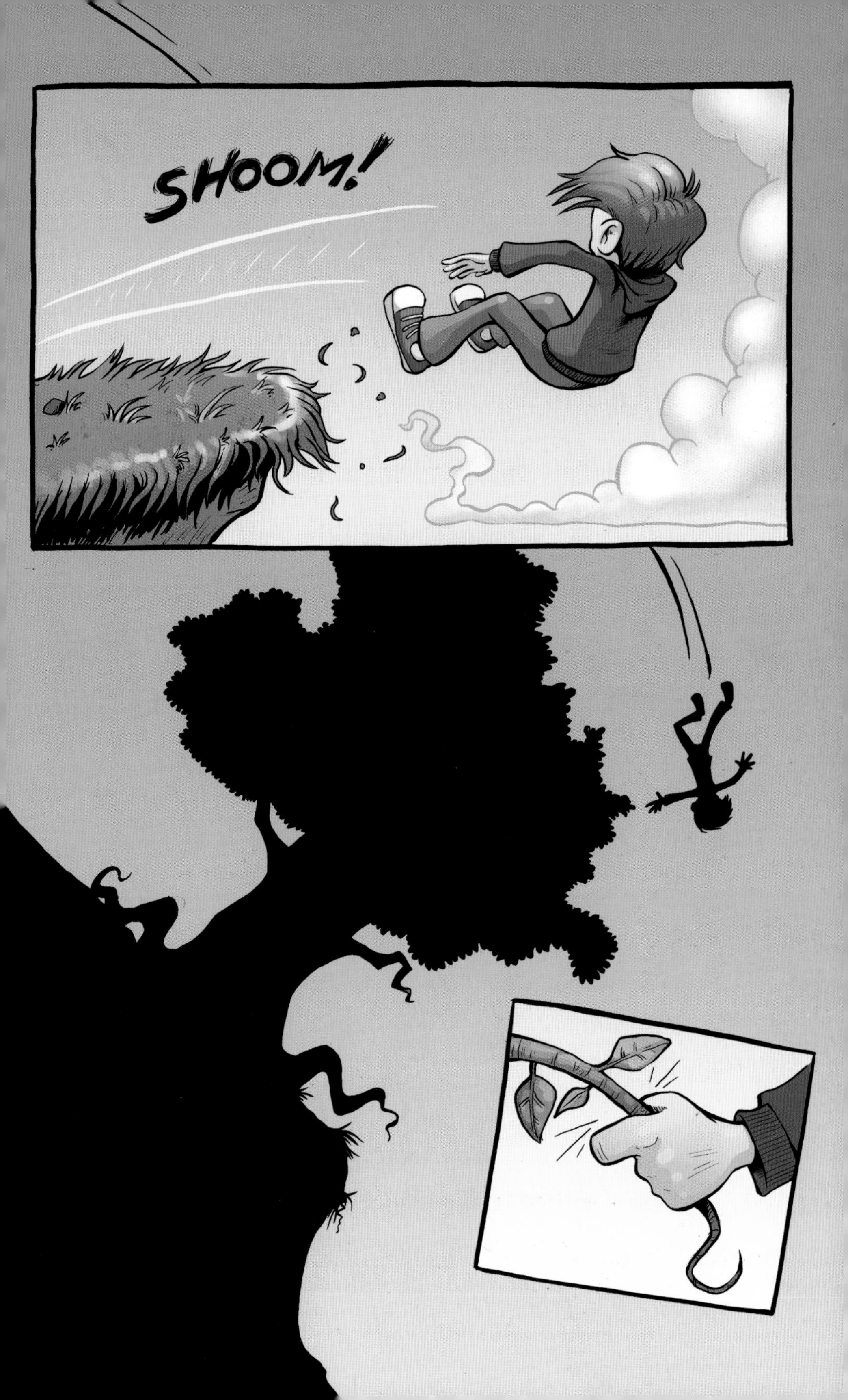
SHOOM!

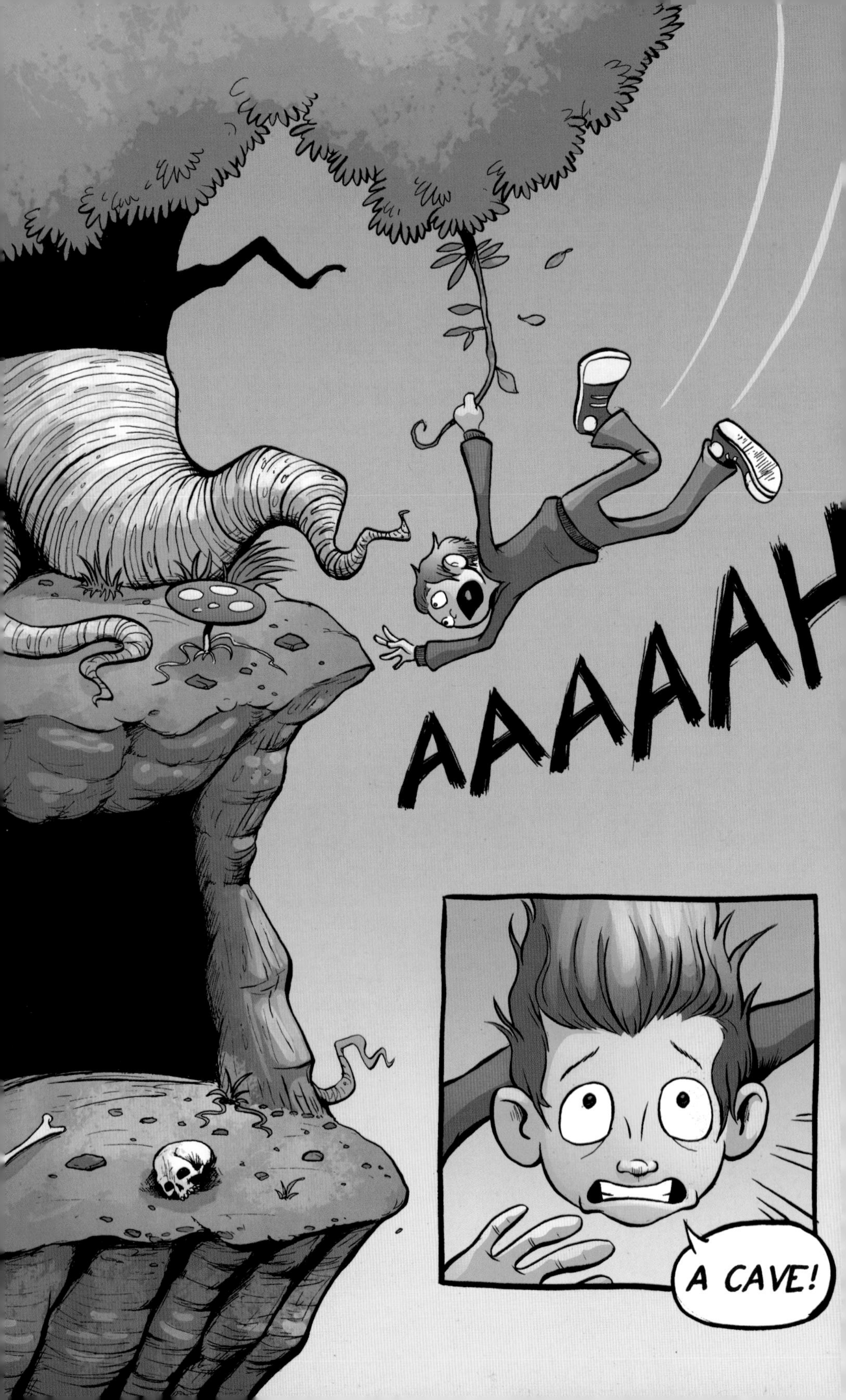
AAAAAH
A CAVE!

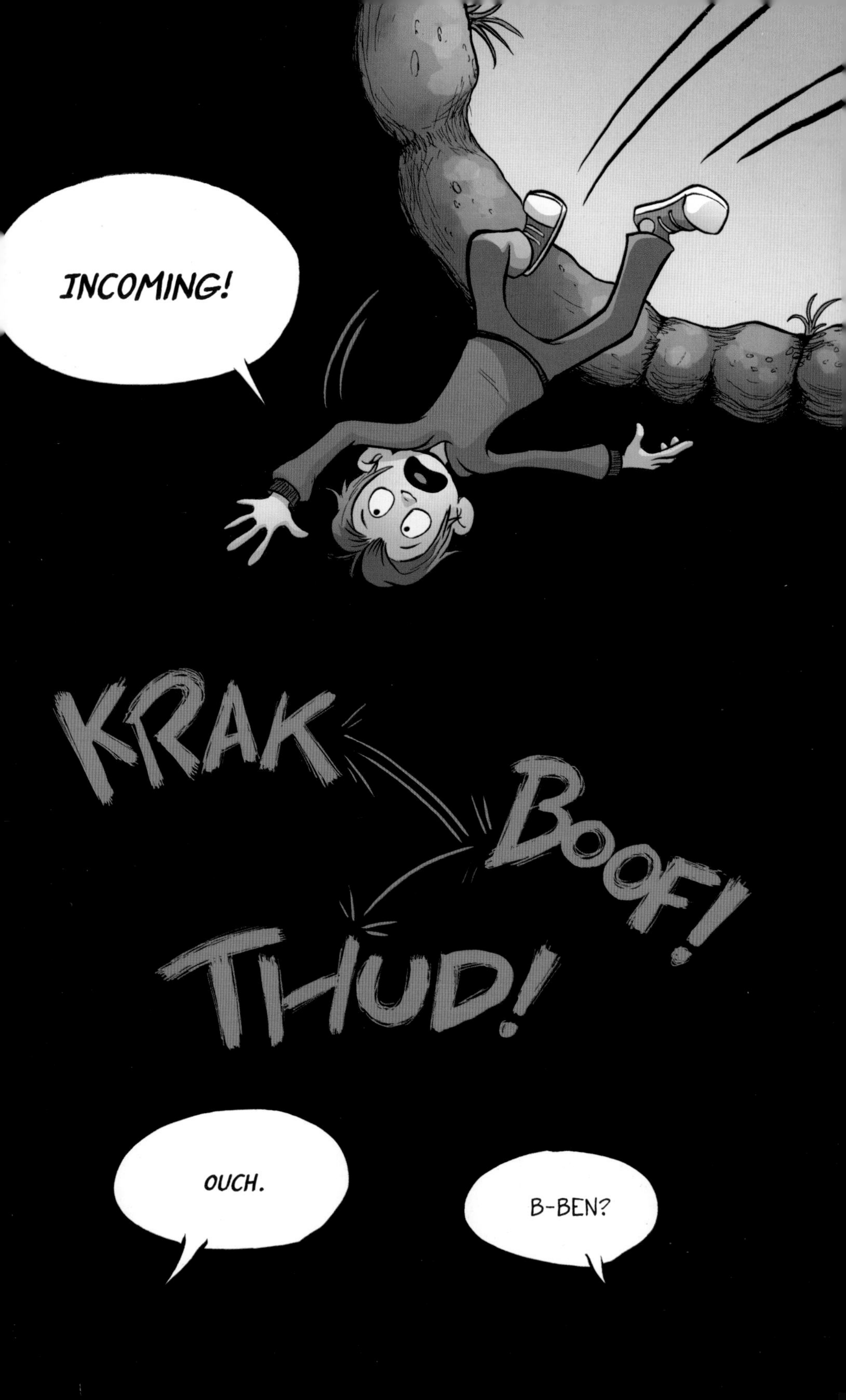
INCOMING!
KRAK
BOOF!
THUD!
OUCH.
B-BEN?

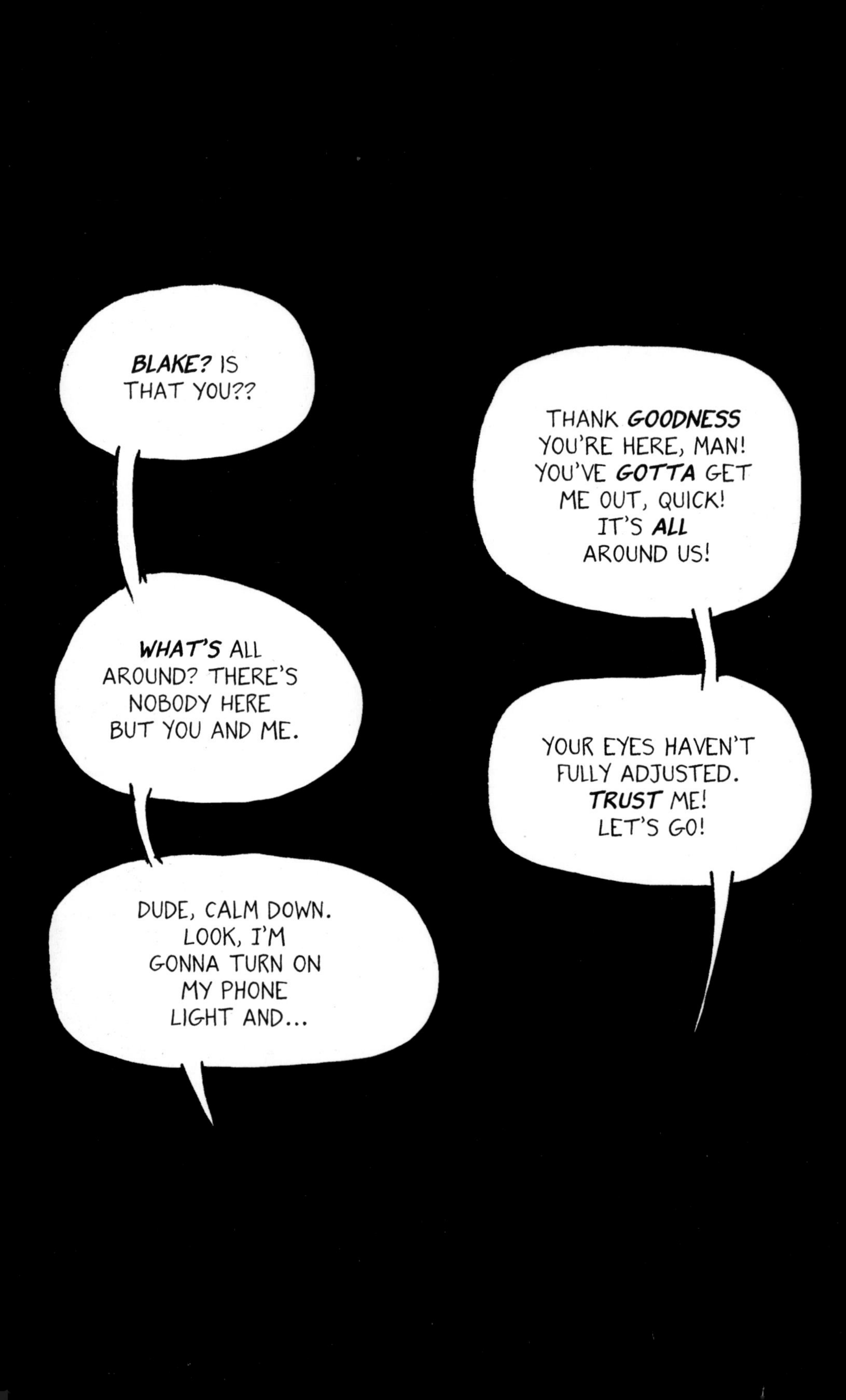
BLAKE? IS THAT YOU??
THANK GOODNESS YOU'RE HERE, MAN! YOU'VE GOTTA GET ME OUT, QUICK! IT'S ALL AROUND US!
WHAT'S ALL AROUND? THERE'S NOBODY HERE BUT YOU AND ME.
YOUR EYES HAVEN'T FULLY ADJUSTED. TRUST ME! LET'S GO!
DUDE, CALM DOWN. LOOK, I'M GONNA TURN ON MY PHONE LIGHT AND...

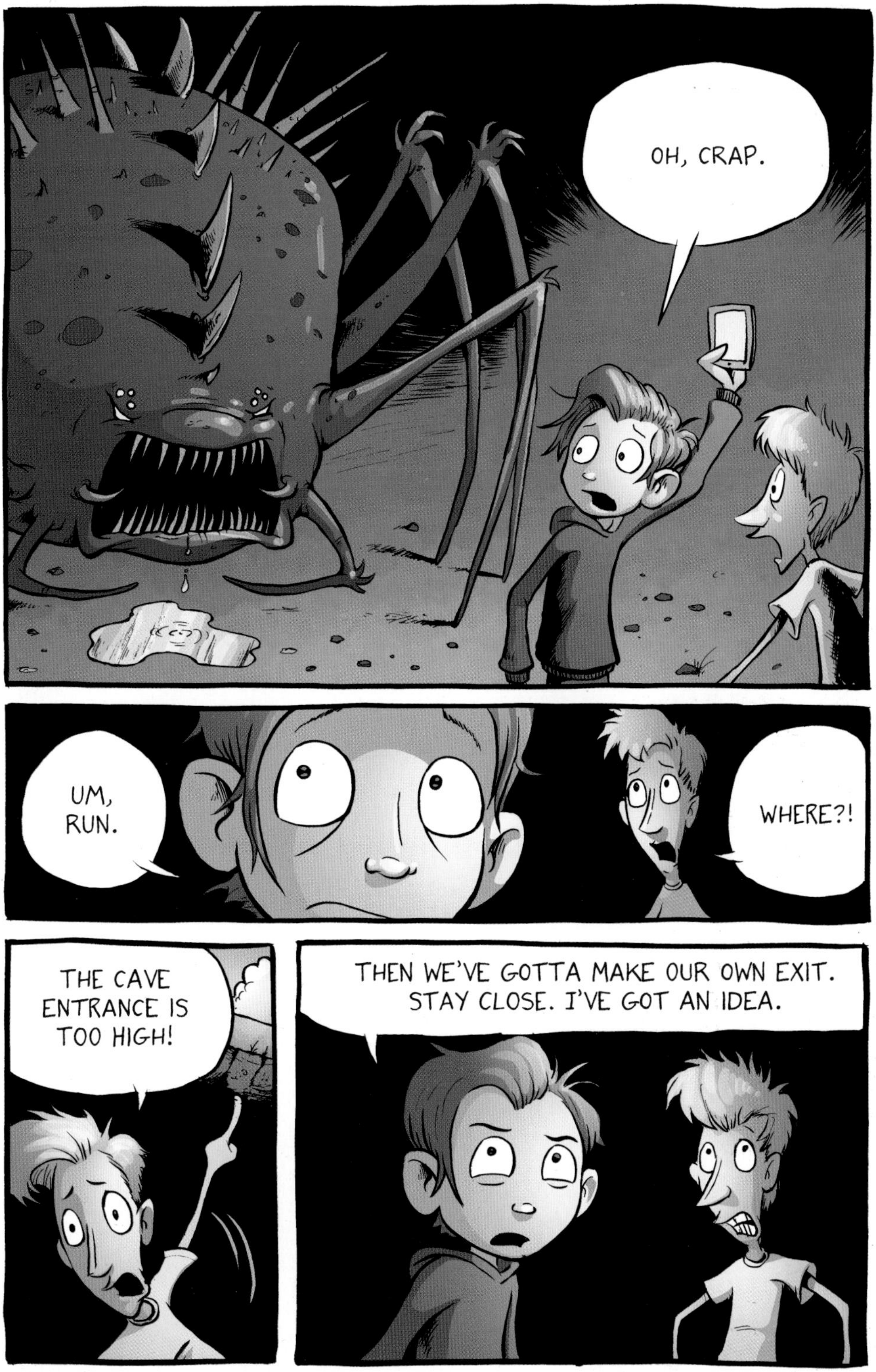
OH, CRAP.
UM, RUN.
WHERE?!
THE CAVE ENTRANCE IS TOO HIGH!
THEN WE'VE GOTTA MAKE OUR OWN EXIT. STAY CLOSE. I'VE GOT AN IDEA.

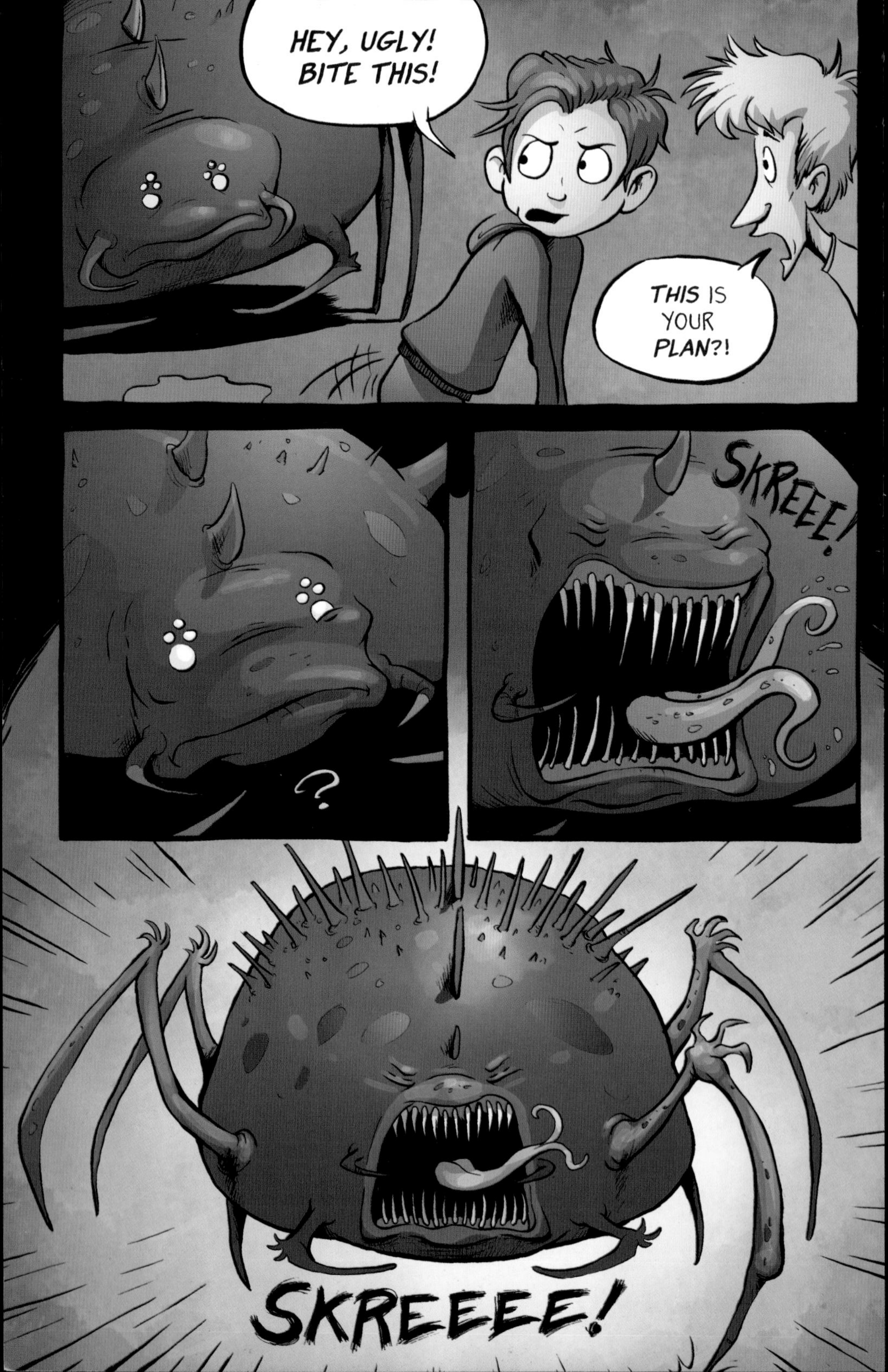
HEY, UGLY! BITE THIS!
THIS IS YOUR PLAN?!
?
SKREEE!
SKREEEE!

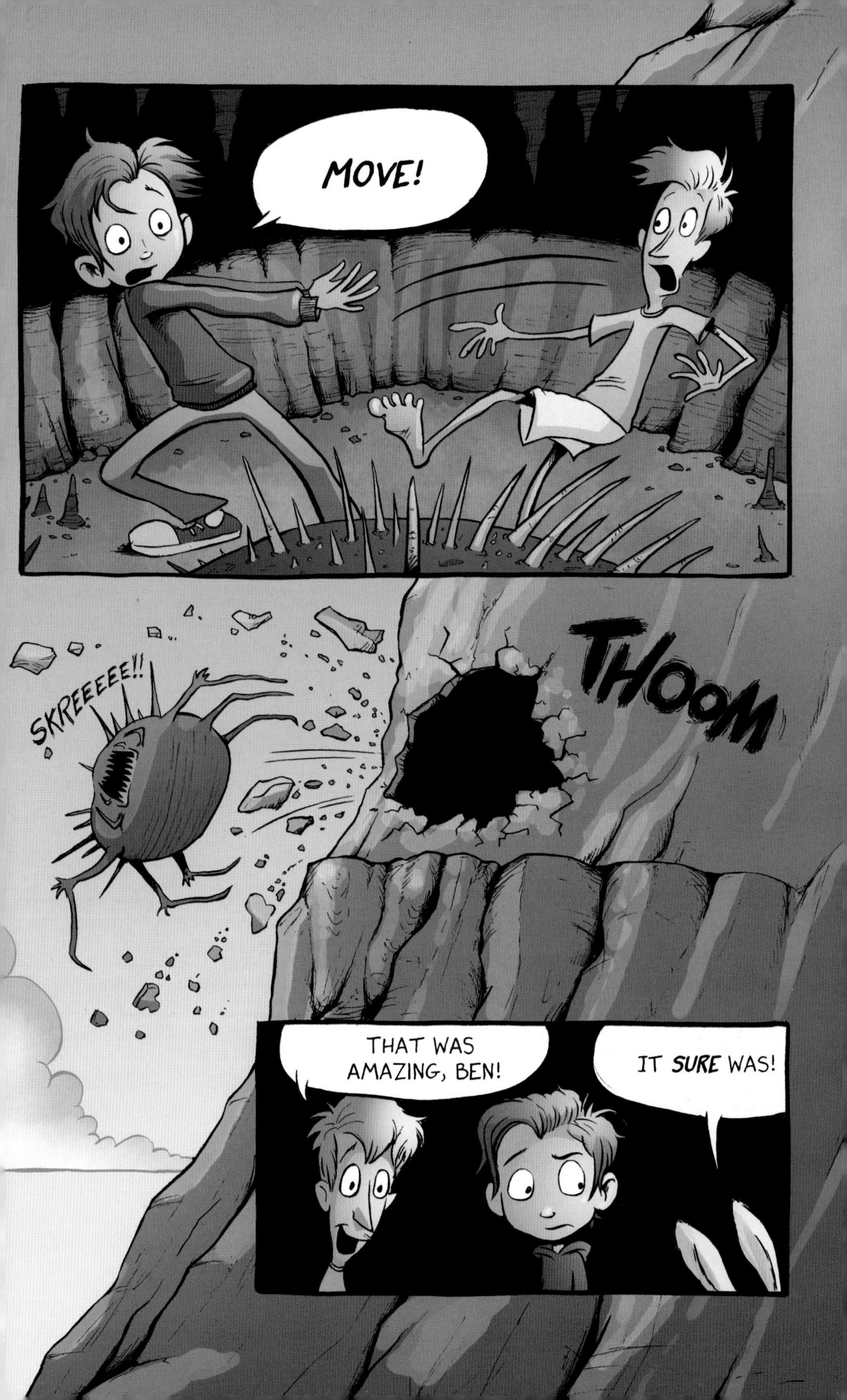
MOVE!
SKREEEEEE!!
THOOM
THAT WAS AMAZING, BEN!
IT SURE WAS!

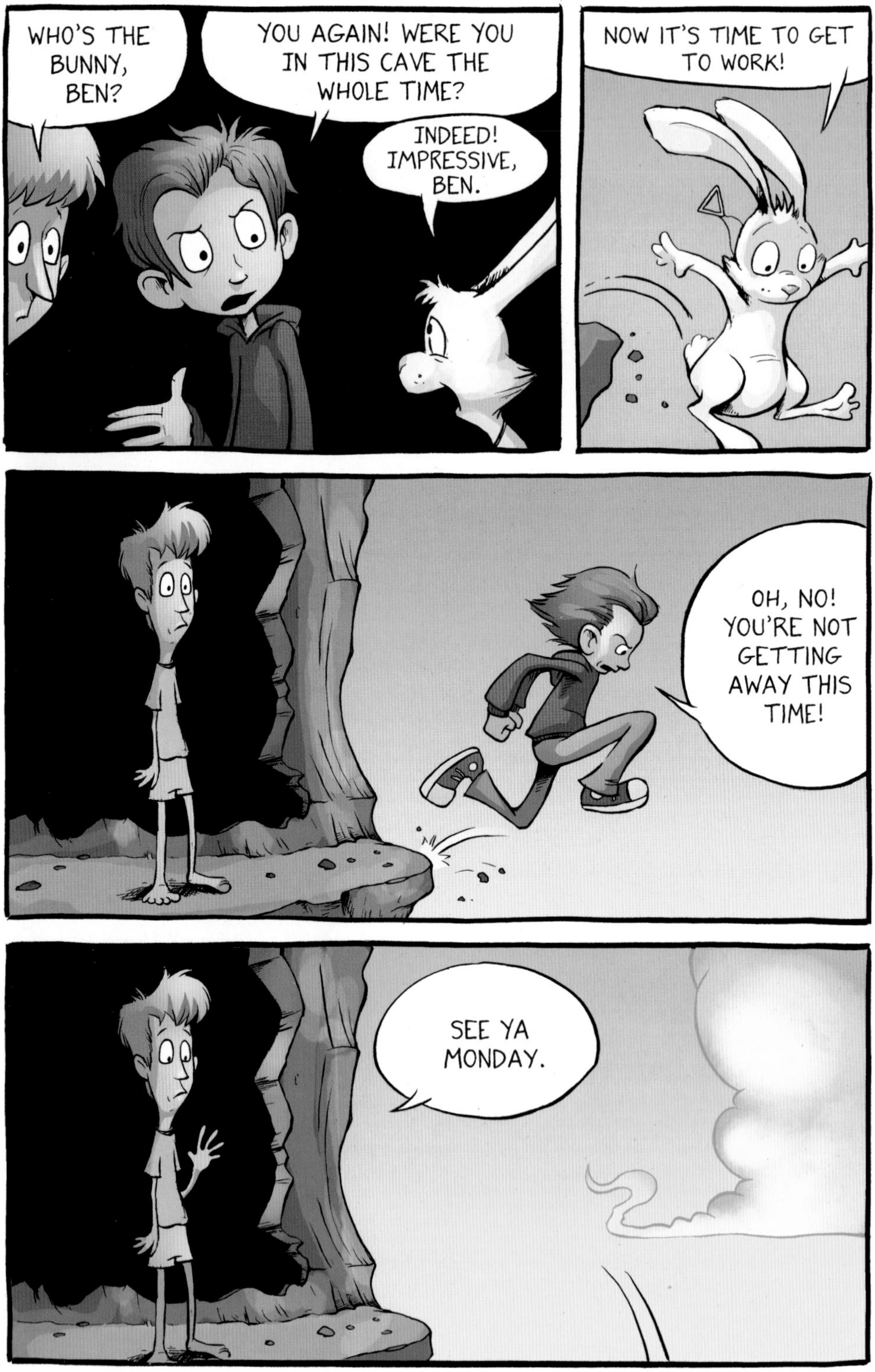
WHO'S THE BUNNY, BEN?
YOU AGAIN! WERE YOU IN THIS CAVE THE WHOLE TIME?
INDEED! IMPRESSIVE, BEN.
NOW IT'S TIME TO GET TO WORK!
OH, NO! YOU'RE NOT GETTING AWAY THIS TIME!
SEE YA MONDAY.

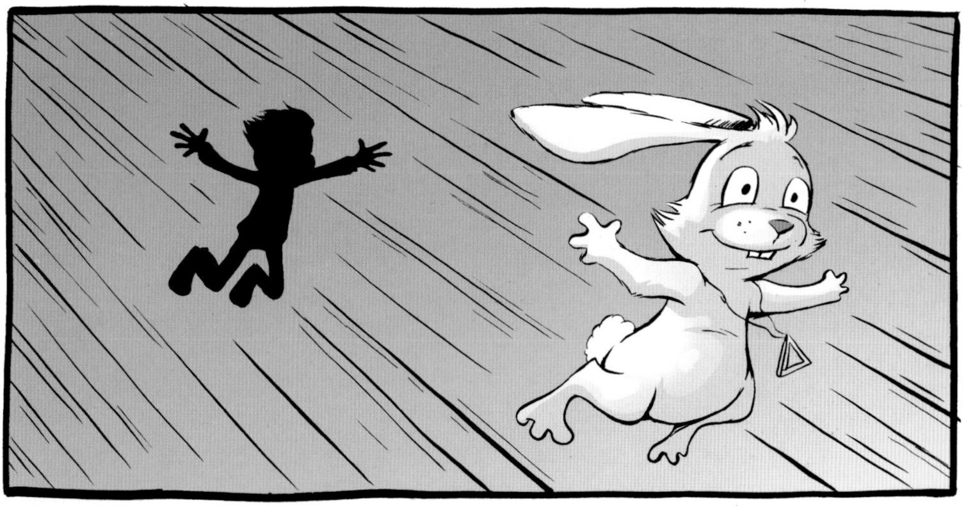

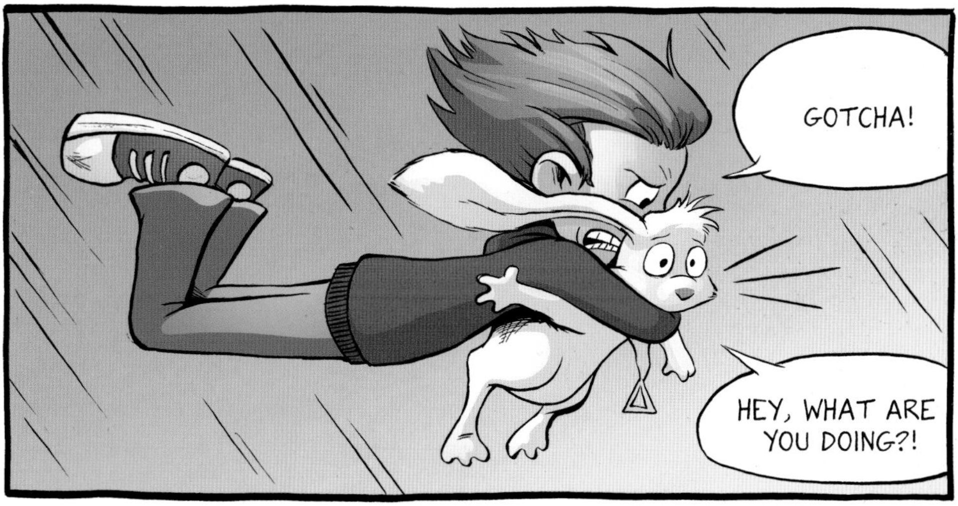
GOTCHA!
HEY, WHAT ARE YOU DOING?!

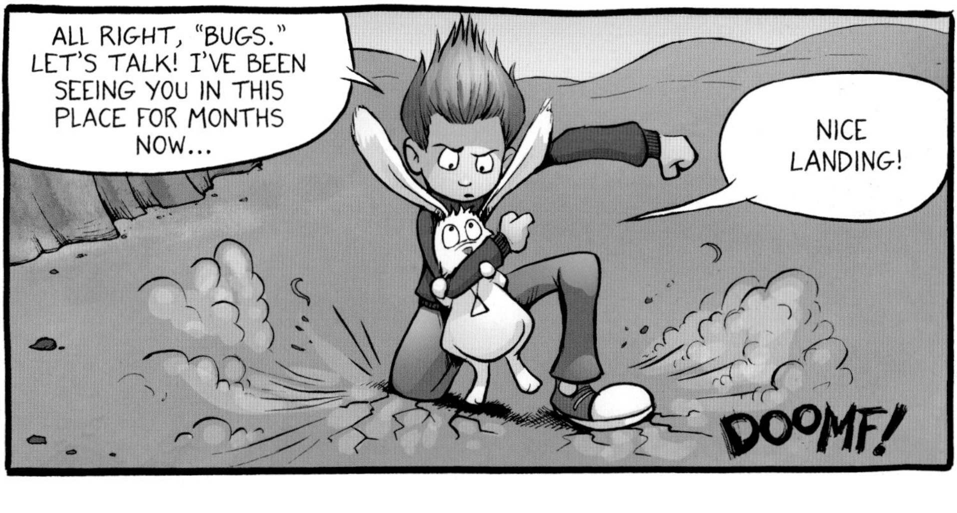
ALL RIGHT, "BUGS." LET'S TALK! I'VE BEEN SEEING YOU IN THIS PLACE FOR MONTHS NOW...
NICE LANDING!
DOOMF!

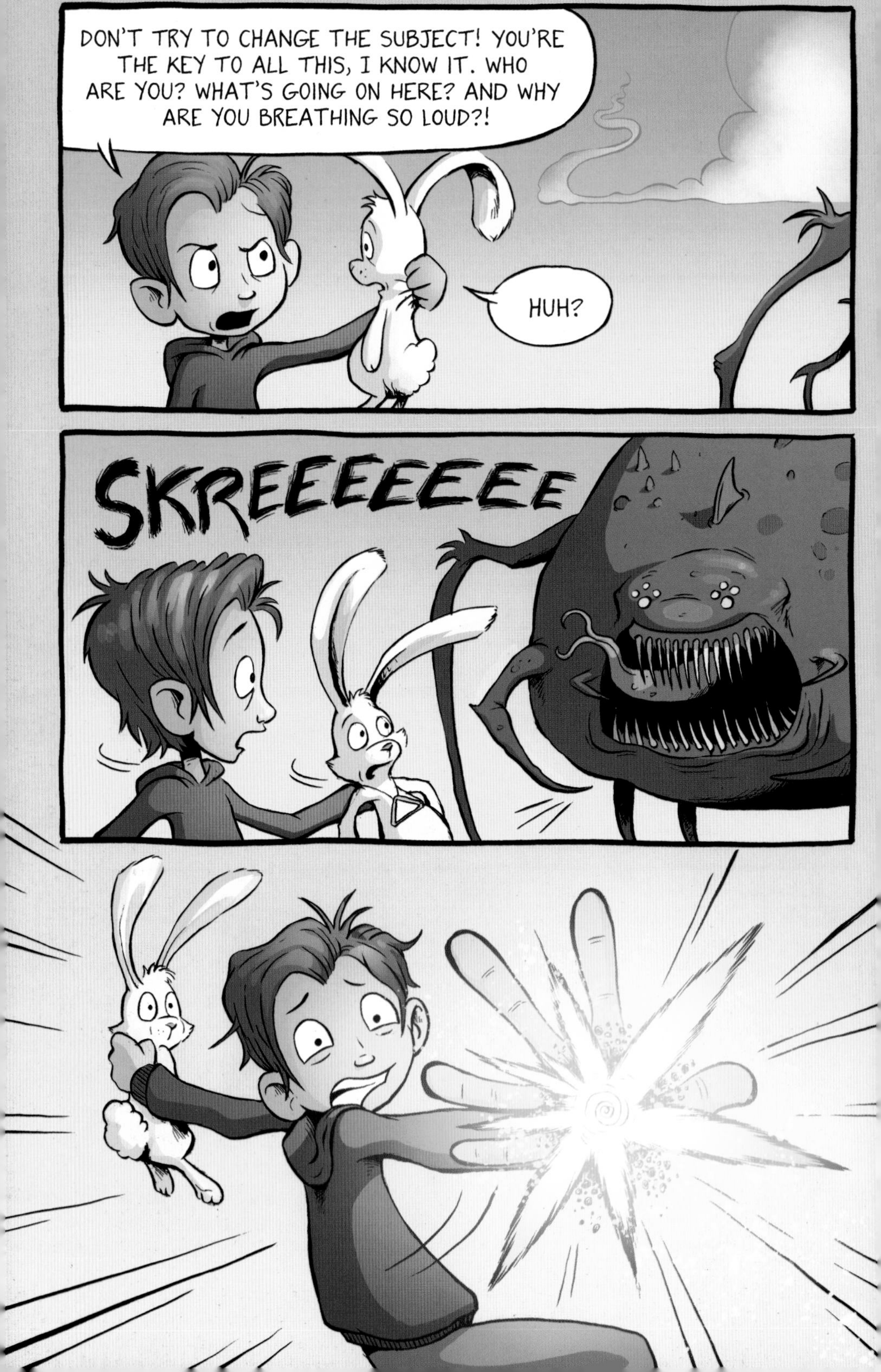
DON'T TRY TO CHANGE THE SUBJECT! YOU'RE THE KEY TO ALL THIS, I KNOW IT. WHO ARE YOU? WHAT'S GOING ON HERE? AND WHY ARE YOU BREATHING SO LOUD?!
HUH?
SKREEEEEEEEE

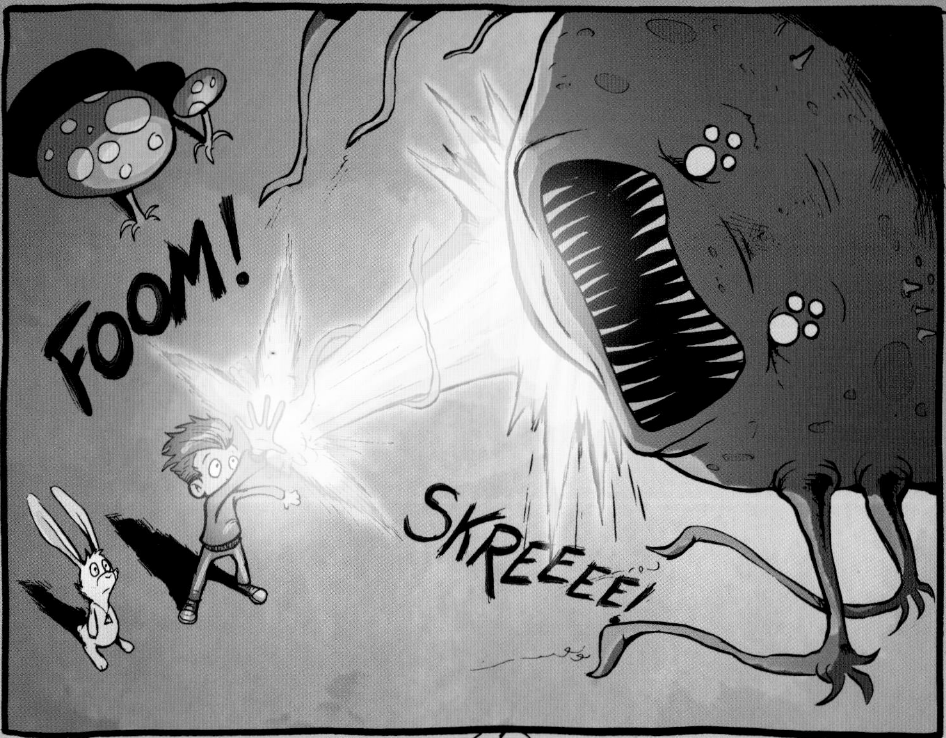
FOOM!
SKREEEEE!

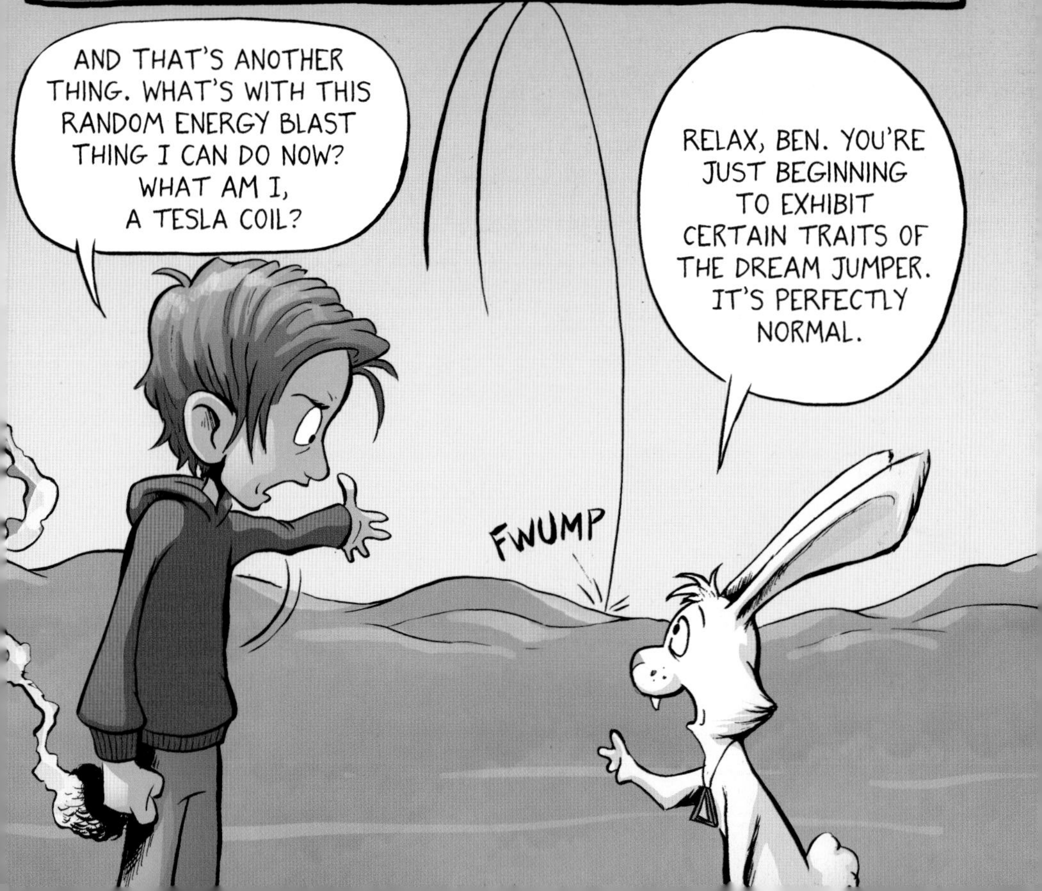
AND THAT'S ANOTHER THING. WHAT'S WITH THIS RANDOM ENERGY BLAST THING I CAN DO NOW? WHAT AM I, A TESLA COIL?
RELAX, BEN. YOU'RE JUST BEGINNING TO EXHIBIT CERTAIN TRAITS OF THE DREAM JUMPER. IT'S PERFECTLY NORMAL.
FWUMP

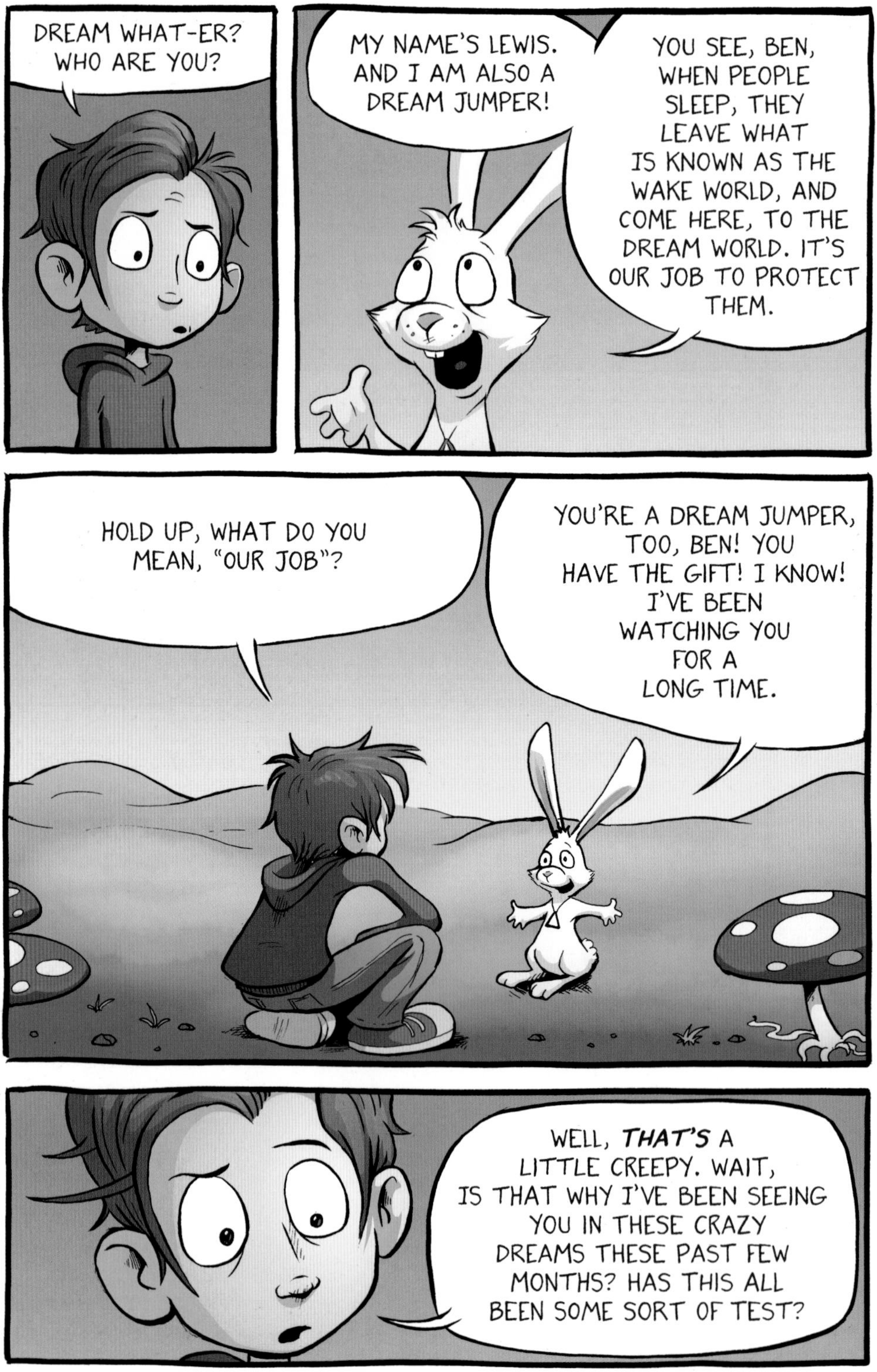
DREAM WHAT-ER? WHO ARE YOU?
MY NAME'S LEWIS. AND I AM ALSO A DREAM JUMPER!
YOU SEE, BEN, WHEN PEOPLE SLEEP, THEY LEAVE WHAT IS KNOWN AS THE WAKE WORLD, AND COME HERE, TO THE DREAM WORLD. IT'S OUR JOB TO PROTECT THEM.
HOLD UP, WHAT DO YOU MEAN, "OUR JOB"?
YOU'RE A DREAM JUMPER, TOO, BEN! YOU HAVE THE GIFT! I KNOW! I'VE BEEN WATCHING YOU FOR A LONG TIME.
WELL, ***THAT'S*** A LITTLE CREEPY. WAIT, IS THAT WHY I'VE BEEN SEEING YOU IN THESE CRAZY DREAMS THESE PAST FEW MONTHS? HAS THIS ALL BEEN SOME SORT OF TEST?

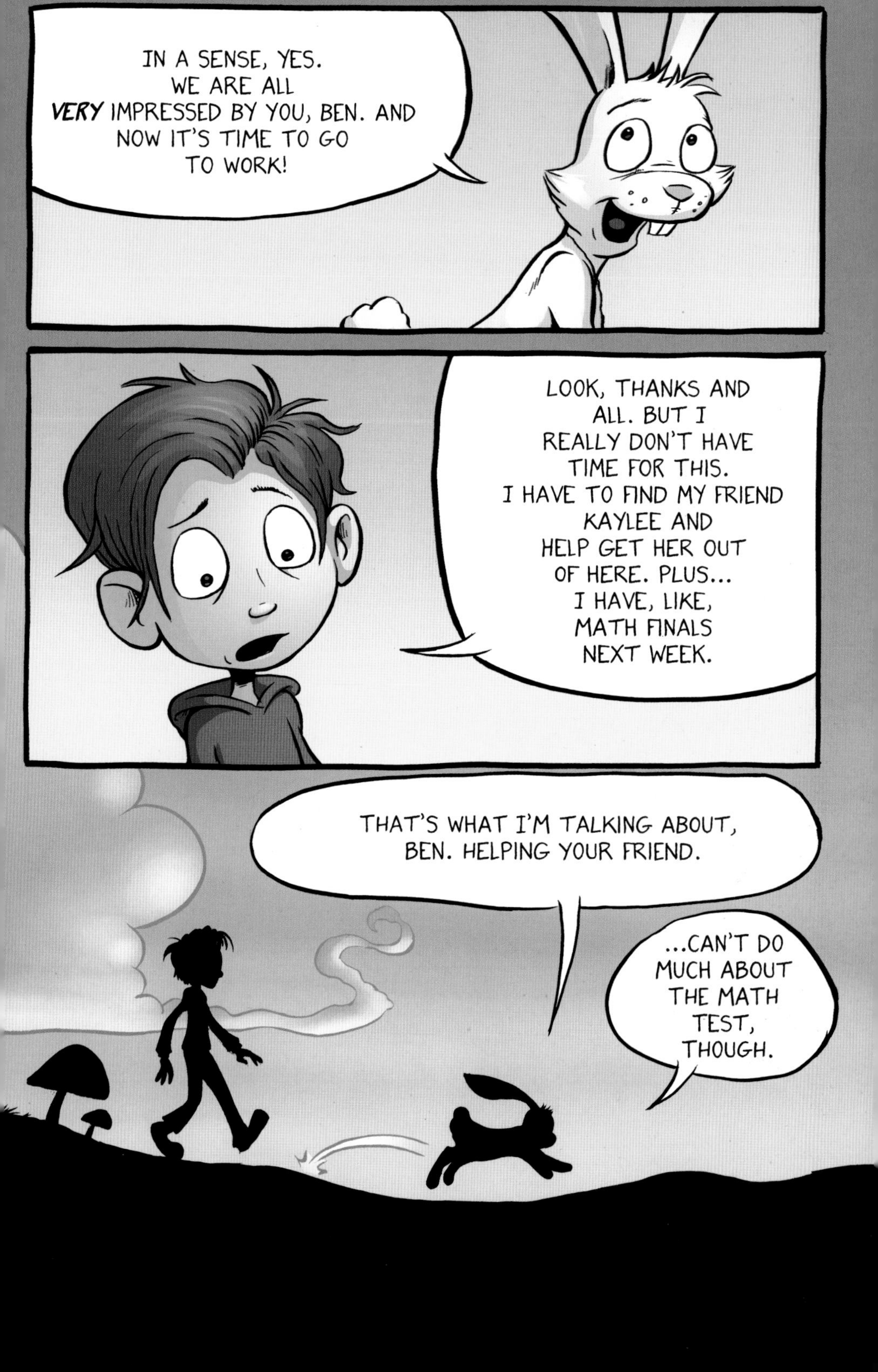
IN A SENSE, YES. WE ARE ALL *VERY* IMPRESSED BY YOU, BEN. AND NOW IT'S TIME TO GO TO WORK!
LOOK, THANKS AND ALL. BUT I REALLY DON'T HAVE TIME FOR THIS. I HAVE TO FIND MY FRIEND KAYLEE AND HELP GET HER OUT OF HERE. PLUS... I HAVE, LIKE, MATH FINALS NEXT WEEK.
THAT'S WHAT I'M TALKING ABOUT, BEN. HELPING YOUR FRIEND.
...CAN'T DO MUCH ABOUT THE MATH TEST, THOUGH.

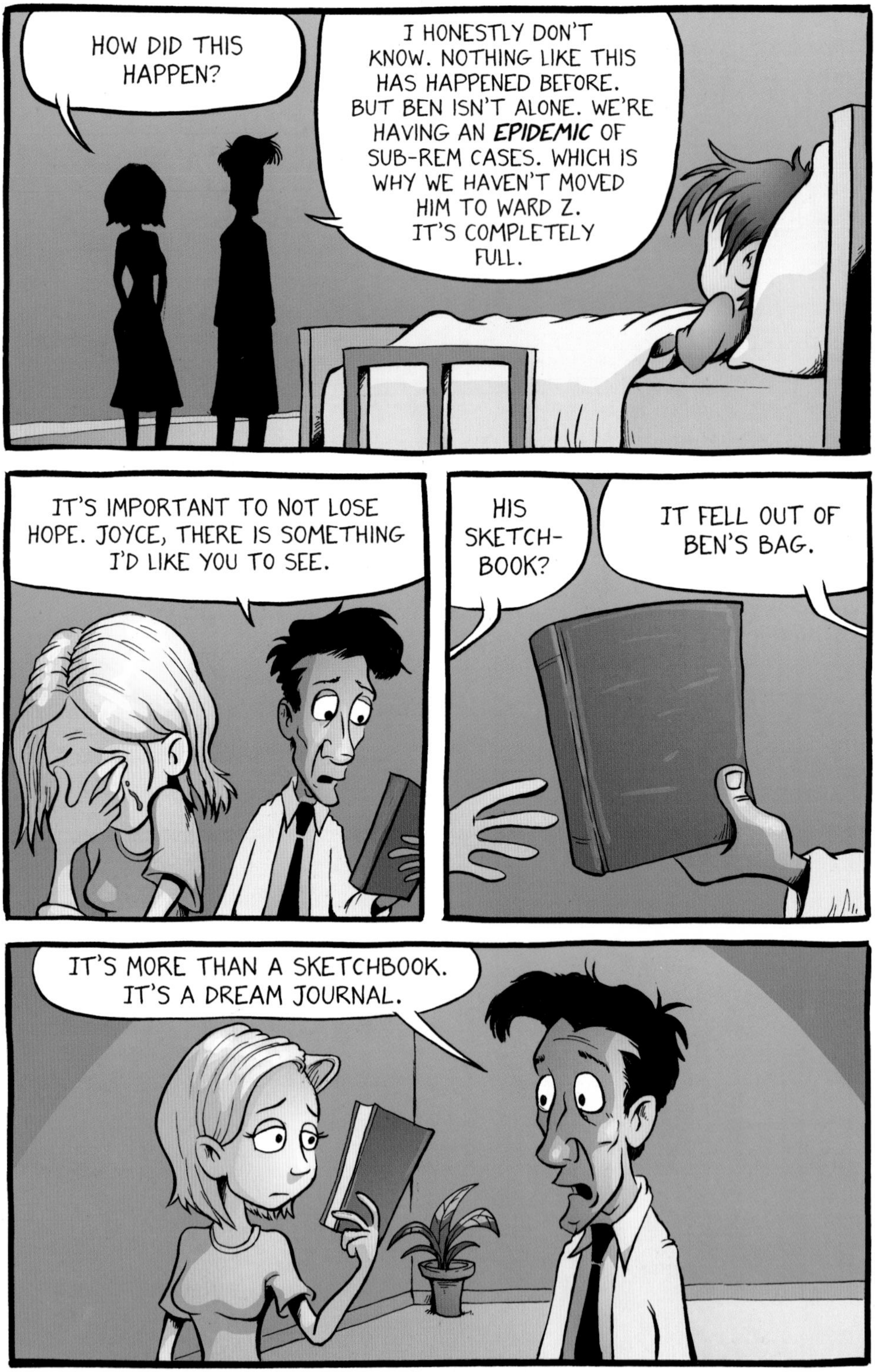
HOW DID THIS HAPPEN?
I HONESTLY DON'T KNOW. NOTHING LIKE THIS HAS HAPPENED BEFORE. BUT BEN ISN'T ALONE. WE'RE HAVING AN EPIDEMIC OF SUB-REM CASES. WHICH IS WHY WE HAVEN'T MOVED HIM TO WARD Z. IT'S COMPLETELY FULL.
IT'S IMPORTANT TO NOT LOSE HOPE. JOYCE, THERE IS SOMETHING I'D LIKE YOU TO SEE.
HIS SKETCH-BOOK?
IT FELL OUT OF BEN'S BAG.
IT'S MORE THAN A SKETCHBOOK. IT'S A DREAM JOURNAL.

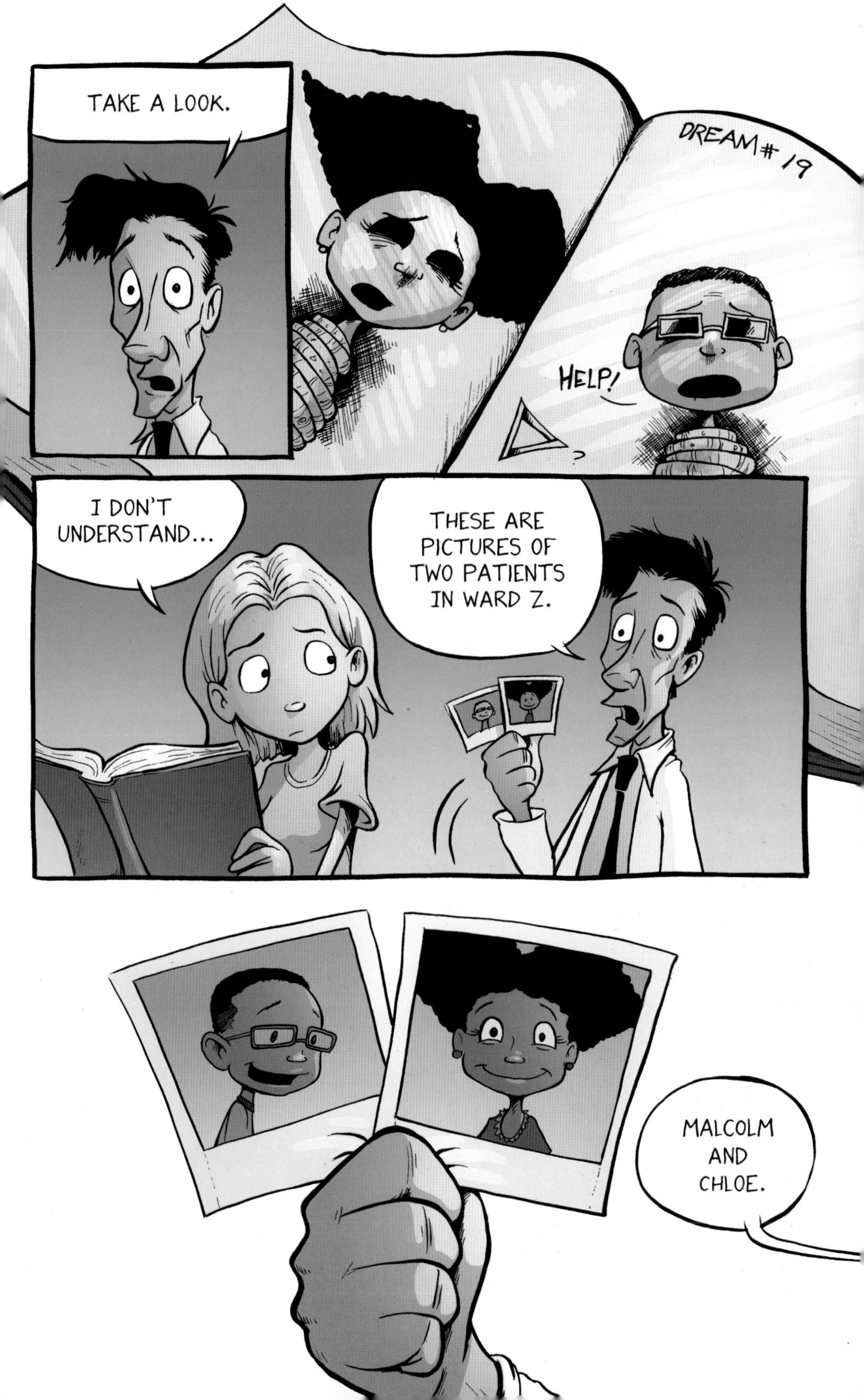
TAKE A LOOK.
DREAM # 19
HELP!
I DON'T UNDERSTAND...
THESE ARE PICTURES OF TWO PATIENTS IN WARD Z.
MALCOLM AND CHLOE.

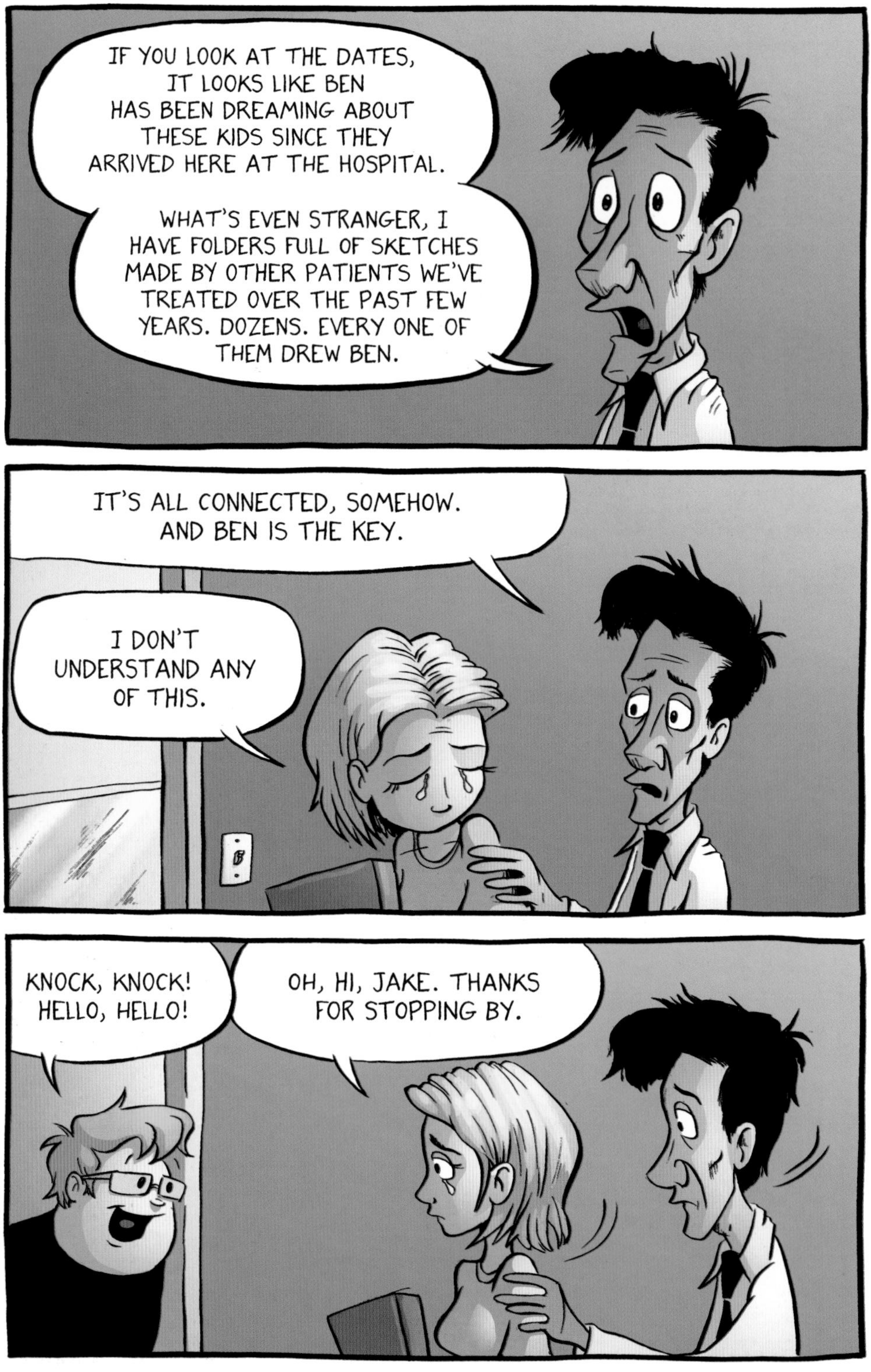
IF YOU LOOK AT THE DATES, IT LOOKS LIKE BEN HAS BEEN DREAMING ABOUT THESE KIDS SINCE THEY ARRIVED HERE AT THE HOSPITAL.
WHAT'S EVEN STRANGER, I HAVE FOLDERS FULL OF SKETCHES MADE BY OTHER PATIENTS WE'VE TREATED OVER THE PAST FEW YEARS. DOZENS. EVERY ONE OF THEM DREW BEN.
IT'S ALL CONNECTED, SOMEHOW. AND BEN IS THE KEY.
I DON'T UNDERSTAND ANY OF THIS.
KNOCK, KNOCK! HELLO, HELLO!
OH, HI, JAKE. THANKS FOR STOPPING BY.

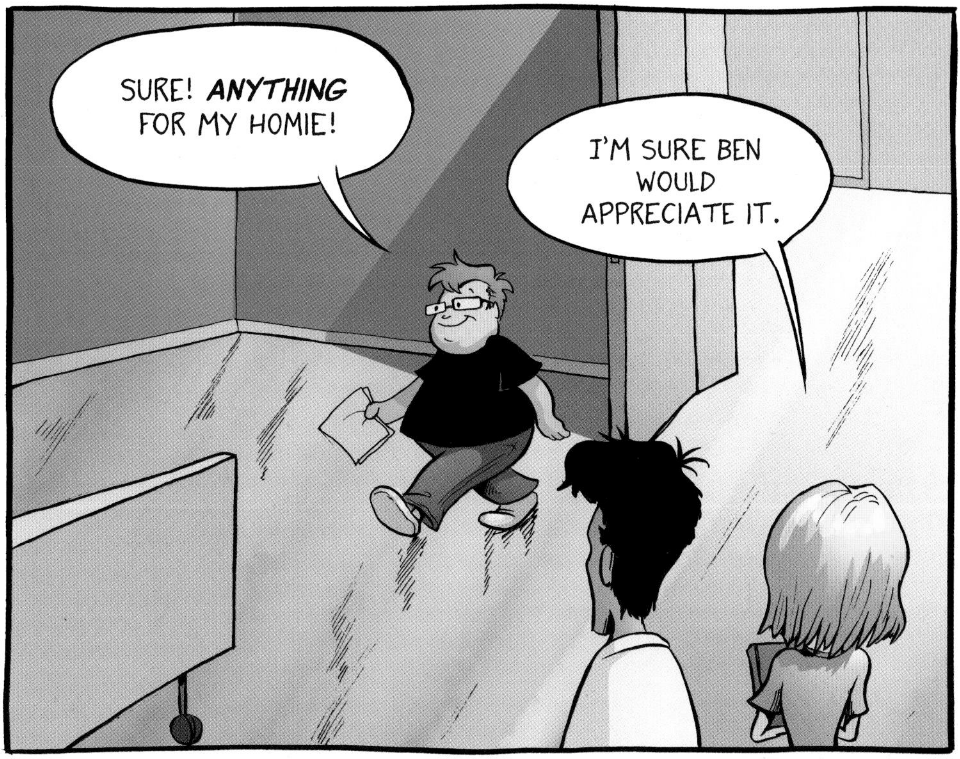
SURE! **ANYTHING** FOR MY HOMIE!
I'M SURE BEN WOULD APPRECIATE IT.

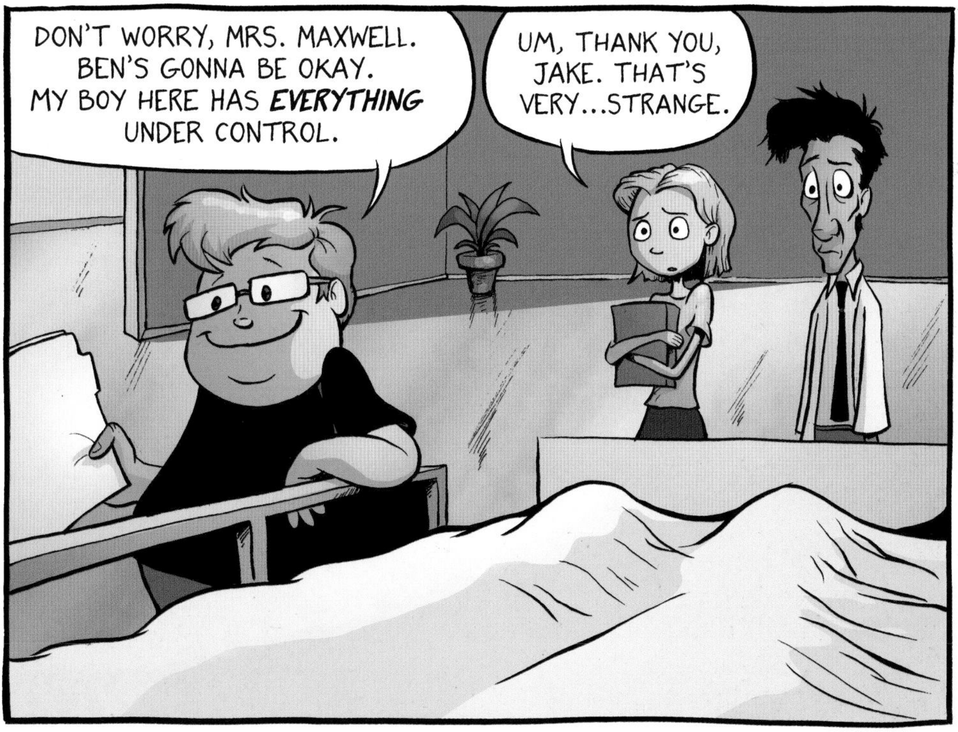
DON'T WORRY, MRS. MAXWELL. BEN'S GONNA BE OKAY. MY BOY HERE HAS **EVERYTHING** UNDER CONTROL.
UM, THANK YOU, JAKE. THAT'S VERY...STRANGE.

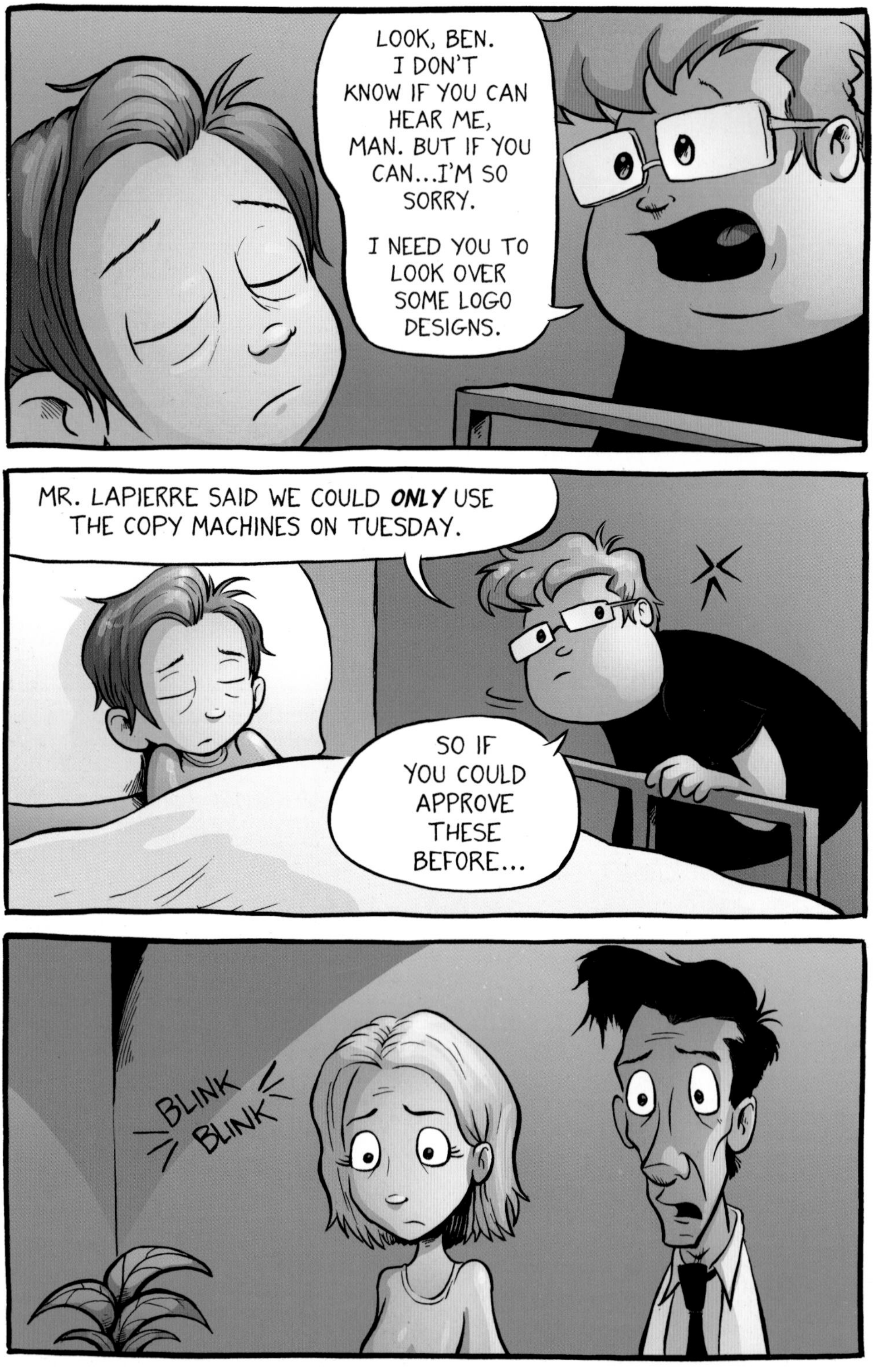
LOOK, BEN. I DON'T KNOW IF YOU CAN HEAR ME, MAN. BUT IF YOU CAN...I'M SO SORRY.
I NEED YOU TO LOOK OVER SOME LOGO DESIGNS.
MR. LAPIERRE SAID WE COULD *ONLY* USE THE COPY MACHINES ON TUESDAY.
SO IF YOU COULD APPROVE THESE BEFORE...
BLINK BLINK

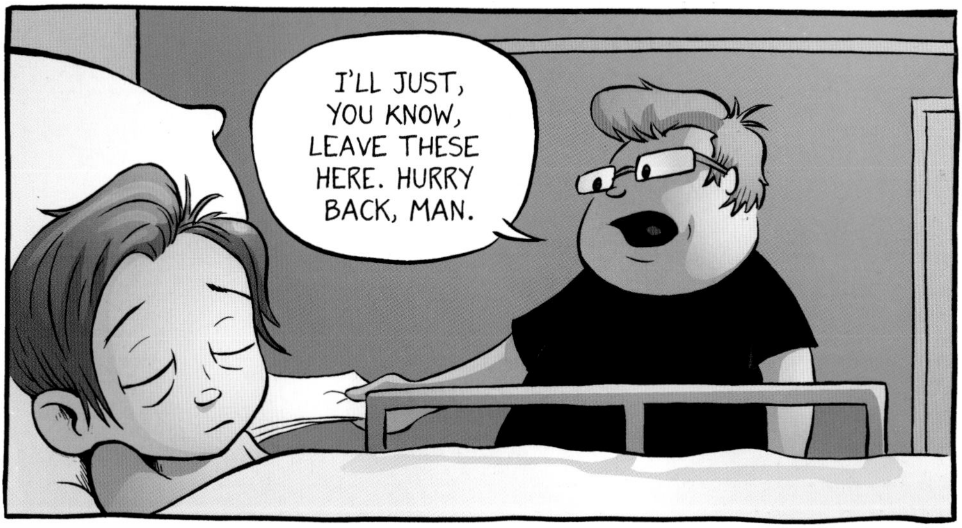
I'LL JUST, YOU KNOW, LEAVE THESE HERE. HURRY BACK, MAN.

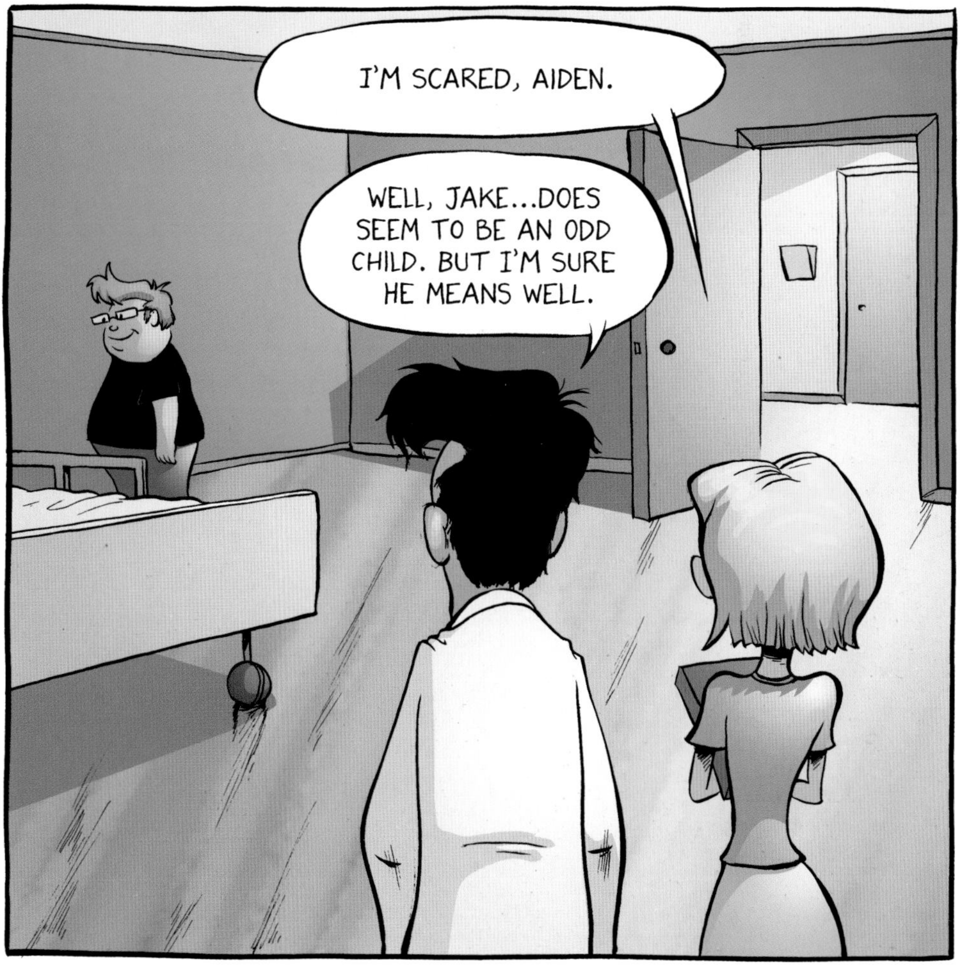
I'M SCARED, AIDEN.
WELL, JAKE...DOES SEEM TO BE AN ODD CHILD. BUT I'M SURE HE MEANS WELL.

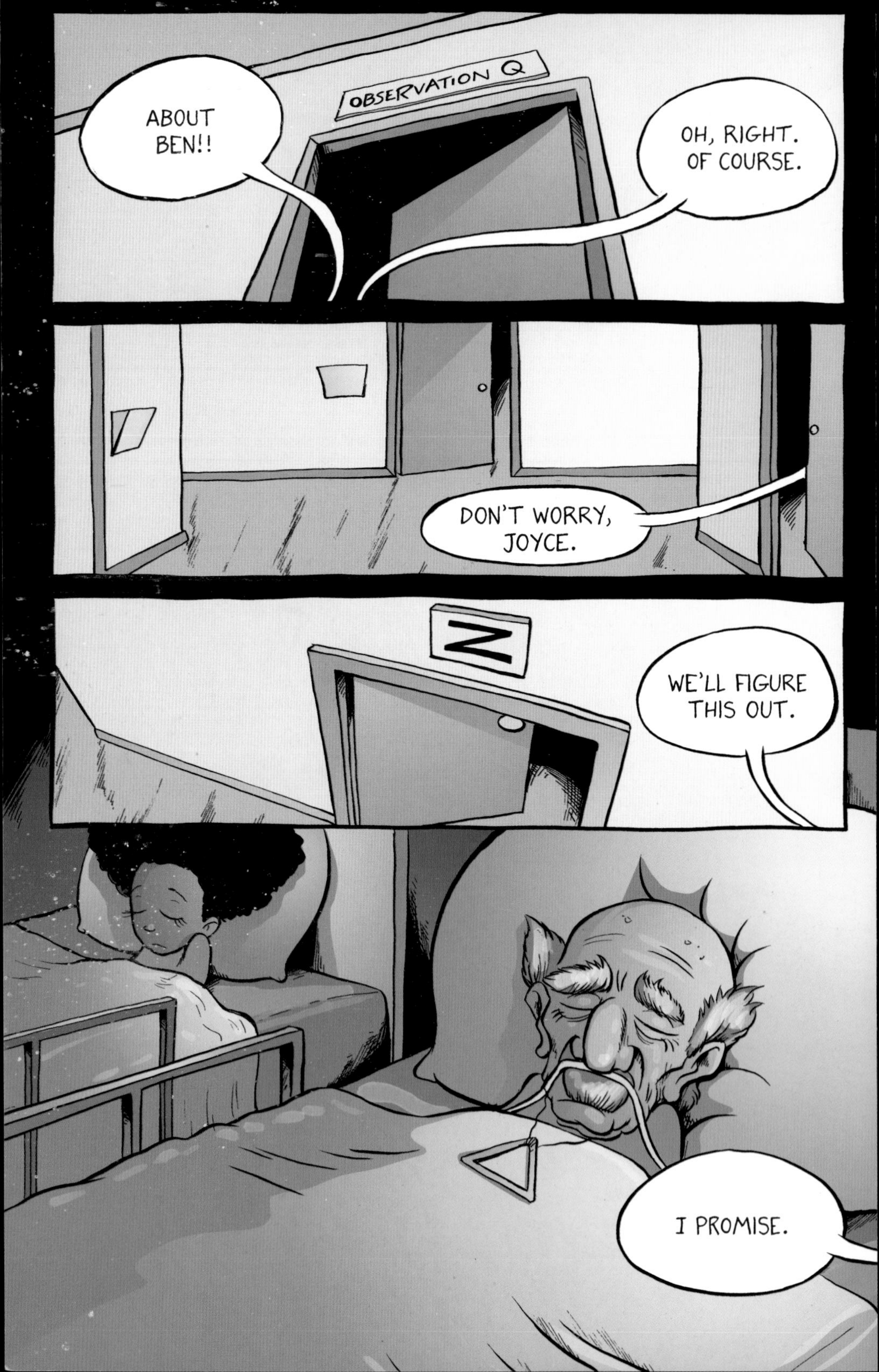
OBSERVATION Q
ABOUT BEN!!
OH, RIGHT. OF COURSE.
DON'T WORRY, JOYCE.
Z
WE'LL FIGURE THIS OUT.
I PROMISE.

ELSEWHERE...

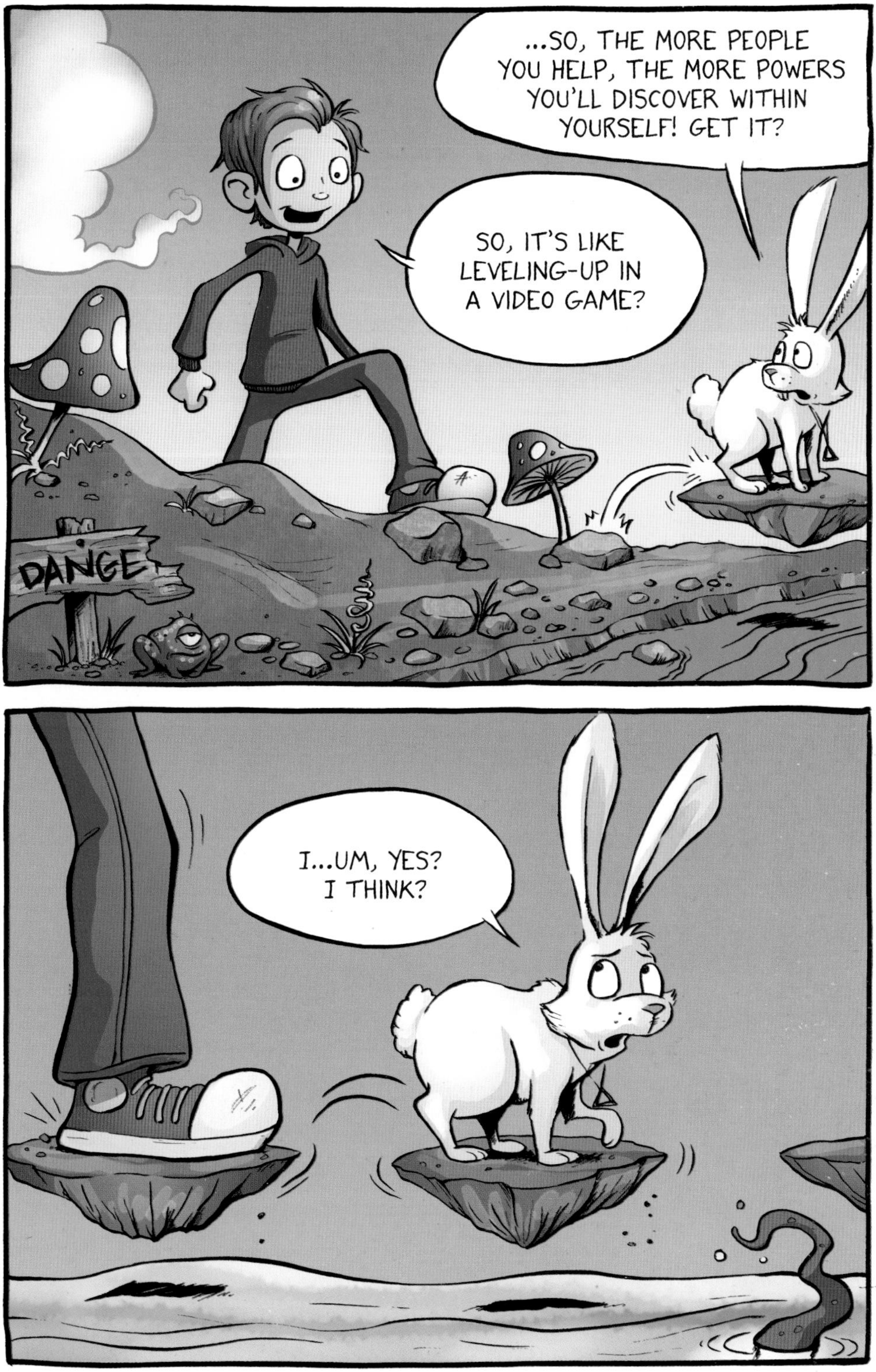
...SO, THE MORE PEOPLE YOU HELP, THE MORE POWERS YOU'LL DISCOVER WITHIN YOURSELF! GET IT?
SO, IT'S LIKE LEVELING-UP IN A VIDEO GAME?
DANGE
I...UM, YES? I THINK?

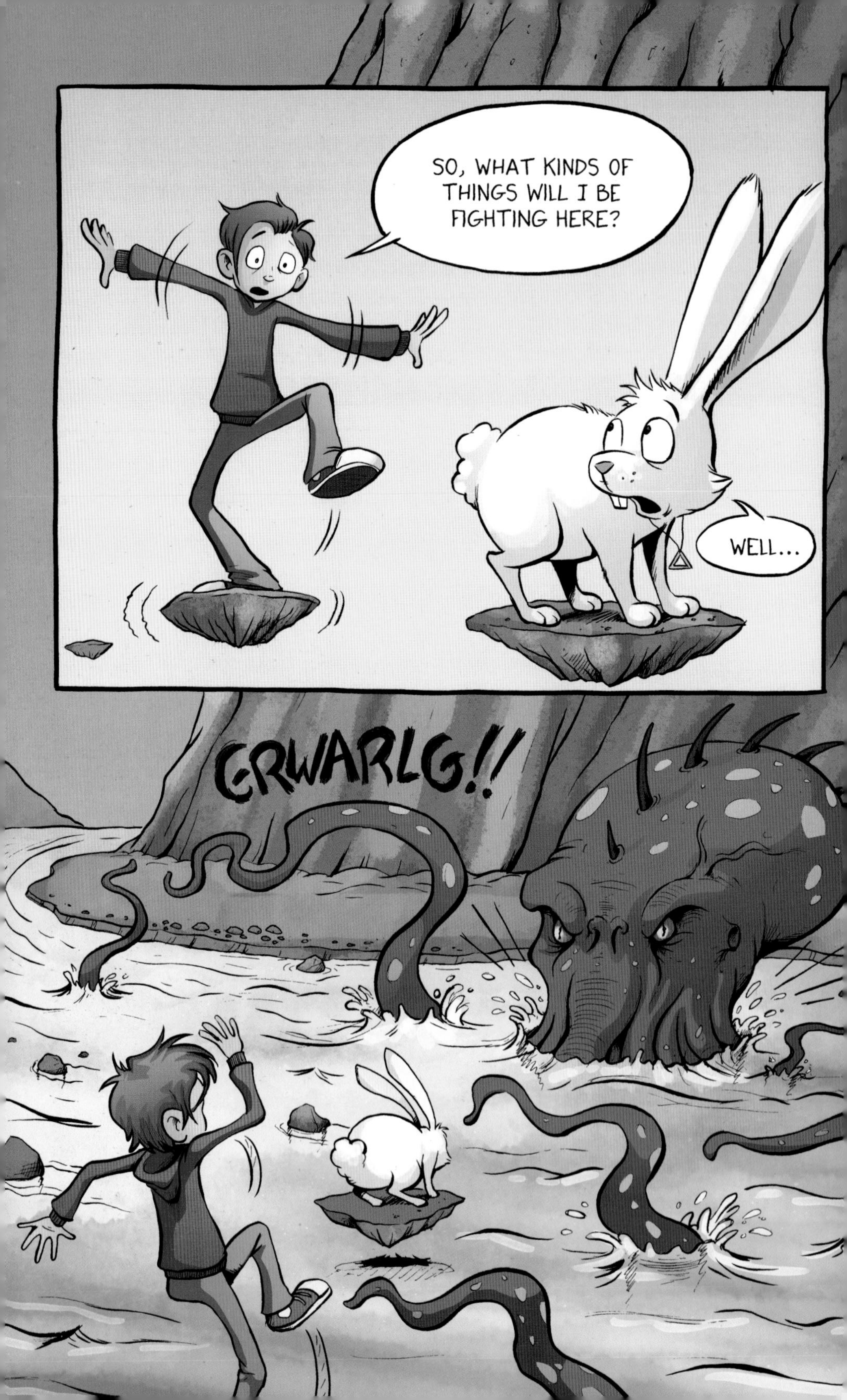
SO, WHAT KINDS OF THINGS WILL I BE FIGHTING HERE?
WELL...
GRWARLG!!

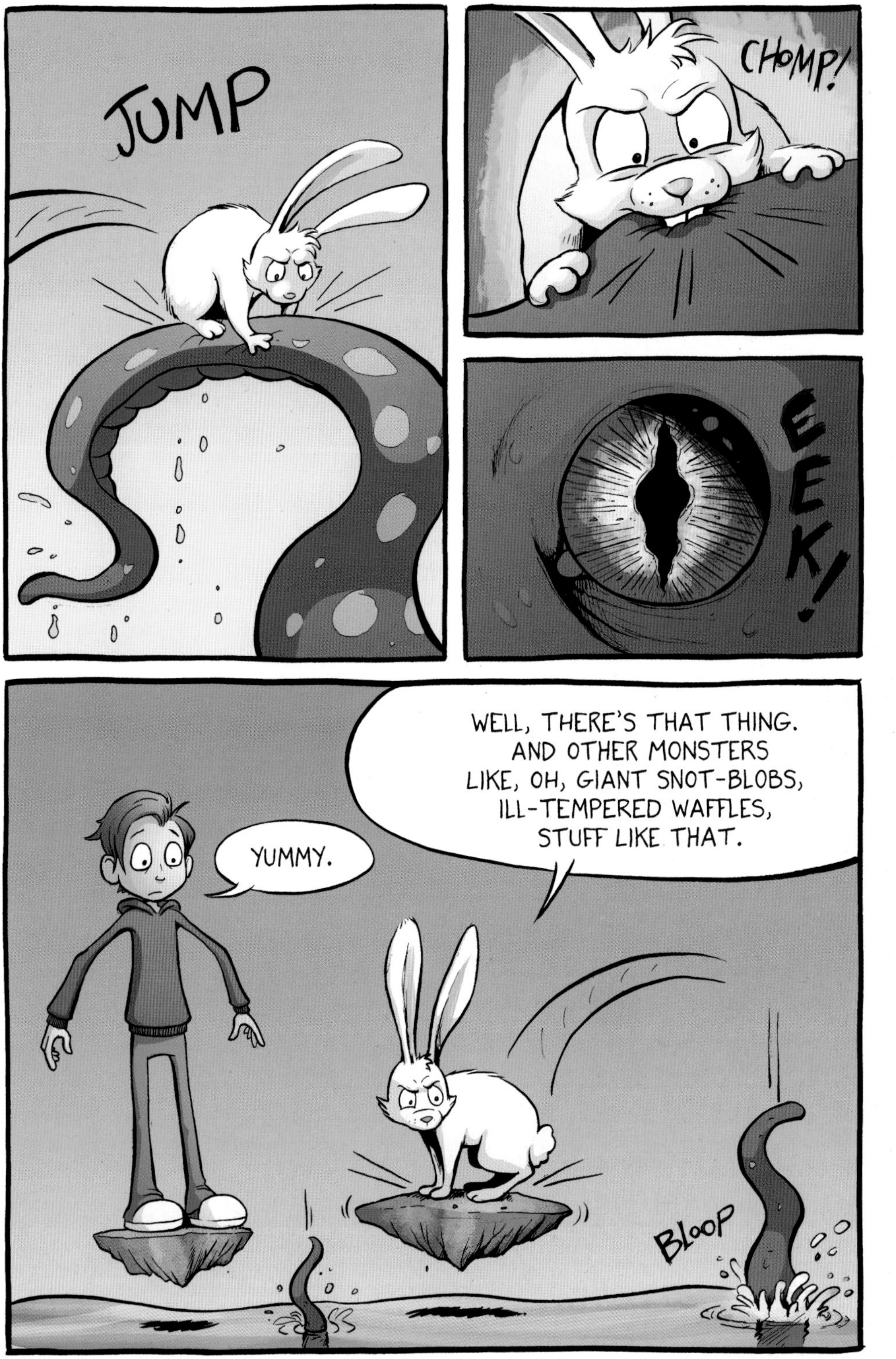
JUMP
CHOMP!
EEK!
WELL, THERE'S THAT THING. AND OTHER MONSTERS LIKE, OH, GIANT SNOT-BLOBS, ILL-TEMPERED WAFFLES, STUFF LIKE THAT.
YUMMY.
BLOOP

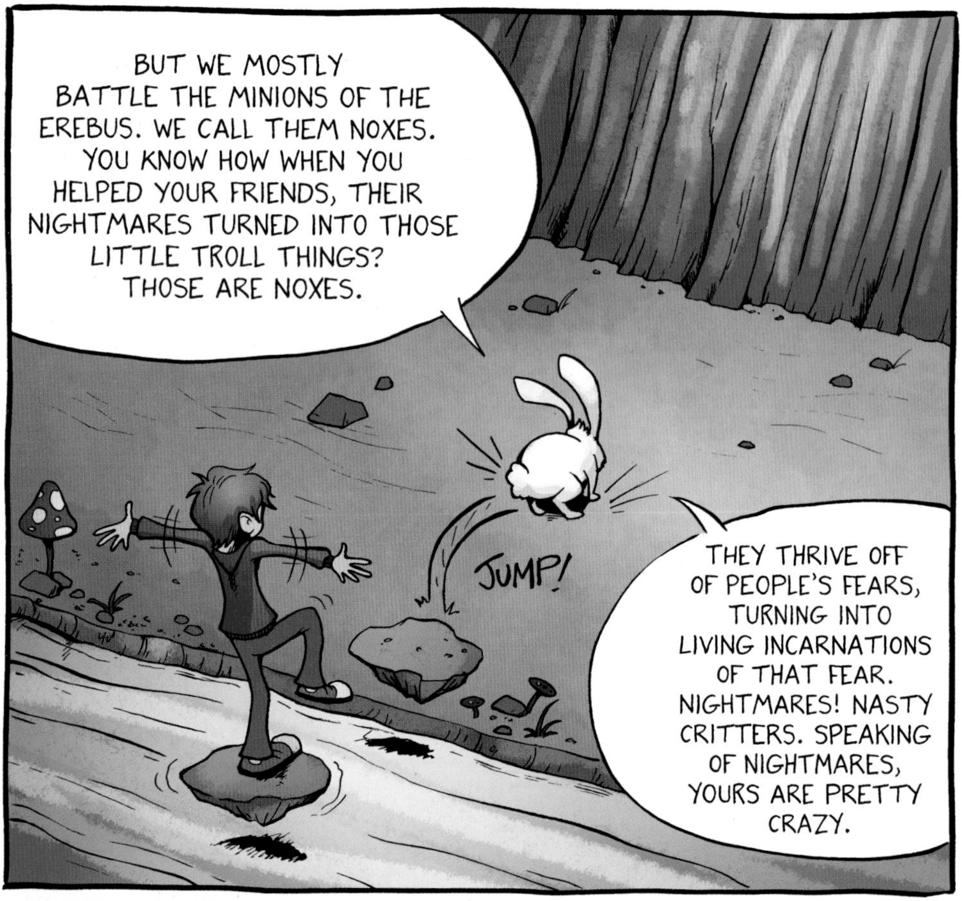
BUT WE MOSTLY BATTLE THE MINIONS OF THE EREBUS. WE CALL THEM NOXES. YOU KNOW HOW WHEN YOU HELPED YOUR FRIENDS, THEIR NIGHTMARES TURNED INTO THOSE LITTLE TROLL THINGS? THOSE ARE NOXES.
JUMP!
THEY THRIVE OFF OF PEOPLE'S FEARS, TURNING INTO LIVING INCARNATIONS OF THAT FEAR. NIGHTMARES! NASTY CRITTERS. SPEAKING OF NIGHTMARES, YOURS ARE PRETTY CRAZY.

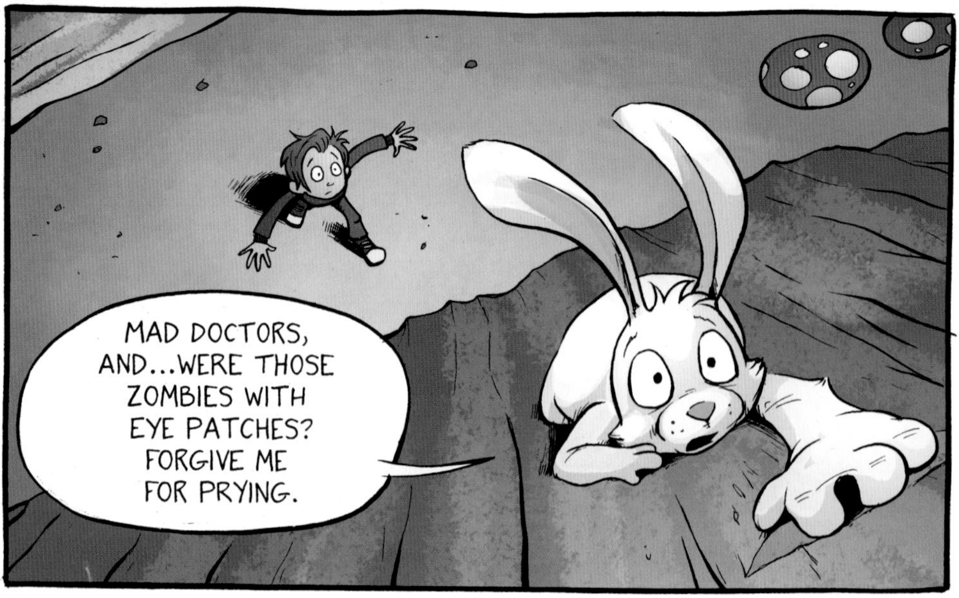
MAD DOCTORS, AND...WERE THOSE ZOMBIES WITH EYE PATCHES? FORGIVE ME FOR PRYING.

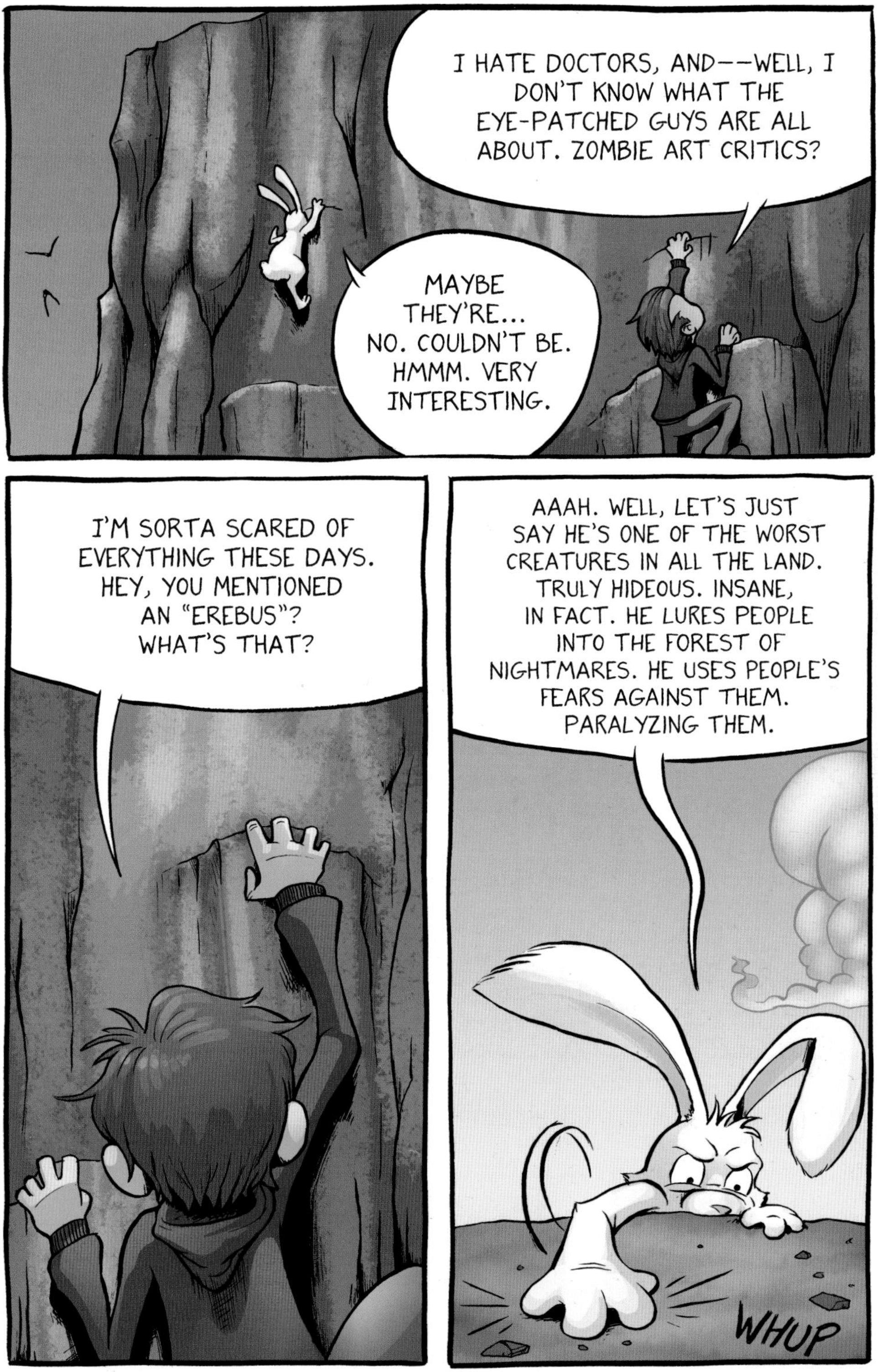
I HATE DOCTORS, AND--WELL, I DON'T KNOW WHAT THE EYE-PATCHED GUYS ARE ALL ABOUT. ZOMBIE ART CRITICS?
MAYBE THEY'RE... NO. COULDN'T BE. HMMM. VERY INTERESTING.
I'M SORTA SCARED OF EVERYTHING THESE DAYS. HEY, YOU MENTIONED AN "EREBUS"? WHAT'S THAT?
AAAH. WELL, LET'S JUST SAY HE'S ONE OF THE WORST CREATURES IN ALL THE LAND. TRULY HIDEOUS. INSANE, IN FACT. HE LURES PEOPLE INTO THE FOREST OF NIGHTMARES. HE USES PEOPLE'S FEARS AGAINST THEM. PARALYZING THEM.
WHUP

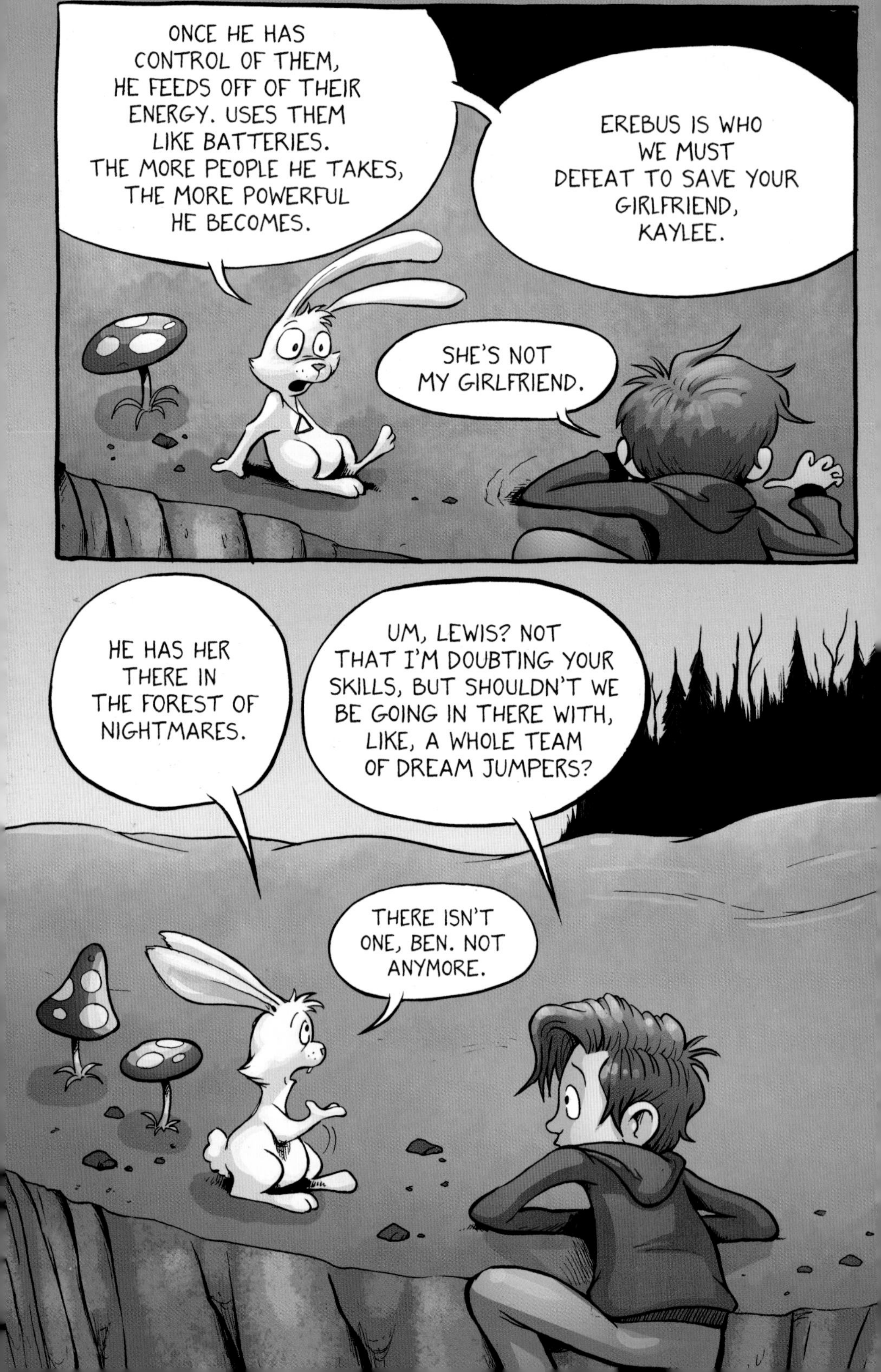
ONCE HE HAS CONTROL OF THEM, HE FEEDS OFF OF THEIR ENERGY. USES THEM LIKE BATTERIES. THE MORE PEOPLE HE TAKES, THE MORE POWERFUL HE BECOMES.
EREBUS IS WHO WE MUST DEFEAT TO SAVE YOUR GIRLFRIEND, KAYLEE.
SHE'S NOT MY GIRLFRIEND.
HE HAS HER THERE IN THE FOREST OF NIGHTMARES.
UM, LEWIS? NOT THAT I'M DOUBTING YOUR SKILLS, BUT SHOULDN'T WE BE GOING IN THERE WITH, LIKE, A WHOLE TEAM OF DREAM JUMPERS?
THERE ISN'T ONE, BEN. NOT ANYMORE.

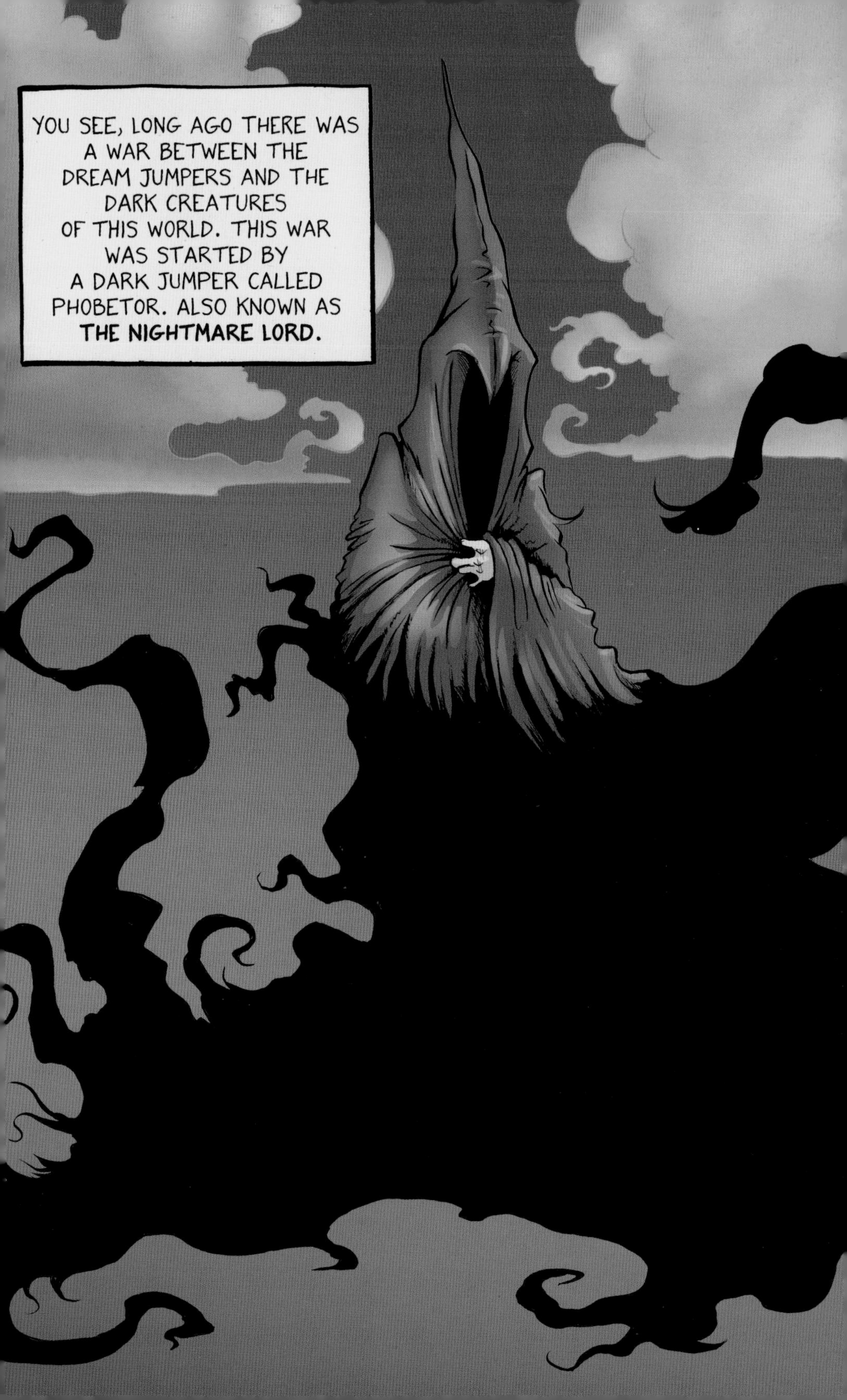
YOU SEE, LONG AGO THERE WAS A WAR BETWEEN THE DREAM JUMPERS AND THE DARK CREATURES OF THIS WORLD. THIS WAR WAS STARTED BY A DARK JUMPER CALLED PHOBETOR. ALSO KNOWN AS **THE NIGHTMARE LORD.**

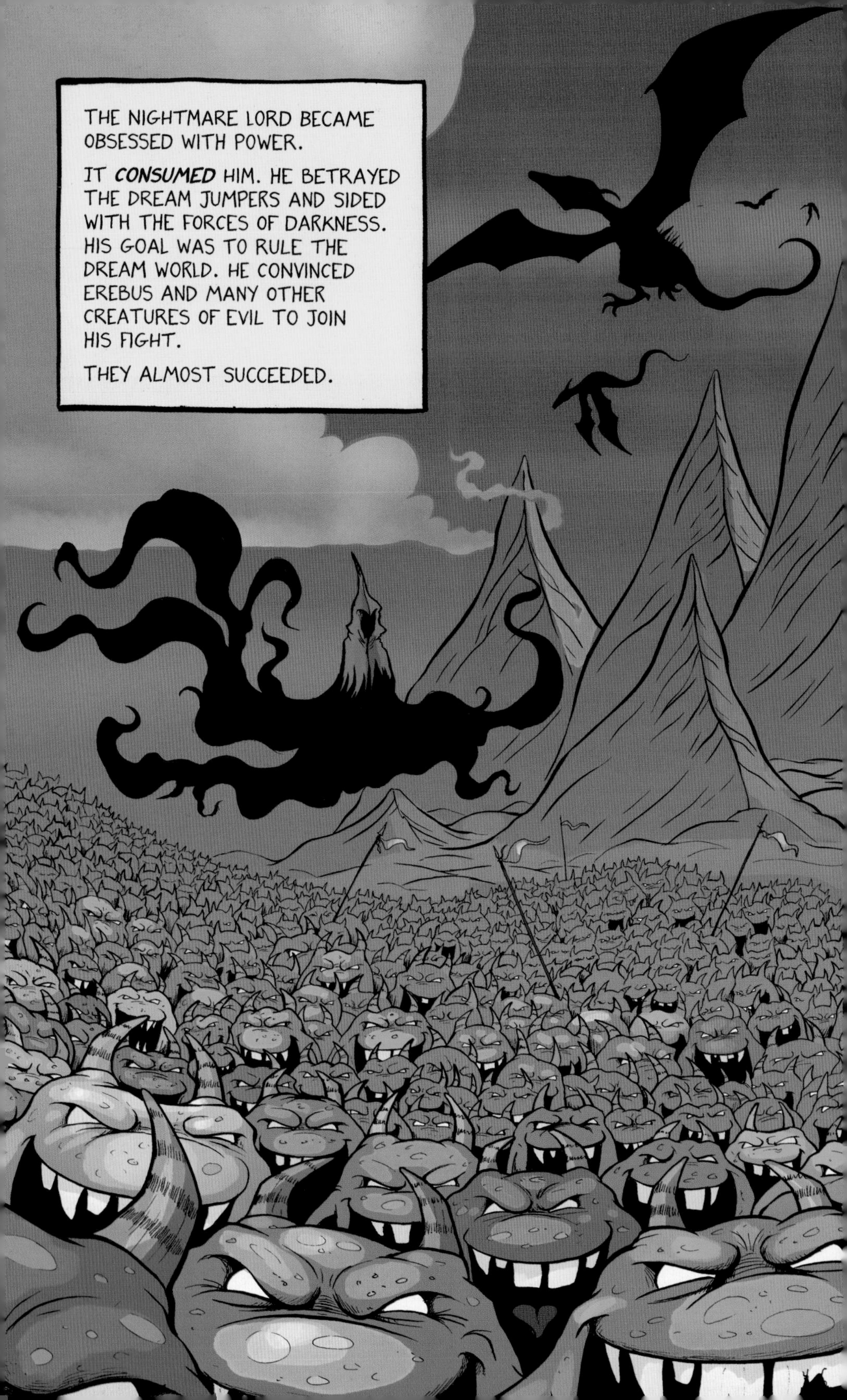
THE NIGHTMARE LORD BECAME OBSESSED WITH POWER.
IT *CONSUMED* HIM. HE BETRAYED THE DREAM JUMPERS AND SIDED WITH THE FORCES OF DARKNESS. HIS GOAL WAS TO RULE THE DREAM WORLD. HE CONVINCED EREBUS AND MANY OTHER CREATURES OF EVIL TO JOIN HIS FIGHT.
THEY ALMOST SUCCEEDED.

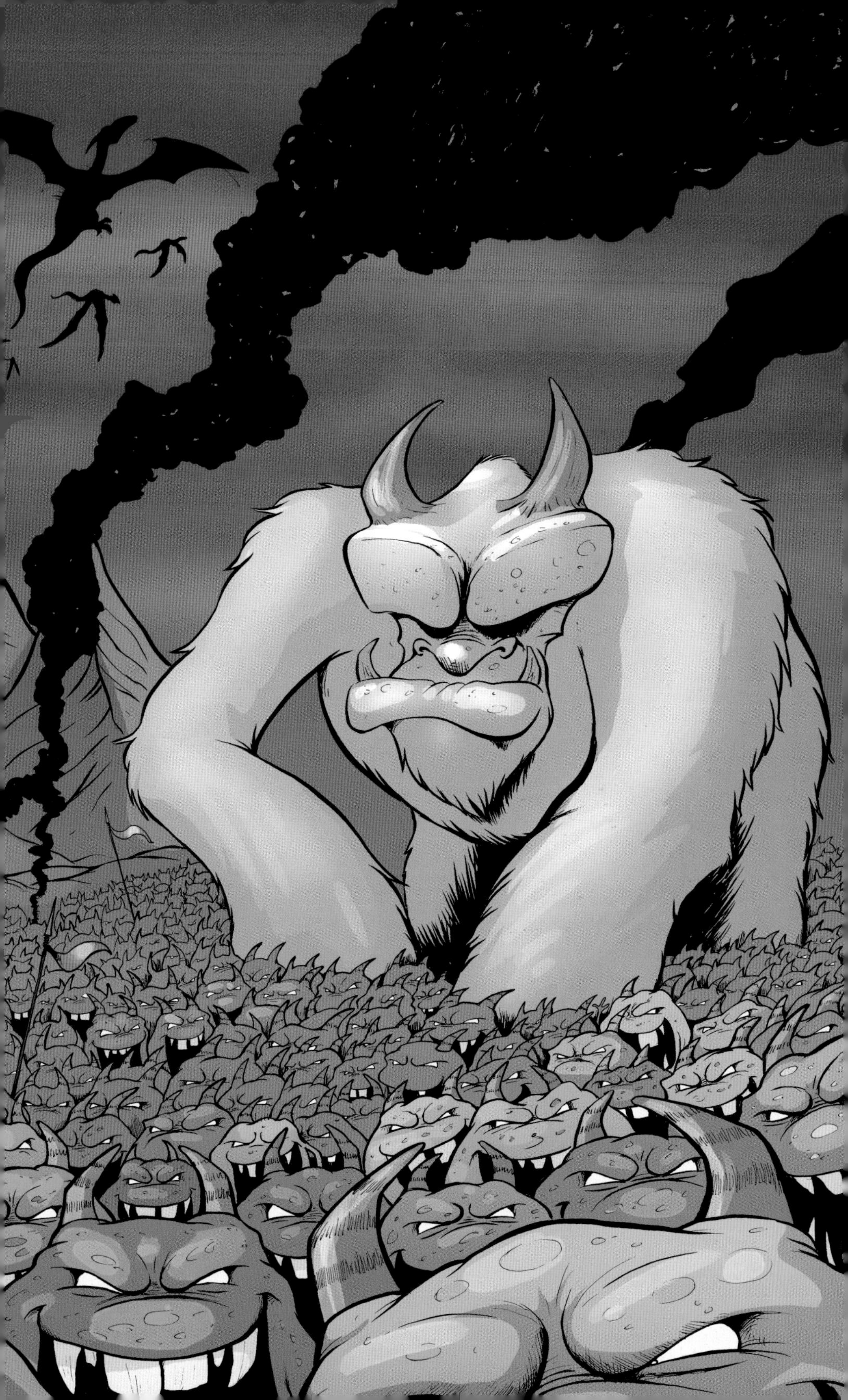

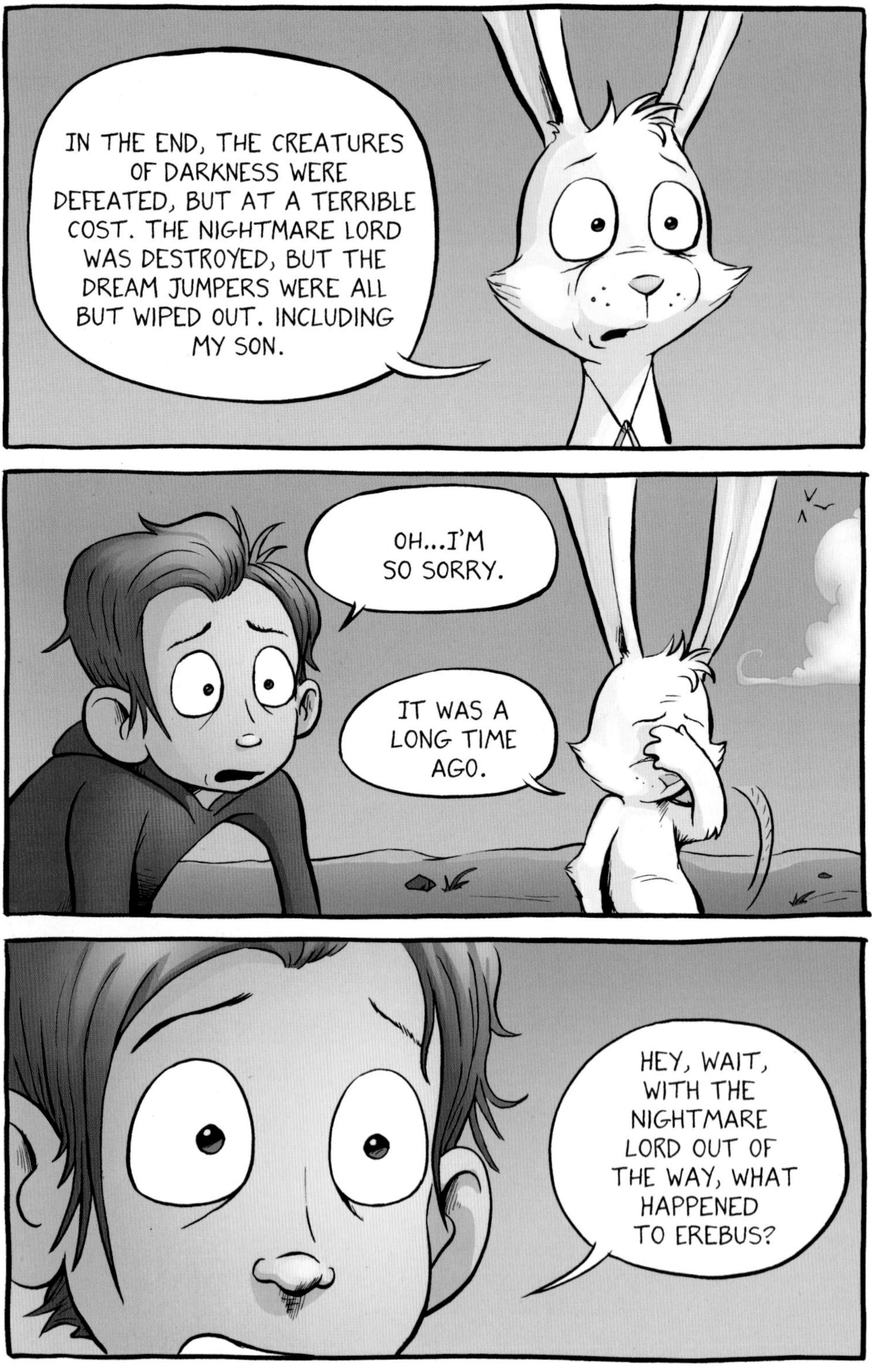
IN THE END, THE CREATURES OF DARKNESS WERE DEFEATED, BUT AT A TERRIBLE COST. THE NIGHTMARE LORD WAS DESTROYED, BUT THE DREAM JUMPERS WERE ALL BUT WIPED OUT. INCLUDING MY SON.
OH...I'M SO SORRY.
IT WAS A LONG TIME AGO.
HEY, WAIT, WITH THE NIGHTMARE LORD OUT OF THE WAY, WHAT HAPPENED TO EREBUS?

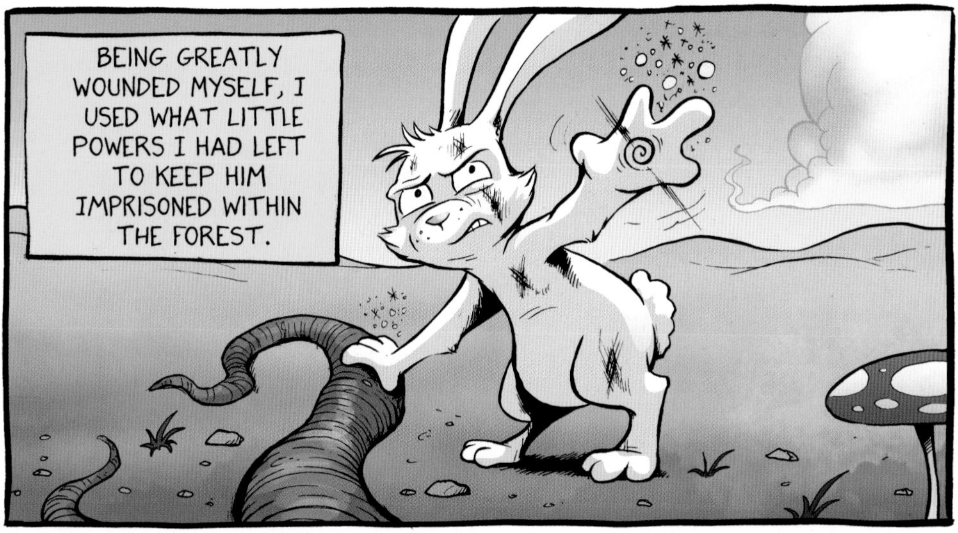
BEING GREATLY WOUNDED MYSELF, I USED WHAT LITTLE POWERS I HAD LEFT TO KEEP HIM IMPRISONED WITHIN THE FOREST.

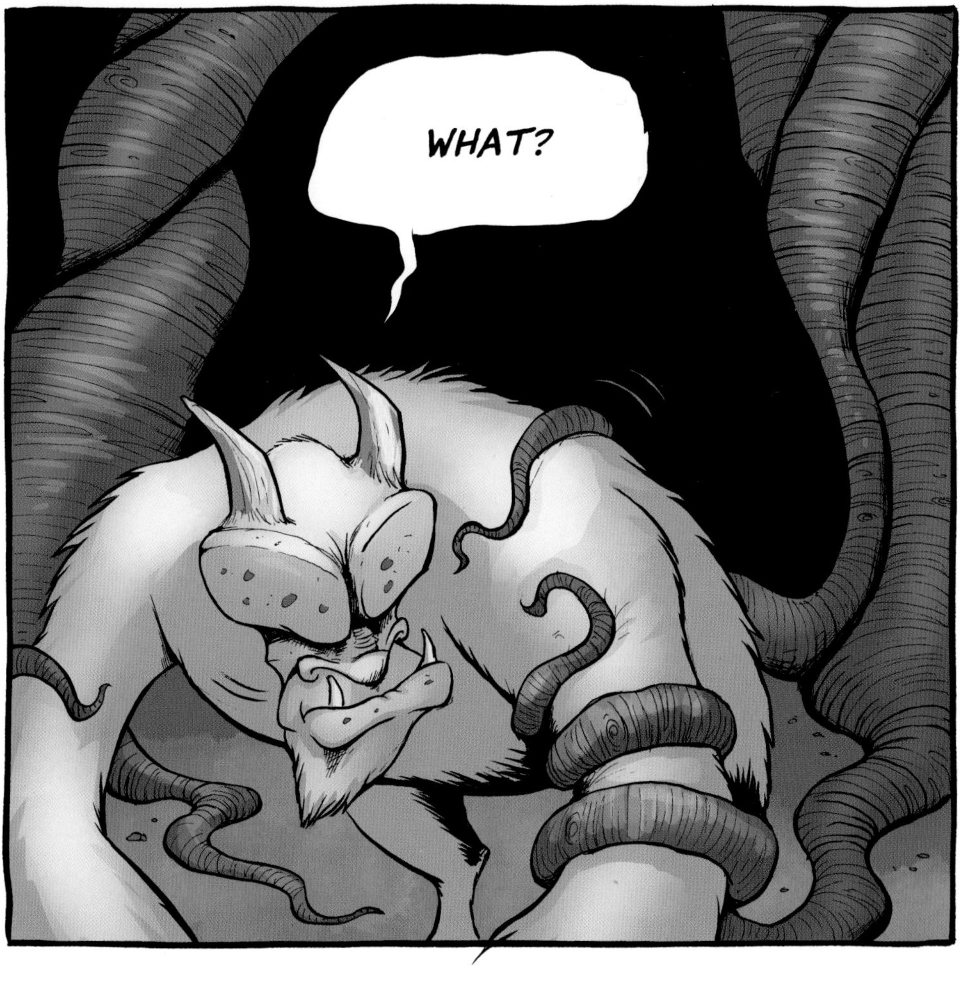
WHAT?

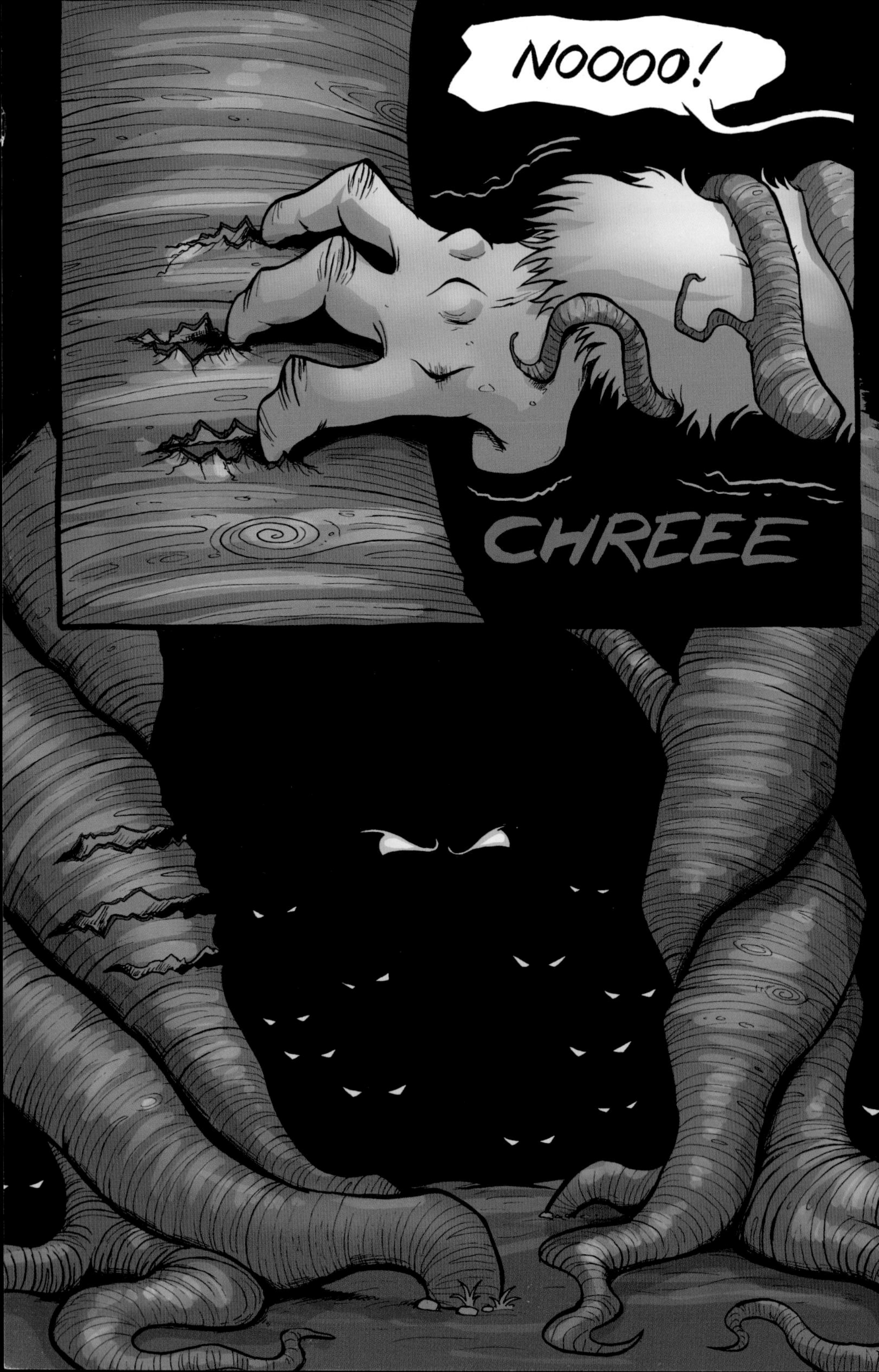
NOOOO!
CHREEE

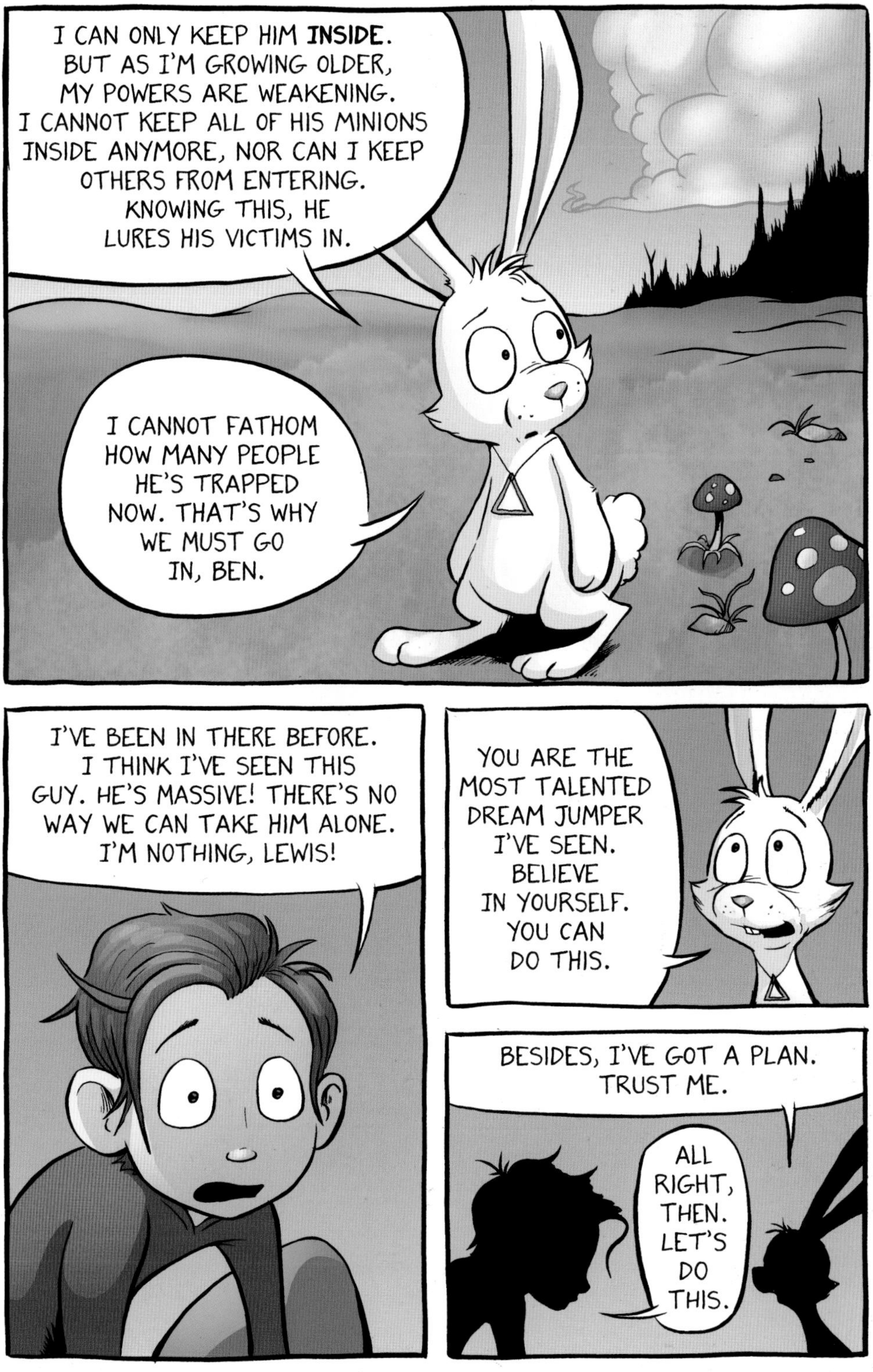
I CAN ONLY KEEP HIM **INSIDE**. BUT AS I'M GROWING OLDER, MY POWERS ARE WEAKENING. I CANNOT KEEP ALL OF HIS MINIONS INSIDE ANYMORE, NOR CAN I KEEP OTHERS FROM ENTERING. KNOWING THIS, HE LURES HIS VICTIMS IN.
I CANNOT FATHOM HOW MANY PEOPLE HE'S TRAPPED NOW. THAT'S WHY WE MUST GO IN, BEN.
I'VE BEEN IN THERE BEFORE. I THINK I'VE SEEN THIS GUY. HE'S MASSIVE! THERE'S NO WAY WE CAN TAKE HIM ALONE. I'M NOTHING, LEWIS!
YOU ARE THE MOST TALENTED DREAM JUMPER I'VE SEEN. BELIEVE IN YOURSELF. YOU CAN DO THIS.
BESIDES, I'VE GOT A PLAN. TRUST ME.
ALL RIGHT, THEN. LET'S DO THIS.

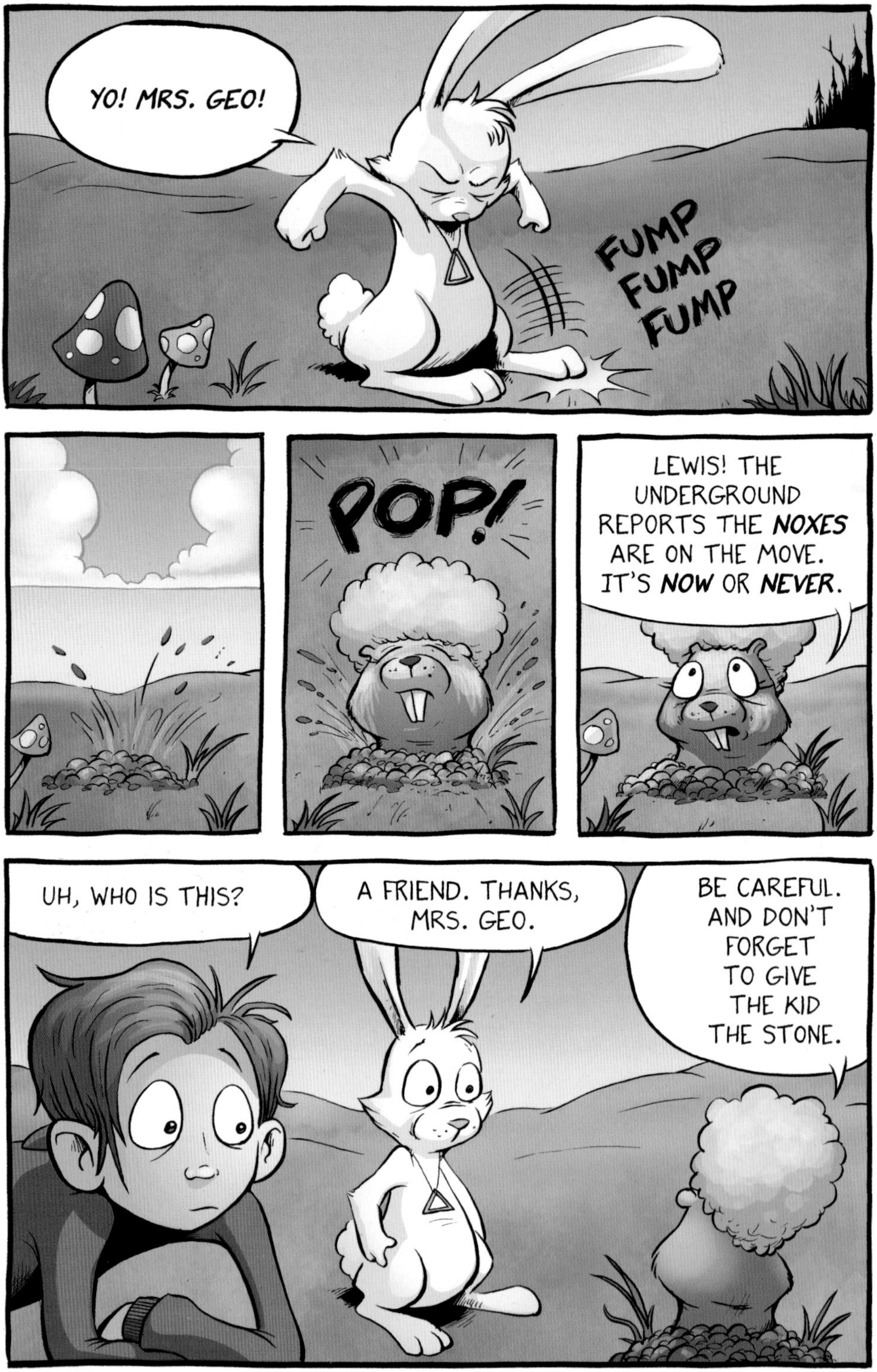
YO! MRS. GEO!
FUMP FUMP FUMP
POP!
LEWIS! THE UNDERGROUND REPORTS THE **NOXES** ARE ON THE MOVE. IT'S **NOW** OR **NEVER**.
UH, WHO IS THIS?
A FRIEND. THANKS, MRS. GEO.
BE CAREFUL. AND DON'T FORGET TO GIVE THE KID THE STONE.

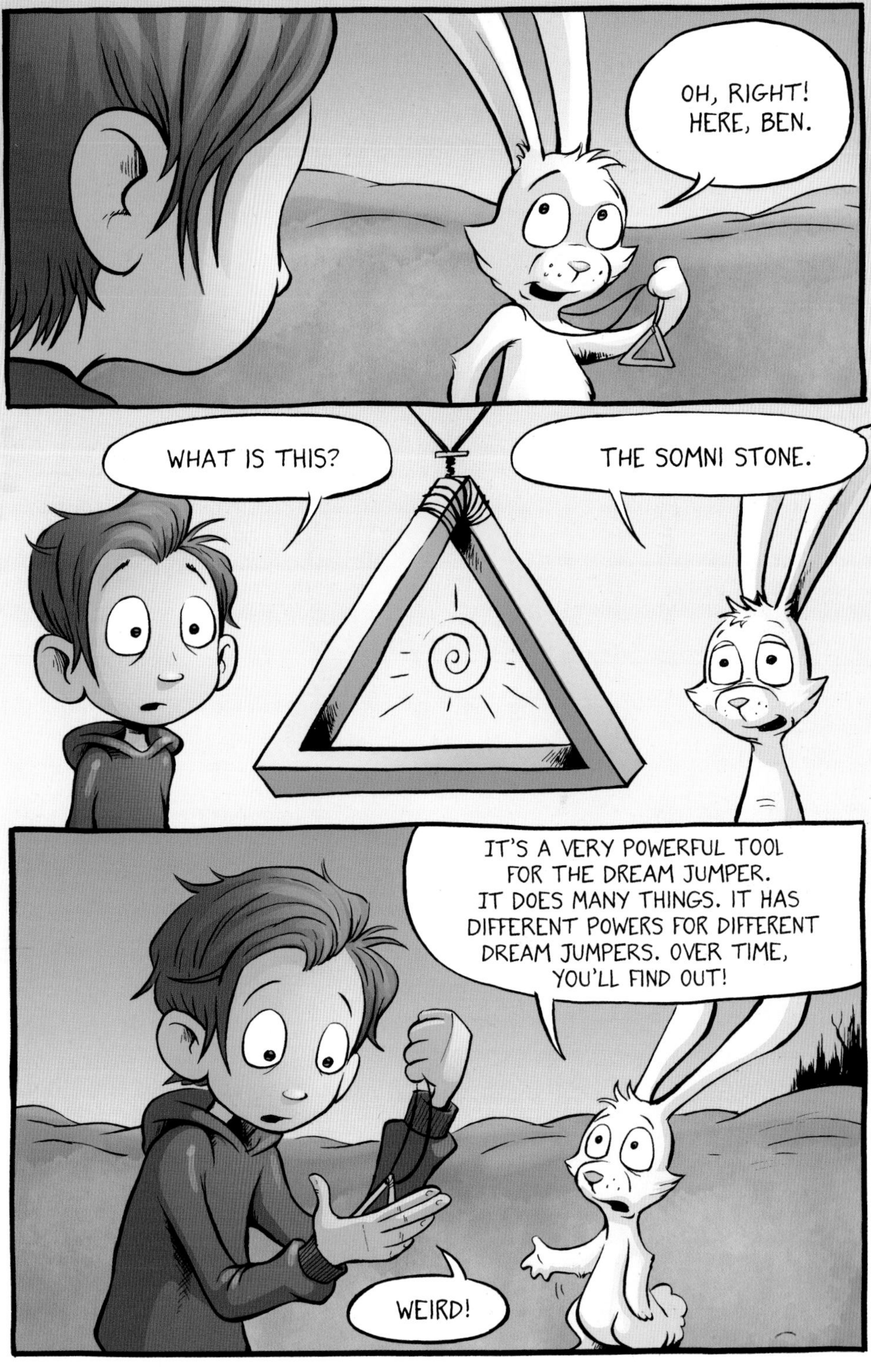
OH, RIGHT! HERE, BEN.
WHAT IS THIS?
THE SOMNI STONE.
IT'S A VERY POWERFUL TOOL FOR THE DREAM JUMPER. IT DOES MANY THINGS. IT HAS DIFFERENT POWERS FOR DIFFERENT DREAM JUMPERS. OVER TIME, YOU'LL FIND OUT!
WEIRD!

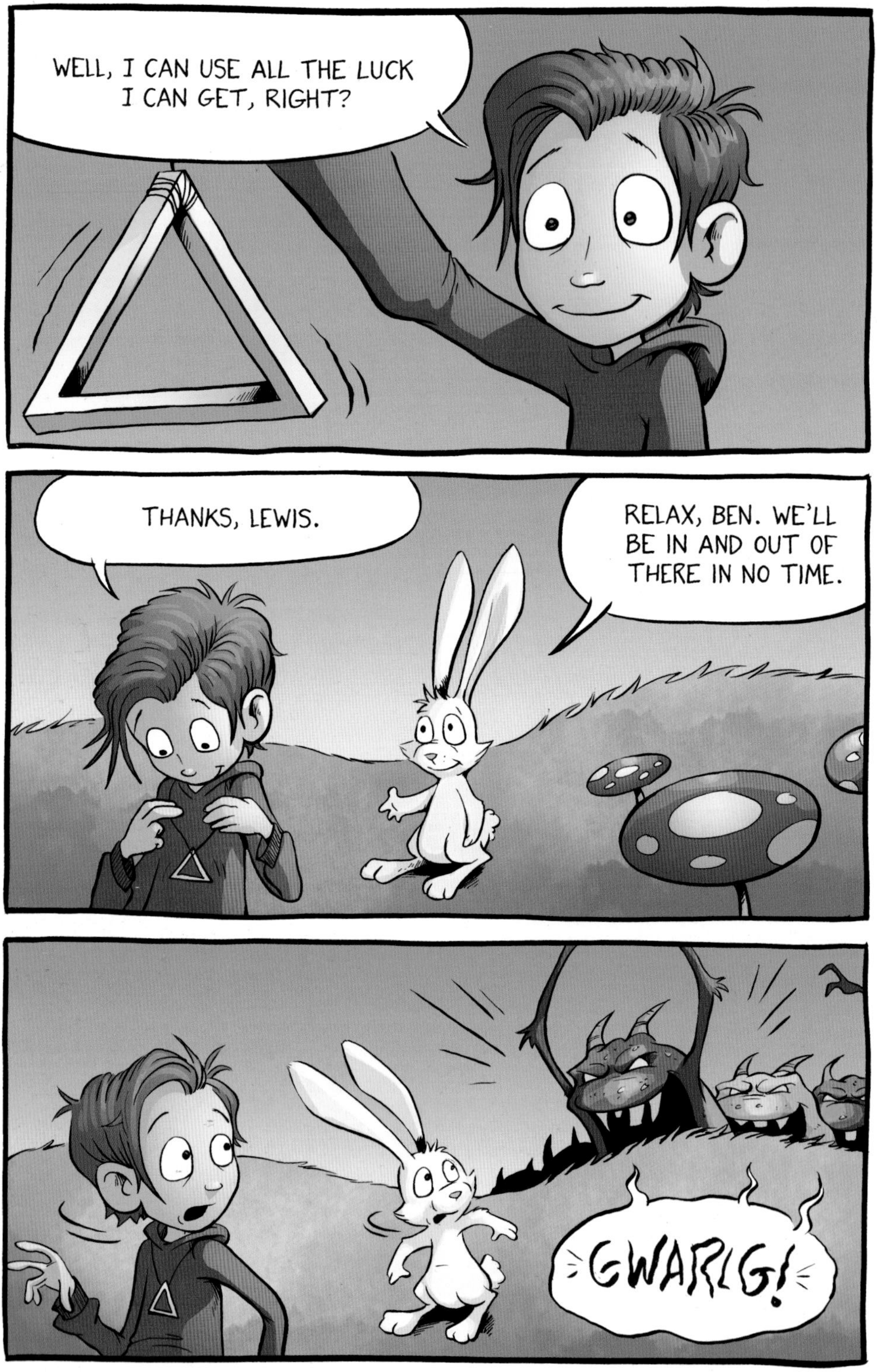
WELL, I CAN USE ALL THE LUCK I CAN GET, RIGHT?
THANKS, LEWIS.
RELAX, BEN. WE'LL BE IN AND OUT OF THERE IN NO TIME.
GWARG!

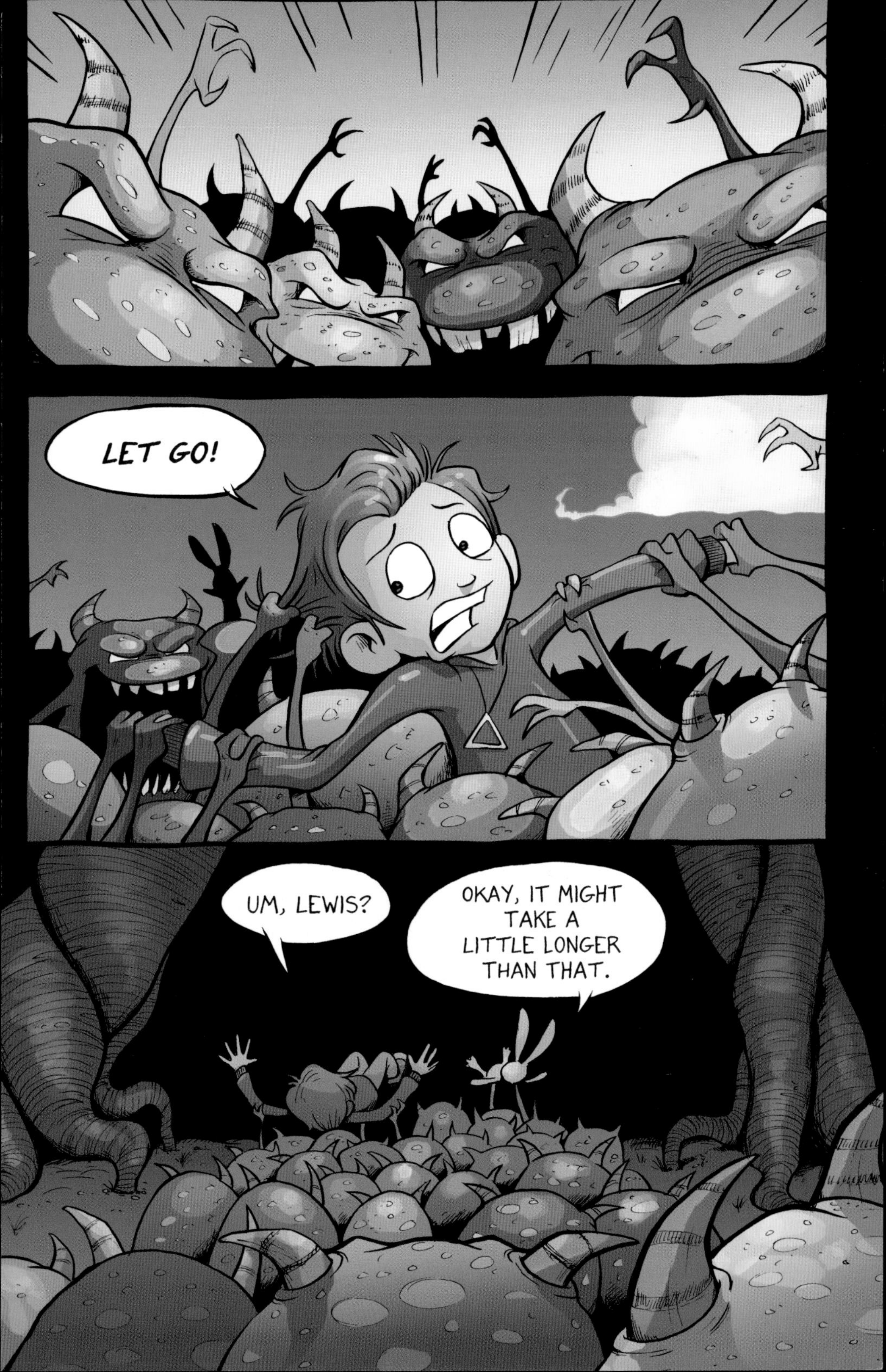
LET GO!
UM, LEWIS?
OKAY, IT MIGHT TAKE A LITTLE LONGER THAN THAT.

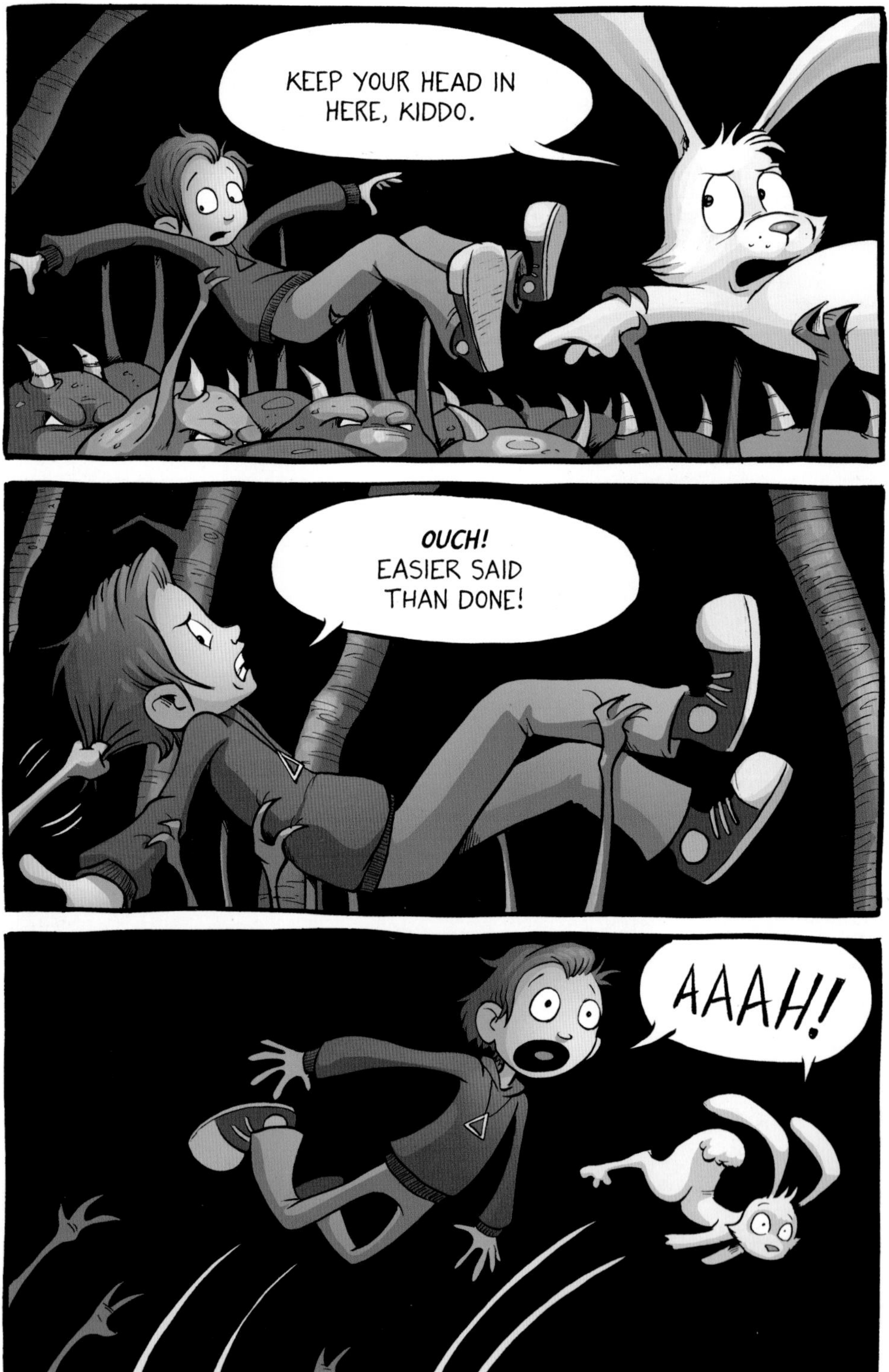
KEEP YOUR HEAD IN HERE, KIDDO.
OUCH! EASIER SAID THAN DONE!
AAAH!

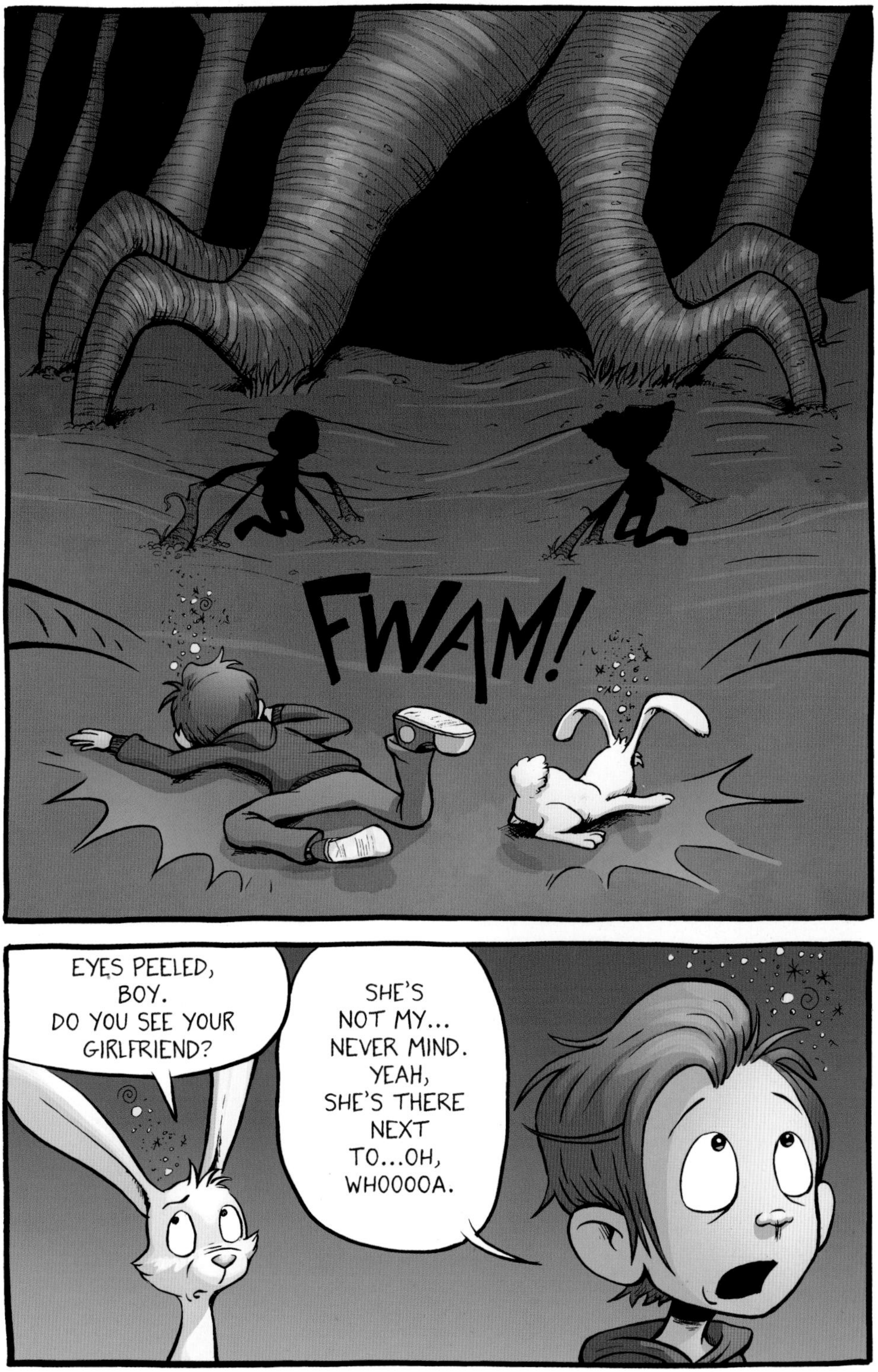
FWAM!
EYES PEELED, BOY. DO YOU SEE YOUR GIRLFRIEND?
SHE'S NOT MY... NEVER MIND. YEAH, SHE'S THERE NEXT TO...OH, WHOOOOA.

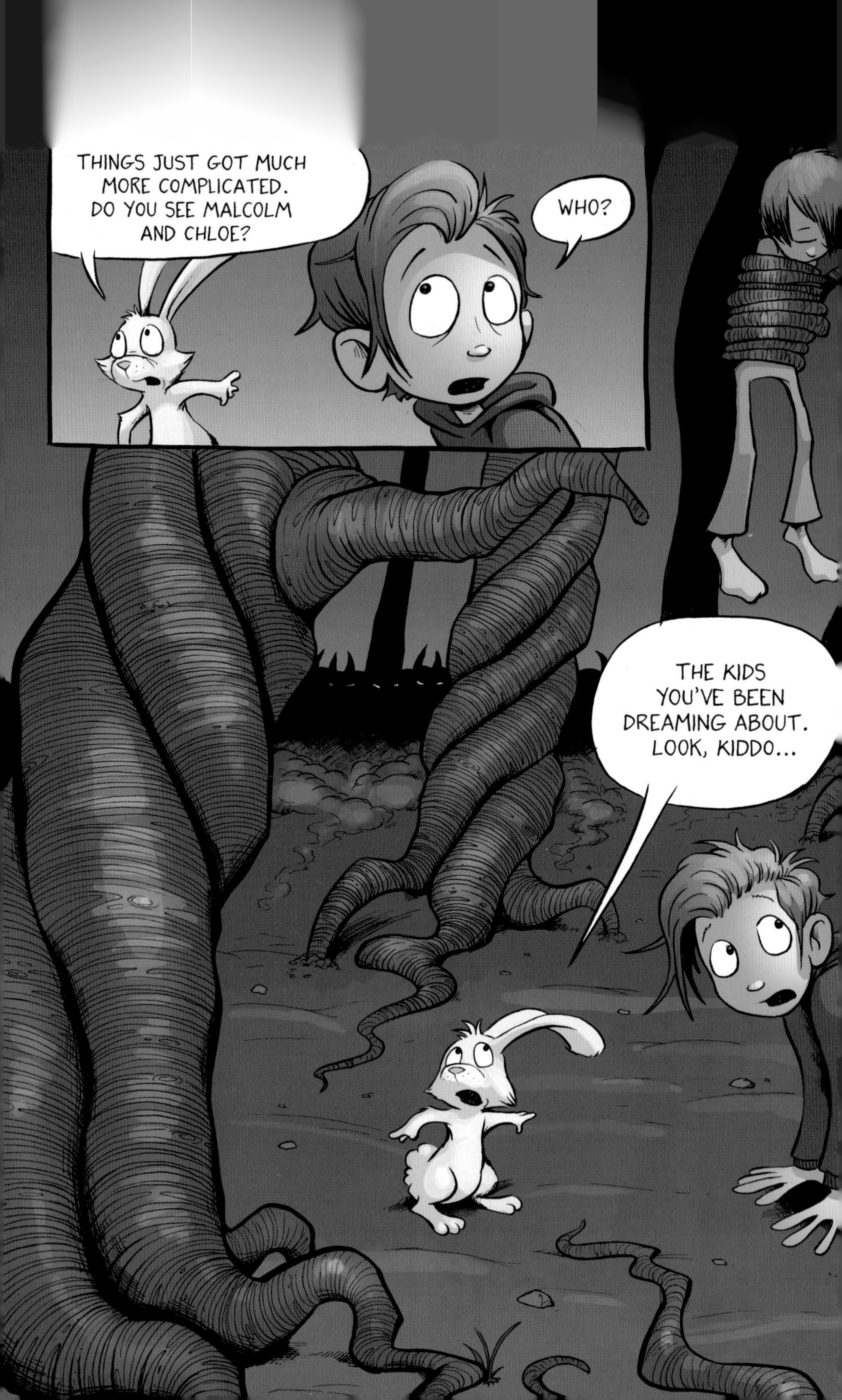
THINGS JUST GOT MUCH MORE COMPLICATED. DO YOU SEE MALCOLM AND CHLOE?
WHO?
THE KIDS YOU'VE BEEN DREAMING ABOUT. LOOK, KIDDO...

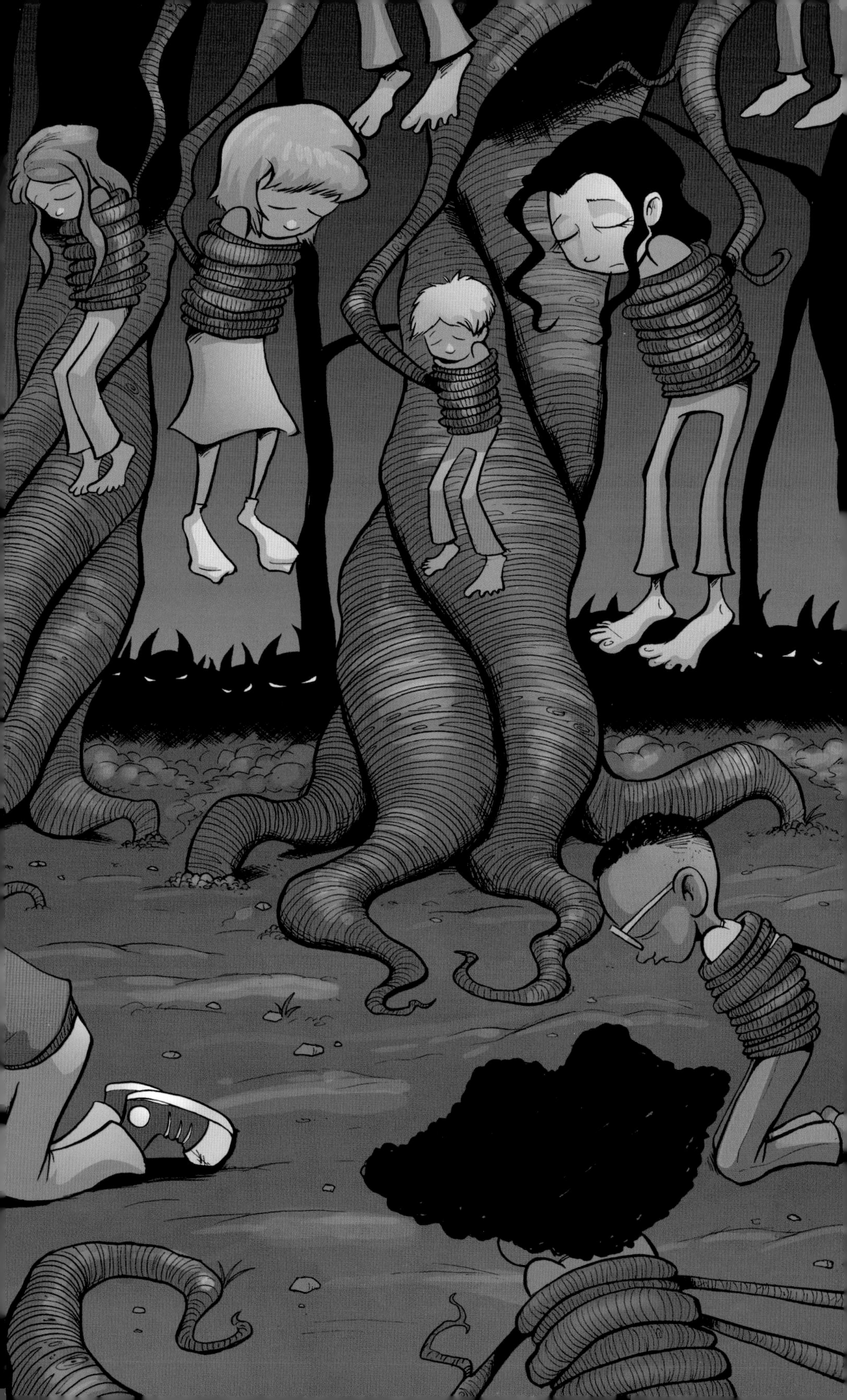

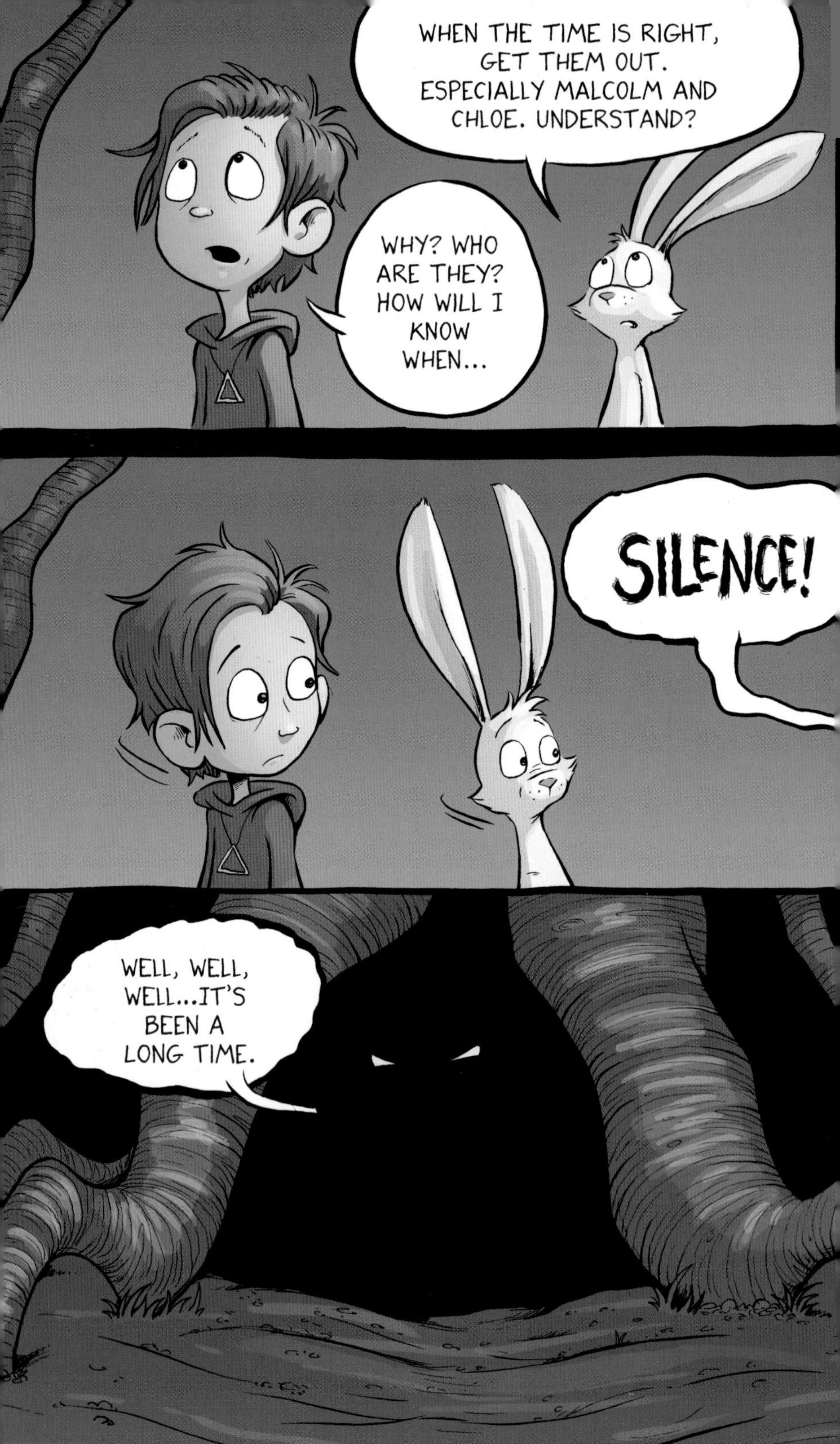
WHEN THE TIME IS RIGHT, GET THEM OUT. ESPECIALLY MALCOLM AND CHLOE. UNDERSTAND?
WHY? WHO ARE THEY? HOW WILL I KNOW WHEN...
SILENCE!
WELL, WELL, WELL...IT'S BEEN A LONG TIME.

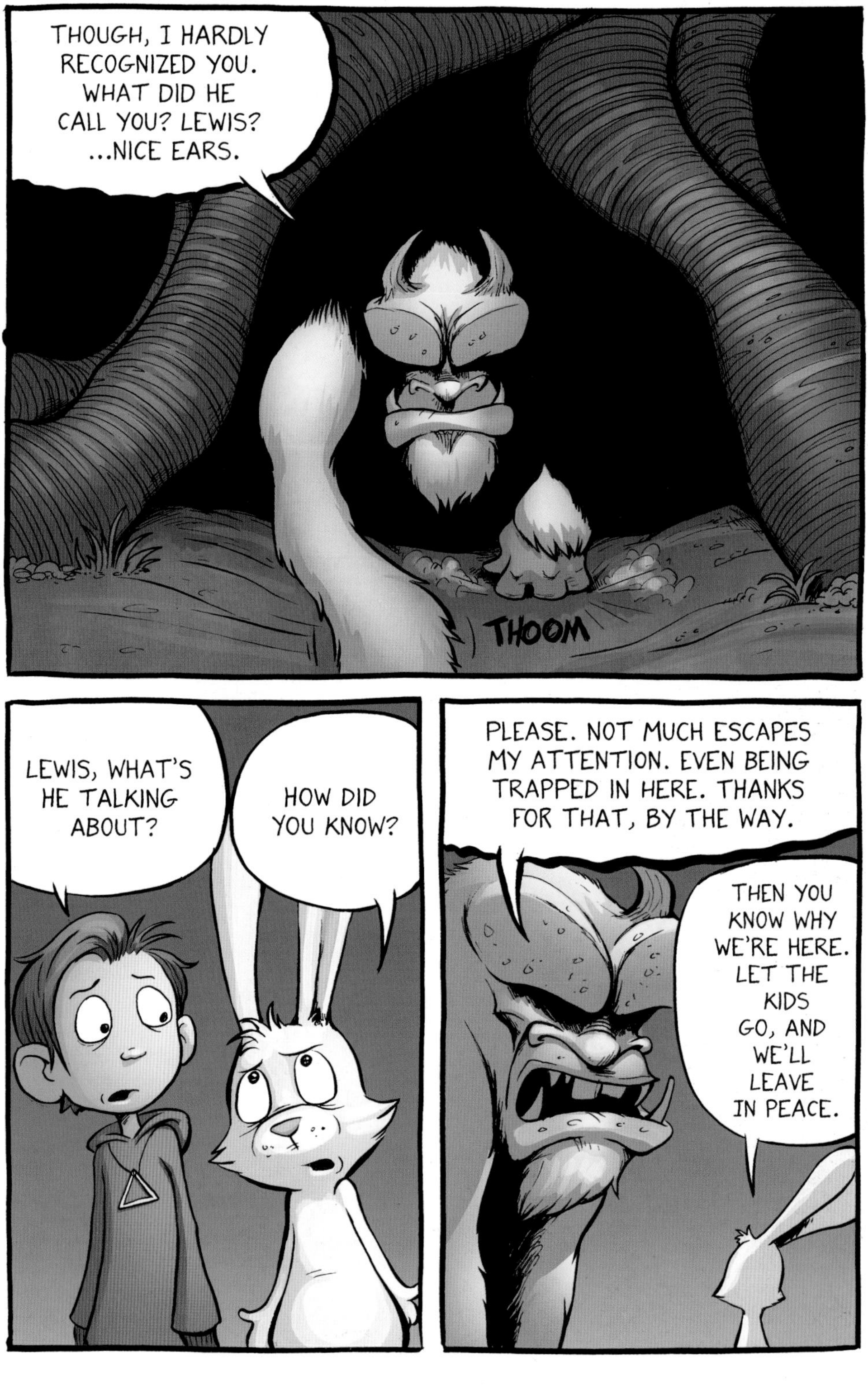
THOUGH, I HARDLY RECOGNIZED YOU. WHAT DID HE CALL YOU? LEWIS? ...NICE EARS.
THOOM
LEWIS, WHAT'S HE TALKING ABOUT?
HOW DID YOU KNOW?
PLEASE. NOT MUCH ESCAPES MY ATTENTION. EVEN BEING TRAPPED IN HERE. THANKS FOR THAT, BY THE WAY.
THEN YOU KNOW WHY WE'RE HERE. LET THE KIDS GO, AND WE'LL LEAVE IN PEACE.

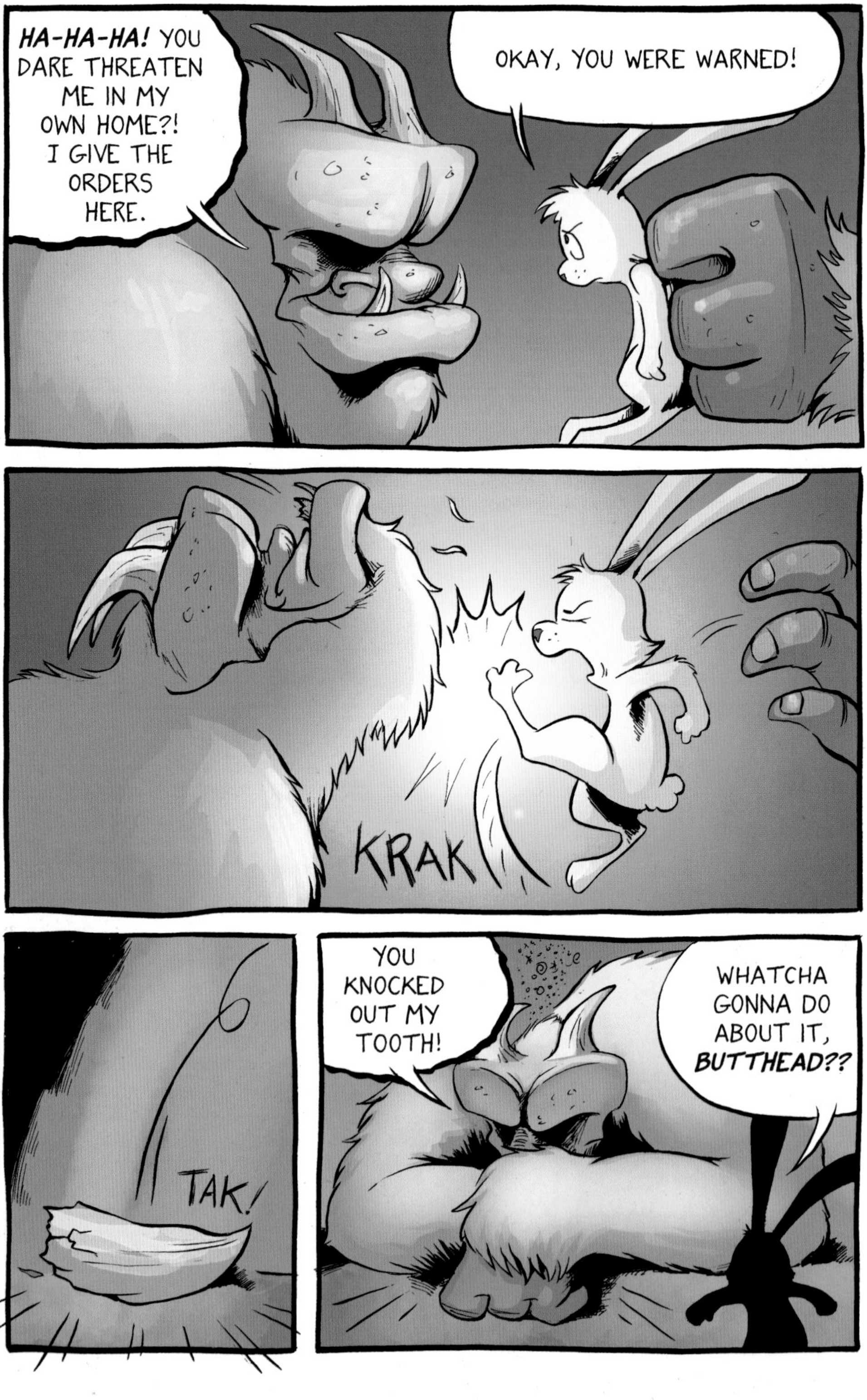
HA-HA-HA! YOU DARE THREATEN ME IN MY OWN HOME?! I GIVE THE ORDERS HERE.
OKAY, YOU WERE WARNED!
KRAK
TAK!
YOU KNOCKED OUT MY TOOTH!
WHATCHA GONNA DO ABOUT IT, BUTTHEAD??

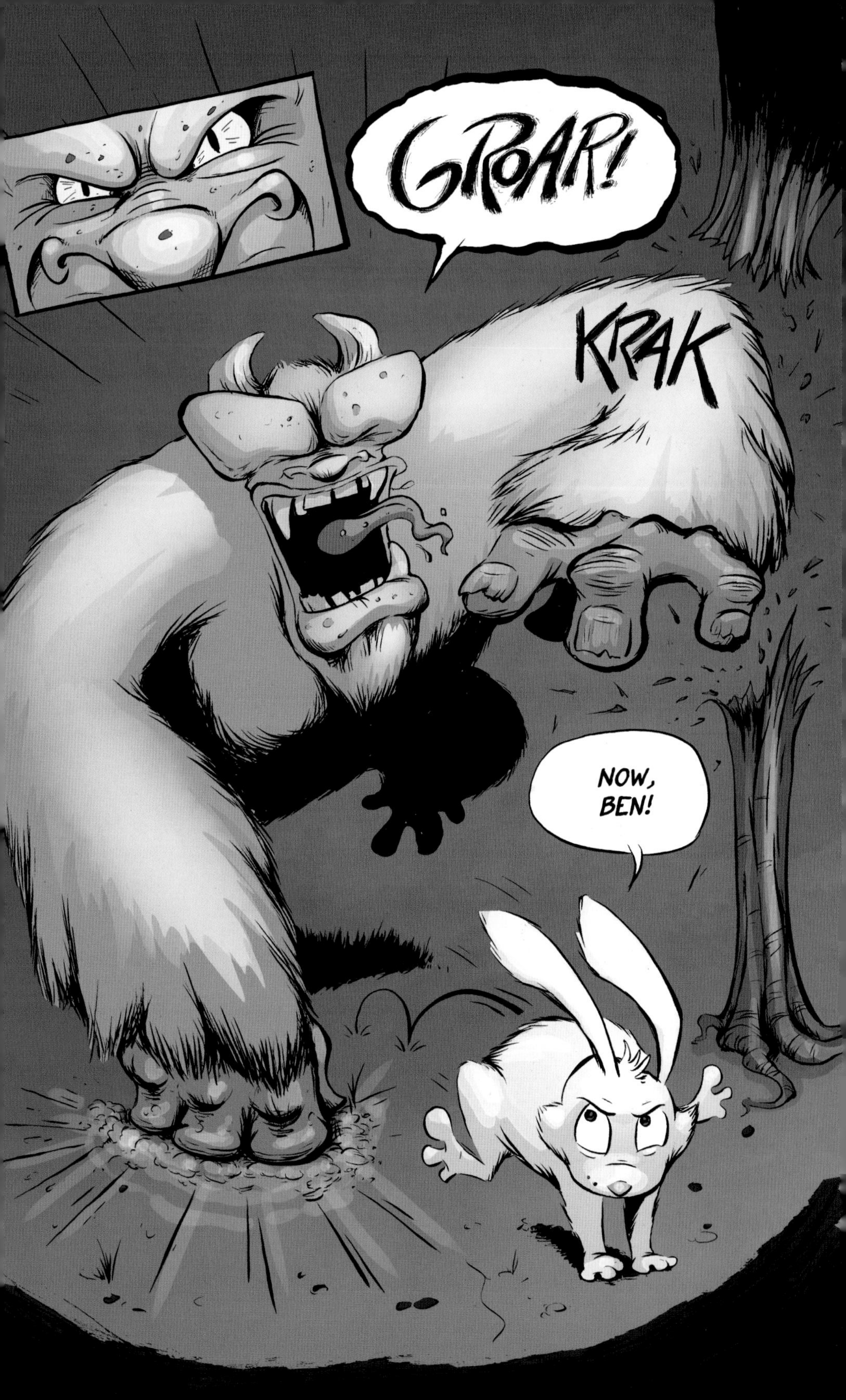
GROAR!
KRAK
NOW, BEN!

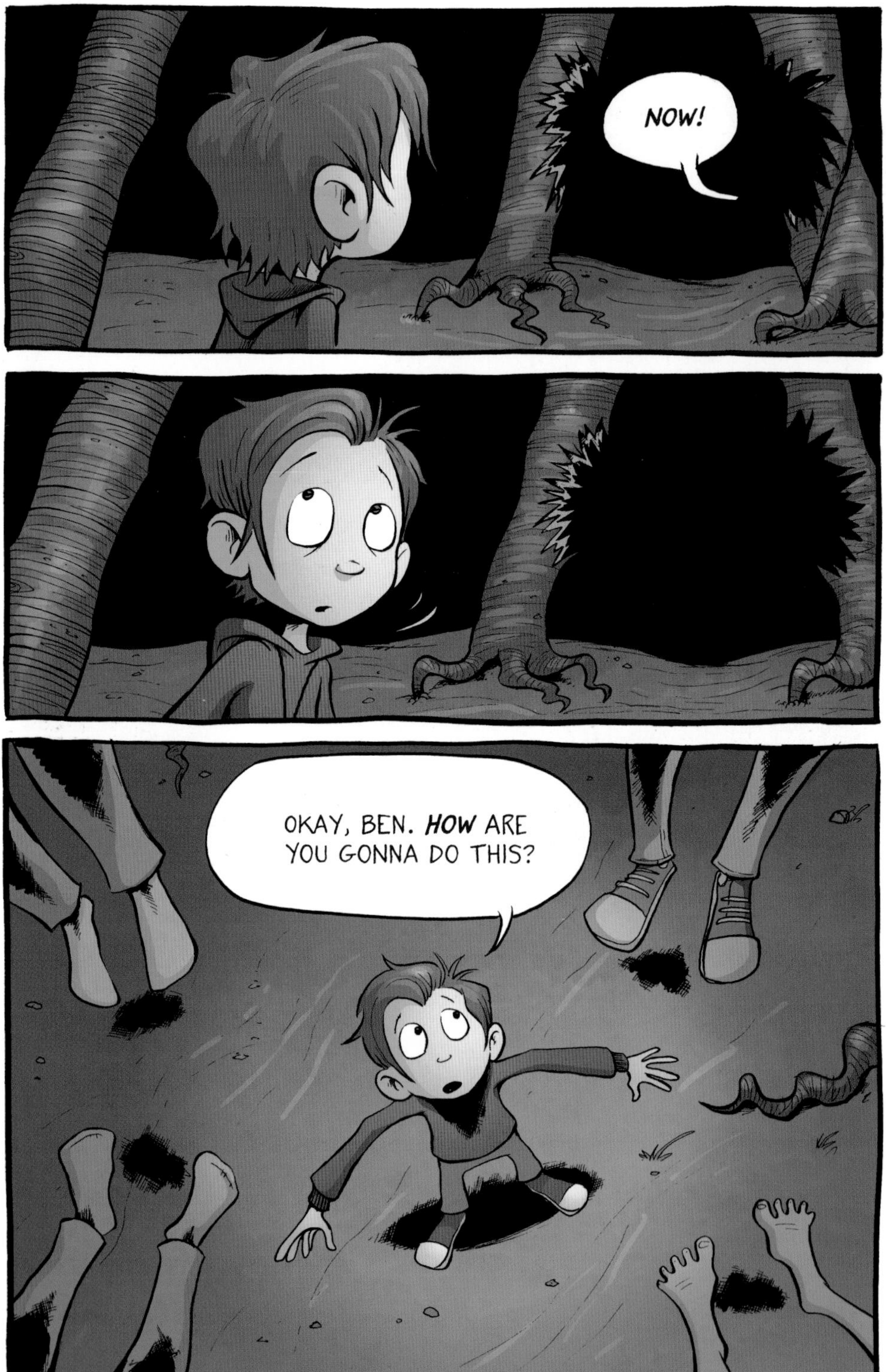
NOW!
OKAY, BEN. HOW ARE YOU GONNA DO THIS?

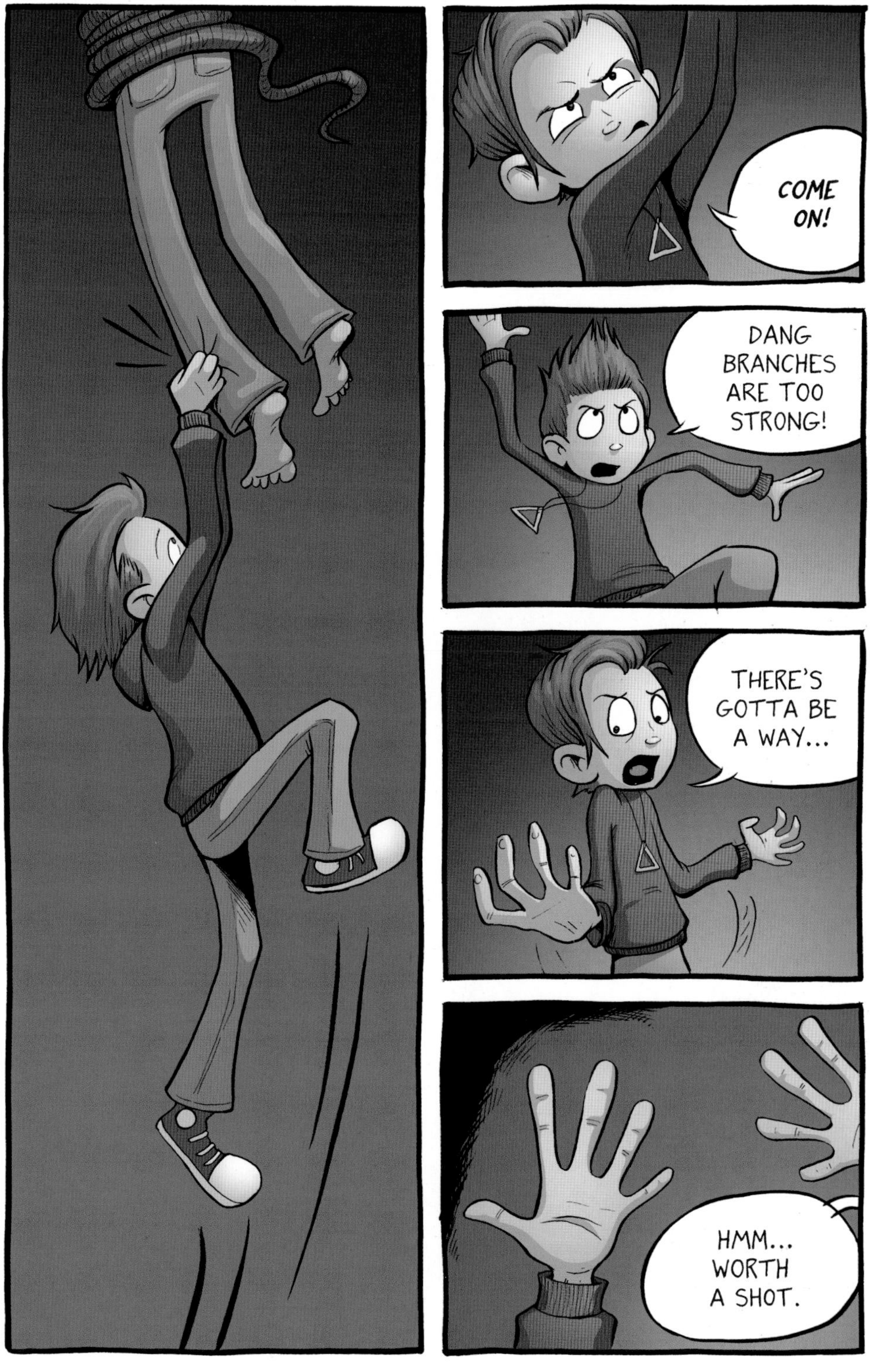
COME ON!
DANG BRANCHES ARE TOO STRONG!
THERE'S GOTTA BE A WAY...
HMM... WORTH A SHOT.

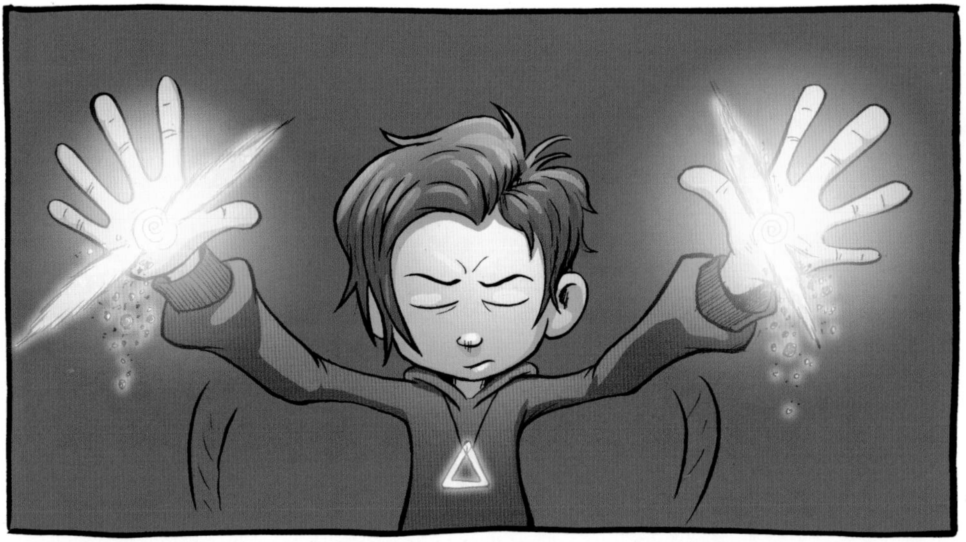

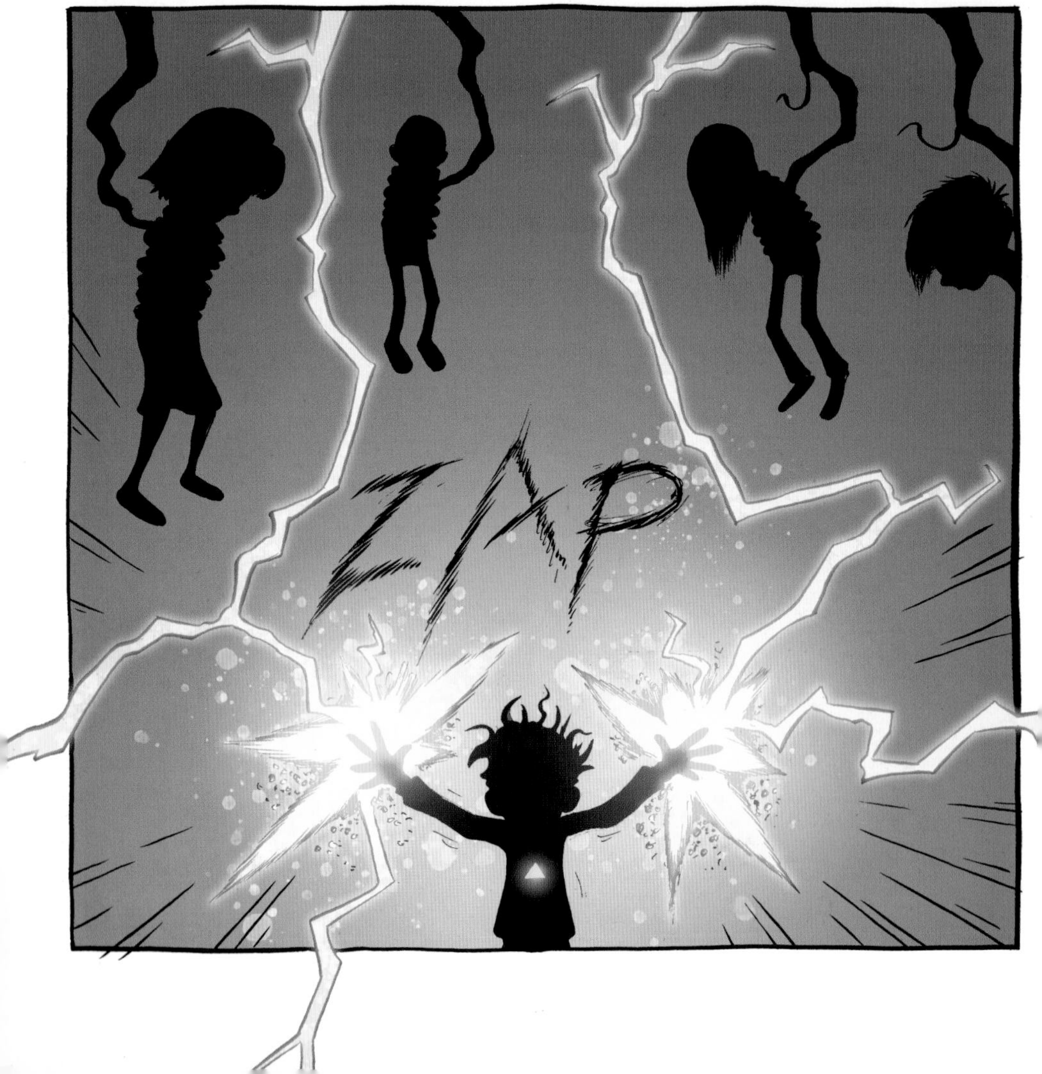
ZAP

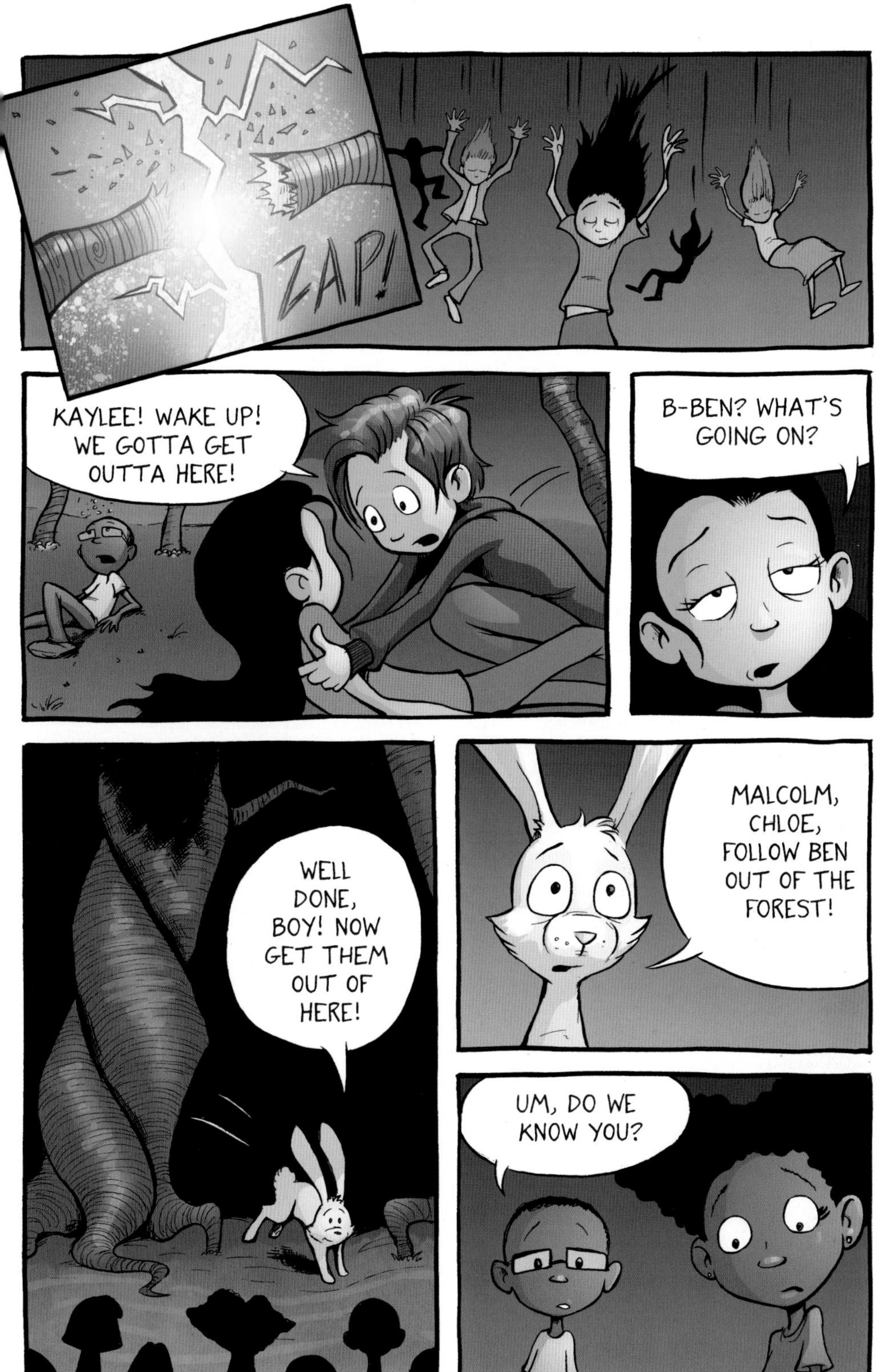
ZAP!
KAYLEE! WAKE UP! WE GOTTA GET OUTTA HERE!
B-BEN? WHAT'S GOING ON?
WELL DONE, BOY! NOW GET THEM OUT OF HERE!
MALCOLM, CHLOE, FOLLOW BEN OUT OF THE FOREST!
UM, DO WE KNOW YOU?

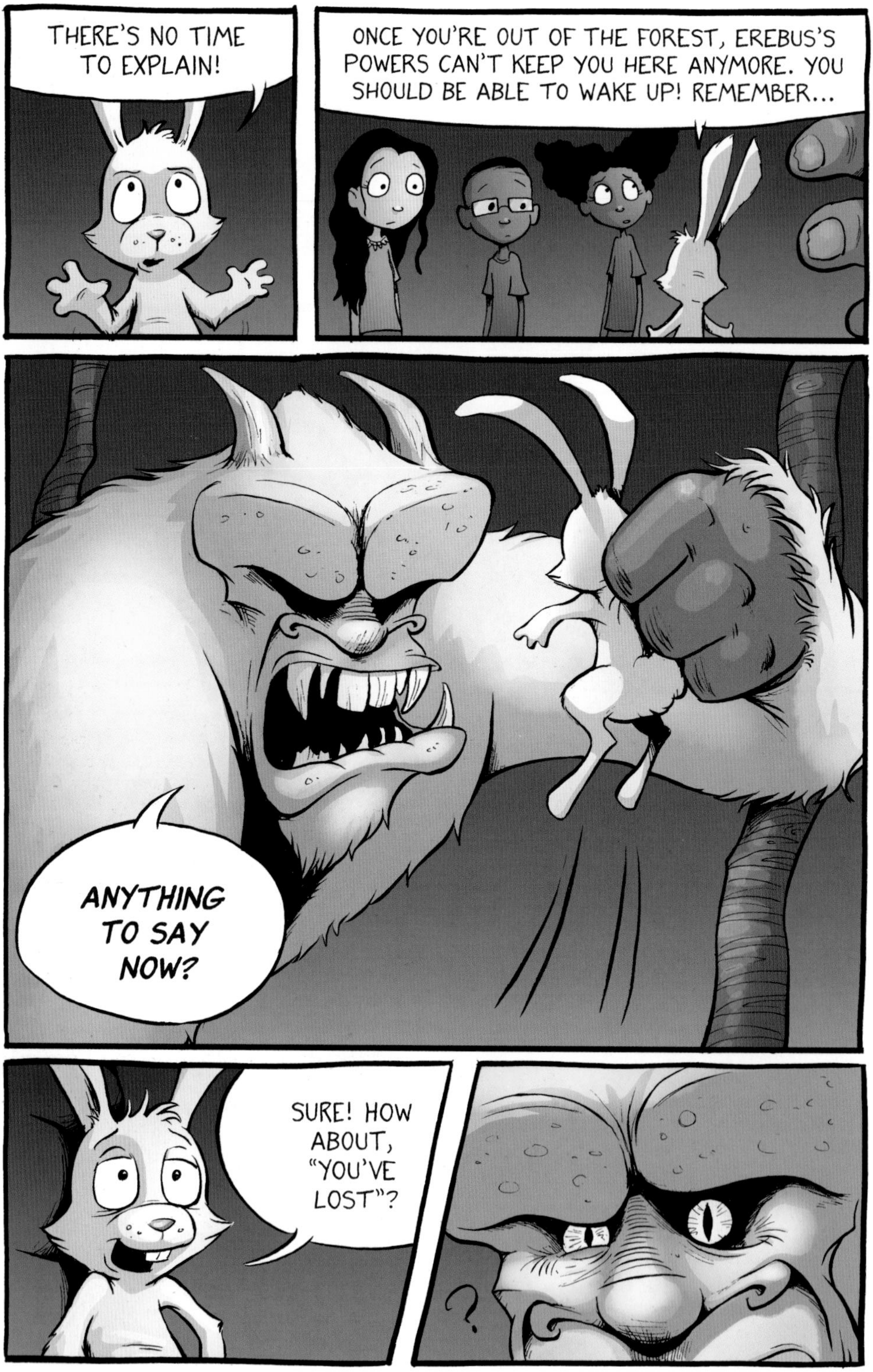
THERE'S NO TIME TO EXPLAIN!
ONCE YOU'RE OUT OF THE FOREST, EREBUS'S POWERS CAN'T KEEP YOU HERE ANYMORE. YOU SHOULD BE ABLE TO WAKE UP! REMEMBER...
ANYTHING TO SAY NOW?
SURE! HOW ABOUT, "YOU'VE LOST"?
?

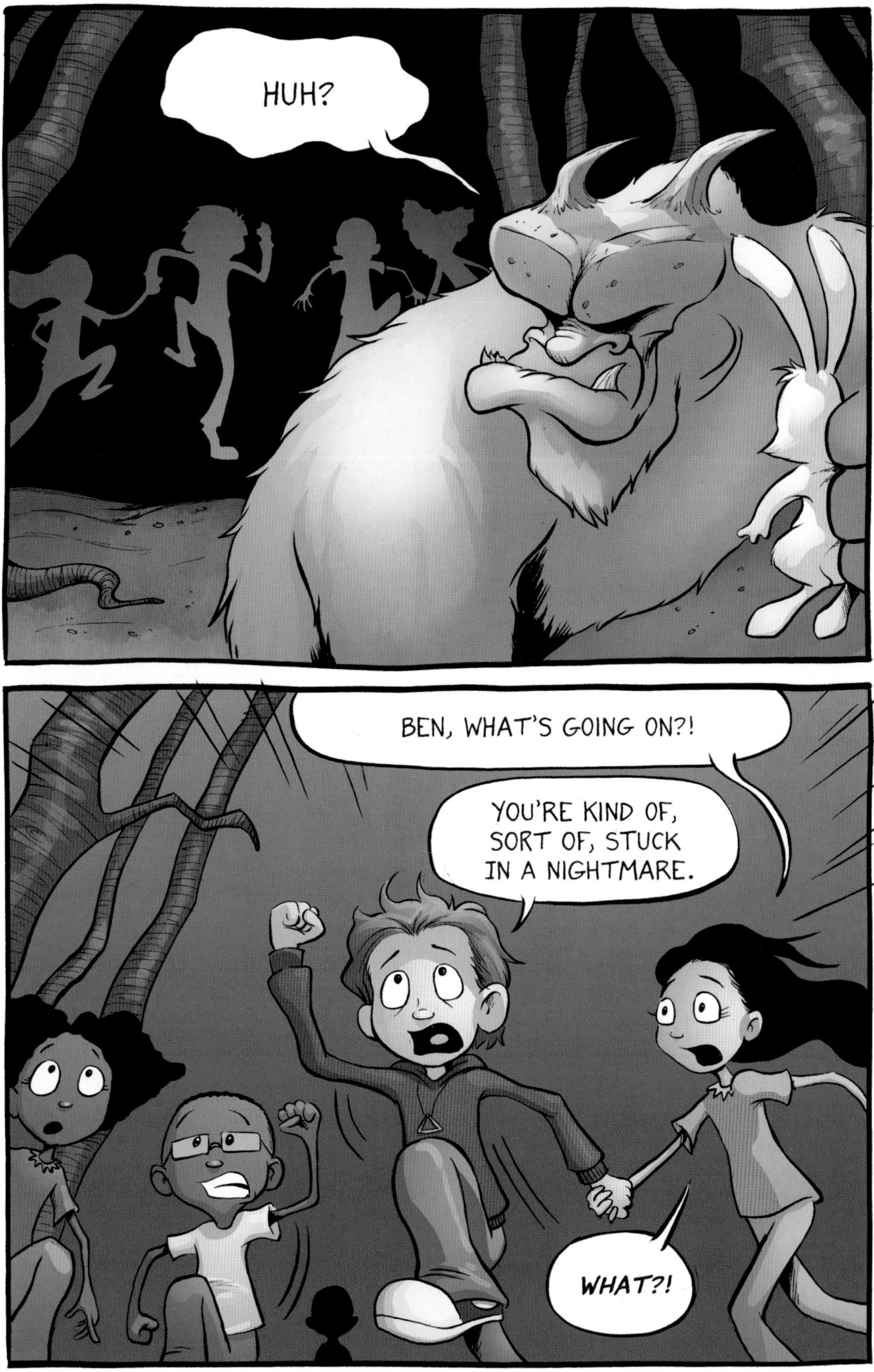
HUH?
BEN, WHAT'S GOING ON?!
YOU'RE KIND OF, SORT OF, STUCK IN A NIGHTMARE.
WHAT?!

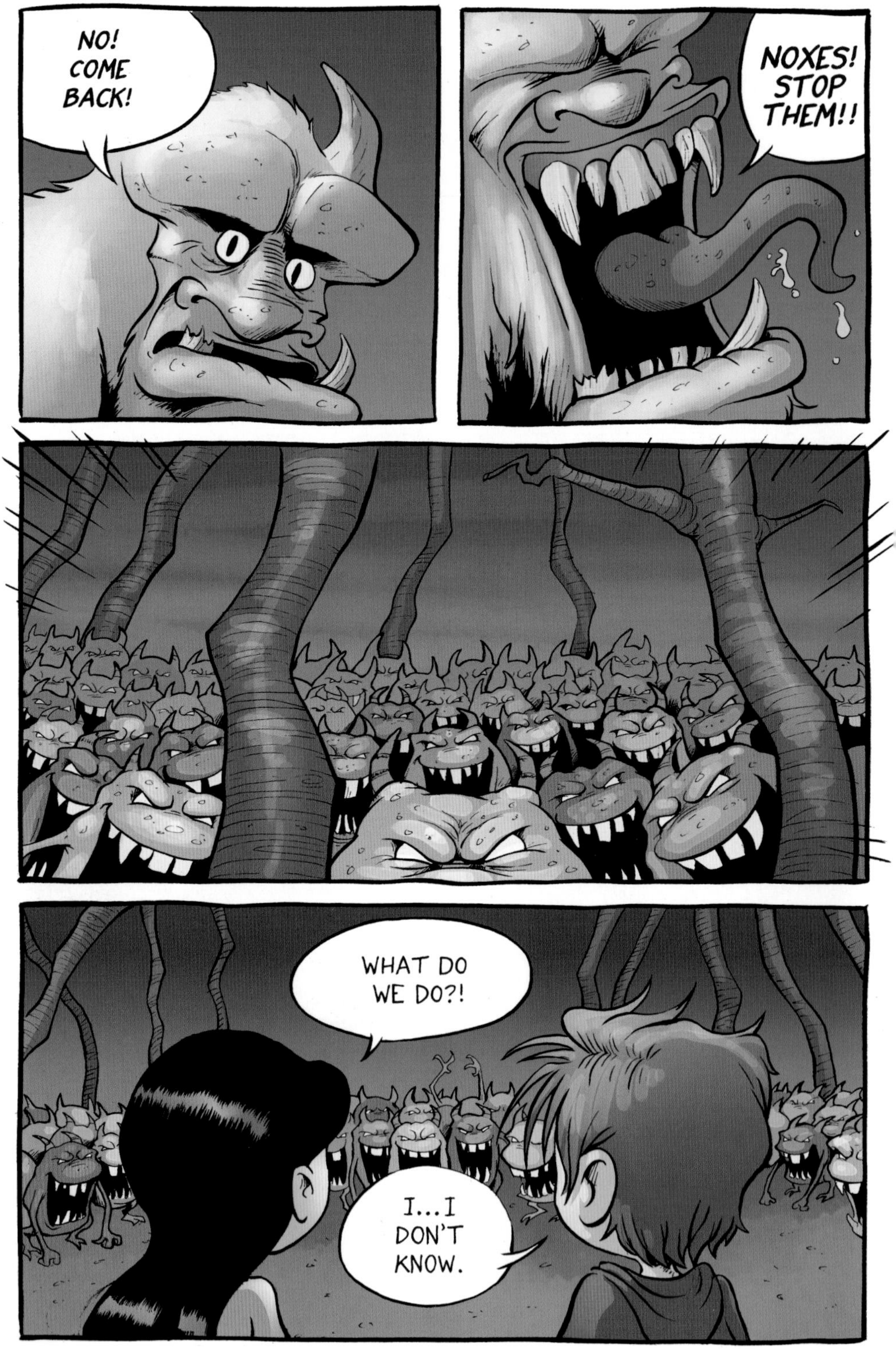
NO! COME BACK!
NOXES! STOP THEM!!
WHAT DO WE DO?!
I...I DON'T KNOW.

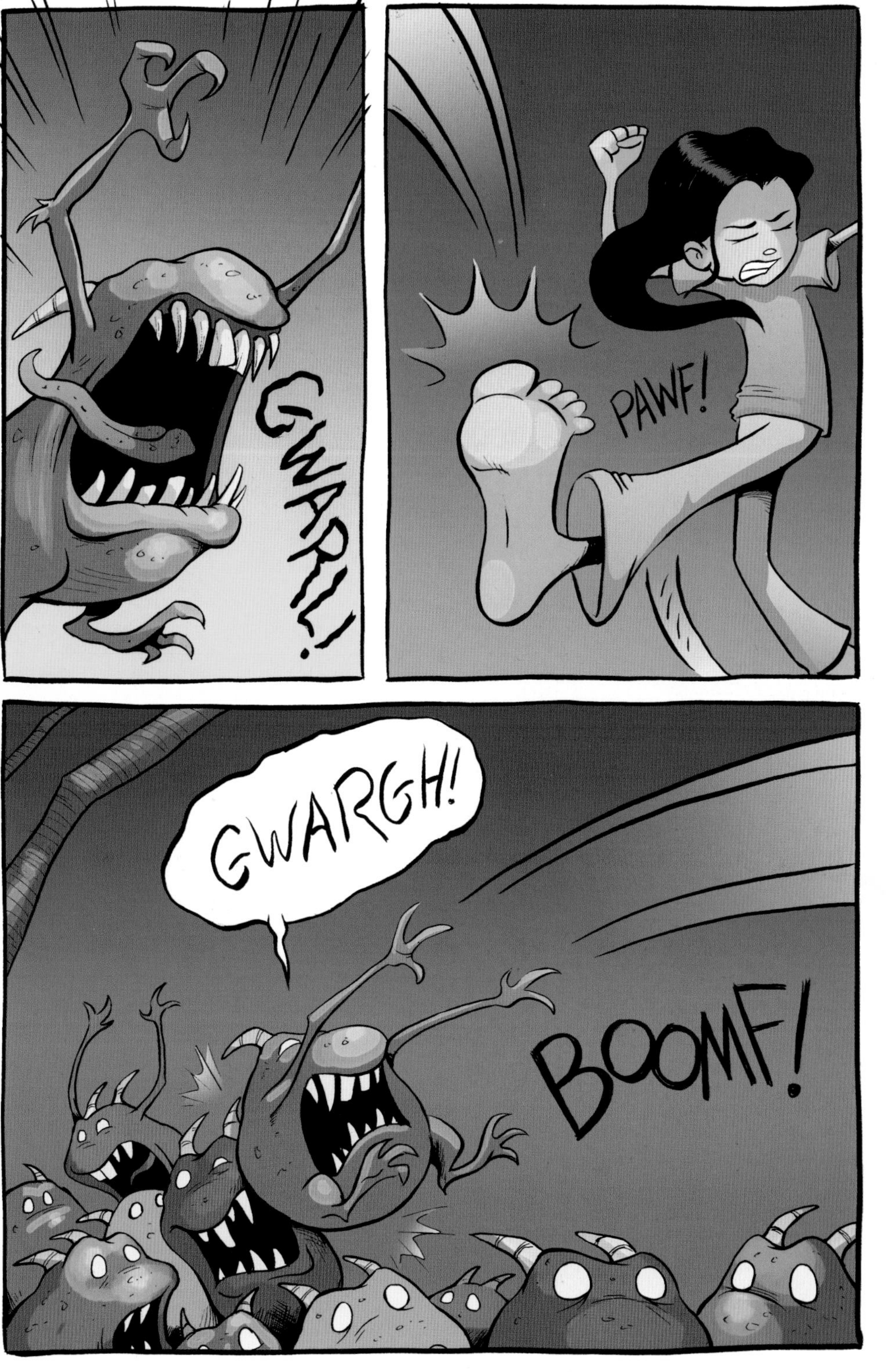
GWARRL!
PAWF!
GWARGH!
BOOMF!

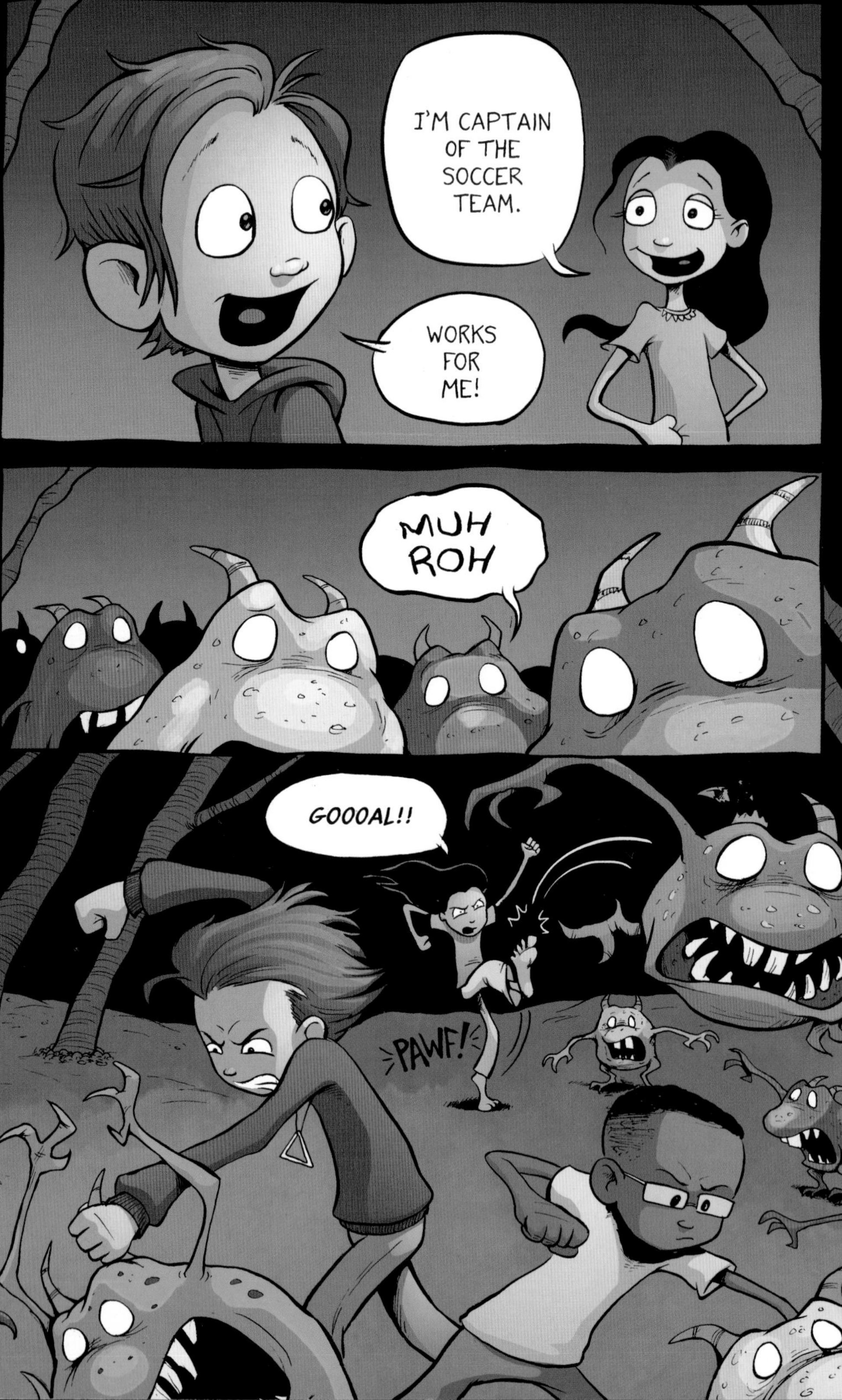

I'M CAPTAIN OF THE SOCCER TEAM.
WORKS FOR ME!
MUH ROH
GOOOAL!!
PAWF!

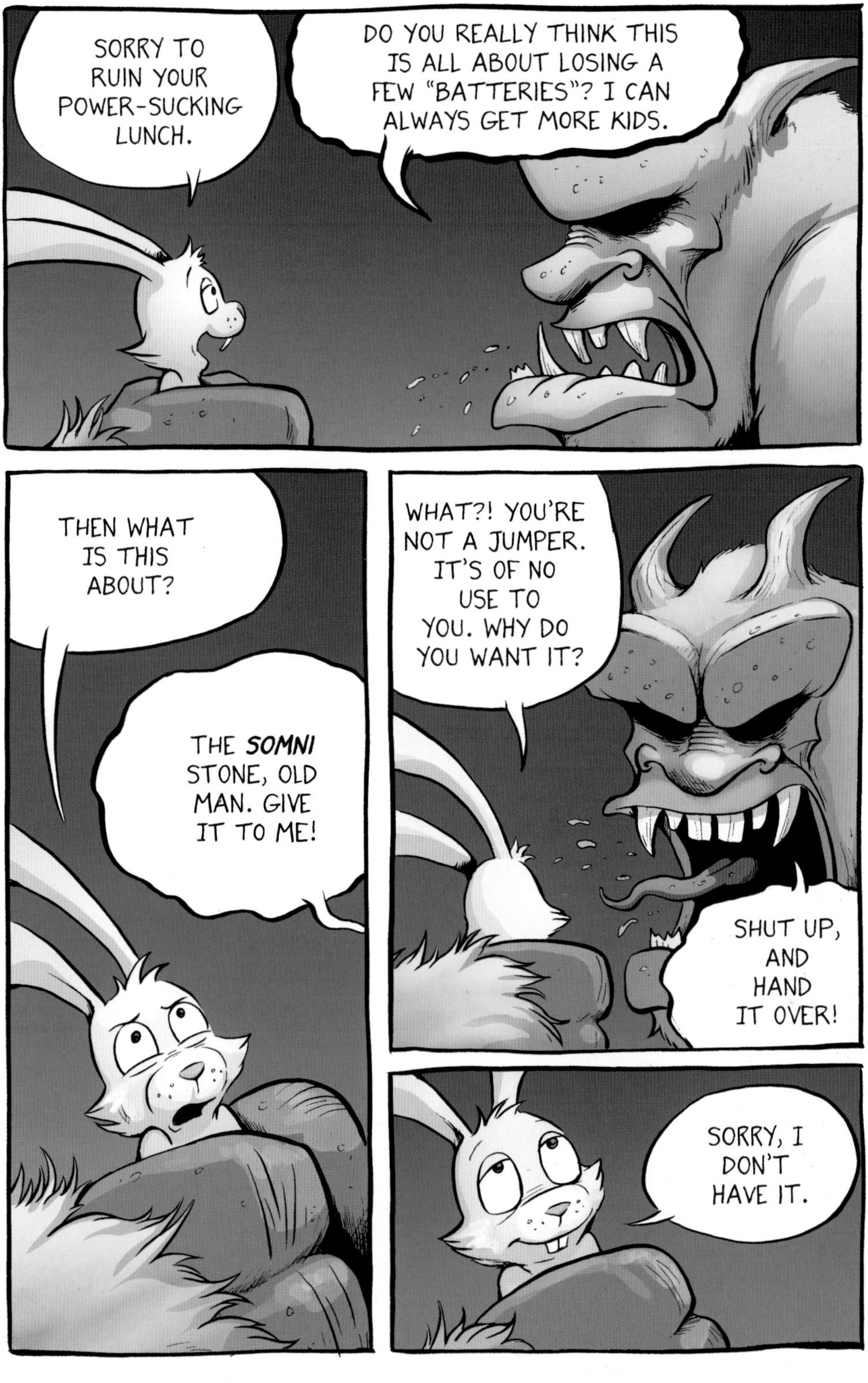
SORRY TO RUIN YOUR POWER-SUCKING LUNCH.
DO YOU REALLY THINK THIS IS ALL ABOUT LOSING A FEW "BATTERIES"? I CAN ALWAYS GET MORE KIDS.
THEN WHAT IS THIS ABOUT?
THE *SOMNI* STONE, OLD MAN. GIVE IT TO ME!
WHAT?! YOU'RE NOT A JUMPER. IT'S OF NO USE TO YOU. WHY DO YOU WANT IT?
SHUT UP, AND HAND IT OVER!
SORRY, I DON'T HAVE IT.

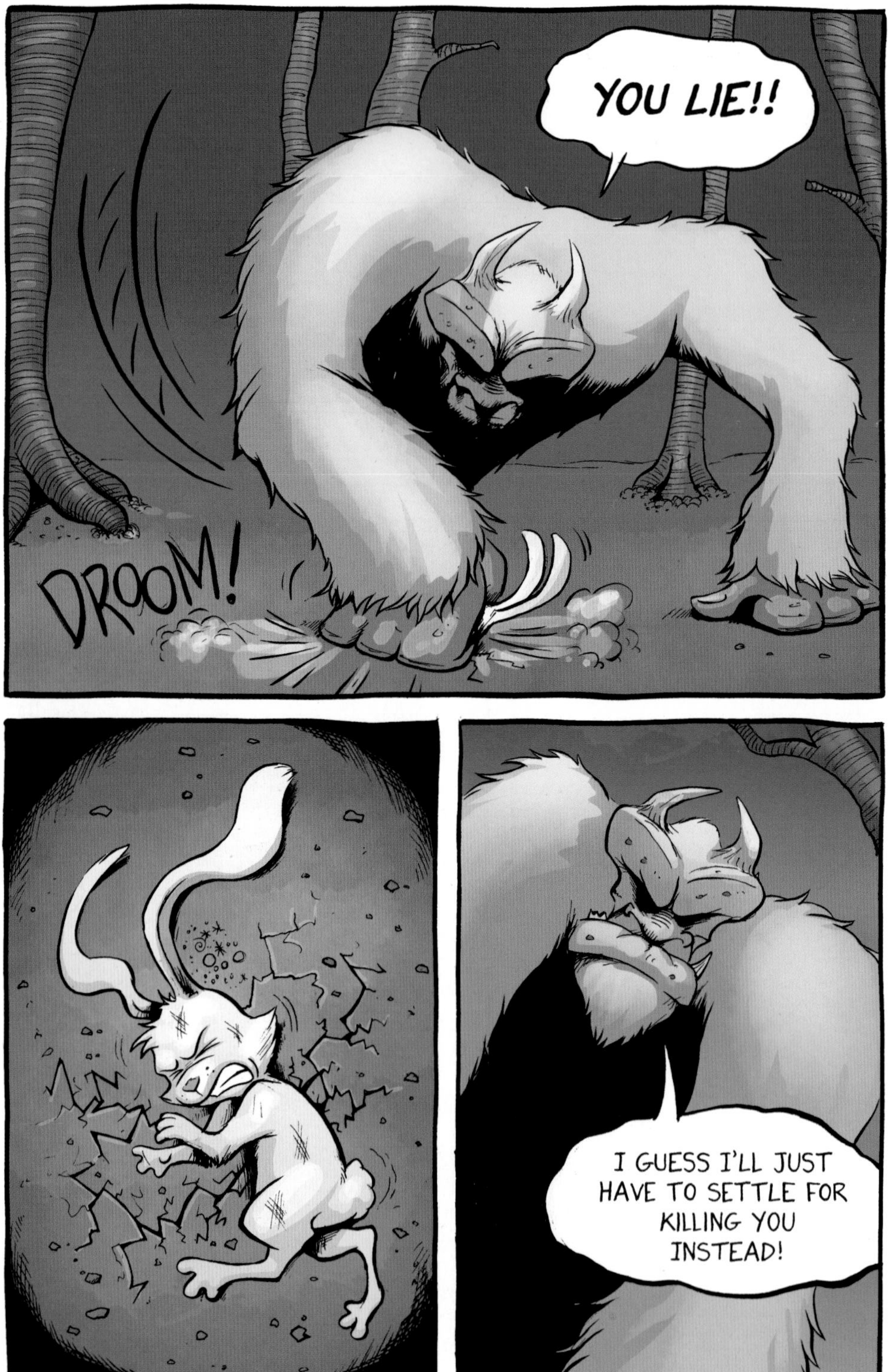
YOU LIE!!
DROOM!
I GUESS I'LL JUST HAVE TO SETTLE FOR KILLING YOU INSTEAD!

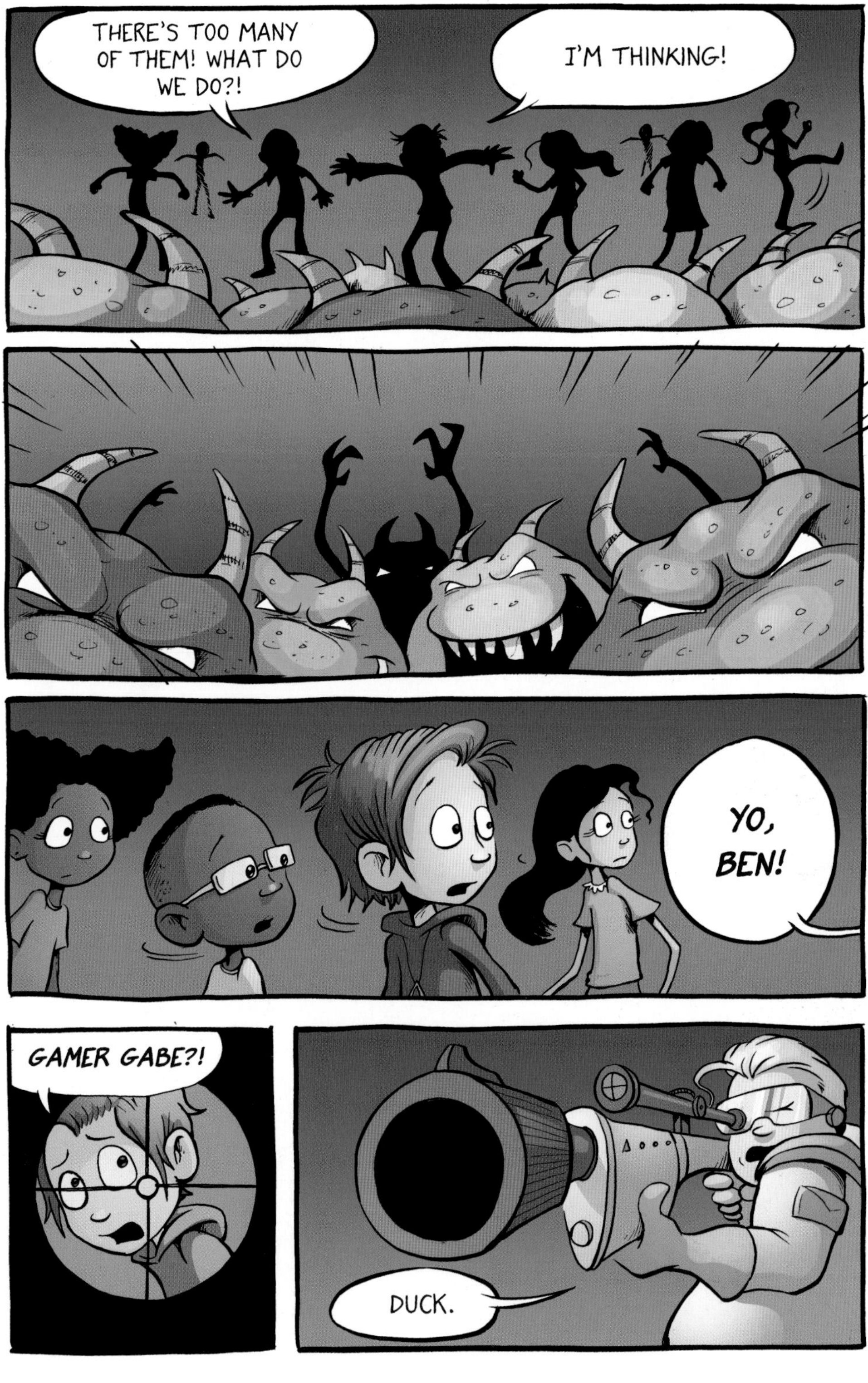

THERE'S TOO MANY OF THEM! WHAT DO WE DO?!
I'M THINKING!
YO, BEN!
GAMER GABE?!
DUCK.

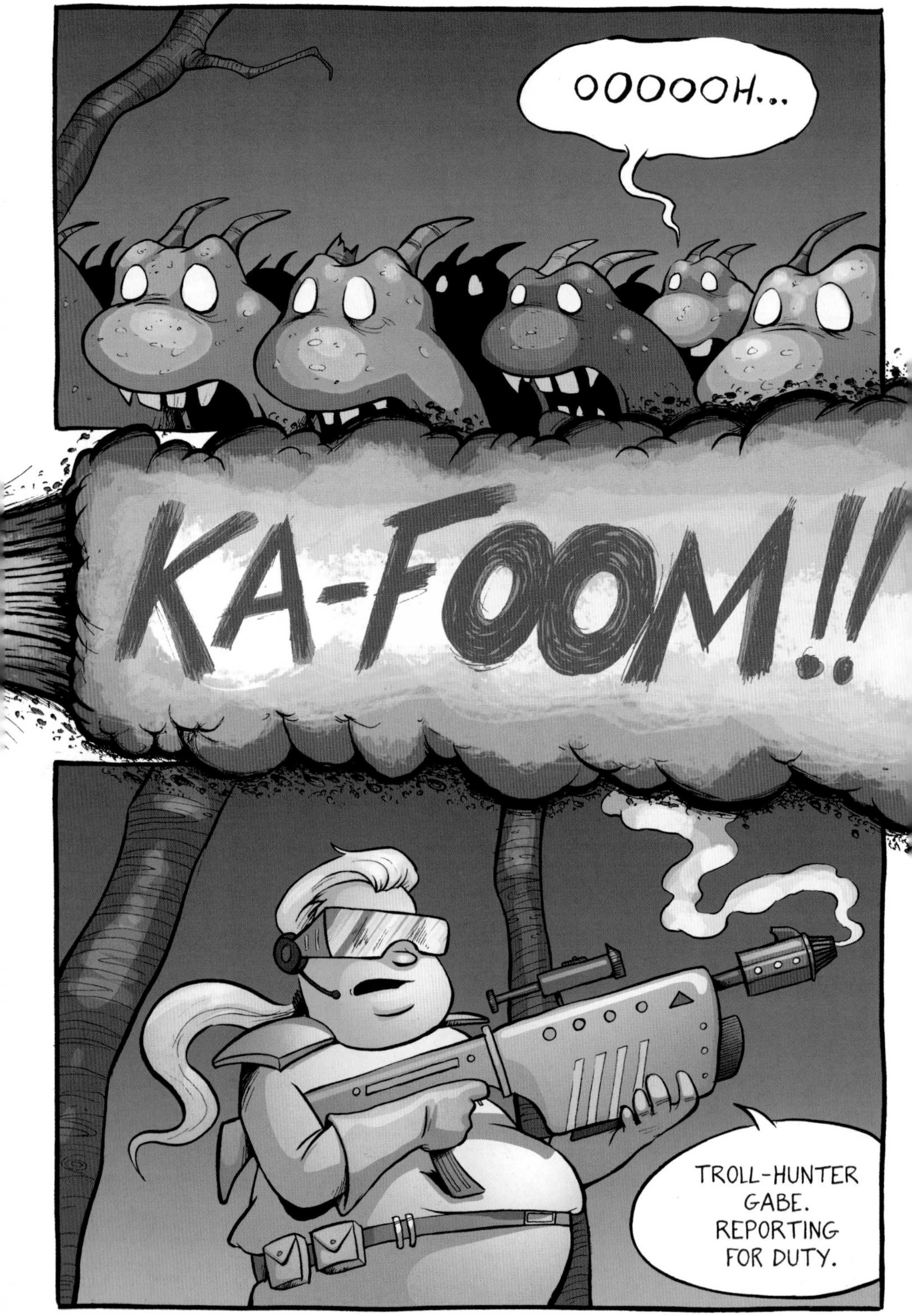
OOOOOH...
KA-FOOM!!
TROLL-HUNTER GABE. REPORTING FOR DUTY.

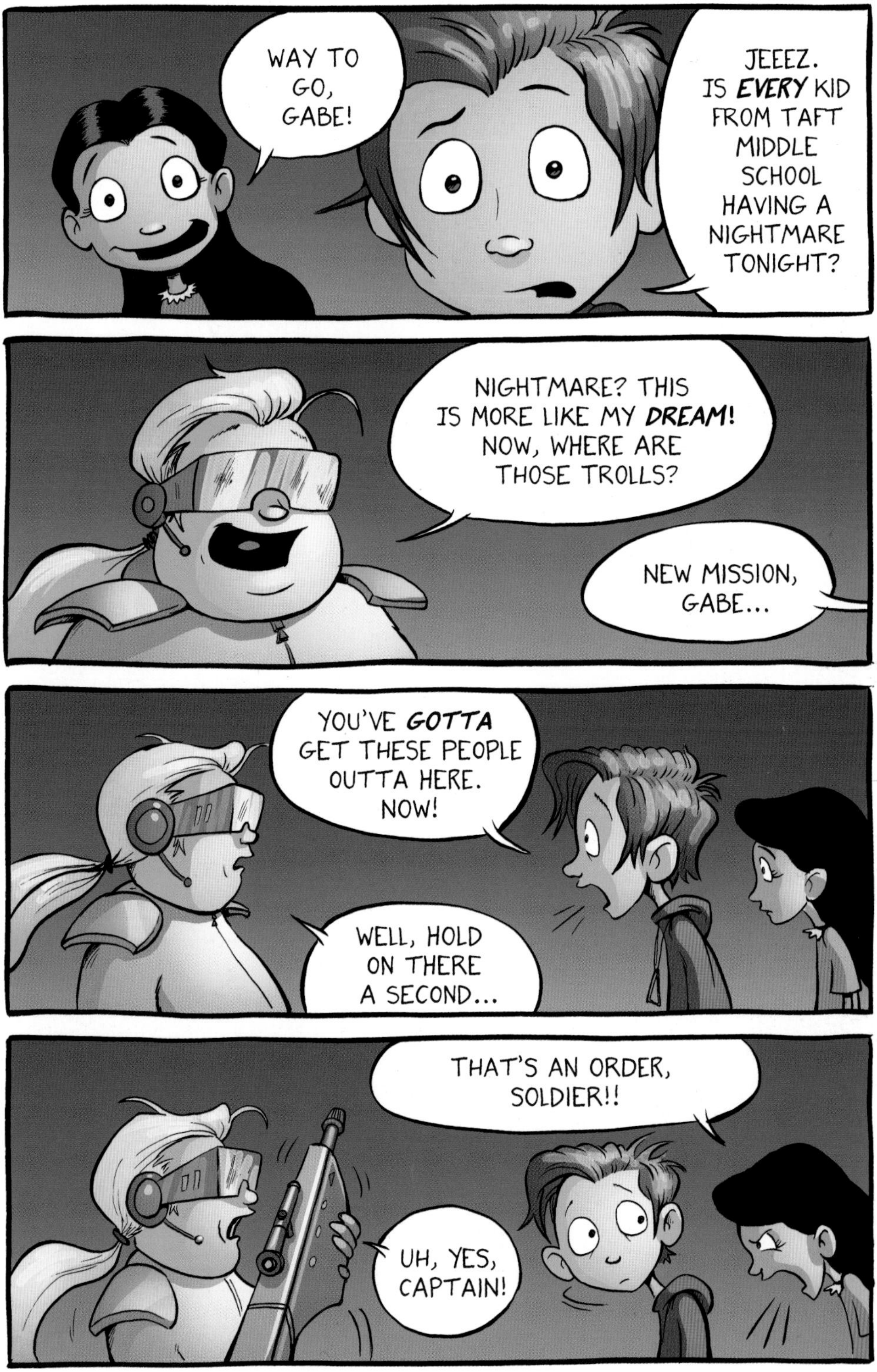
WAY TO GO, GABE!
JEEEZ. IS EVERY KID FROM TAFT MIDDLE SCHOOL HAVING A NIGHTMARE TONIGHT?
NIGHTMARE? THIS IS MORE LIKE MY DREAM! NOW, WHERE ARE THOSE TROLLS?
NEW MISSION, GABE...
YOU'VE GOTTA GET THESE PEOPLE OUTTA HERE. NOW!
WELL, HOLD ON THERE A SECOND...
THAT'S AN ORDER, SOLDIER!!
UH, YES, CAPTAIN!

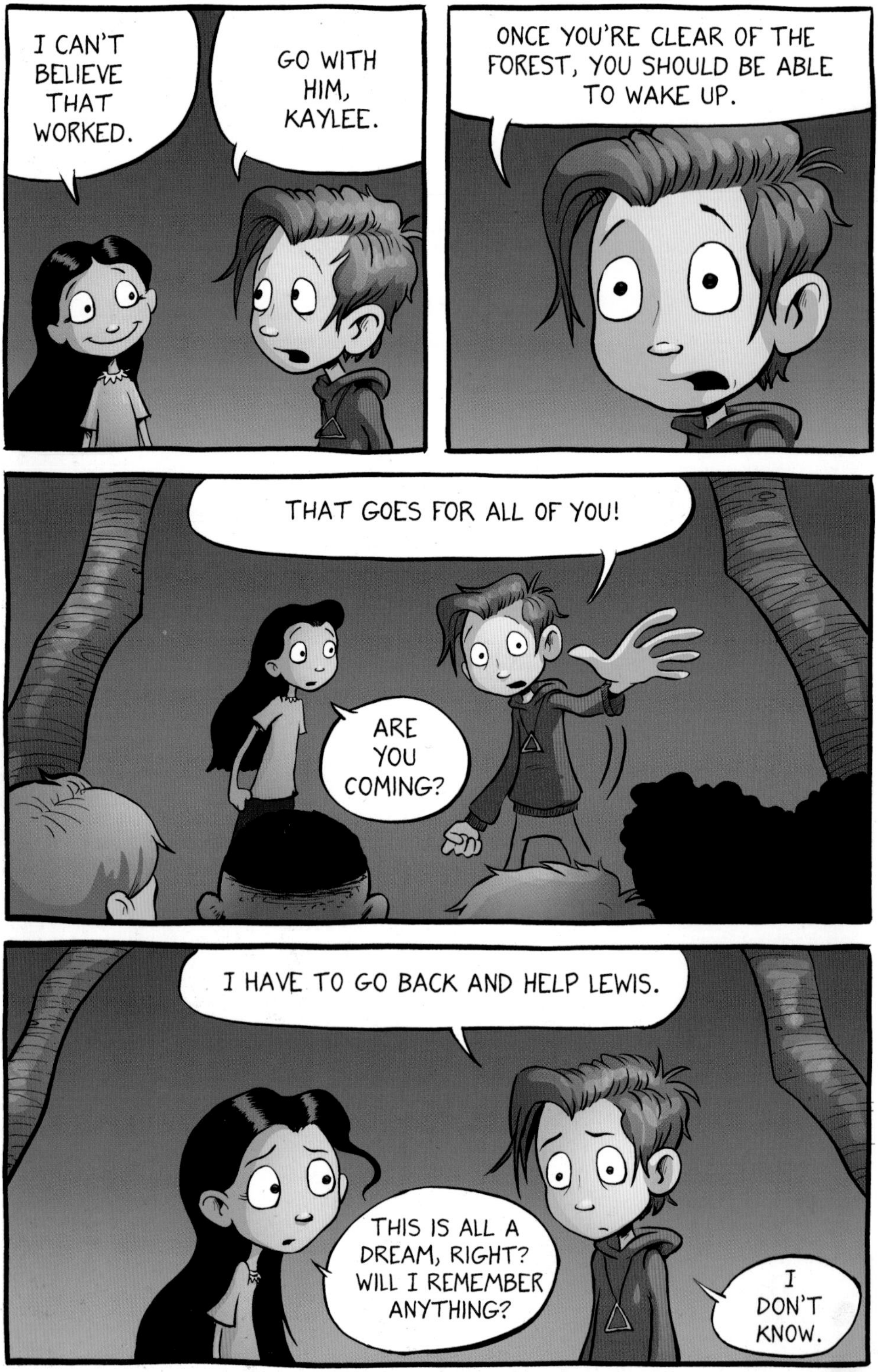
I CAN'T BELIEVE THAT WORKED.
GO WITH HIM, KAYLEE.
ONCE YOU'RE CLEAR OF THE FOREST, YOU SHOULD BE ABLE TO WAKE UP.
THAT GOES FOR ALL OF YOU!
ARE YOU COMING?
I HAVE TO GO BACK AND HELP LEWIS.
THIS IS ALL A DREAM, RIGHT? WILL I REMEMBER ANYTHING?
I DON'T KNOW.

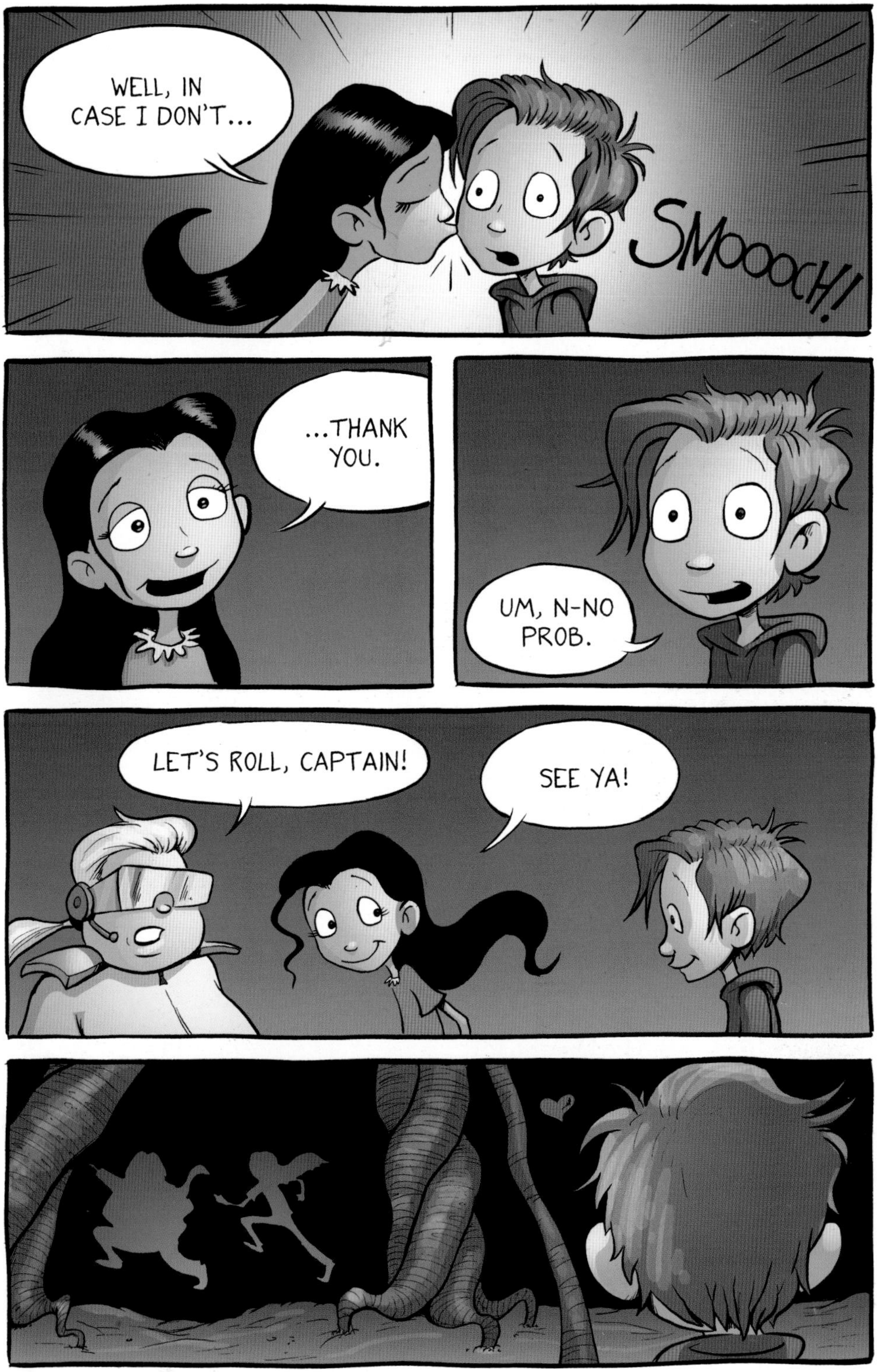
WELL, IN CASE I DON'T...
SMOOOCH!
...THANK YOU.
UM, N-NO PROB.
LET'S ROLL, CAPTAIN!
SEE YA!

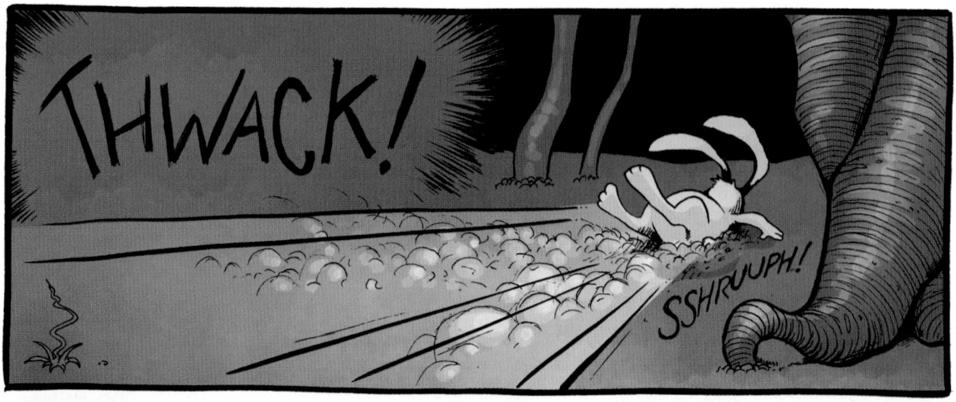
THWACK!
SSHRUUPH!

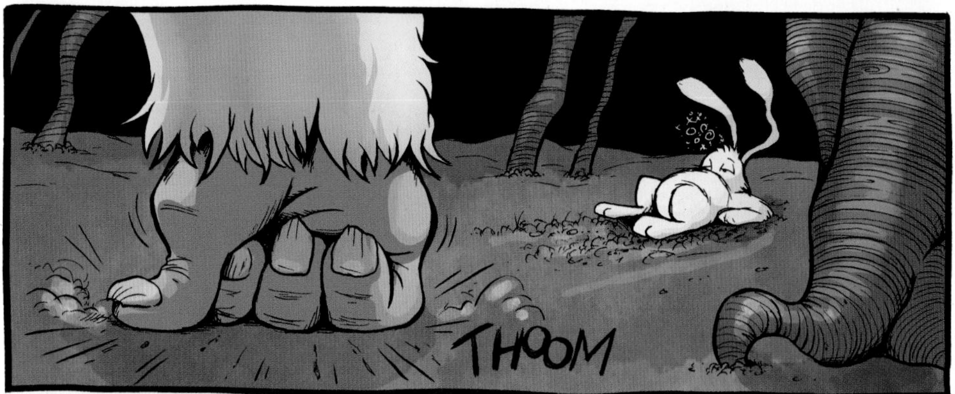
THOOM

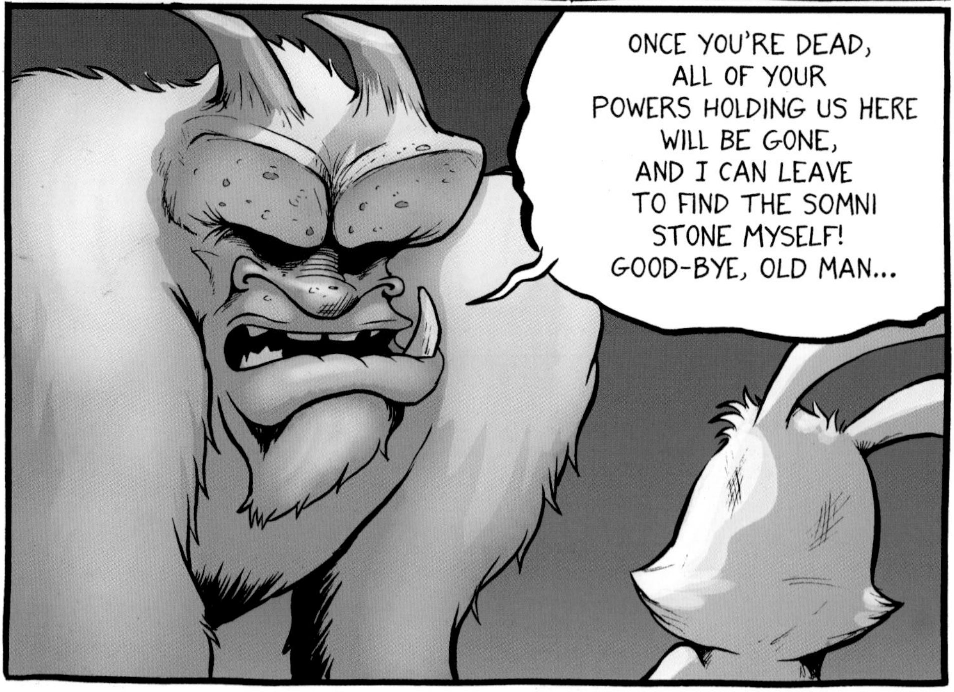
ONCE YOU'RE DEAD, ALL OF YOUR POWERS HOLDING US HERE WILL BE GONE, AND I CAN LEAVE TO FIND THE SOMNI STONE MYSELF! GOOD-BYE, OLD MAN...

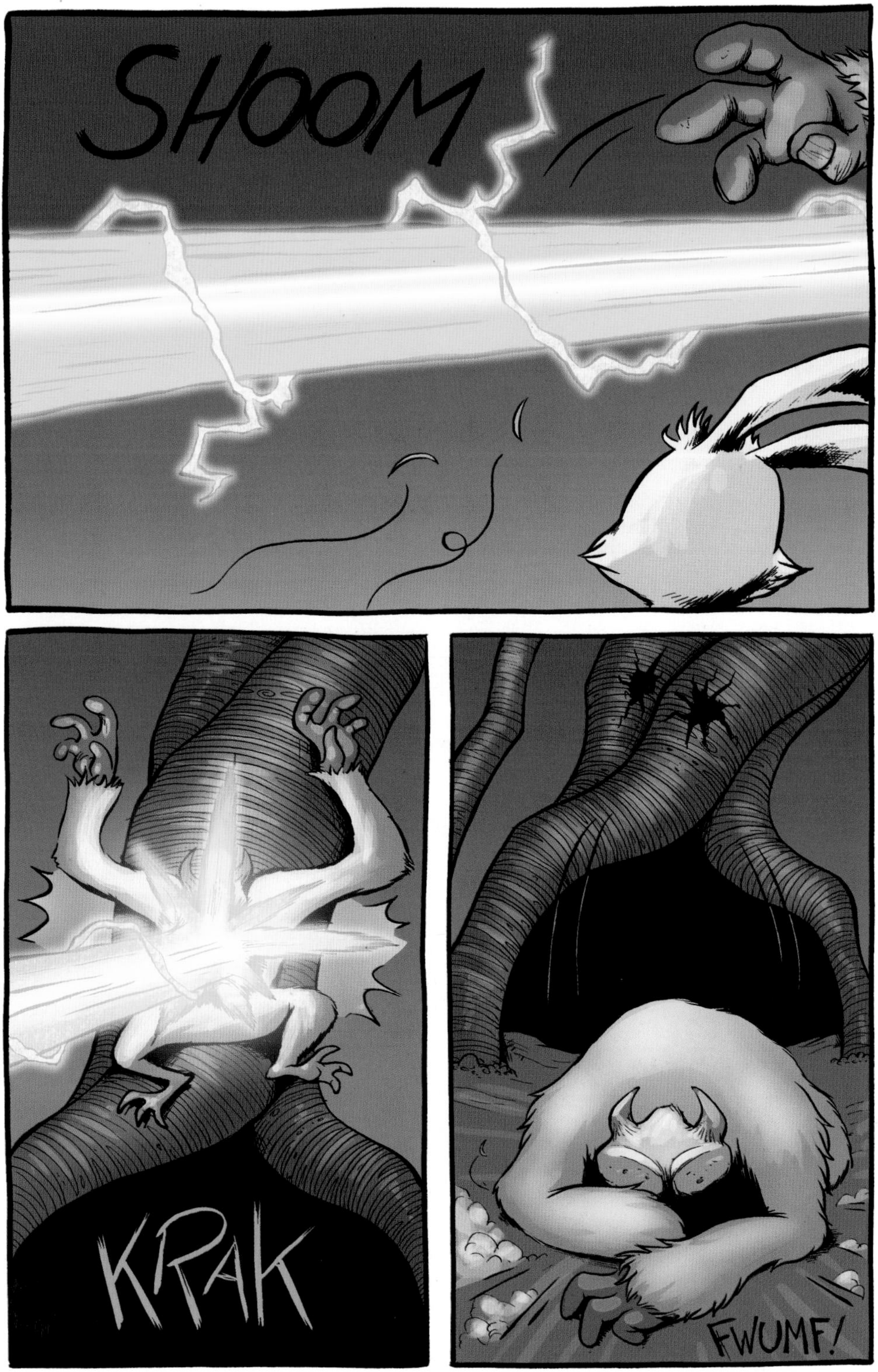
SHOOM
KRAK
FWUMF!

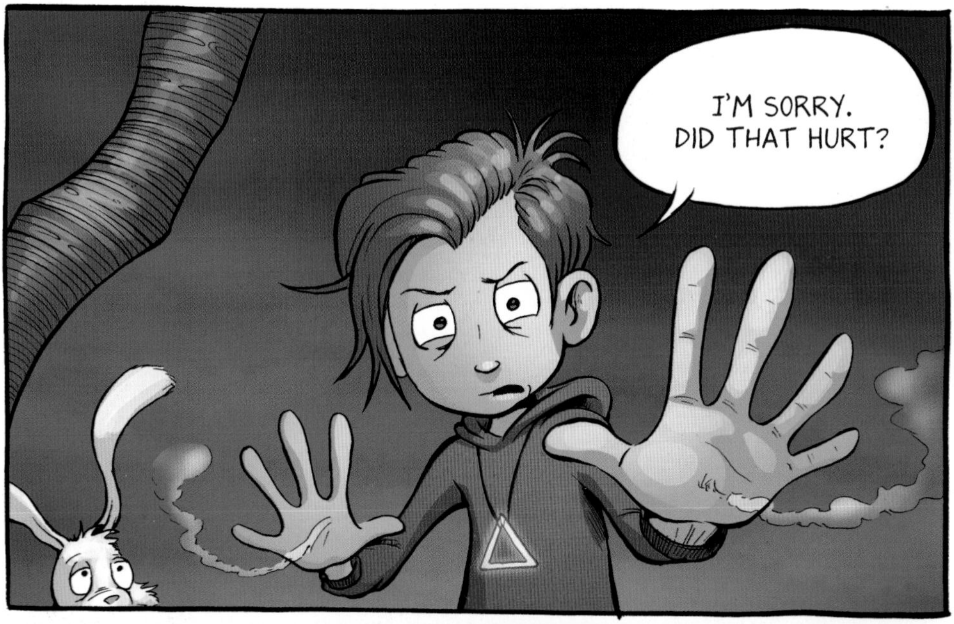
I'M SORRY.
DID THAT HURT?

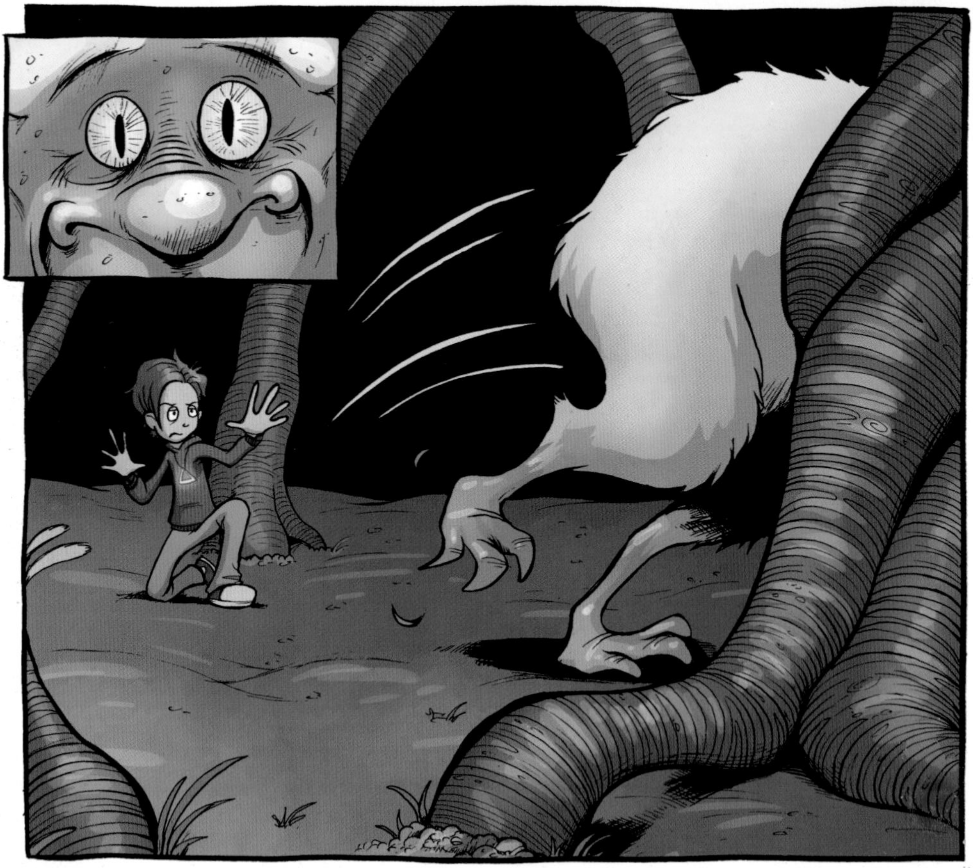

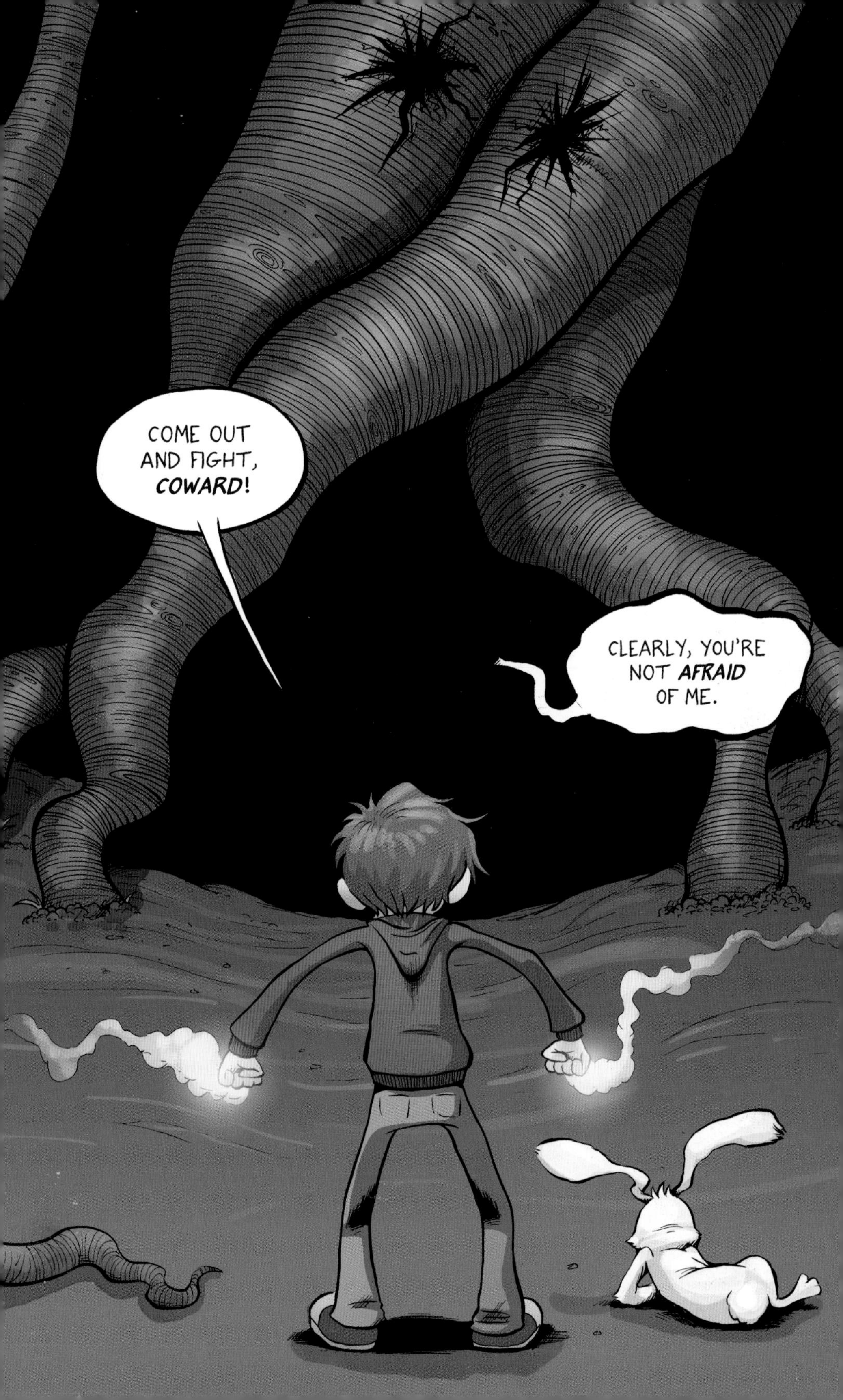
COME OUT AND FIGHT, *COWARD!*
CLEARLY, YOU'RE NOT *AFRAID* OF ME.

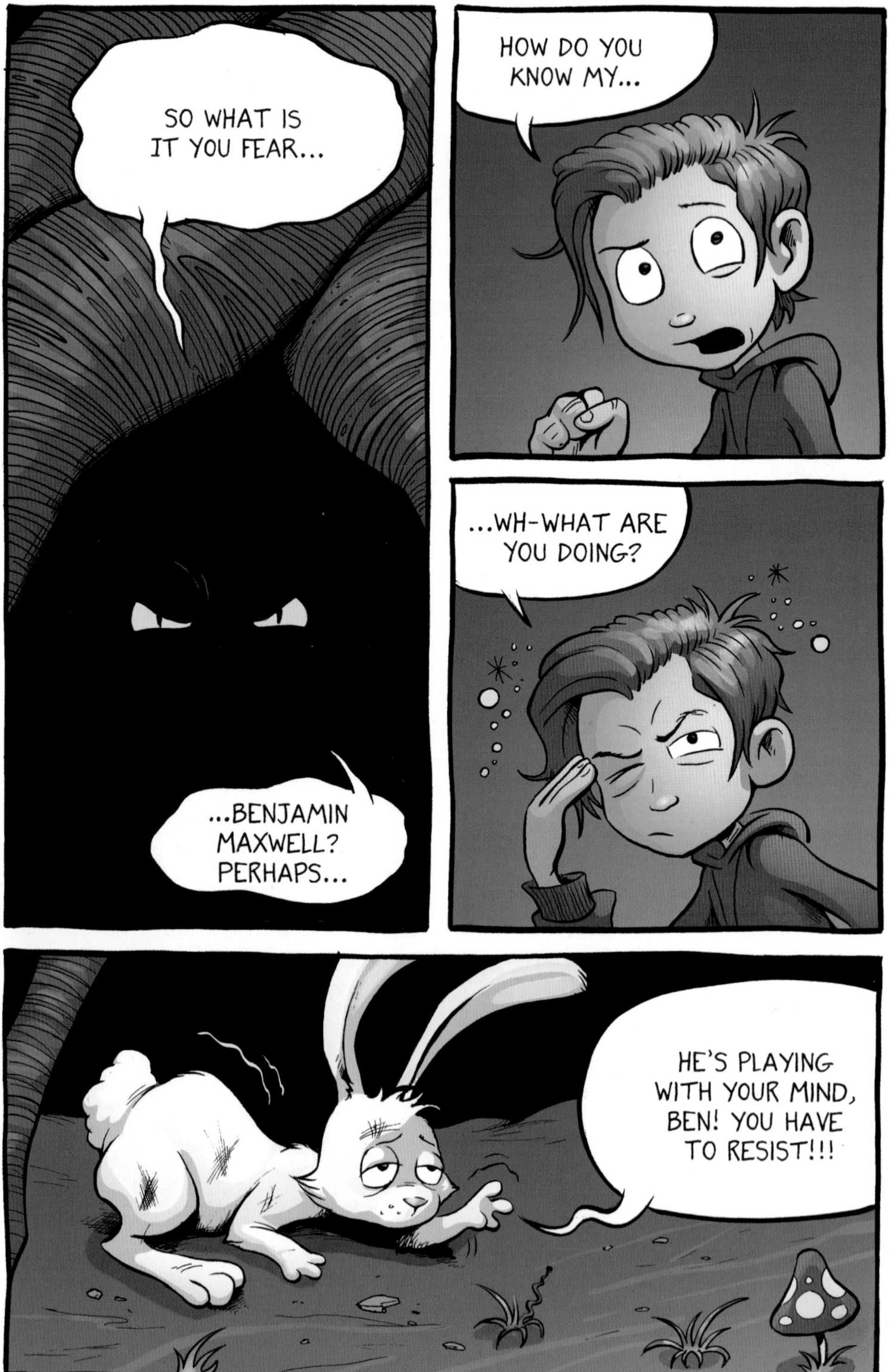
SO WHAT IS IT YOU FEAR...
...BENJAMIN MAXWELL? PERHAPS...
HOW DO YOU KNOW MY...
...WH-WHAT ARE YOU DOING?
HE'S PLAYING WITH YOUR MIND, BEN! YOU HAVE TO RESIST!!!

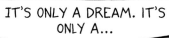
IT'S ONLY A DREAM. IT'S ONLY A...

NO? WELL THEN...

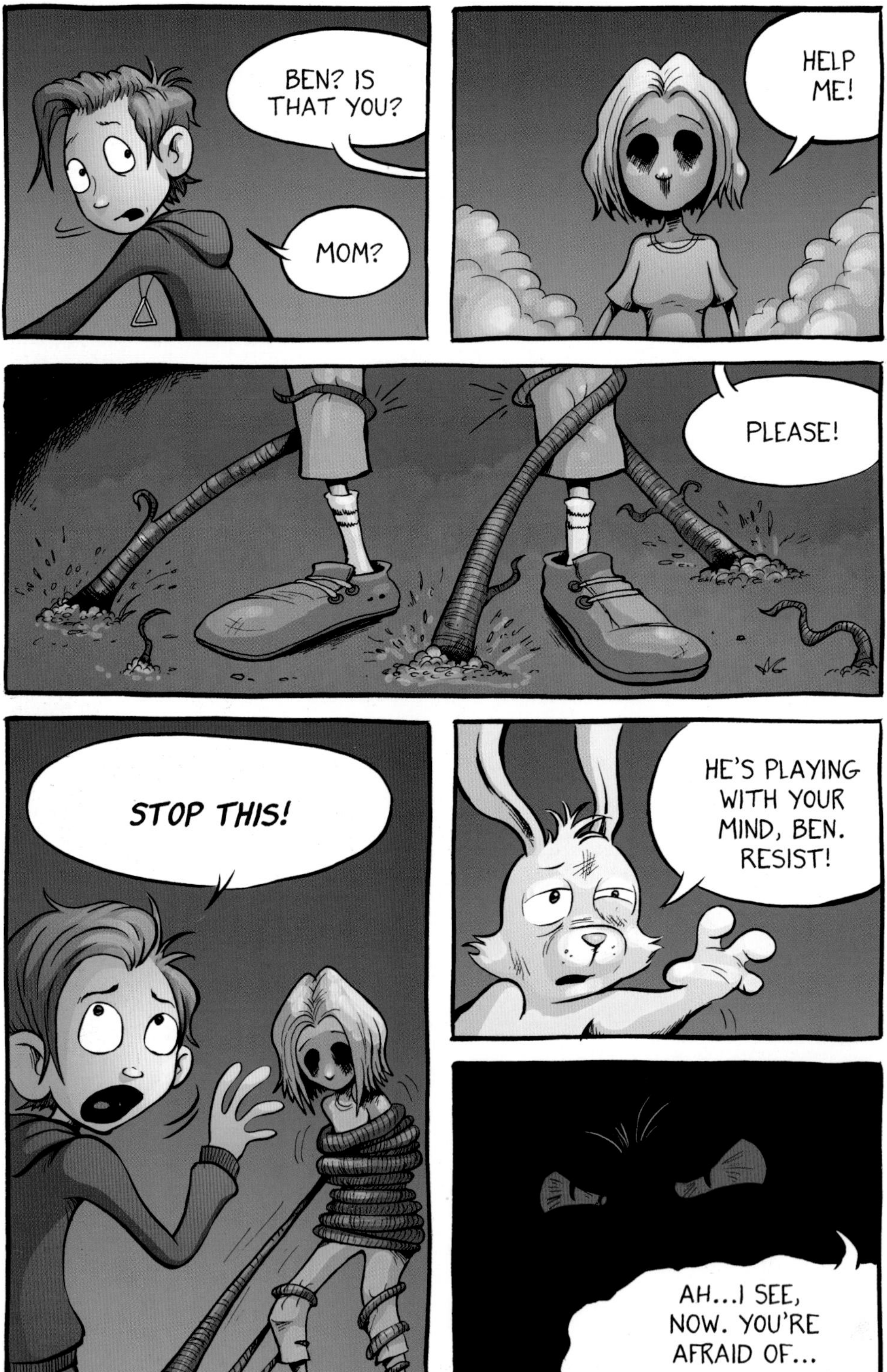
BEN? IS THAT YOU?
MOM?
HELP ME!
PLEASE!
STOP THIS!
HE'S PLAYING WITH YOUR MIND, BEN. RESIST!
AH...I SEE, NOW. YOU'RE AFRAID OF...

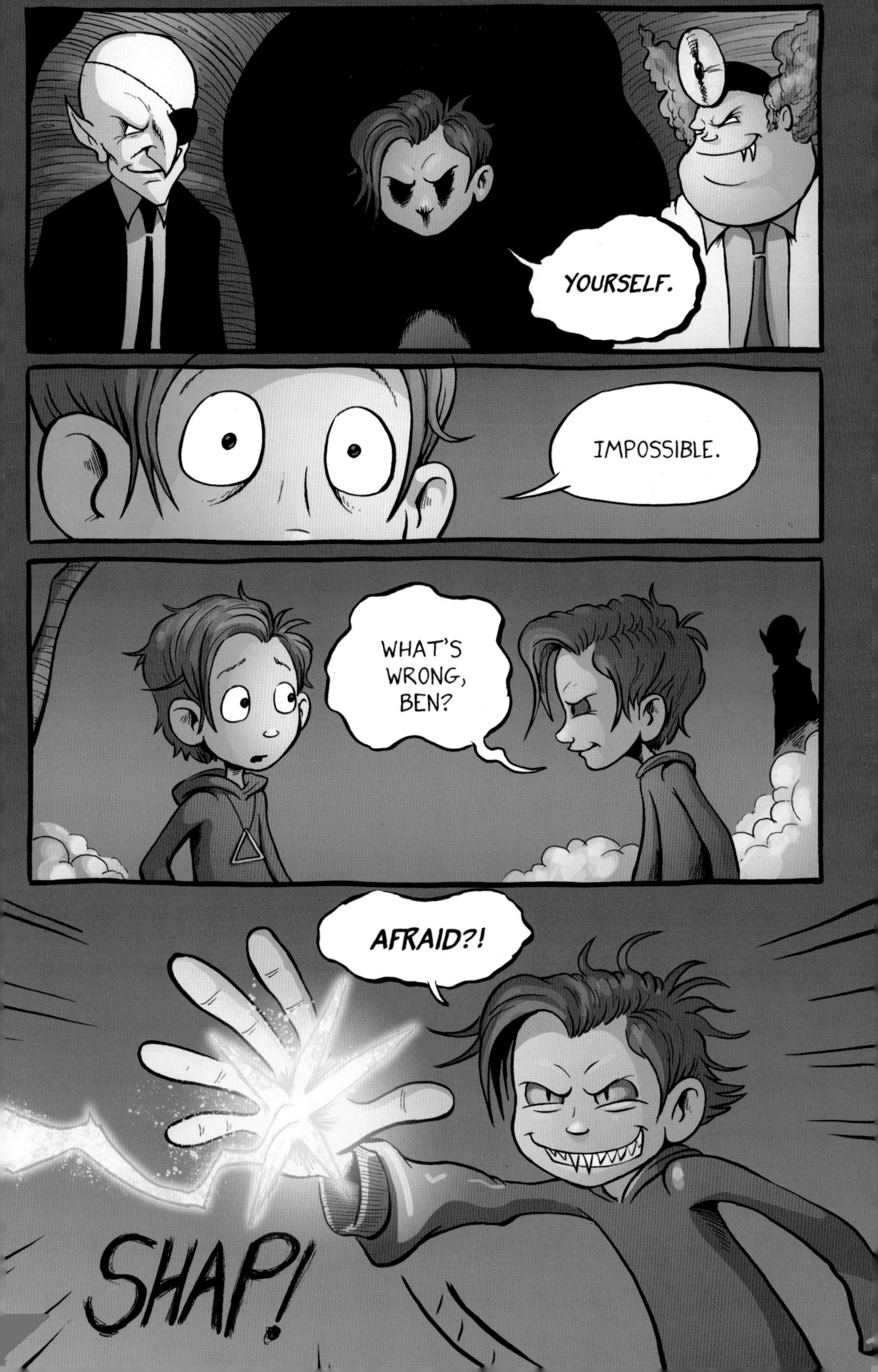
YOURSELF.
IMPOSSIBLE.
WHAT'S WRONG, BEN?
AFRAID?!
SHAP!

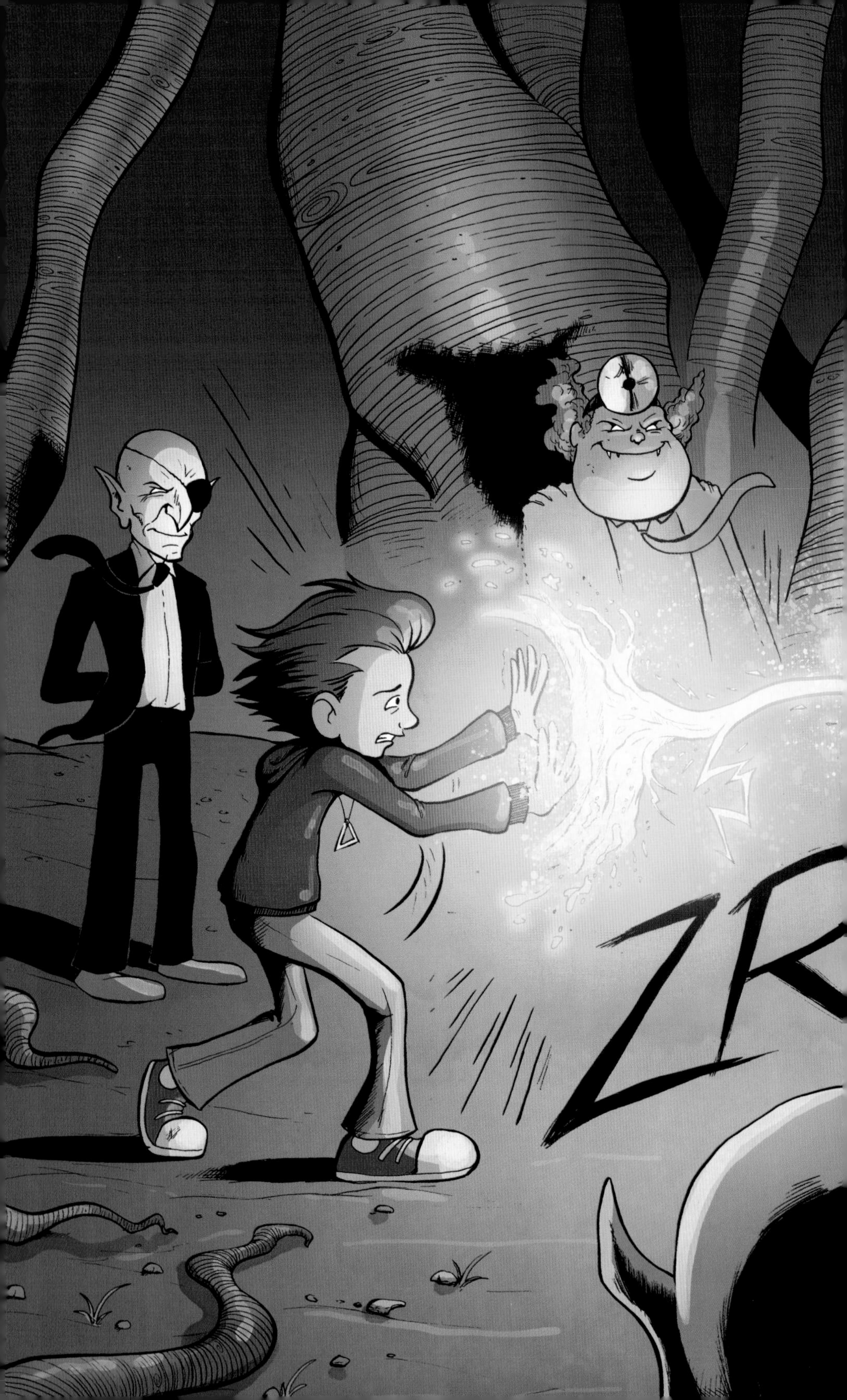
ZR

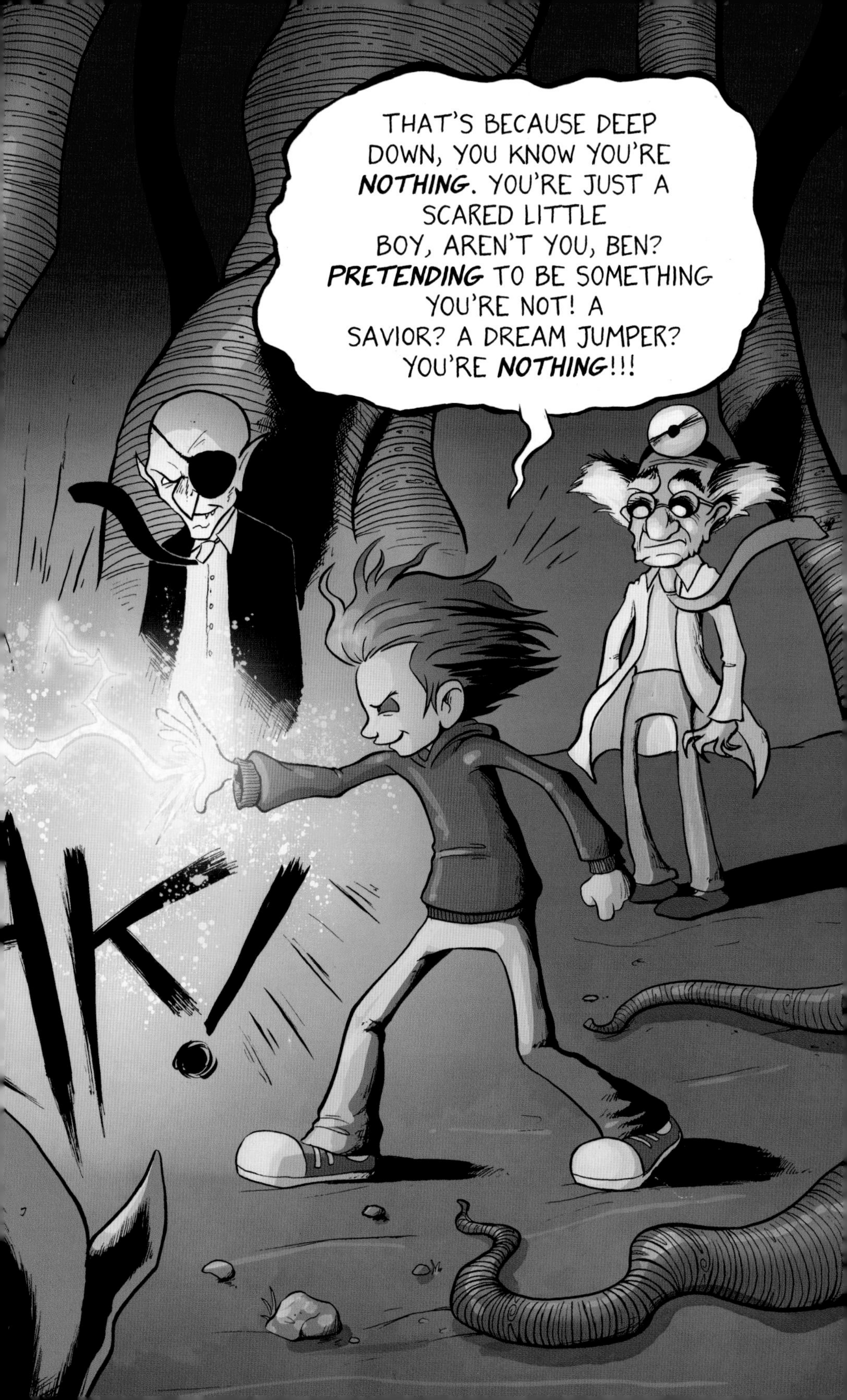
THAT'S BECAUSE DEEP DOWN, YOU KNOW YOU'RE ***NOTHING***. YOU'RE JUST A SCARED LITTLE BOY, AREN'T YOU, BEN? ***PRETENDING*** TO BE SOMETHING YOU'RE NOT! A SAVIOR? A DREAM JUMPER? YOU'RE ***NOTHING***!!!

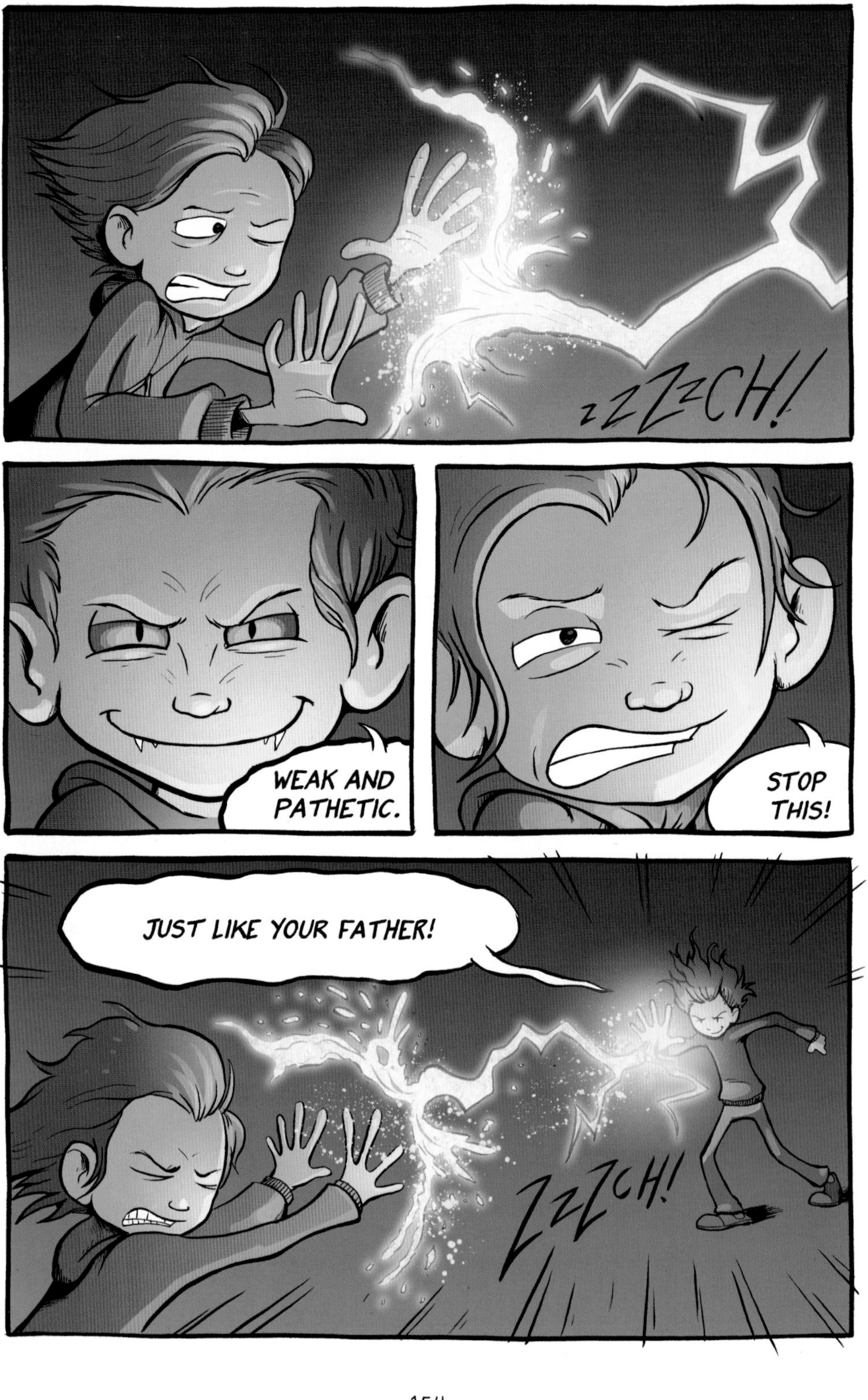
zzZzCH!
WEAK AND PATHETIC.
STOP THIS!
JUST LIKE YOUR FATHER!
ZzZCH!

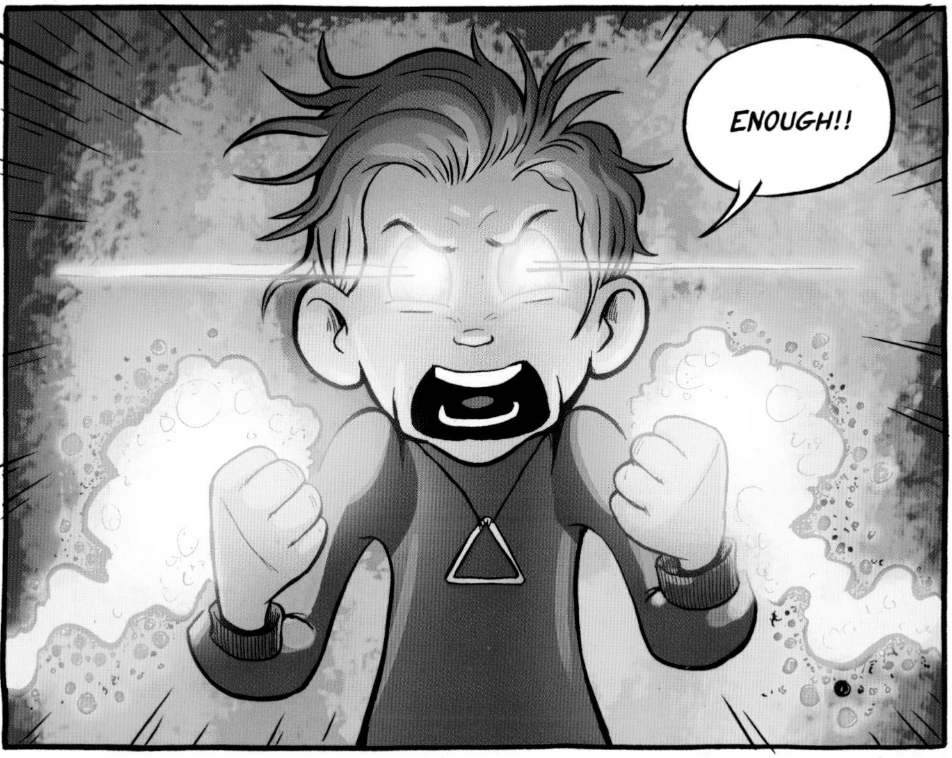
ENOUGH!!

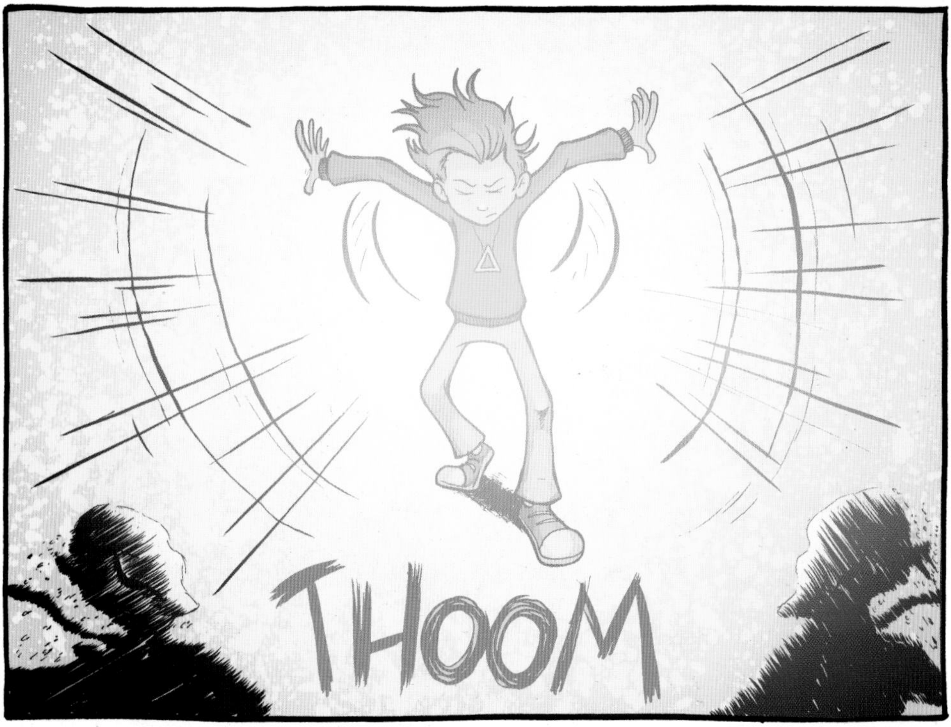
THOOM

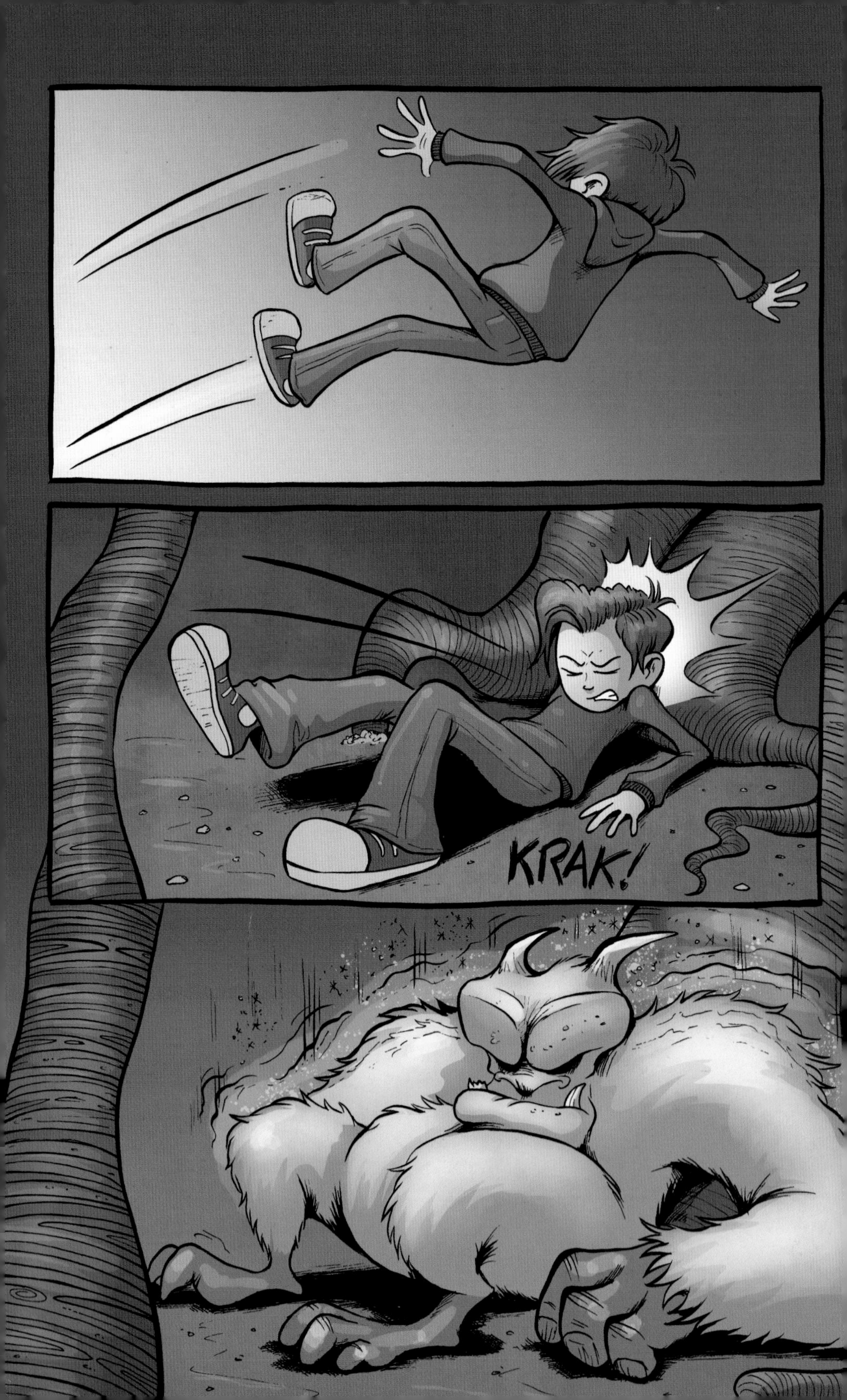
KRAK!

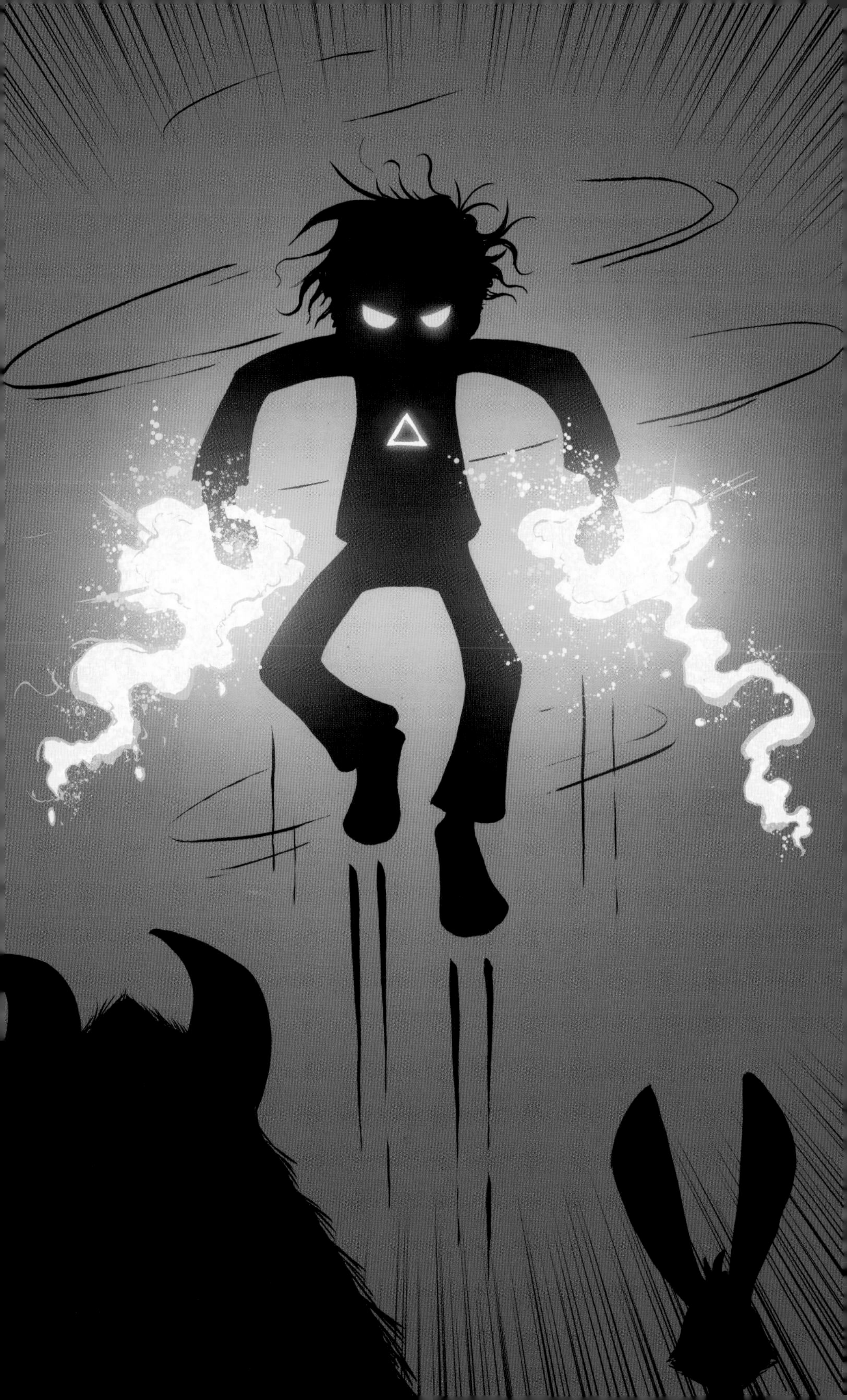

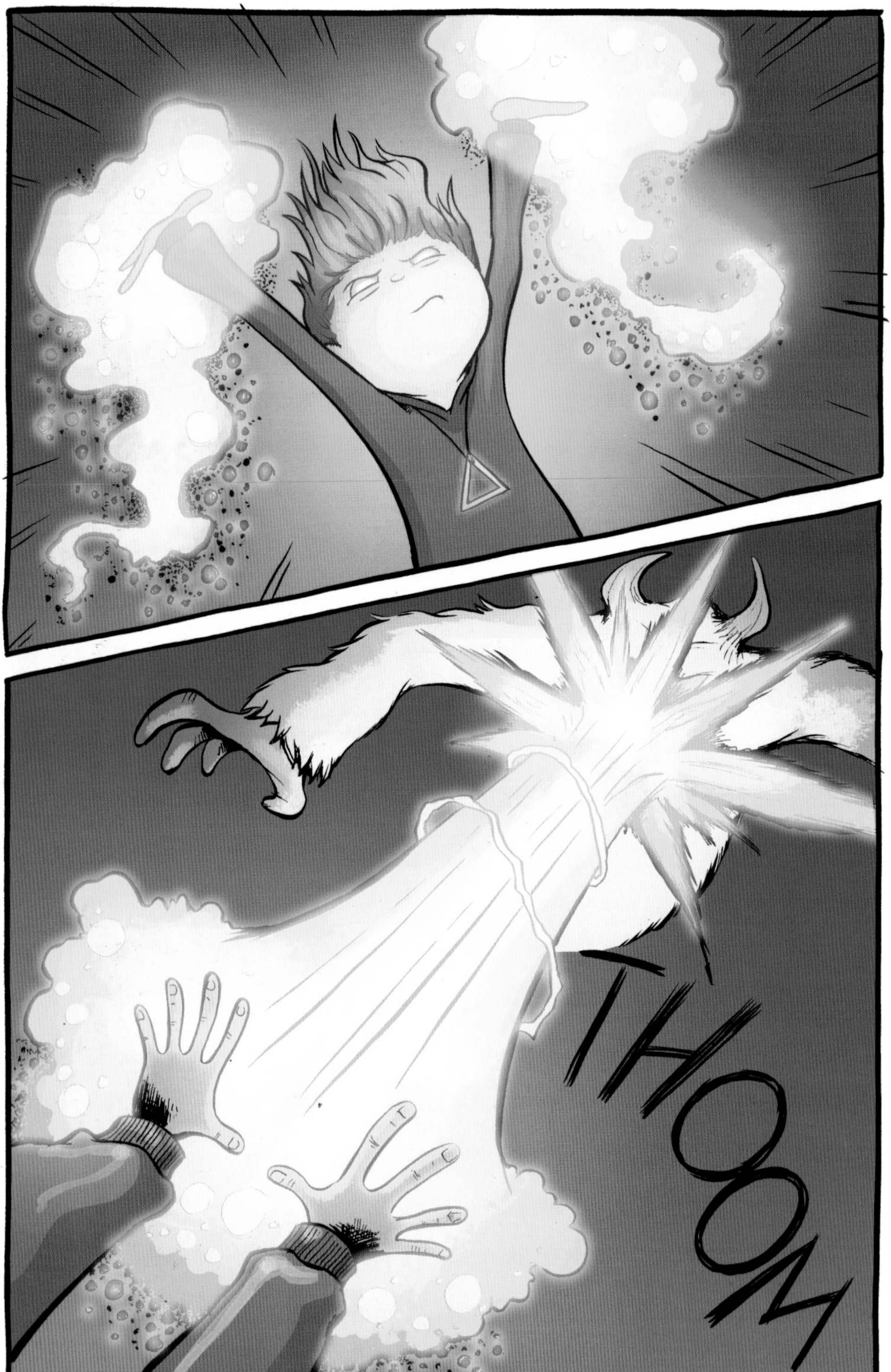
THOOM

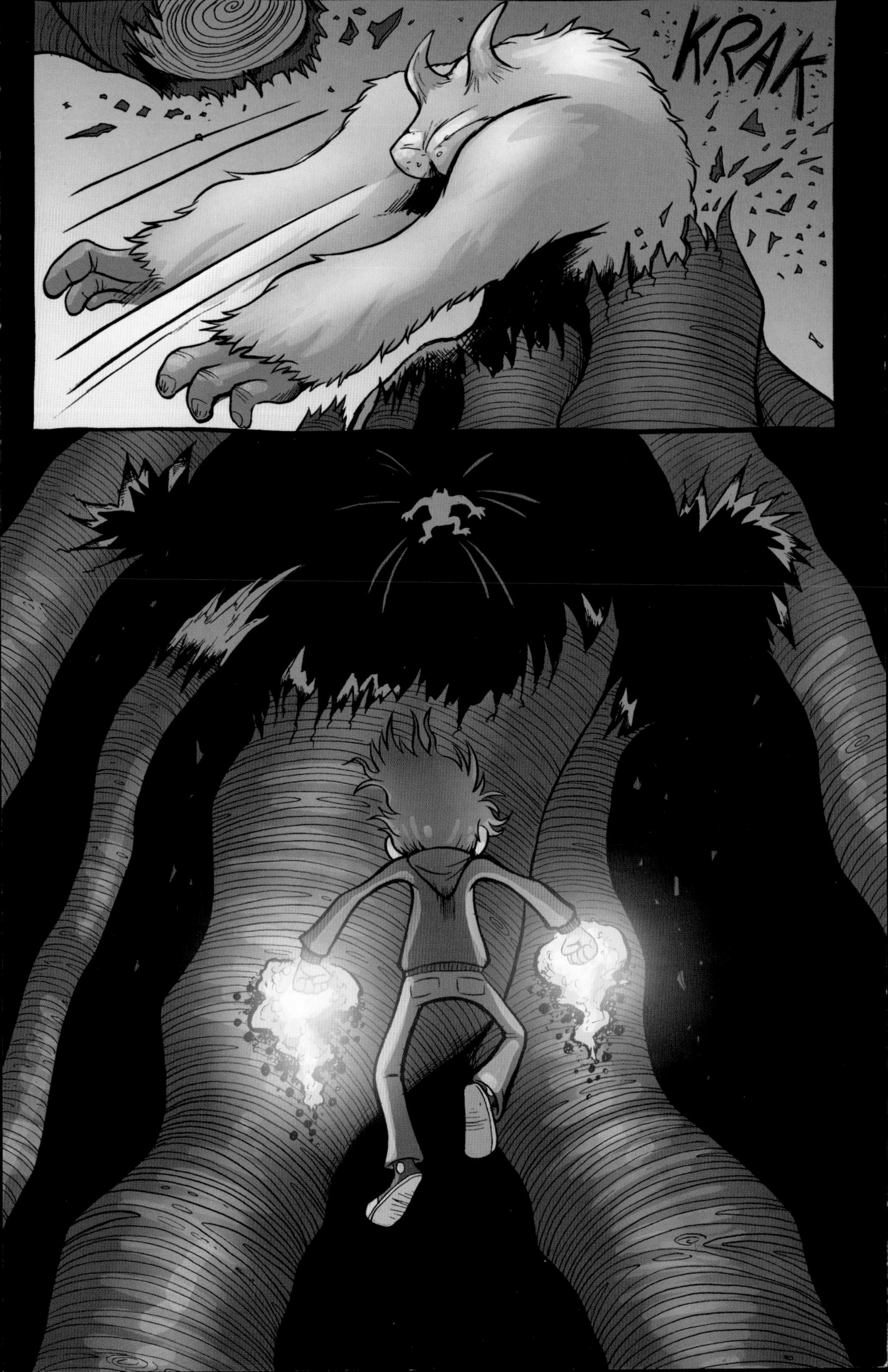
KRAK

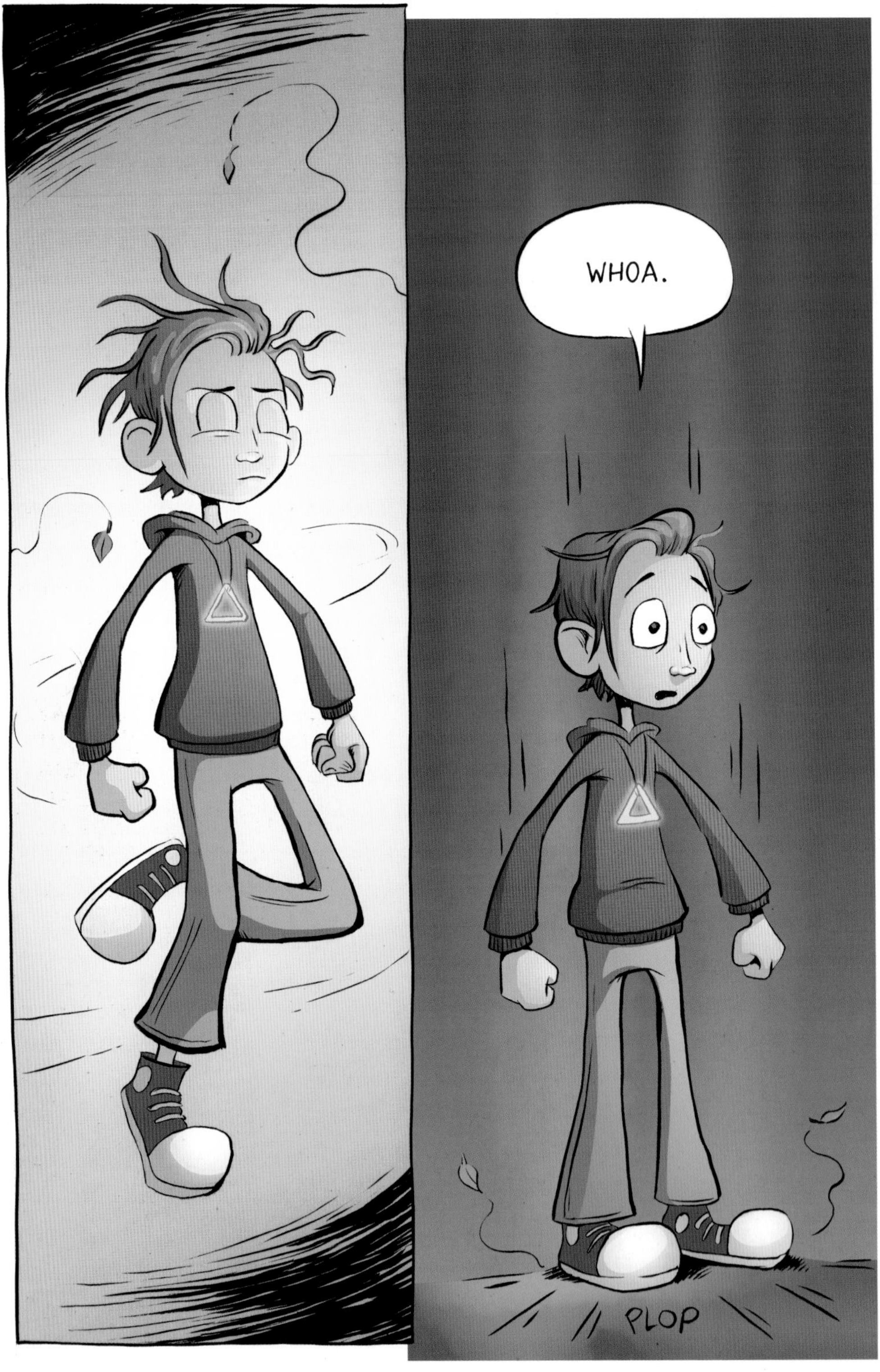
WHOA.
PLOP

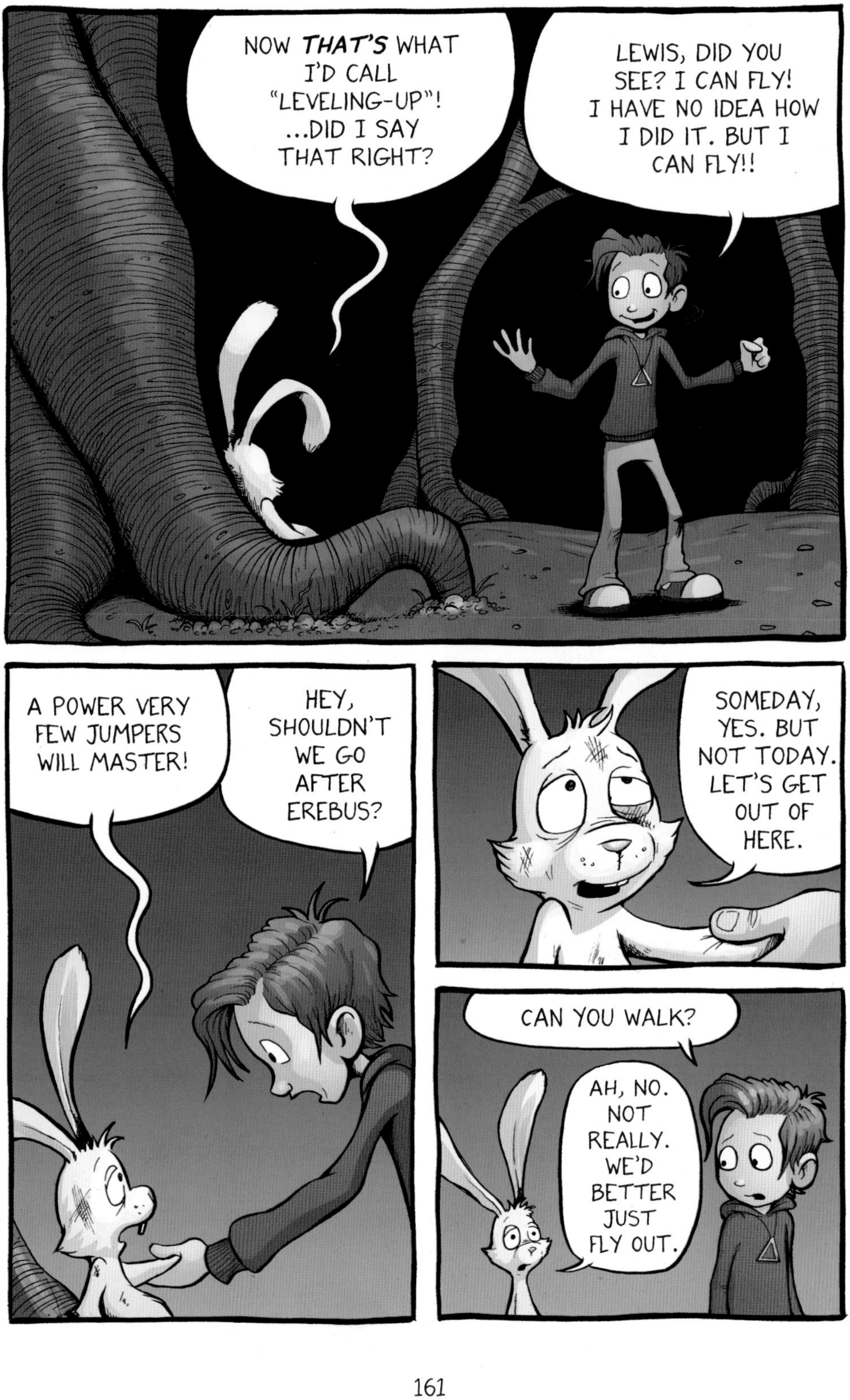
NOW *THAT'S* WHAT I'D CALL "LEVELING-UP"! ...DID I SAY THAT RIGHT?
LEWIS, DID YOU SEE? I CAN FLY! I HAVE NO IDEA HOW I DID IT. BUT I CAN FLY!!
A POWER VERY FEW JUMPERS WILL MASTER!
HEY, SHOULDN'T WE GO AFTER EREBUS?
SOMEDAY, YES. BUT NOT TODAY. LET'S GET OUT OF HERE.
CAN YOU WALK?
AH, NO. NOT REALLY. WE'D BETTER JUST FLY OUT.

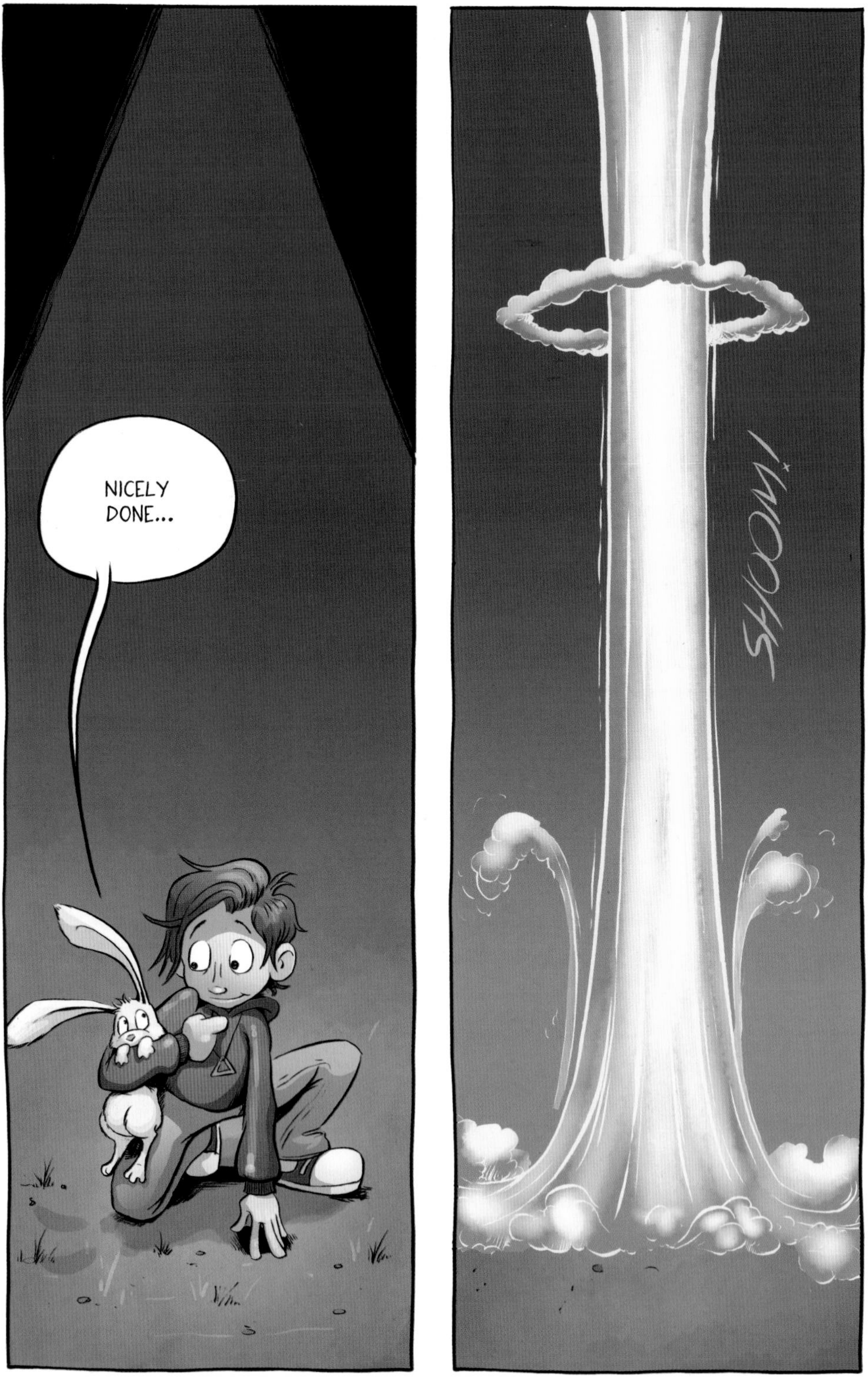
NICELY DONE...
SHOOM!

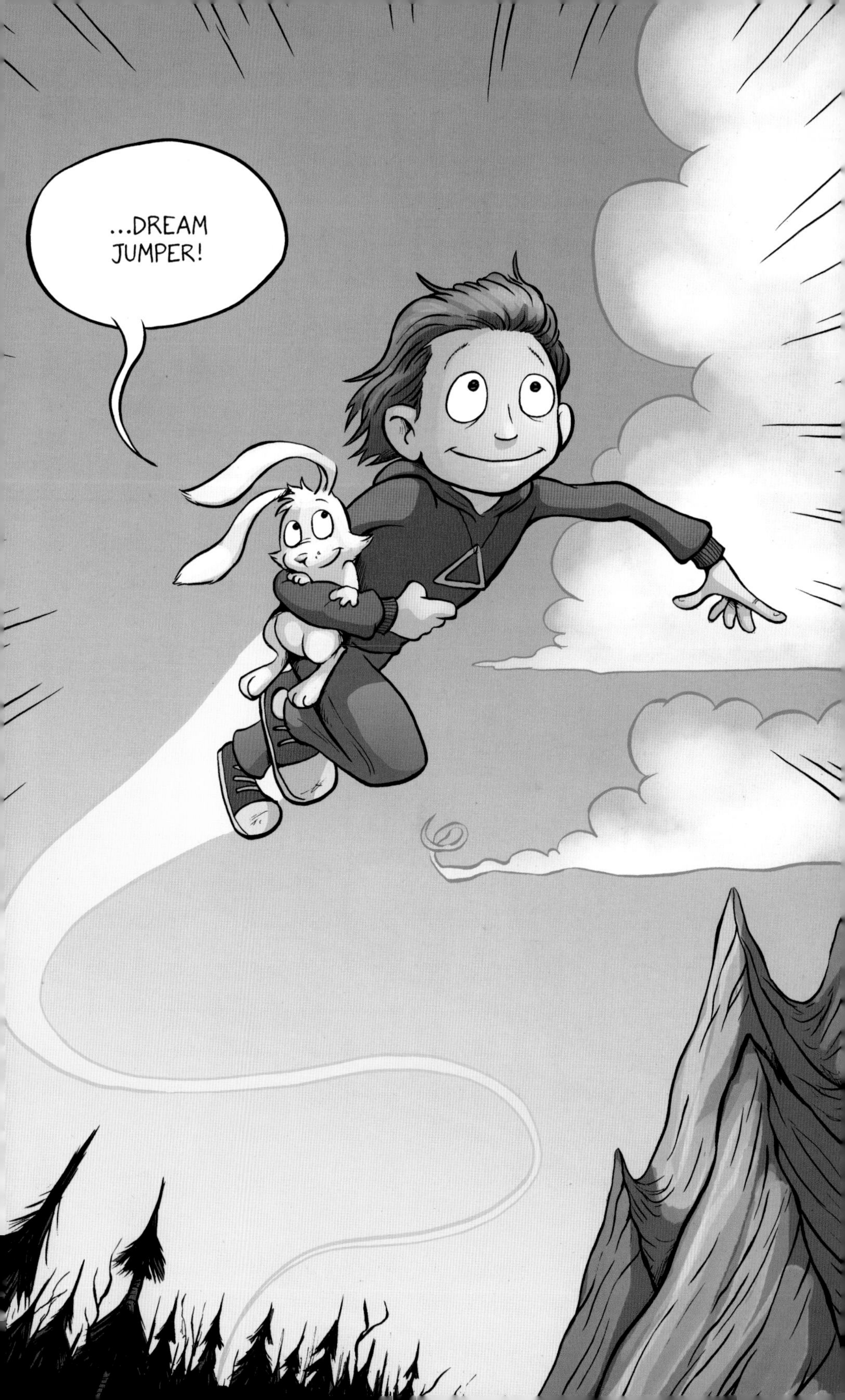
...DREAM JUMPER!

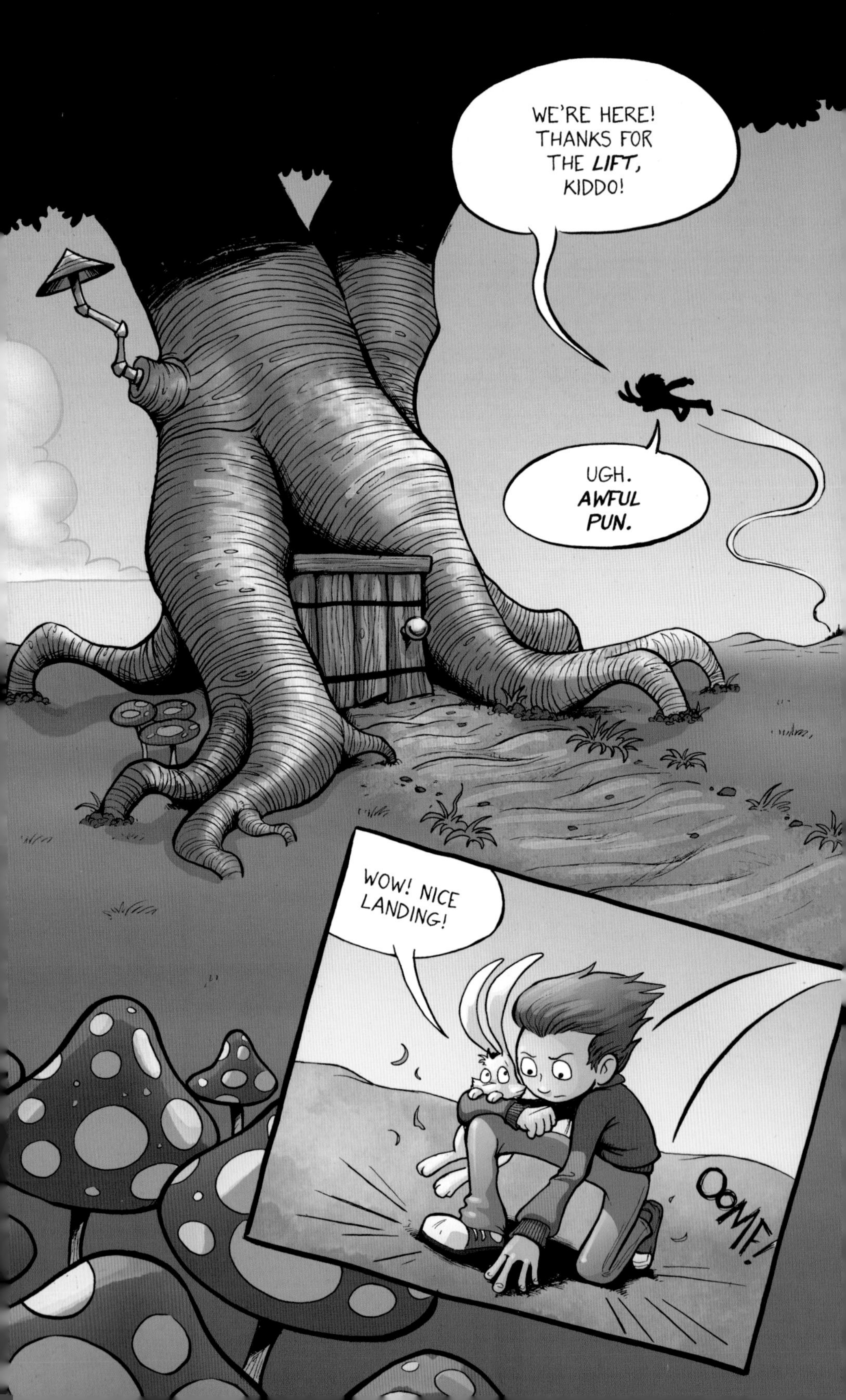
WE'RE HERE! THANKS FOR THE *LIFT,* KIDDO!
UGH. **AWFUL PUN.**
WOW! NICE LANDING!
OOMF!

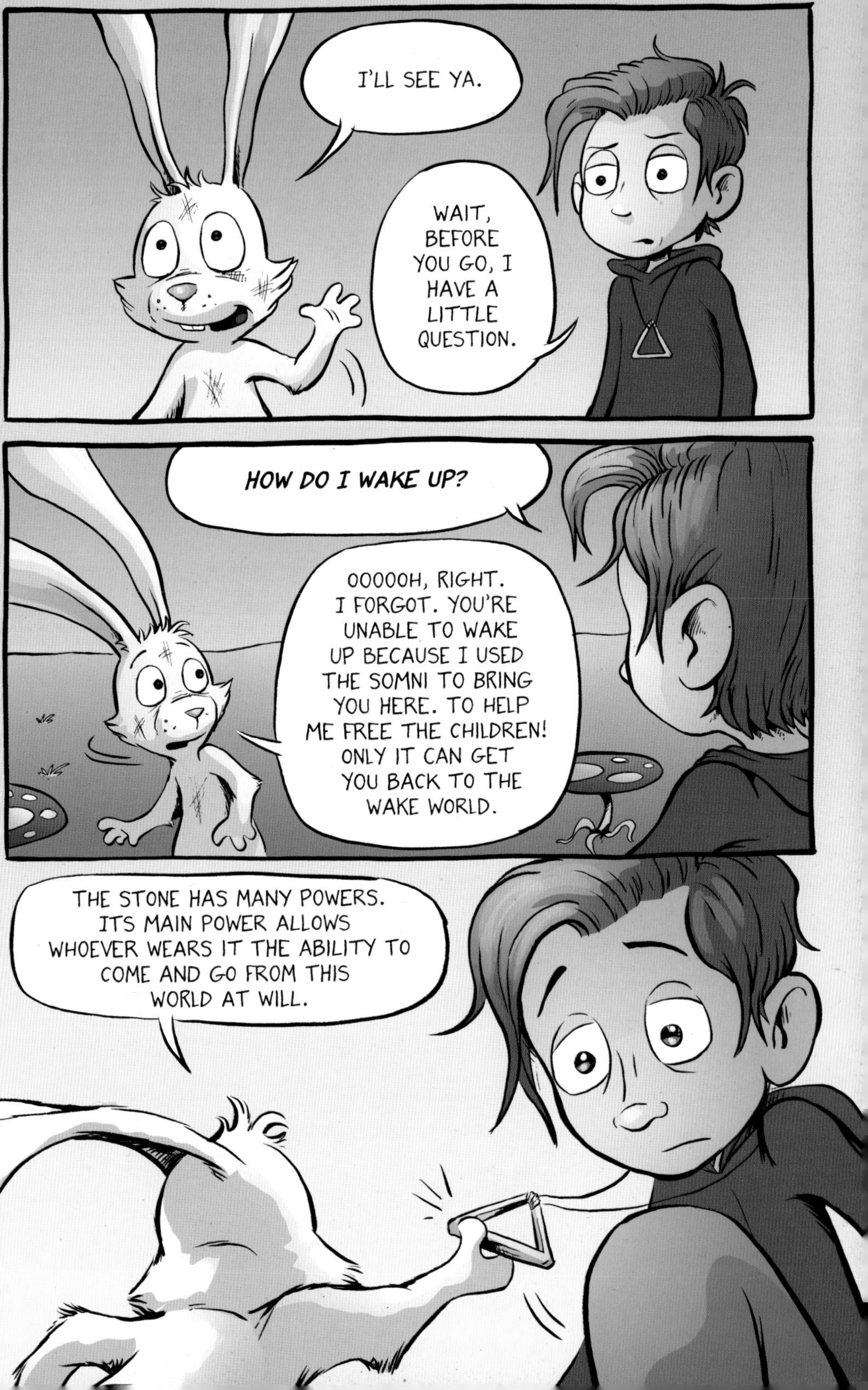
I'LL SEE YA.
WAIT, BEFORE YOU GO, I HAVE A LITTLE QUESTION.
HOW DO I WAKE UP?
OOOOOH, RIGHT. I FORGOT. YOU'RE UNABLE TO WAKE UP BECAUSE I USED THE SOMNI TO BRING YOU HERE. TO HELP ME FREE THE CHILDREN! ONLY IT CAN GET YOU BACK TO THE WAKE WORLD.
THE STONE HAS MANY POWERS. ITS MAIN POWER ALLOWS WHOEVER WEARS IT THE ABILITY TO COME AND GO FROM THIS WORLD AT WILL.

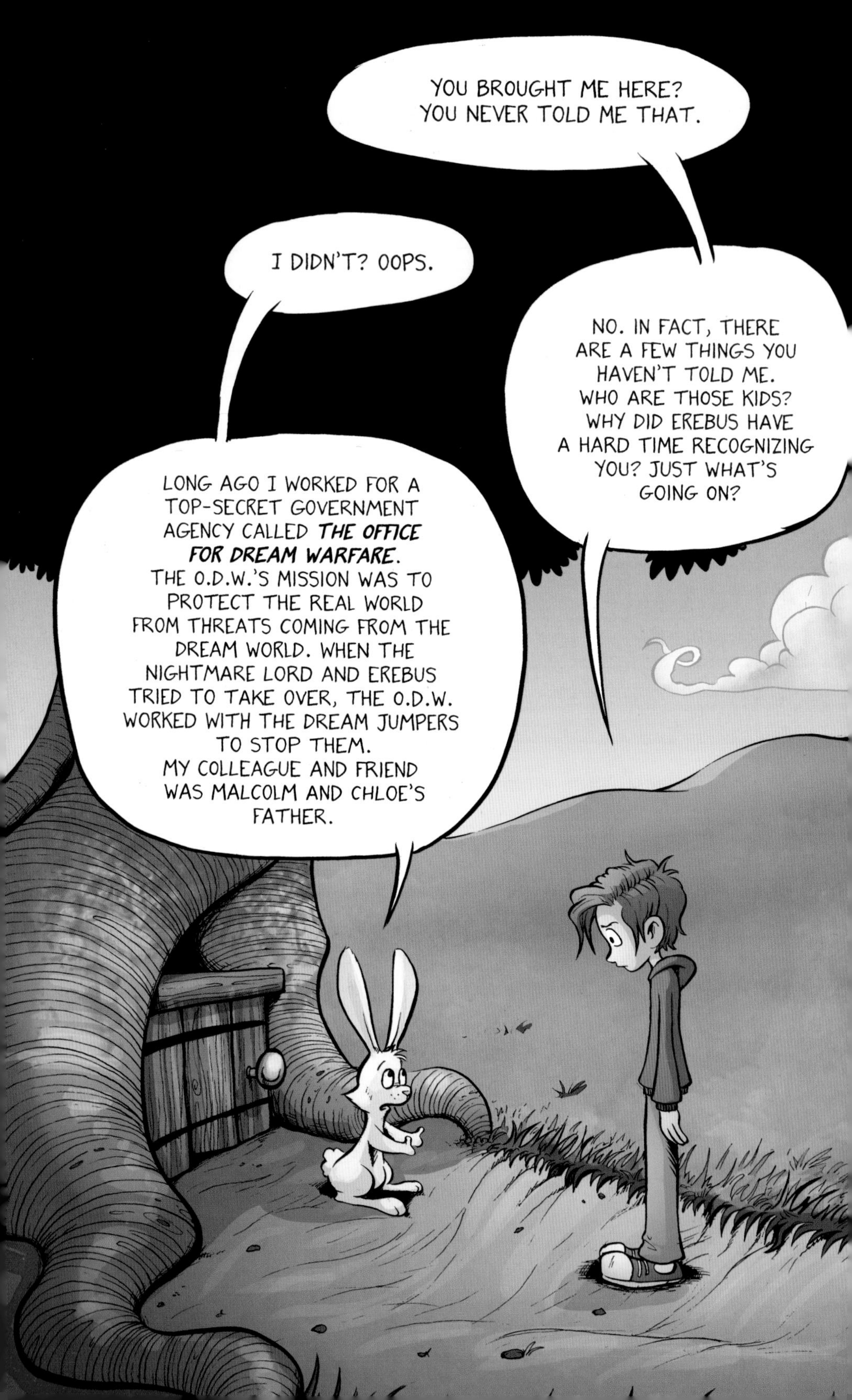

YOU BROUGHT ME HERE? YOU NEVER TOLD ME THAT.
I DIDN'T? OOPS.
NO. IN FACT, THERE ARE A FEW THINGS YOU HAVEN'T TOLD ME. WHO ARE THOSE KIDS? WHY DID EREBUS HAVE A HARD TIME RECOGNIZING YOU? JUST WHAT'S GOING ON?
LONG AGO I WORKED FOR A TOP-SECRET GOVERNMENT AGENCY CALLED ***THE OFFICE FOR DREAM WARFARE***. THE O.D.W.'S MISSION WAS TO PROTECT THE REAL WORLD FROM THREATS COMING FROM THE DREAM WORLD. WHEN THE NIGHTMARE LORD AND EREBUS TRIED TO TAKE OVER, THE O.D.W. WORKED WITH THE DREAM JUMPERS TO STOP THEM. MY COLLEAGUE AND FRIEND WAS MALCOLM AND CHLOE'S FATHER.

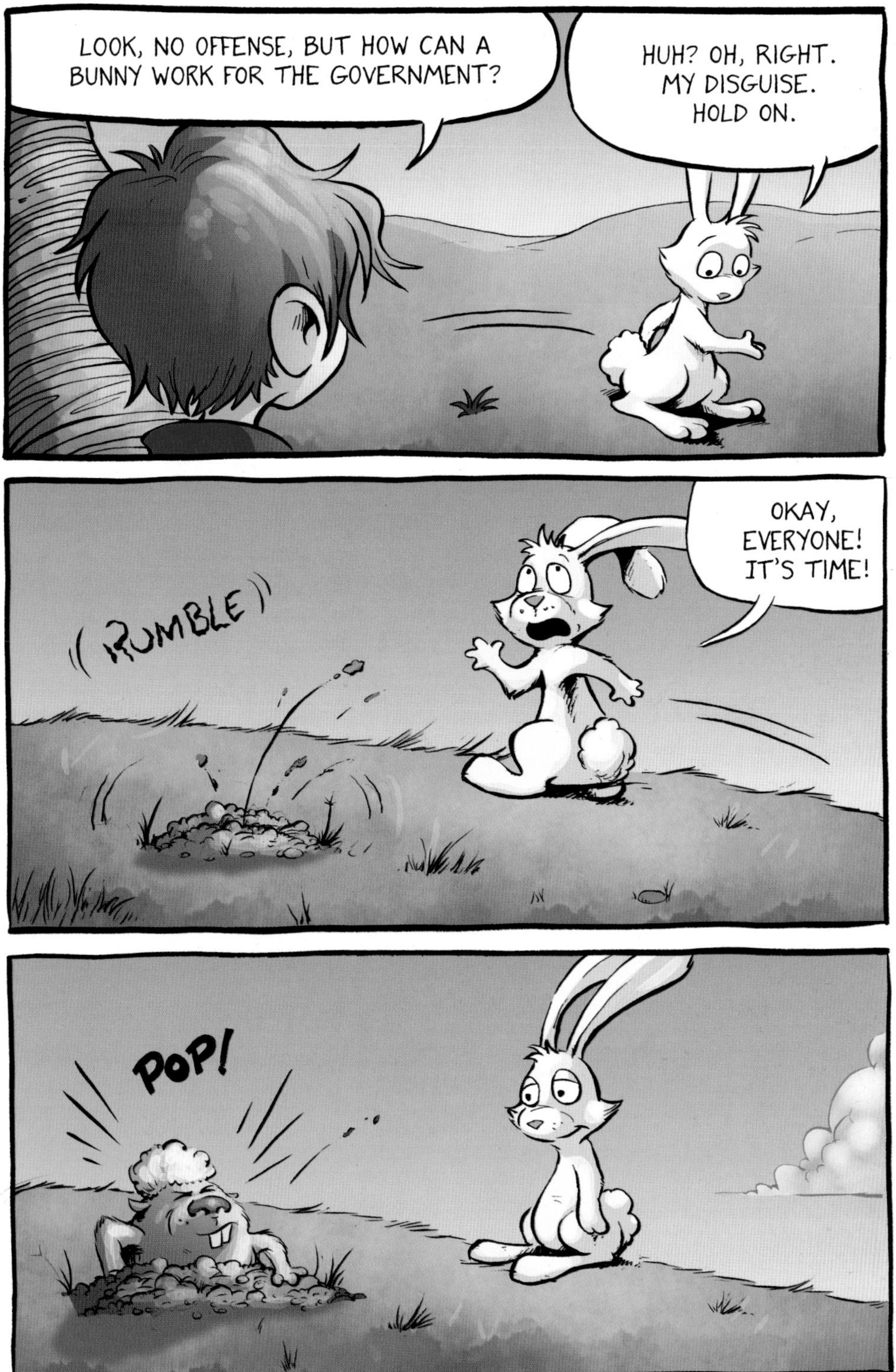
LOOK, NO OFFENSE, BUT HOW CAN A BUNNY WORK FOR THE GOVERNMENT?
HUH? OH, RIGHT. MY DISGUISE. HOLD ON.
RUMBLE
OKAY, EVERYONE! IT'S TIME!
POP!

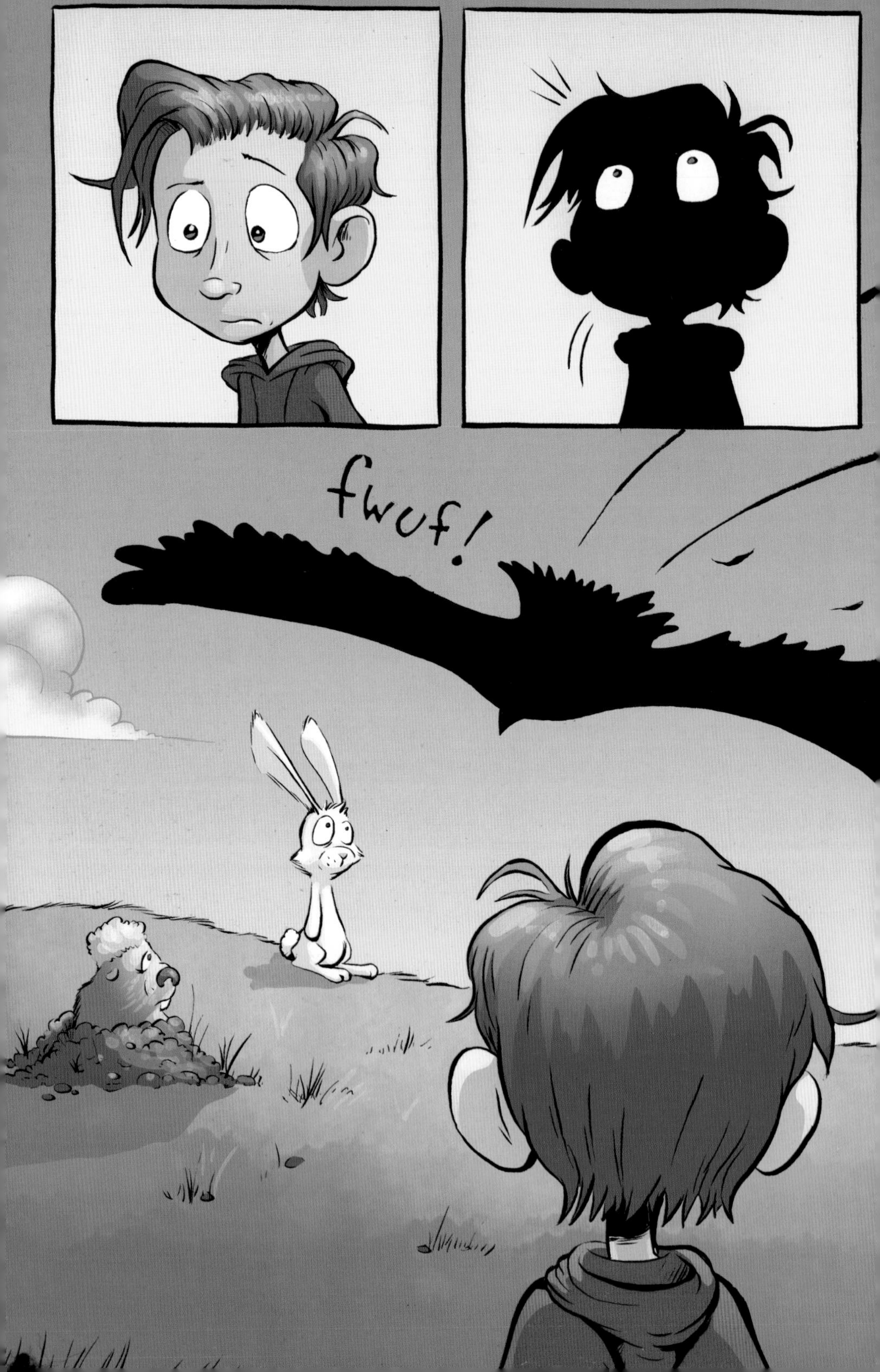
fwuf!

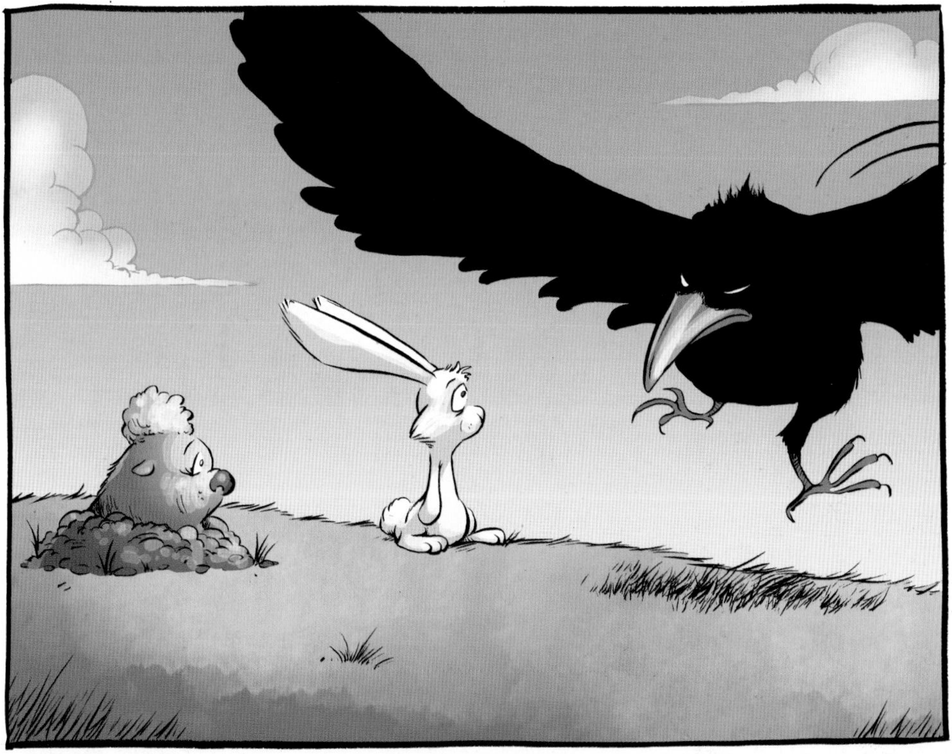

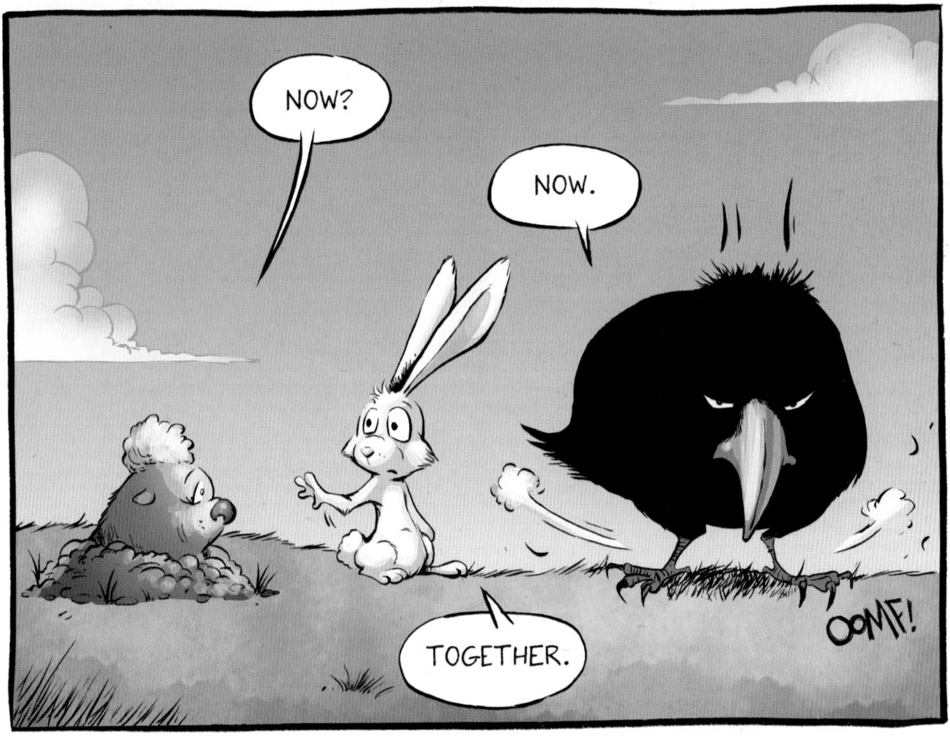
NOW?
NOW.
TOGETHER.
OOMF!

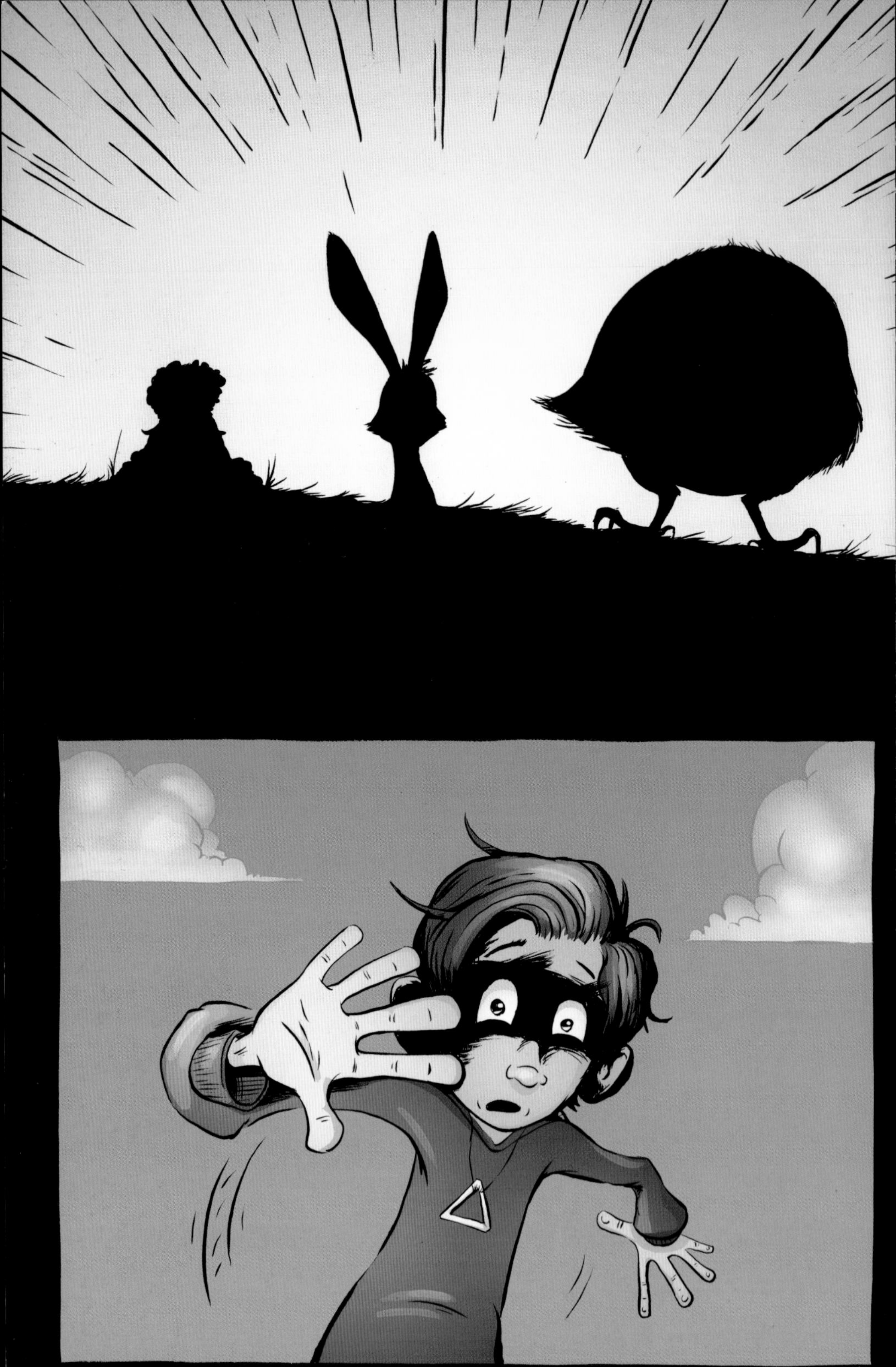

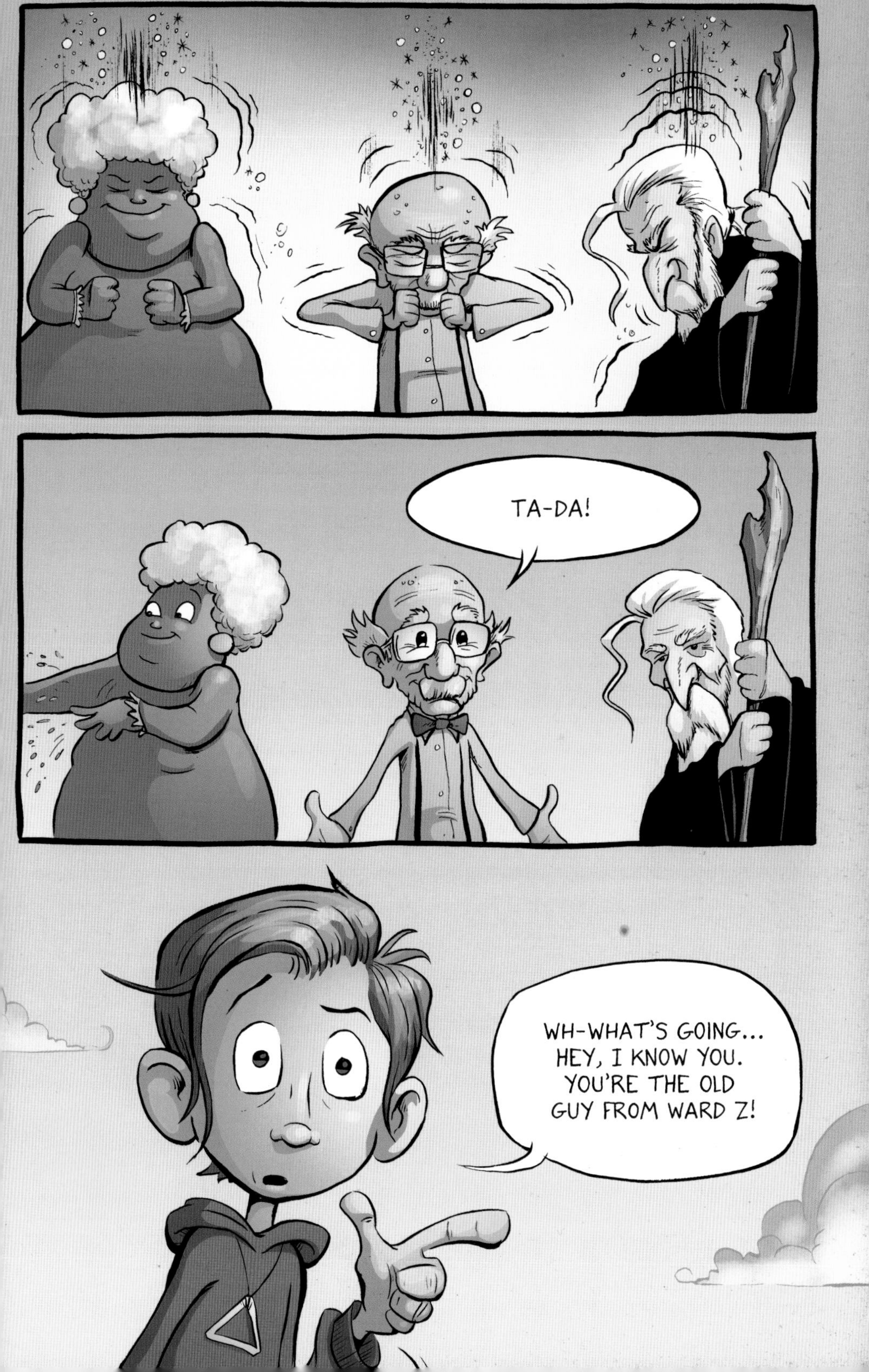
TA-DA!
WH-WHAT'S GOING... HEY, I KNOW YOU. YOU'RE THE OLD GUY FROM WARD Z!

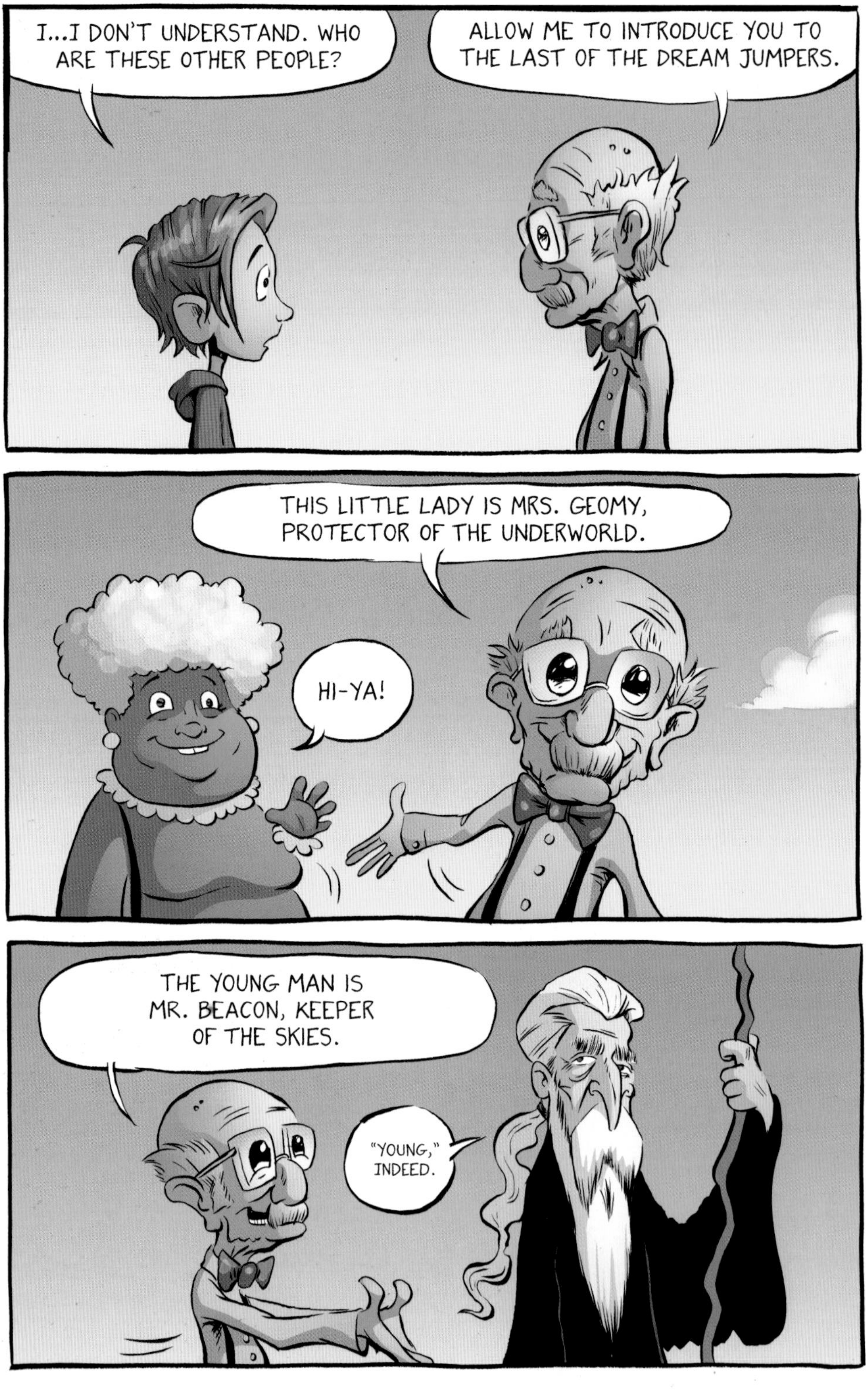
I...I DON'T UNDERSTAND. WHO ARE THESE OTHER PEOPLE?
ALLOW ME TO INTRODUCE YOU TO THE LAST OF THE DREAM JUMPERS.
THIS LITTLE LADY IS MRS. GEOMY, PROTECTOR OF THE UNDERWORLD.
HI-YA!
THE YOUNG MAN IS MR. BEACON, KEEPER OF THE SKIES.
"YOUNG," INDEED.

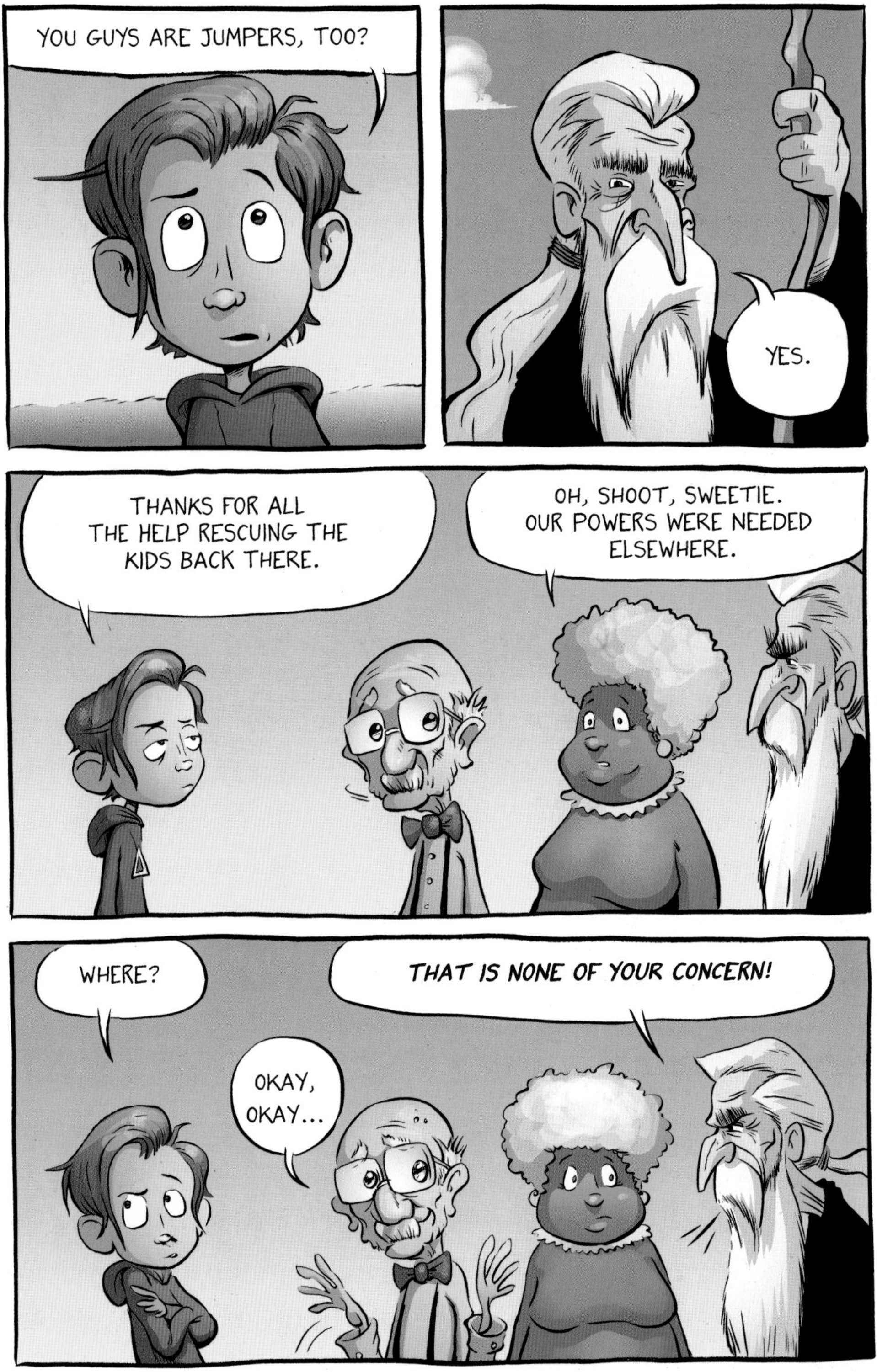

YOU GUYS ARE JUMPERS, TOO?
YES.
THANKS FOR ALL THE HELP RESCUING THE KIDS BACK THERE.
OH, SHOOT, SWEETIE. OUR POWERS WERE NEEDED ELSEWHERE.
WHERE?
THAT IS NONE OF YOUR CONCERN!
OKAY, OKAY...

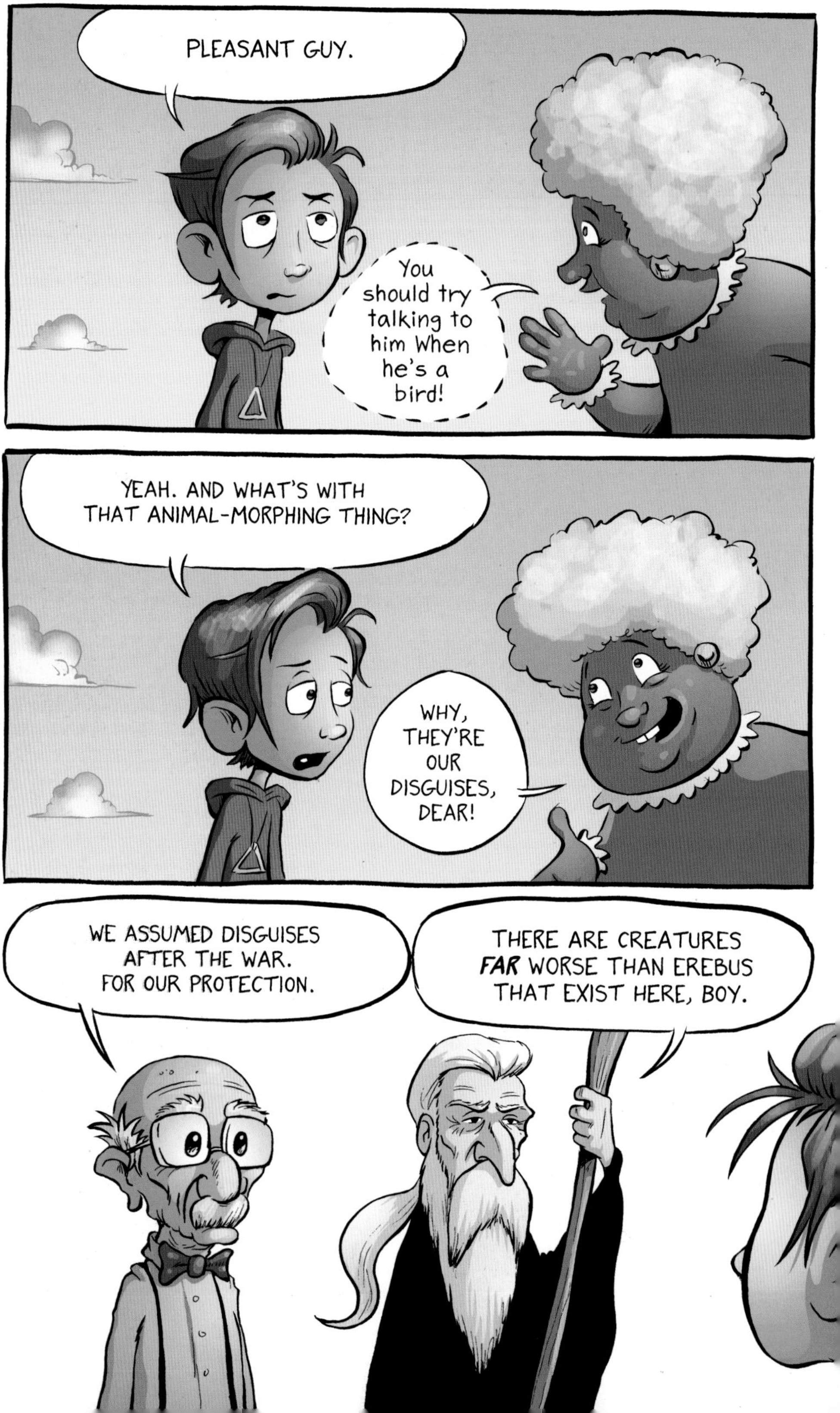
PLEASANT GUY.
You should try talking to him When he's a bird!
YEAH. AND WHAT'S WITH THAT ANIMAL-MORPHING THING?
WHY, THEY'RE OUR DISGUISES, DEAR!
WE ASSUMED DISGUISES AFTER THE WAR. FOR OUR PROTECTION.
THERE ARE CREATURES *FAR* WORSE THAN EREBUS THAT EXIST HERE, BOY.

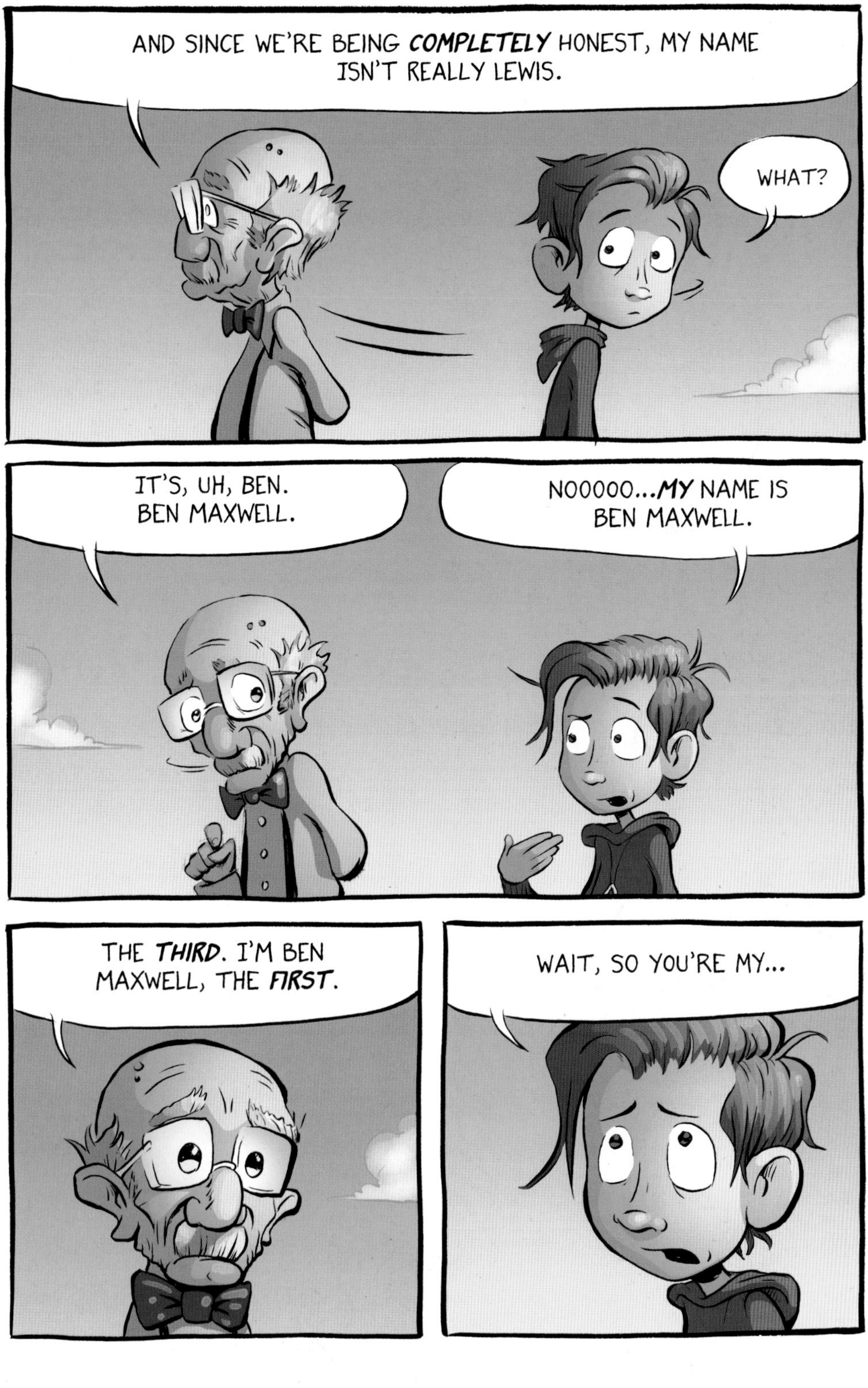
AND SINCE WE'RE BEING COMPLETELY HONEST, MY NAME ISN'T REALLY LEWIS.
WHAT?
IT'S, UH, BEN. BEN MAXWELL.
NOOOOO...MY NAME IS BEN MAXWELL.
THE THIRD. I'M BEN MAXWELL, THE FIRST.
WAIT, SO YOU'RE MY...

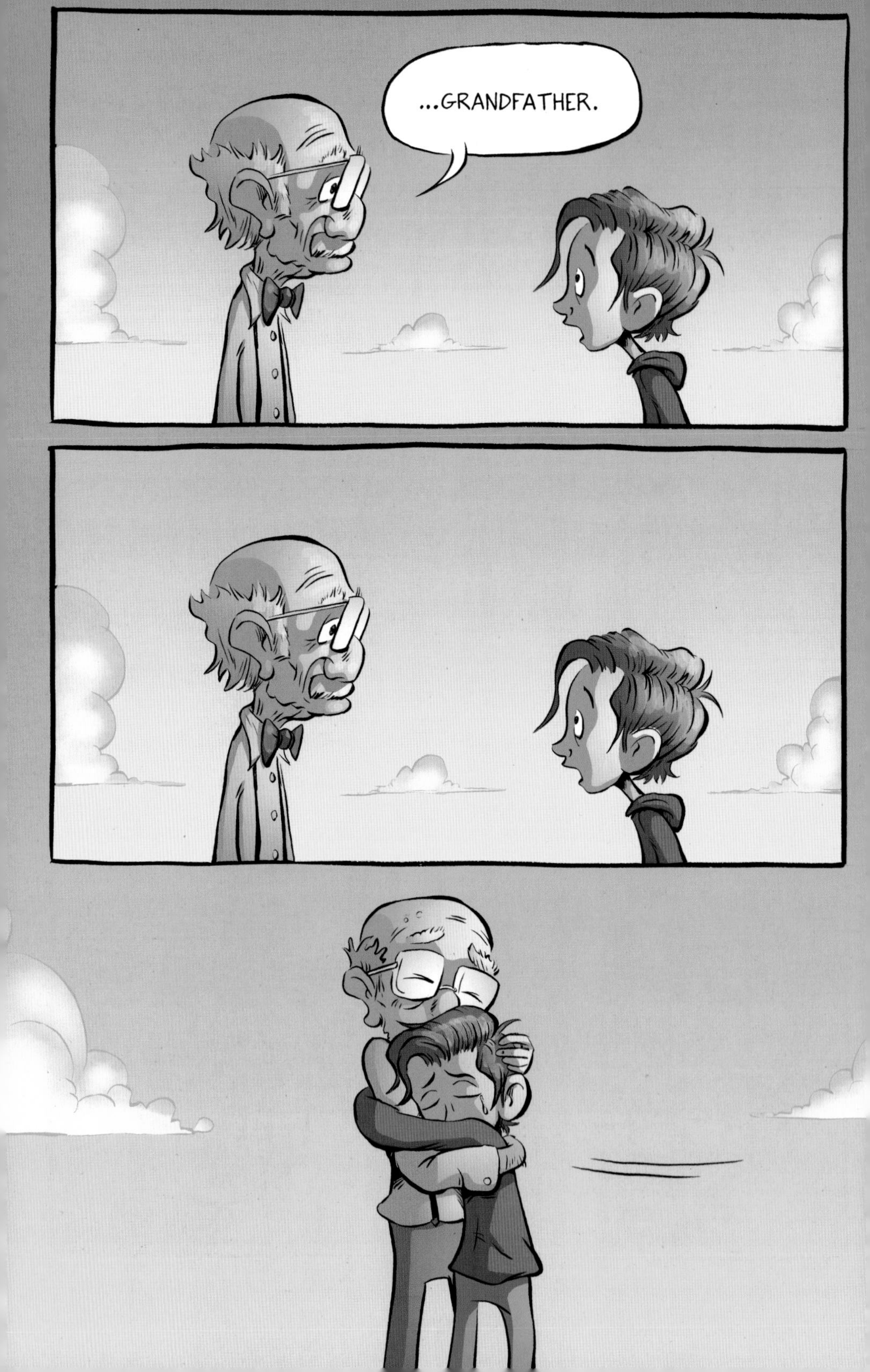
...GRANDFATHER.

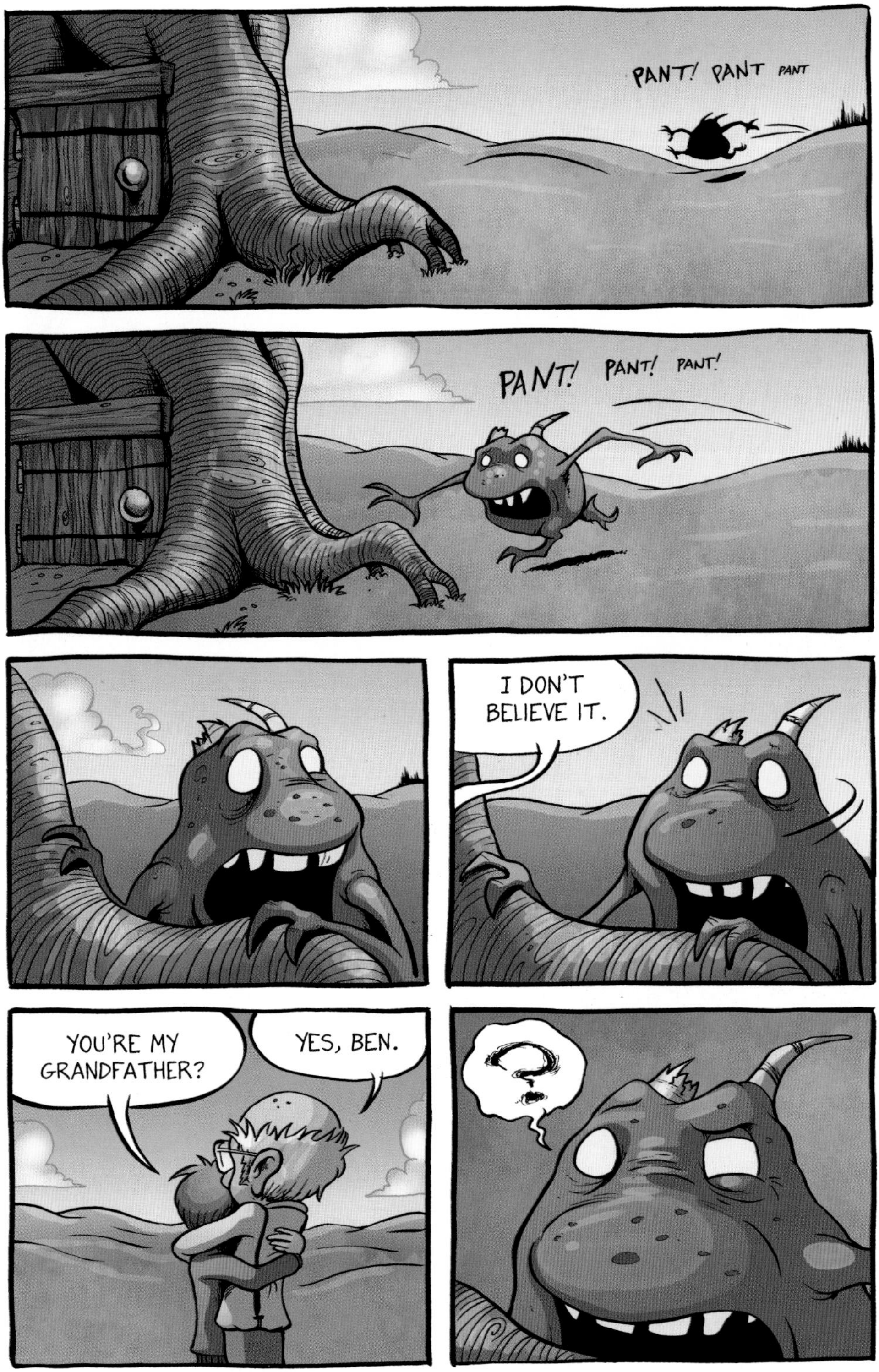
PANT! PANT PANT
PANT! PANT! PANT!
I DON'T BELIEVE IT.
YOU'RE MY GRANDFATHER?
YES, BEN.

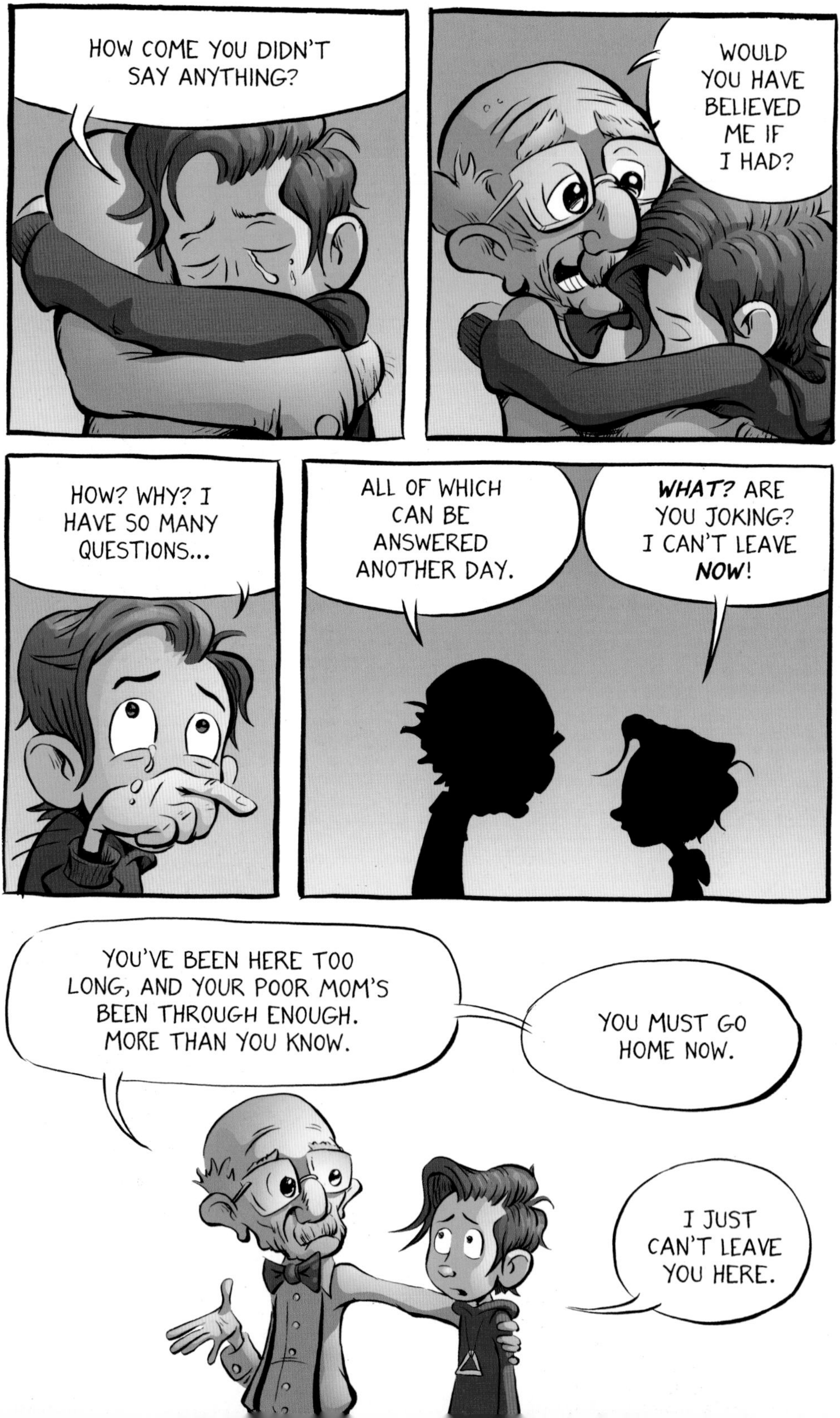
HOW COME YOU DIDN'T SAY ANYTHING?
WOULD YOU HAVE BELIEVED ME IF I HAD?
HOW? WHY? I HAVE SO MANY QUESTIONS...
ALL OF WHICH CAN BE ANSWERED ANOTHER DAY.
WHAT? ARE YOU JOKING? I CAN'T LEAVE NOW!
YOU'VE BEEN HERE TOO LONG, AND YOUR POOR MOM'S BEEN THROUGH ENOUGH. MORE THAN YOU KNOW.
YOU MUST GO HOME NOW.
I JUST CAN'T LEAVE YOU HERE.

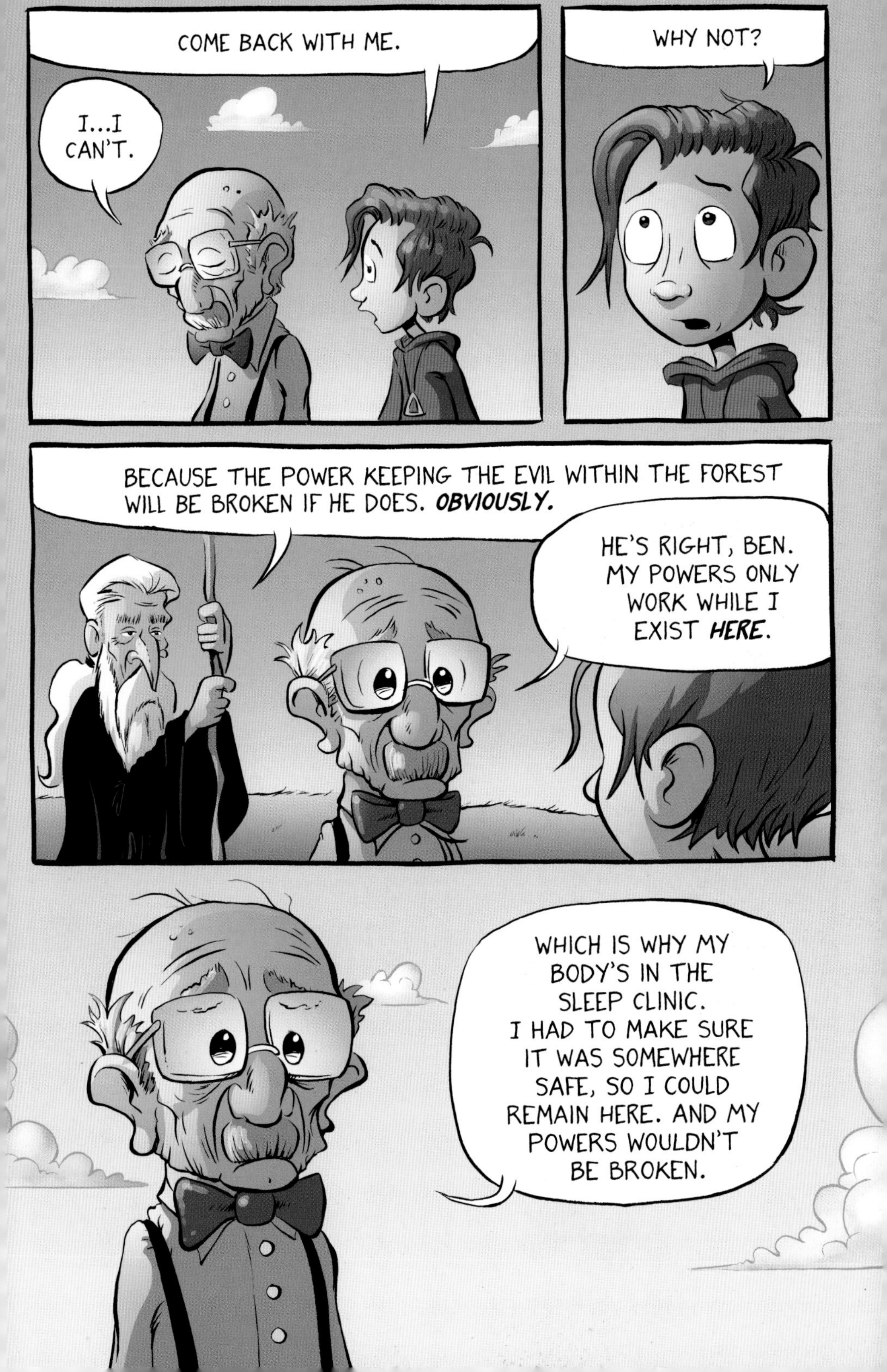
COME BACK WITH ME.
I...I CAN'T.
WHY NOT?
BECAUSE THE POWER KEEPING THE EVIL WITHIN THE FOREST WILL BE BROKEN IF HE DOES. OBVIOUSLY.
HE'S RIGHT, BEN. MY POWERS ONLY WORK WHILE I EXIST HERE.
WHICH IS WHY MY BODY'S IN THE SLEEP CLINIC. I HAD TO MAKE SURE IT WAS SOMEWHERE SAFE, SO I COULD REMAIN HERE. AND MY POWERS WOULDN'T BE BROKEN.

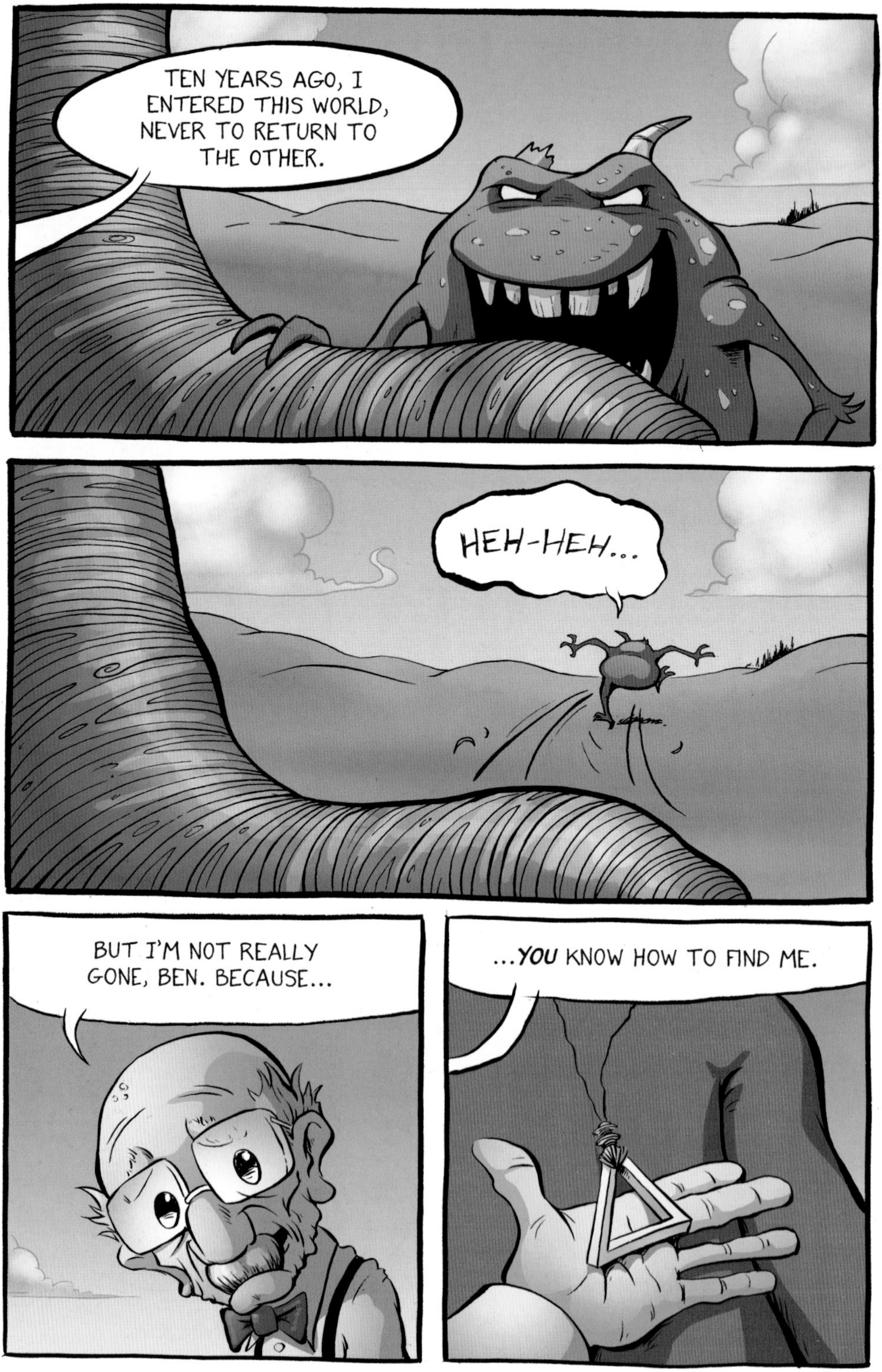
TEN YEARS AGO, I ENTERED THIS WORLD, NEVER TO RETURN TO THE OTHER.
HEH-HEH...
BUT I'M NOT REALLY GONE, BEN. BECAUSE...
...YOU KNOW HOW TO FIND ME.

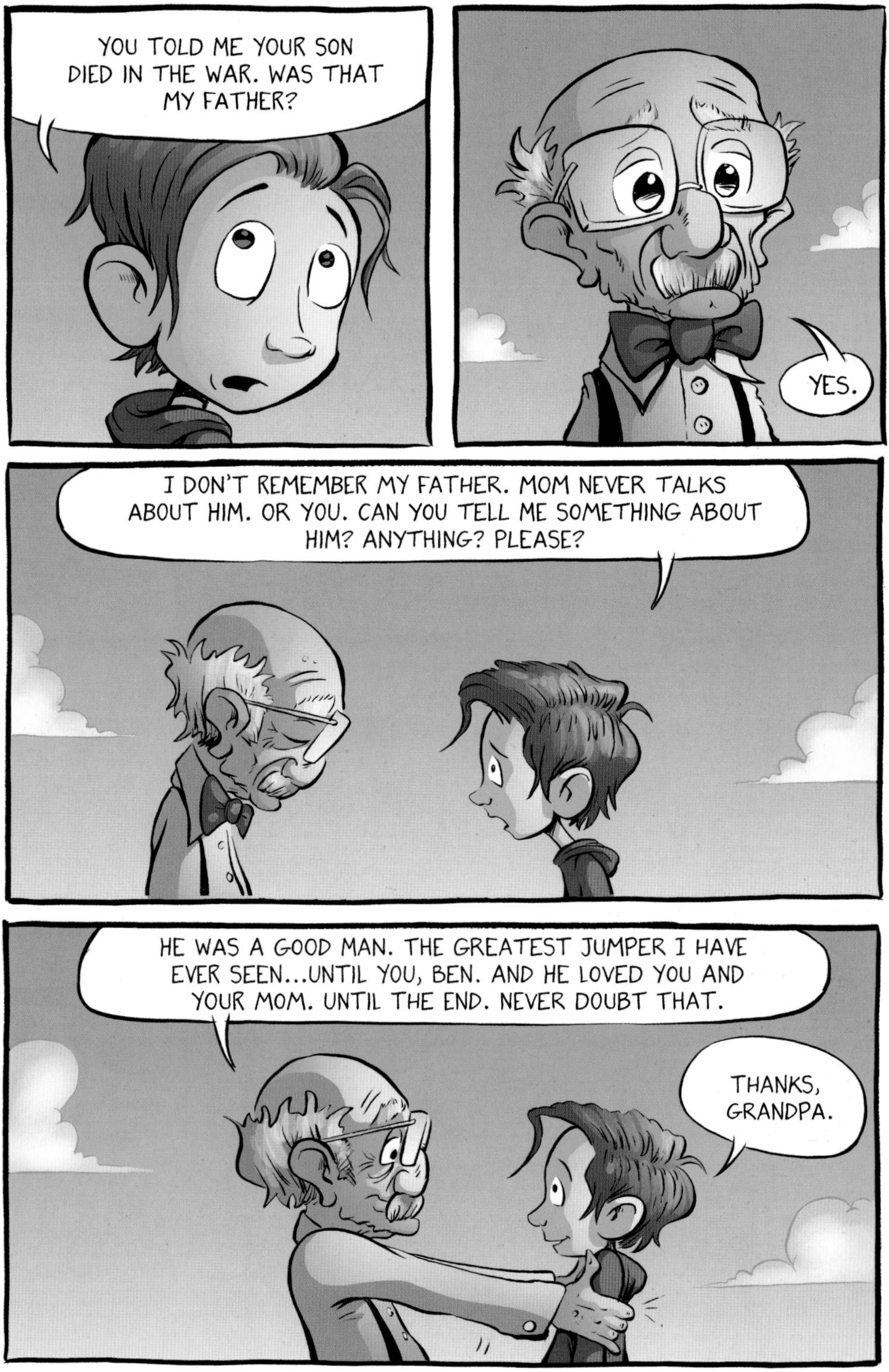
YOU TOLD ME YOUR SON DIED IN THE WAR. WAS THAT MY FATHER?
YES.
I DON'T REMEMBER MY FATHER. MOM NEVER TALKS ABOUT HIM. OR YOU. CAN YOU TELL ME SOMETHING ABOUT HIM? ANYTHING? PLEASE?
HE WAS A GOOD MAN. THE GREATEST JUMPER I HAVE EVER SEEN...UNTIL YOU, BEN. AND HE LOVED YOU AND YOUR MOM. UNTIL THE END. NEVER DOUBT THAT.
THANKS, GRANDPA.

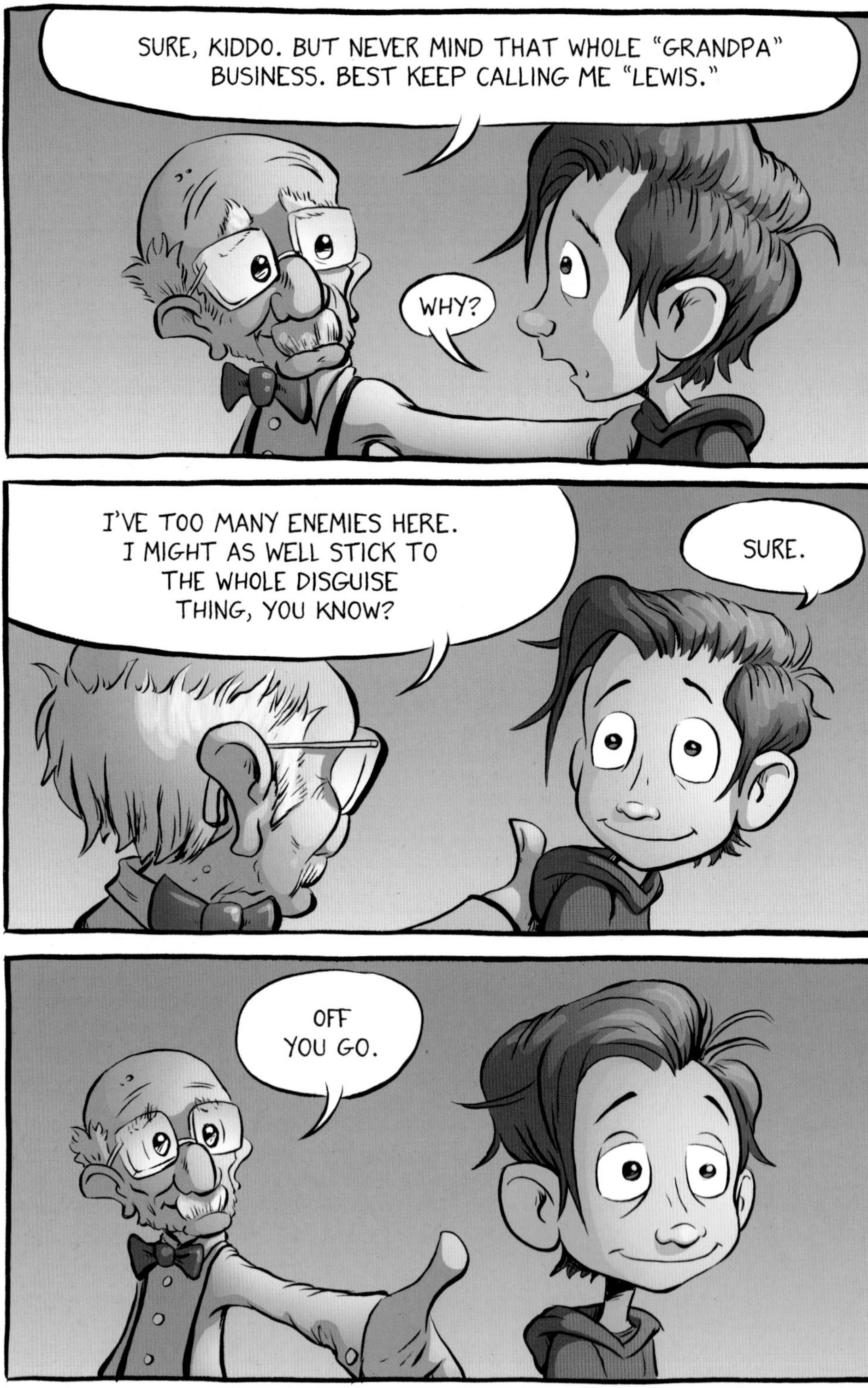
SURE, KIDDO. BUT NEVER MIND THAT WHOLE "GRANDPA" BUSINESS. BEST KEEP CALLING ME "LEWIS."
WHY?
I'VE TOO MANY ENEMIES HERE. I MIGHT AS WELL STICK TO THE WHOLE DISGUISE THING, YOU KNOW?
SURE.
OFF YOU GO.

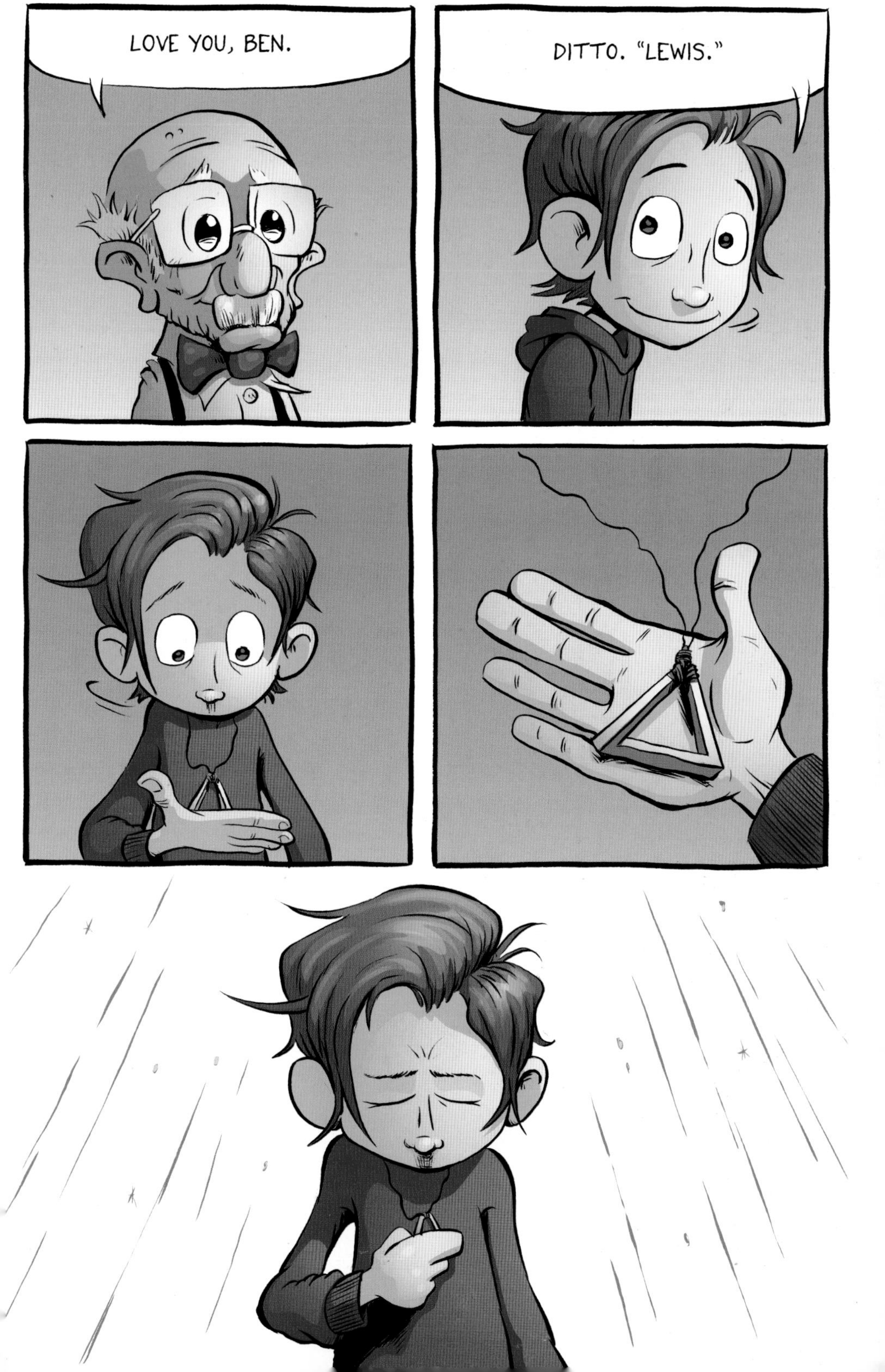
LOVE YOU, BEN.
DITTO. "LEWIS."

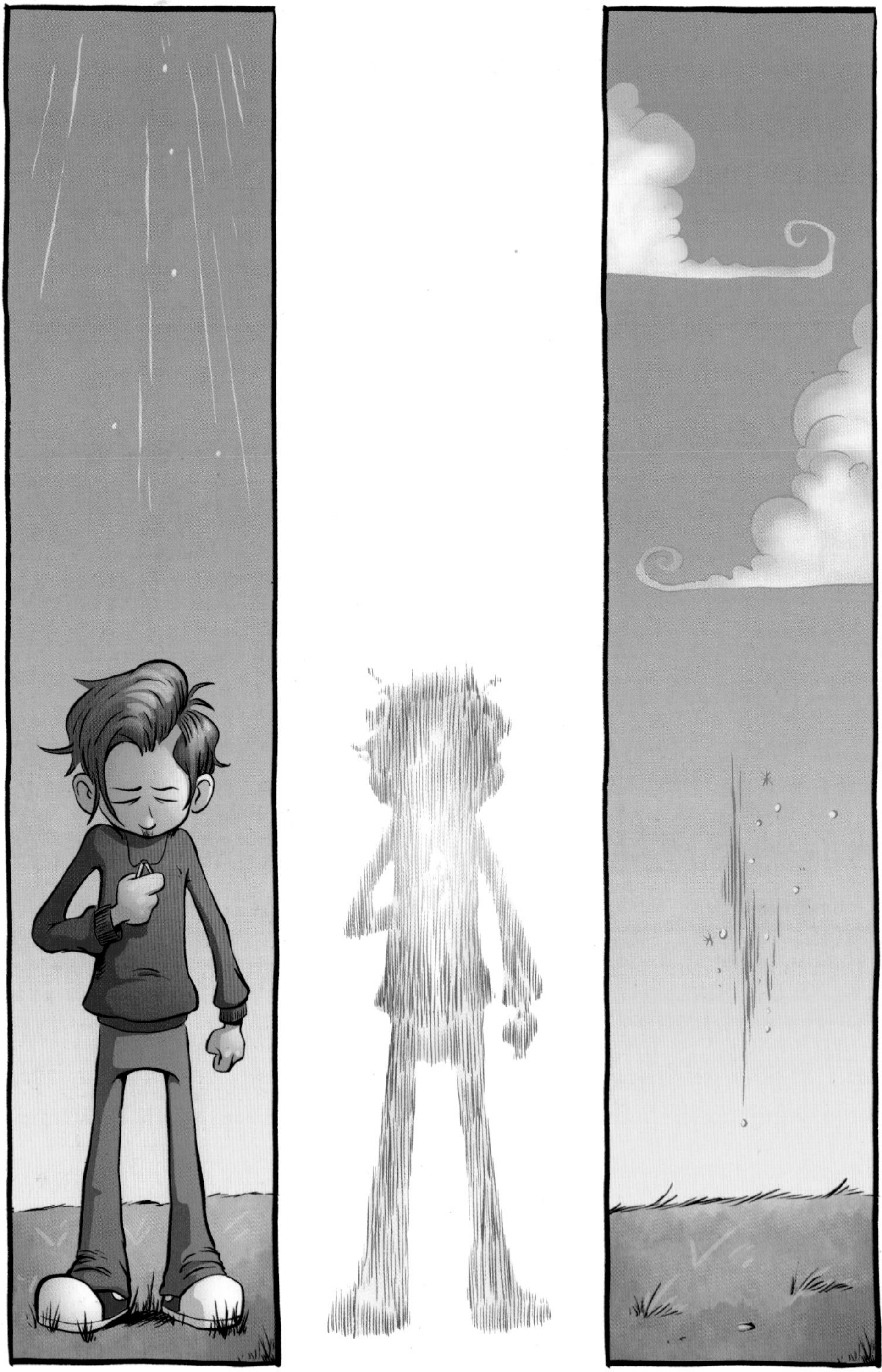

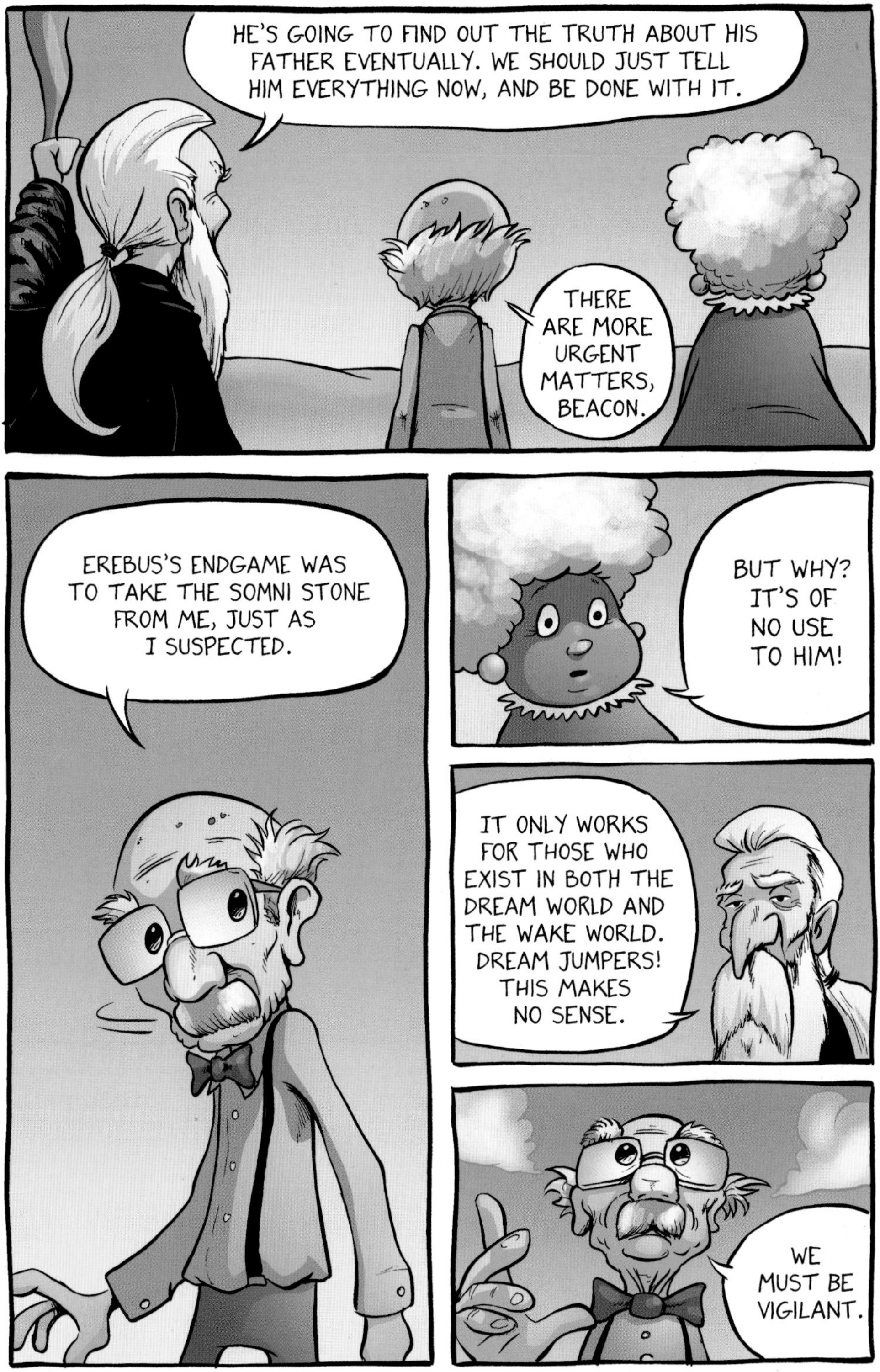
HE'S GOING TO FIND OUT THE TRUTH ABOUT HIS FATHER EVENTUALLY. WE SHOULD JUST TELL HIM EVERYTHING NOW, AND BE DONE WITH IT.
THERE ARE MORE URGENT MATTERS, BEACON.
EREBUS'S ENDGAME WAS TO TAKE THE SOMNI STONE FROM ME, JUST AS I SUSPECTED.
BUT WHY? IT'S OF NO USE TO HIM!
IT ONLY WORKS FOR THOSE WHO EXIST IN BOTH THE DREAM WORLD AND THE WAKE WORLD. DREAM JUMPERS! THIS MAKES NO SENSE.
WE MUST BE VIGILANT.

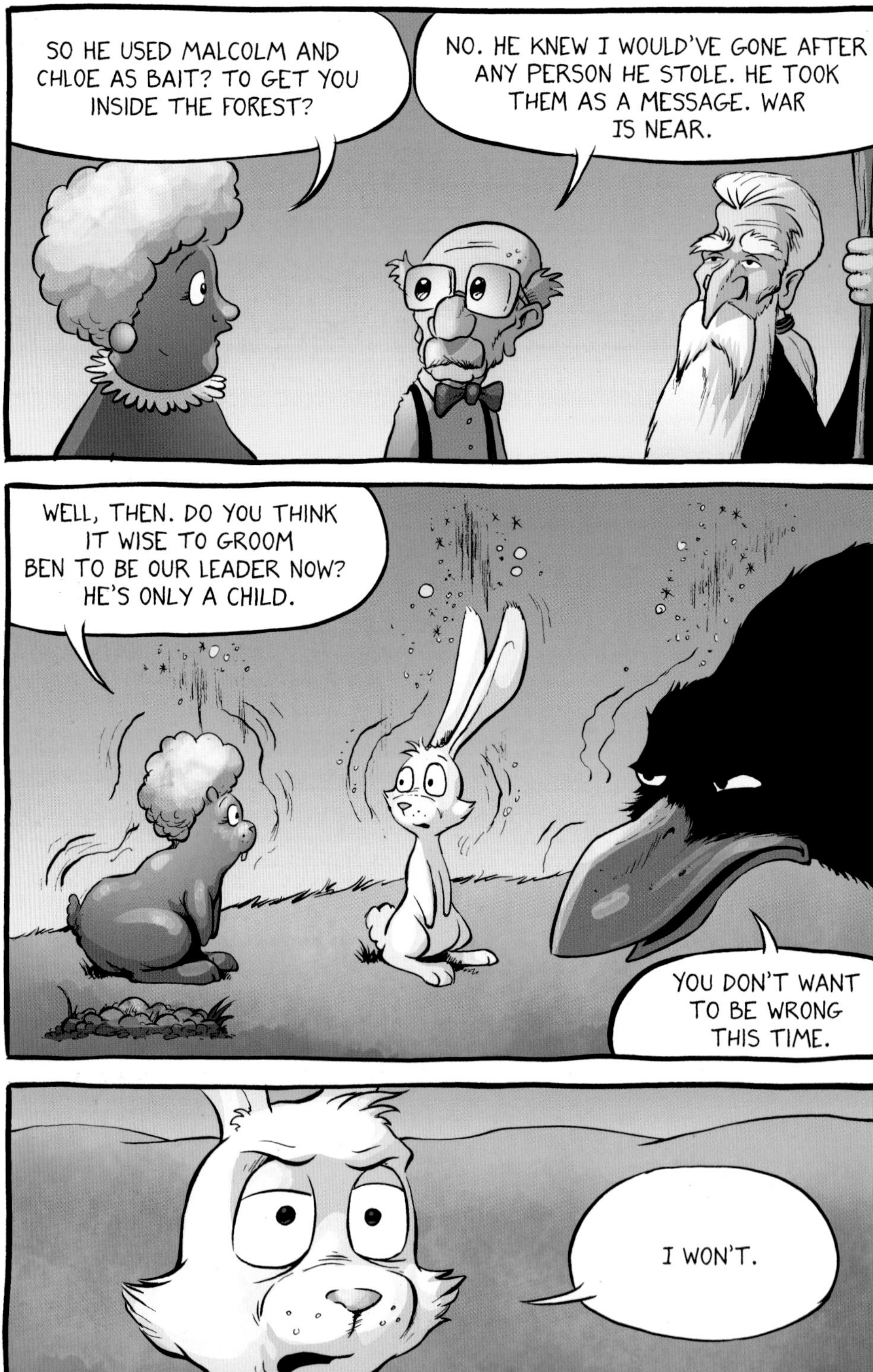
SO HE USED MALCOLM AND CHLOE AS BAIT? TO GET YOU INSIDE THE FOREST?
NO. HE KNEW I WOULD'VE GONE AFTER ANY PERSON HE STOLE. HE TOOK THEM AS A MESSAGE. WAR IS NEAR.
WELL, THEN. DO YOU THINK IT WISE TO GROOM BEN TO BE OUR LEADER NOW? HE'S ONLY A CHILD.
YOU DON'T WANT TO BE WRONG THIS TIME.
I WON'T.

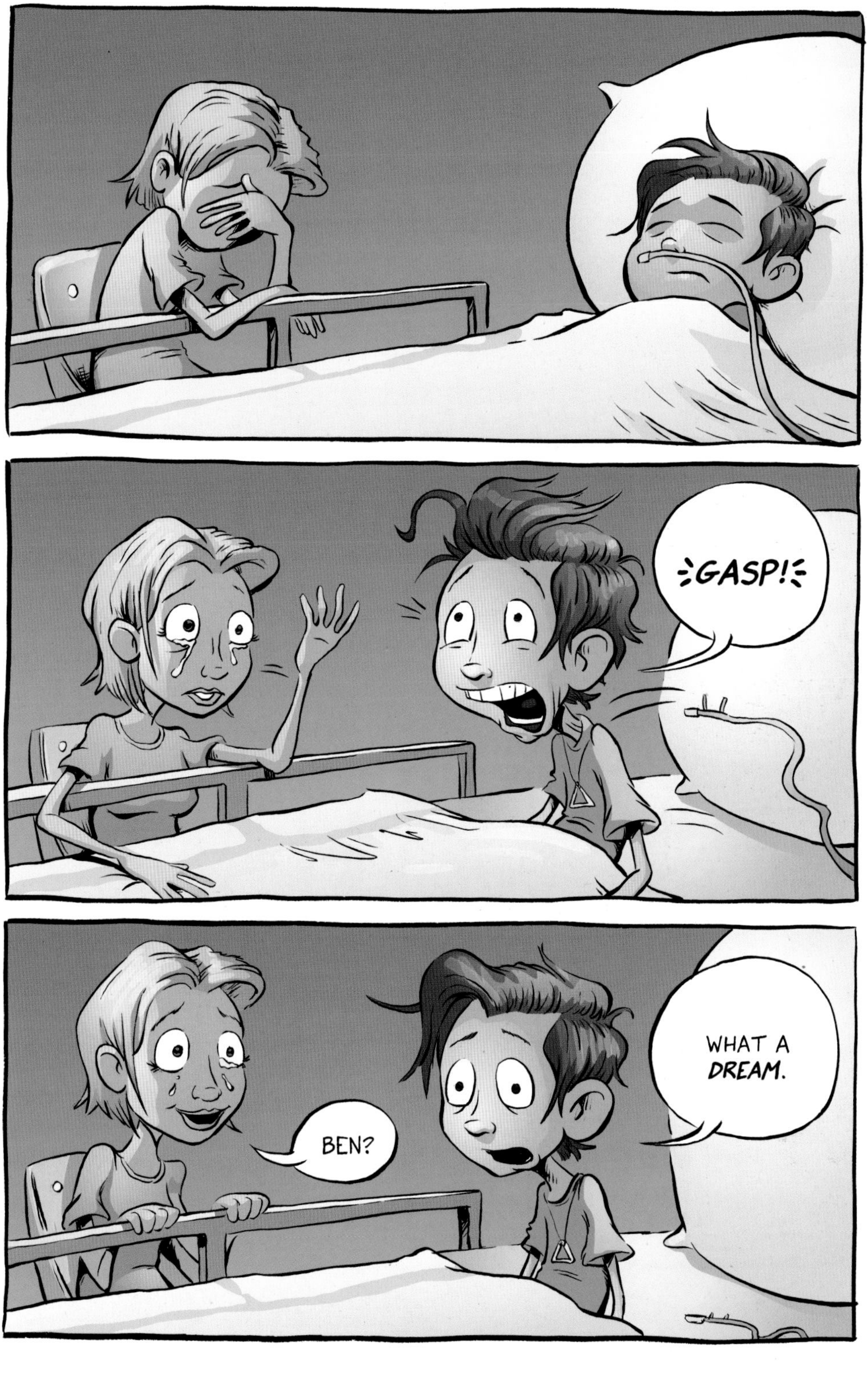
GASP!
BEN?
WHAT A DREAM.

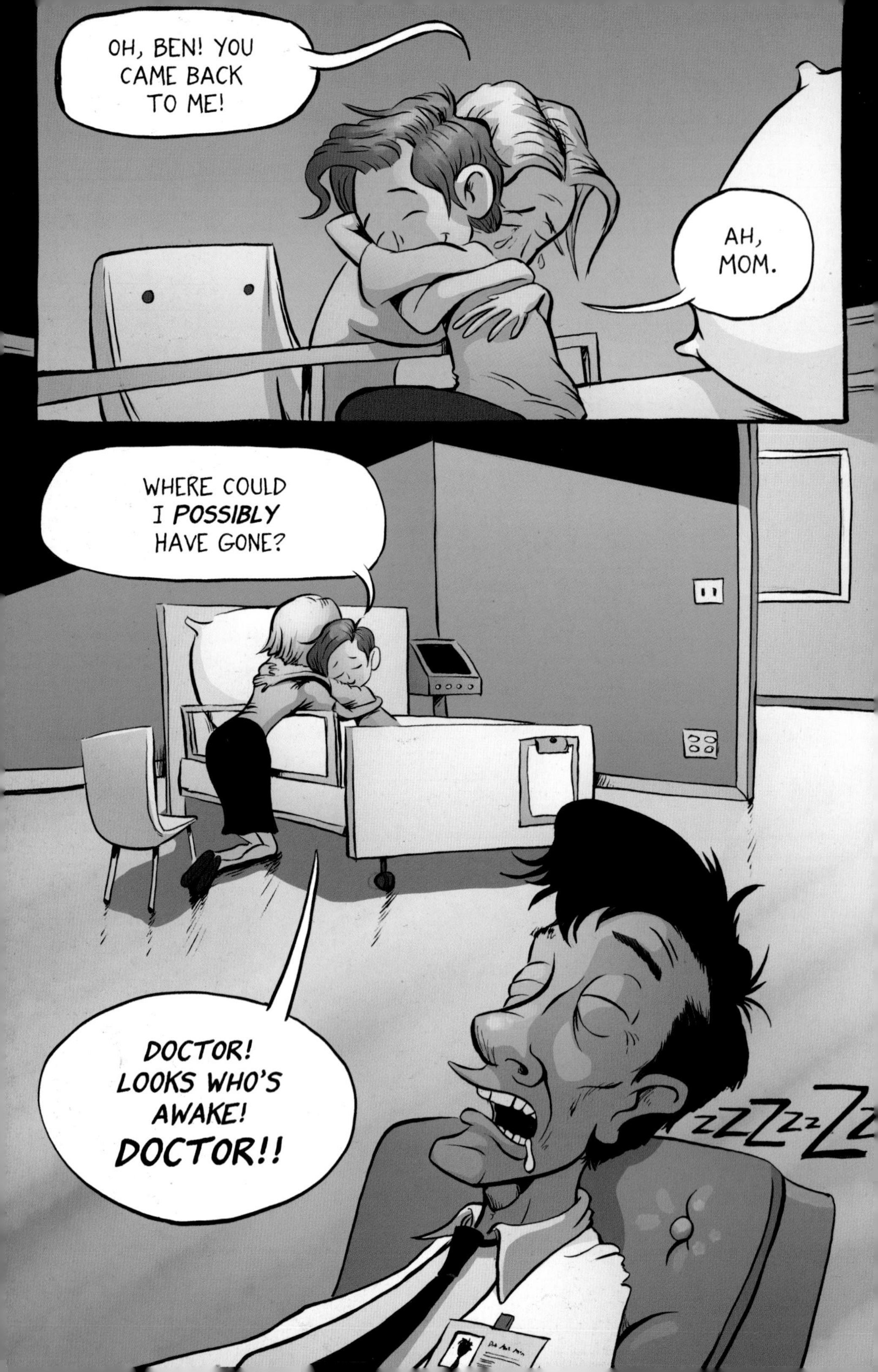

OH, BEN! YOU CAME BACK TO ME!
AH, MOM.
WHERE COULD I *POSSIBLY* HAVE GONE?
DOCTOR! LOOKS WHO'S AWAKE! **DOCTOR!!**
ZZZZZZZ

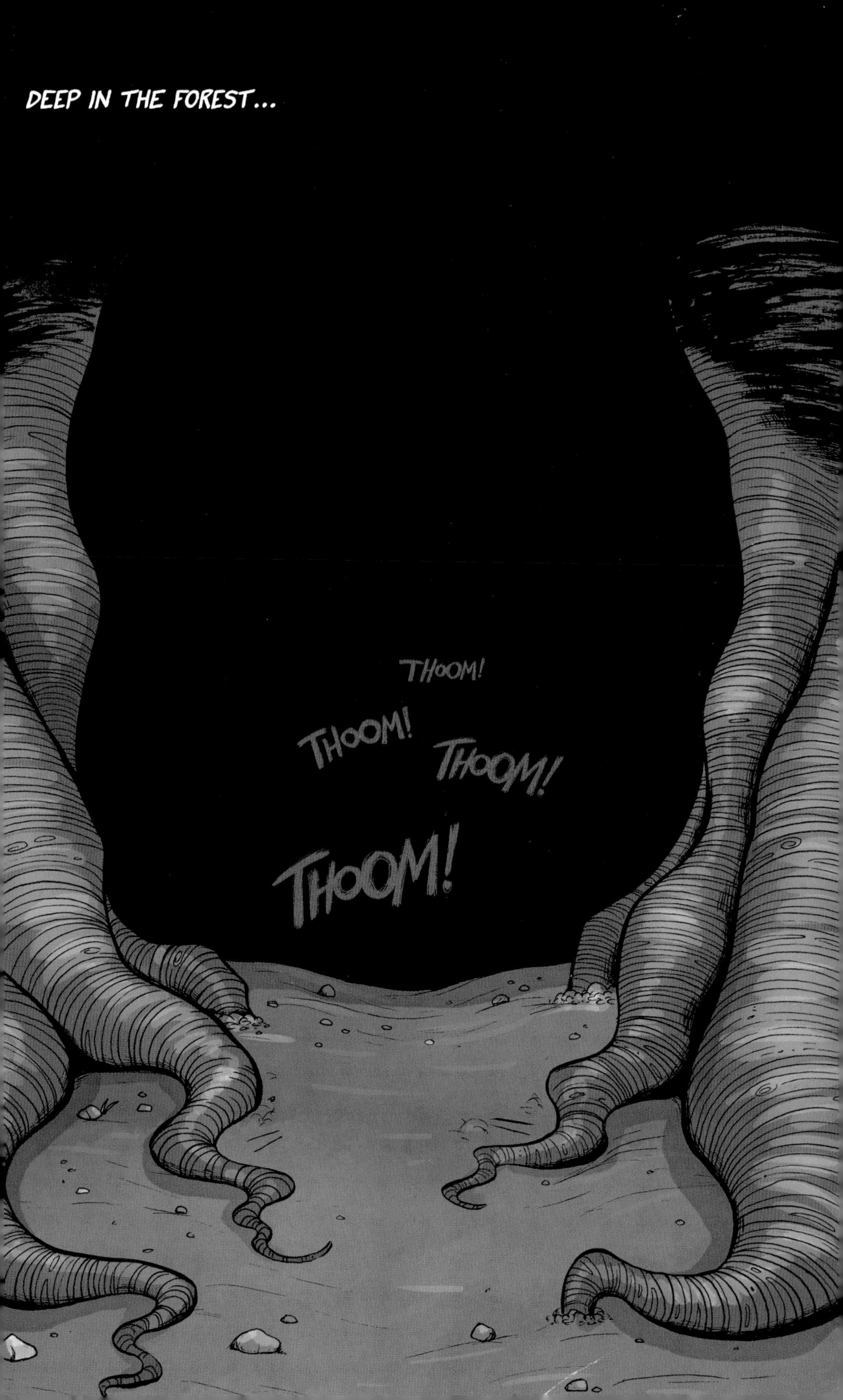
DEEP IN THE FOREST...
THOOM!
THOOM!
THOOM!
THOOM!

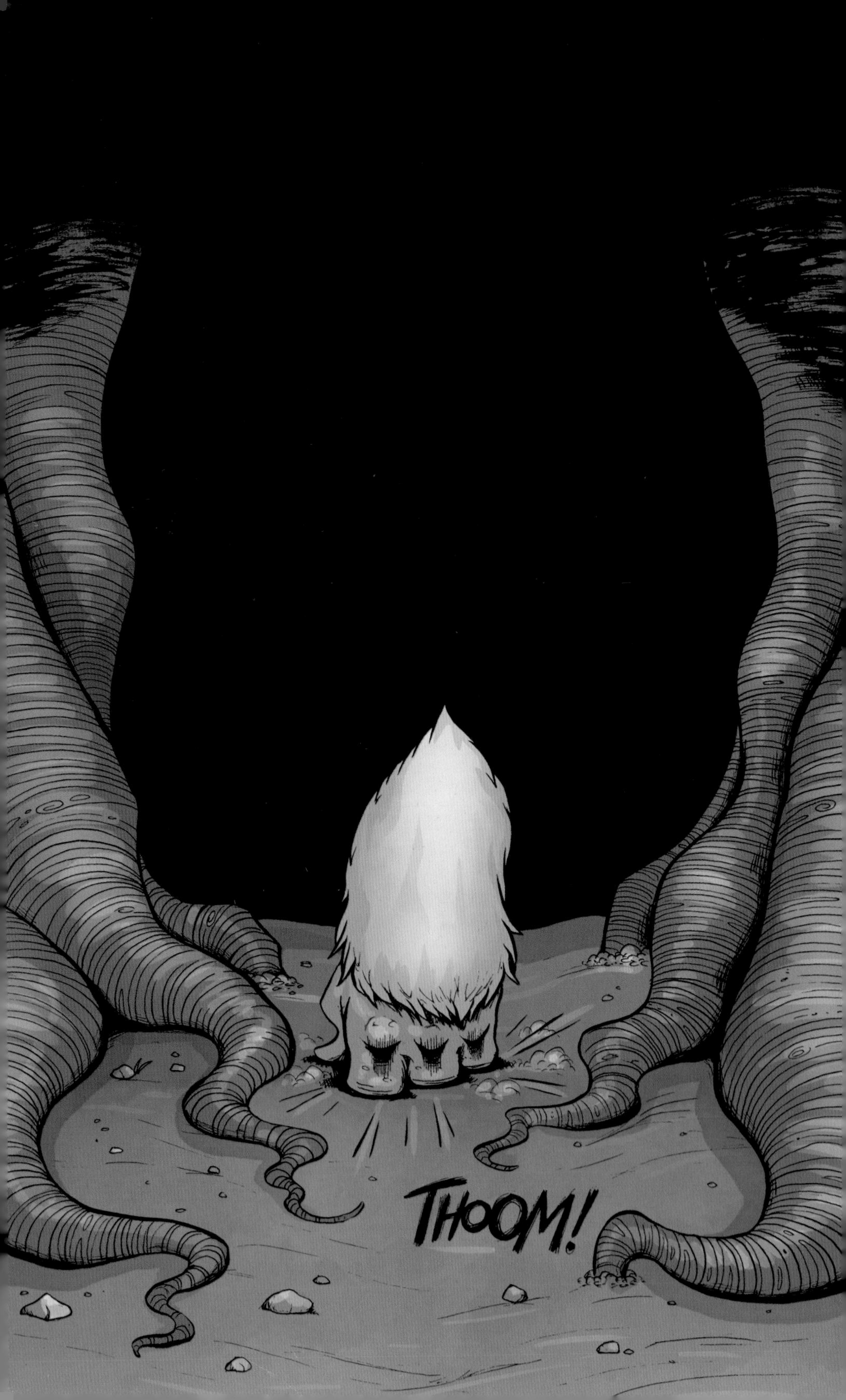
THOOM!

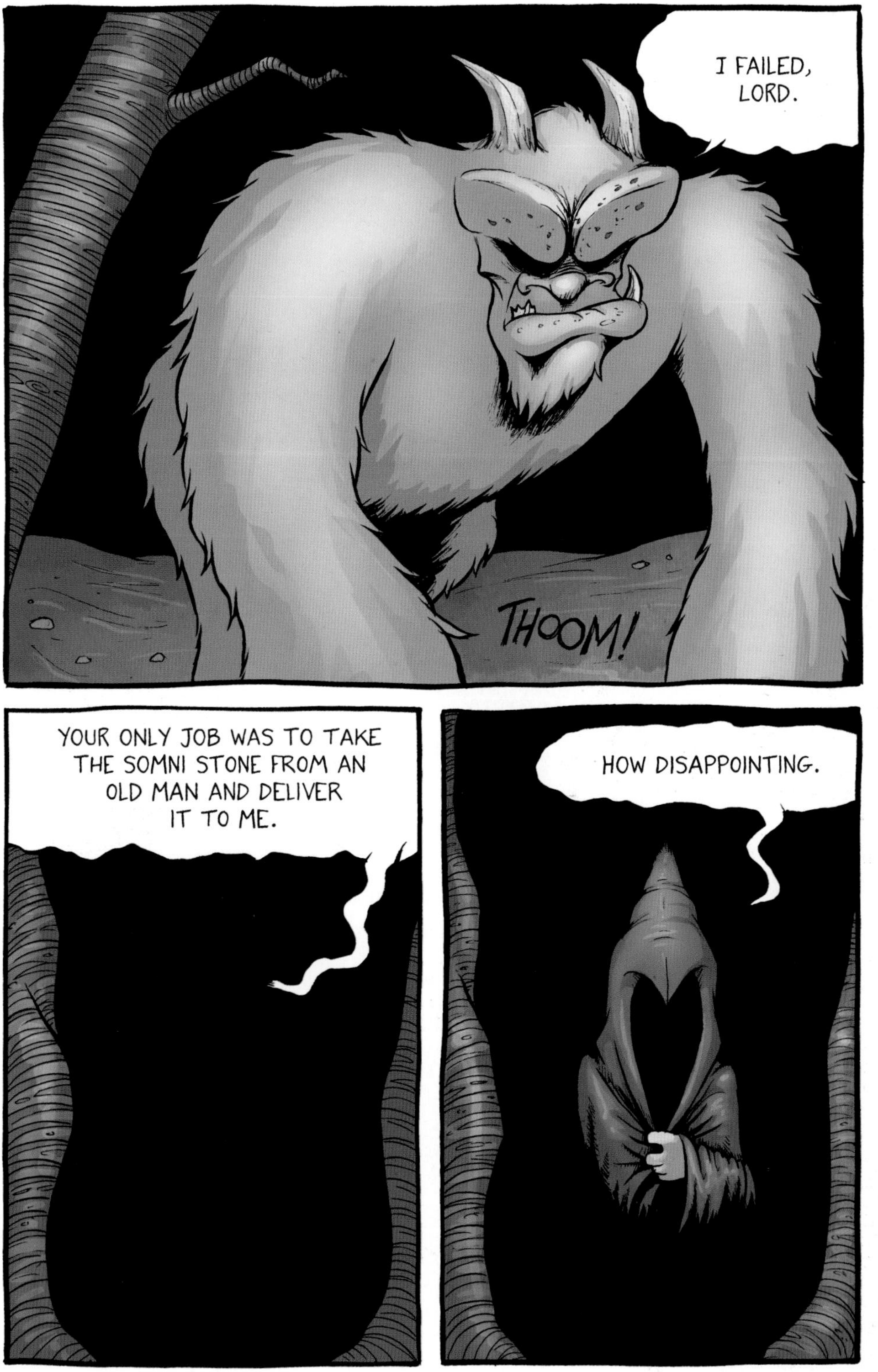
I FAILED, LORD.
THOOM!
YOUR ONLY JOB WAS TO TAKE THE SOMNI STONE FROM AN OLD MAN AND DELIVER IT TO ME.
HOW DISAPPOINTING.

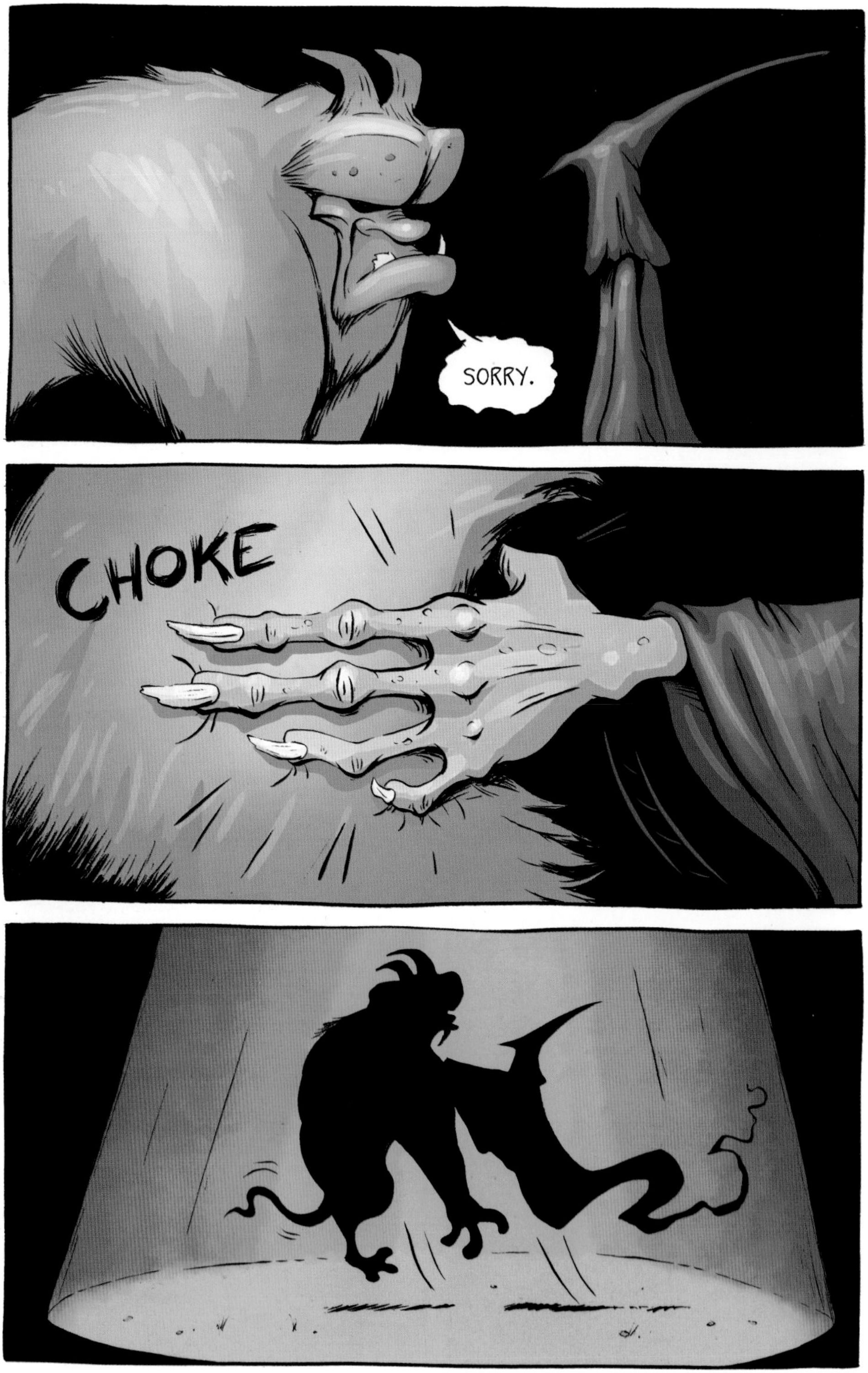
SORRY.
CHOKE

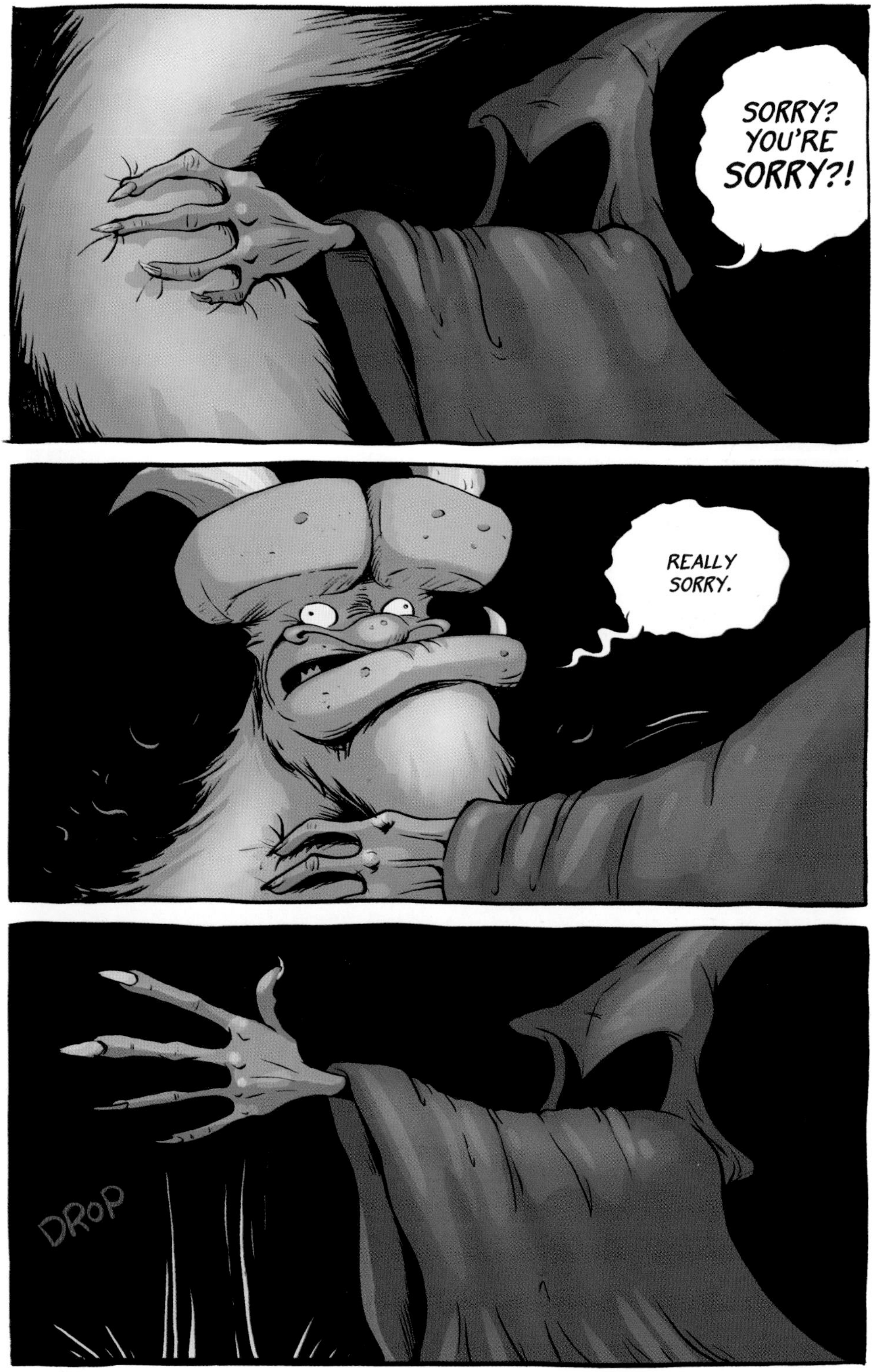
SORRY? YOU'RE SORRY?!
REALLY SORRY.
DROP

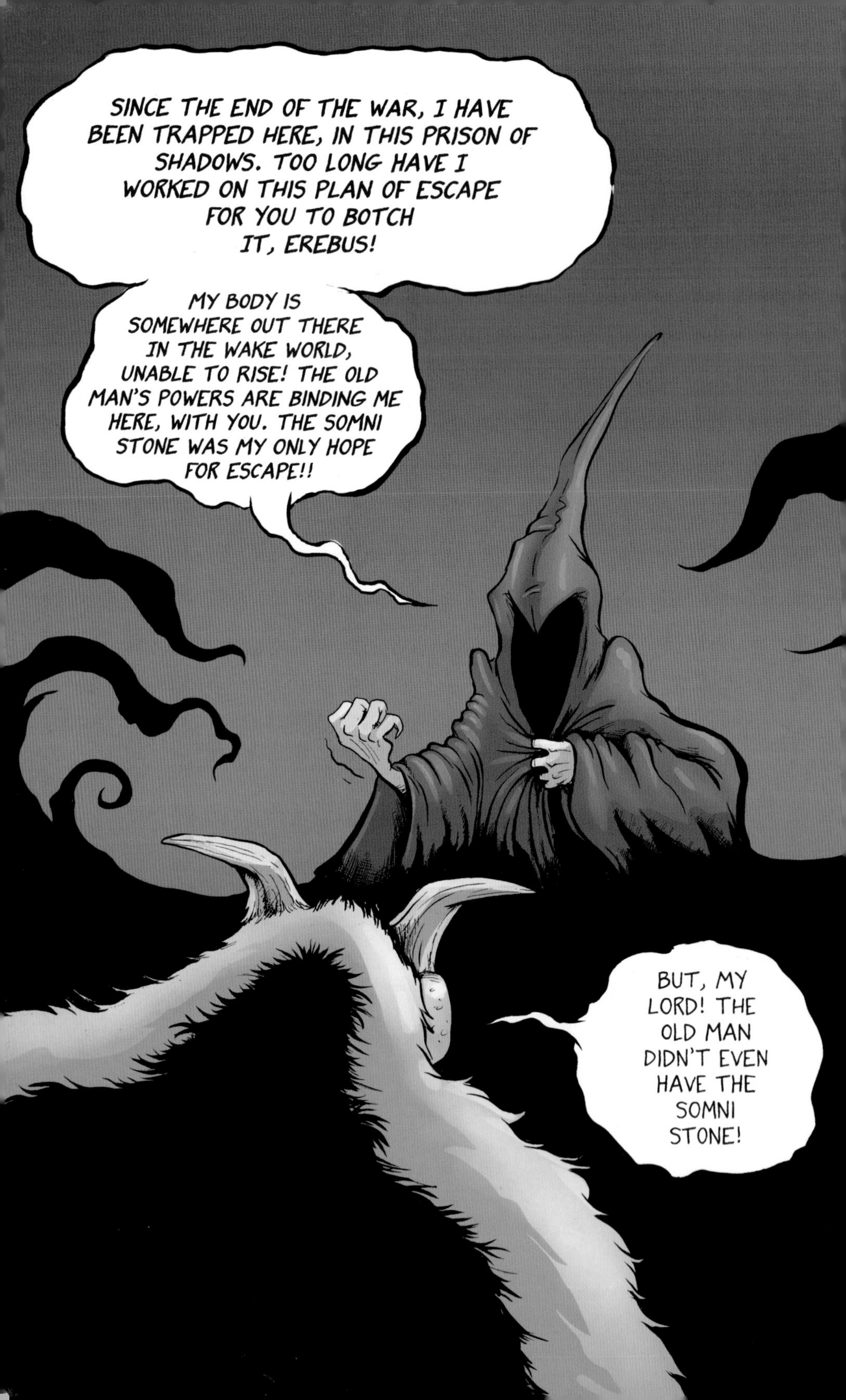
SINCE THE END OF THE WAR, I HAVE BEEN TRAPPED HERE, IN THIS PRISON OF SHADOWS. TOO LONG HAVE I WORKED ON THIS PLAN OF ESCAPE FOR YOU TO BOTCH IT, EREBUS!
MY BODY IS SOMEWHERE OUT THERE IN THE WAKE WORLD, UNABLE TO RISE! THE OLD MAN'S POWERS ARE BINDING ME HERE, WITH YOU. THE SOMNI STONE WAS MY ONLY HOPE FOR ESCAPE!!
BUT, MY LORD! THE OLD MAN DIDN'T EVEN HAVE THE SOMNI STONE!

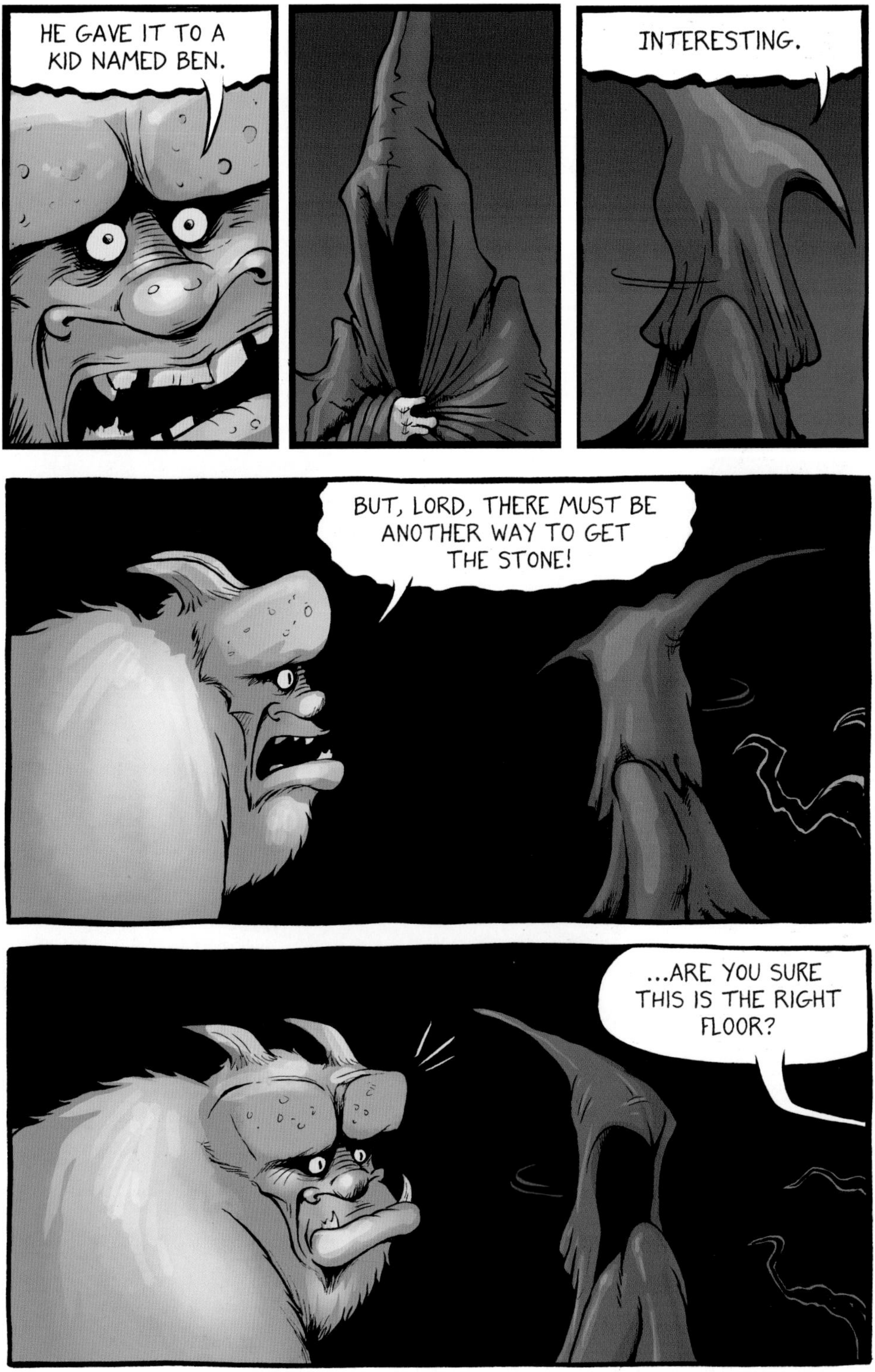
HE GAVE IT TO A KID NAMED BEN.
INTERESTING.
BUT, LORD, THERE MUST BE ANOTHER WAY TO GET THE STONE!
...ARE YOU SURE THIS IS THE RIGHT FLOOR?

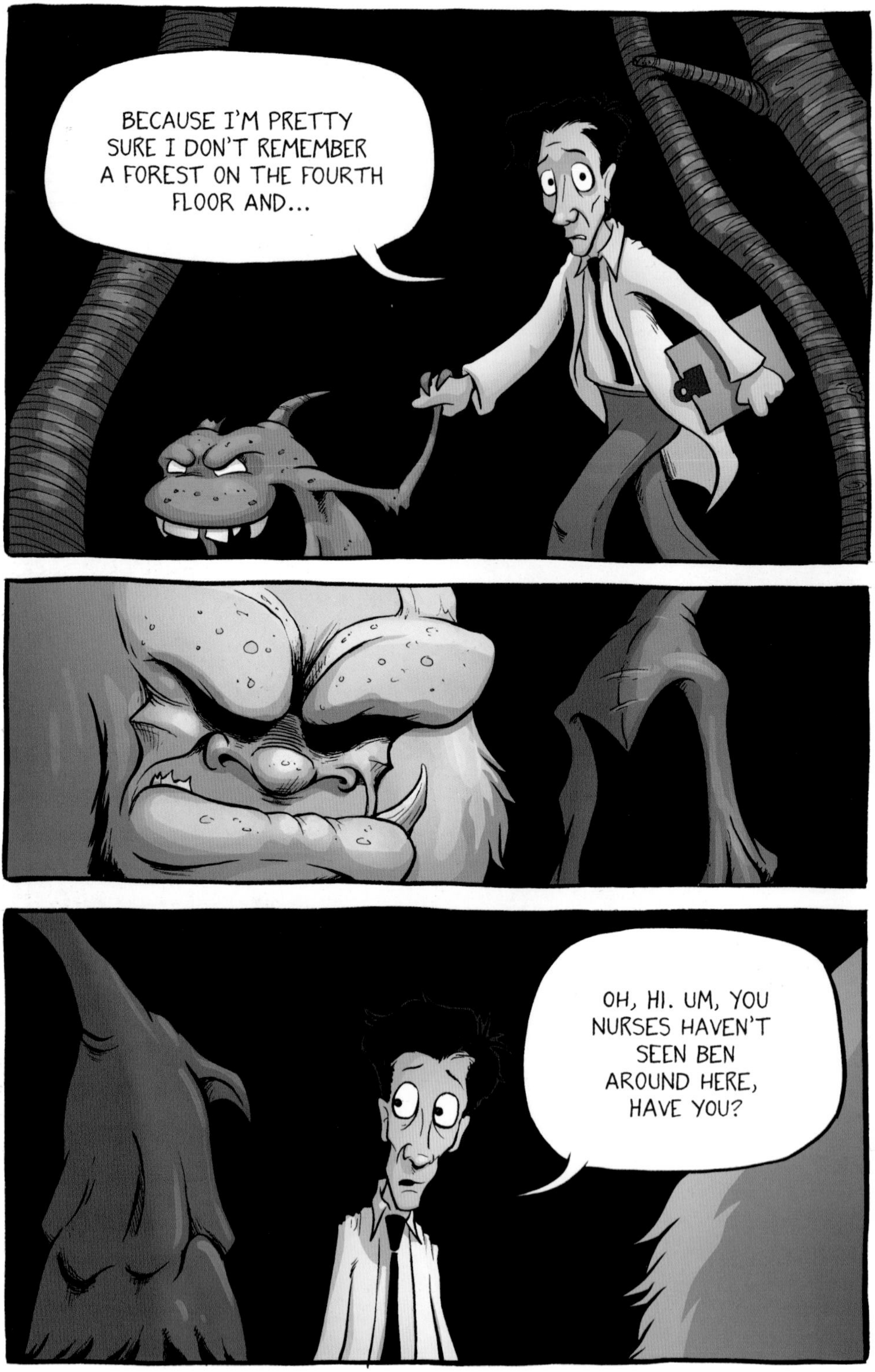
BECAUSE I'M PRETTY SURE I DON'T REMEMBER A FOREST ON THE FOURTH FLOOR AND...
OH, HI. UM, YOU NURSES HAVEN'T SEEN BEN AROUND HERE, HAVE YOU?

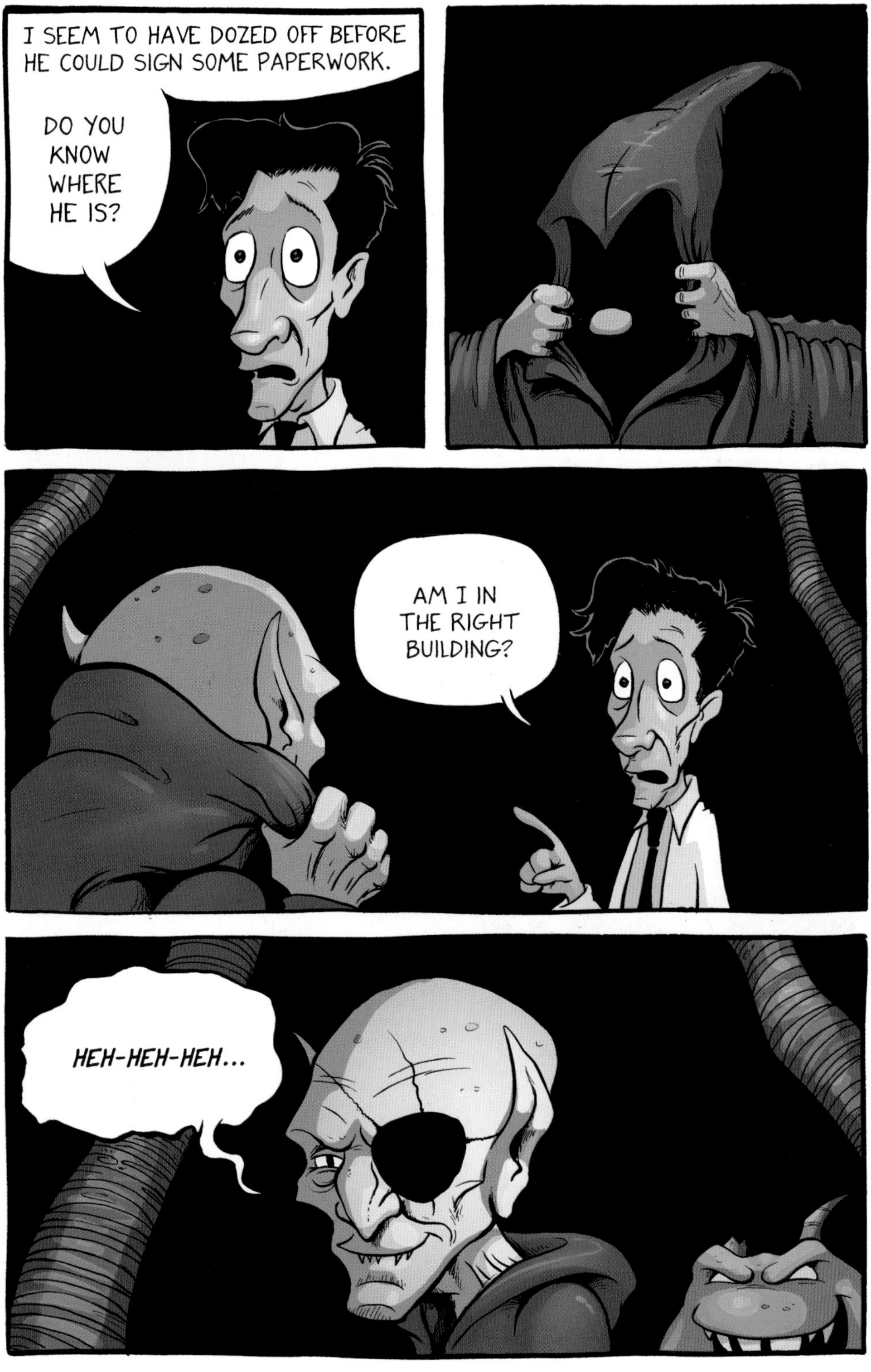
I SEEM TO HAVE DOZED OFF BEFORE HE COULD SIGN SOME PAPERWORK.
DO YOU KNOW WHERE HE IS?
AM I IN THE RIGHT BUILDING?
HEH-HEH-HEH...

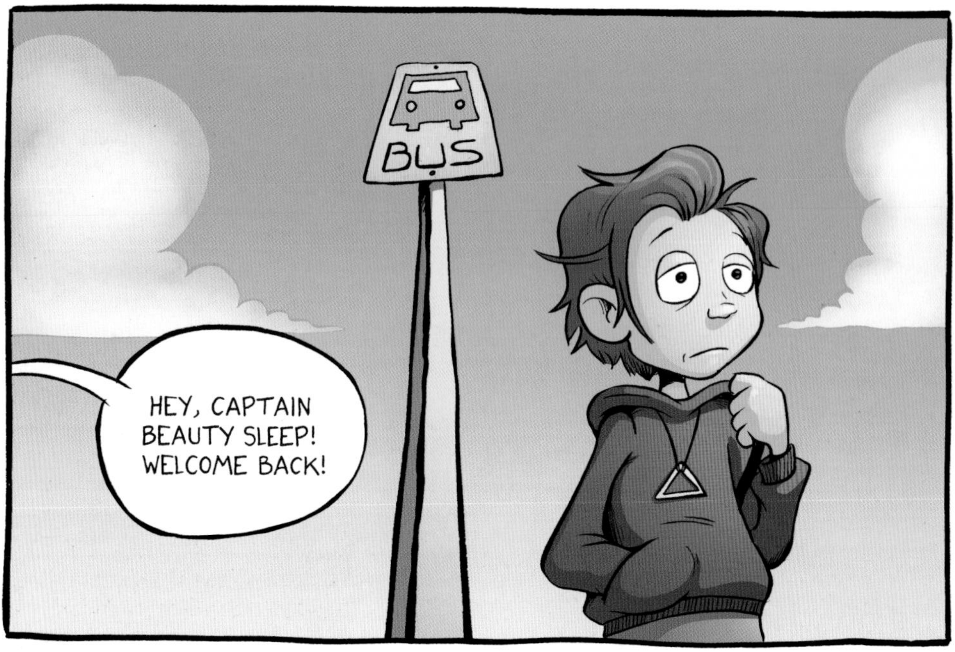
BUS
HEY, CAPTAIN BEAUTY SLEEP! WELCOME BACK!

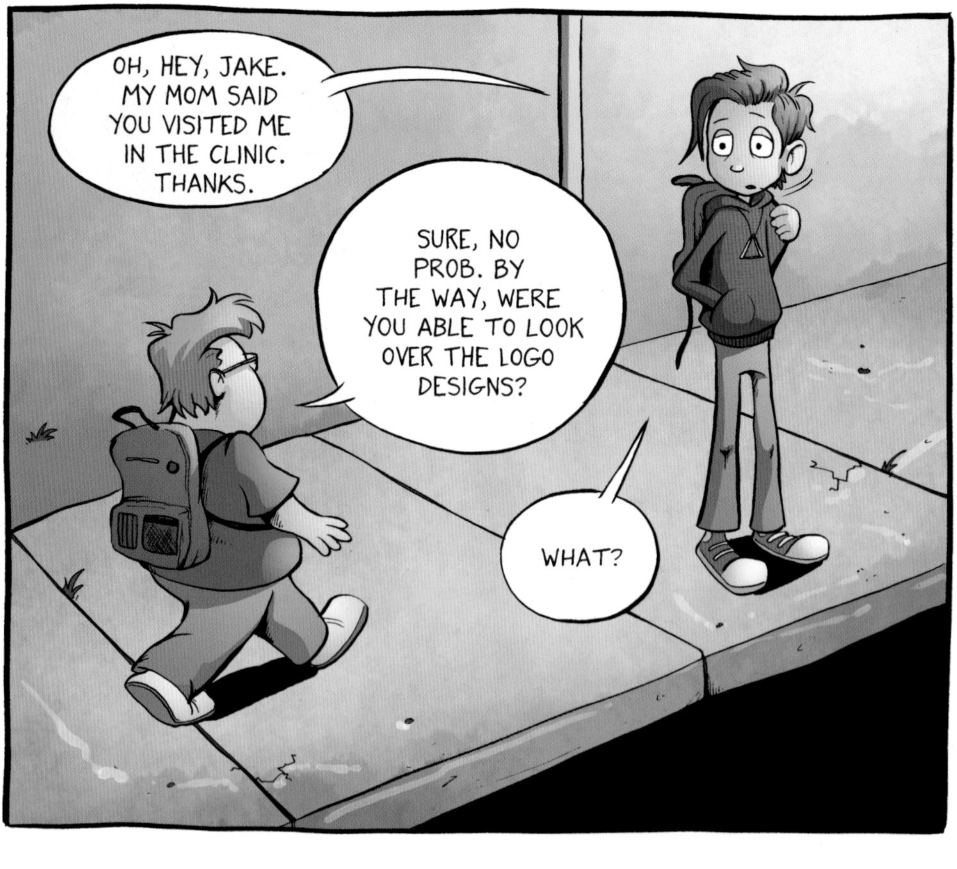
OH, HEY, JAKE. MY MOM SAID YOU VISITED ME IN THE CLINIC. THANKS.
SURE, NO PROB. BY THE WAY, WERE YOU ABLE TO LOOK OVER THE LOGO DESIGNS?
WHAT?

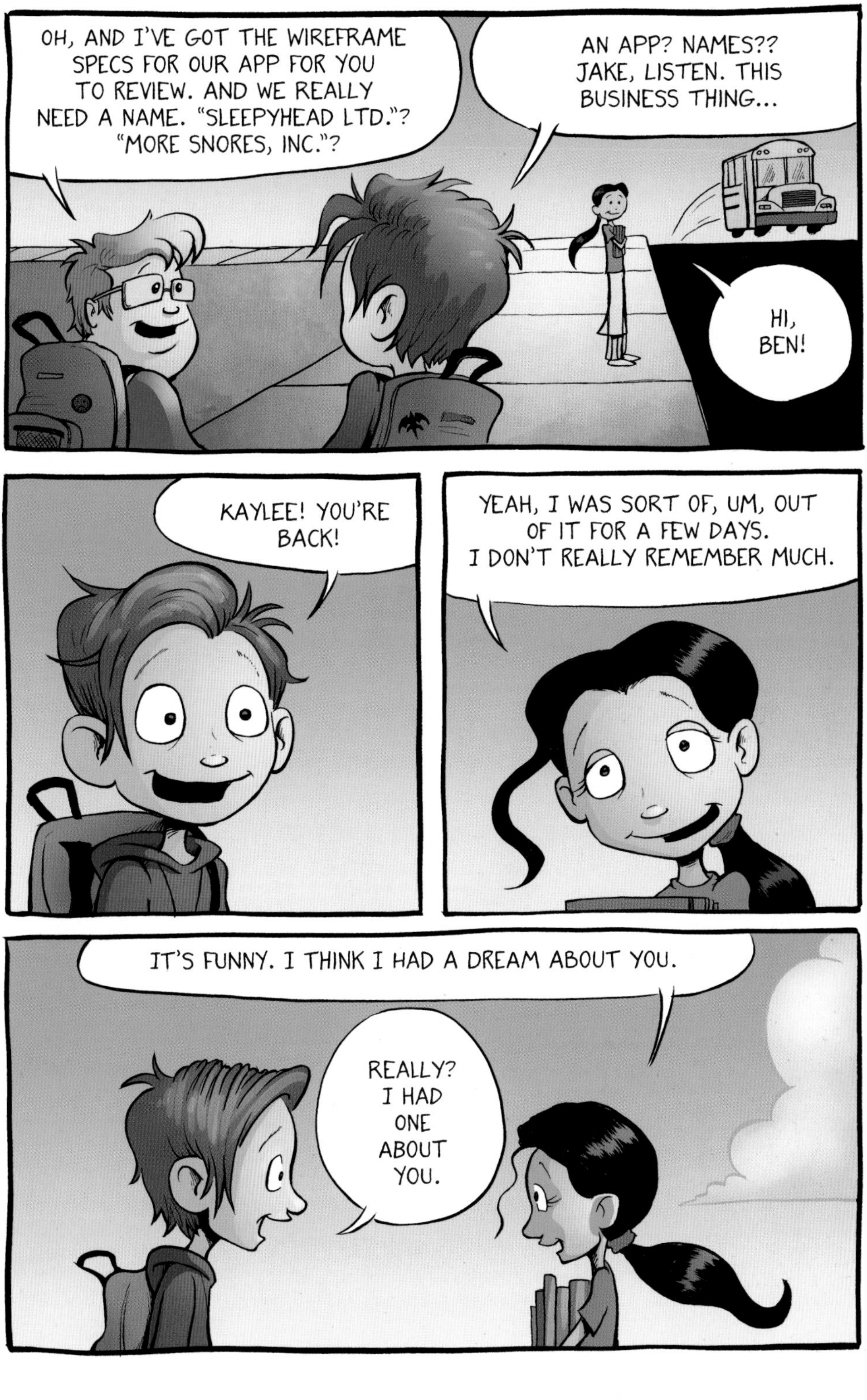
OH, AND I'VE GOT THE WIREFRAME SPECS FOR OUR APP FOR YOU TO REVIEW. AND WE REALLY NEED A NAME. "SLEEPYHEAD LTD."? "MORE SNORES, INC."?
AN APP? NAMES?? JAKE, LISTEN. THIS BUSINESS THING...
HI, BEN!
KAYLEE! YOU'RE BACK!
YEAH, I WAS SORT OF, UM, OUT OF IT FOR A FEW DAYS. I DON'T REALLY REMEMBER MUCH.
IT'S FUNNY. I THINK I HAD A DREAM ABOUT YOU.
REALLY? I HAD ONE ABOUT YOU.

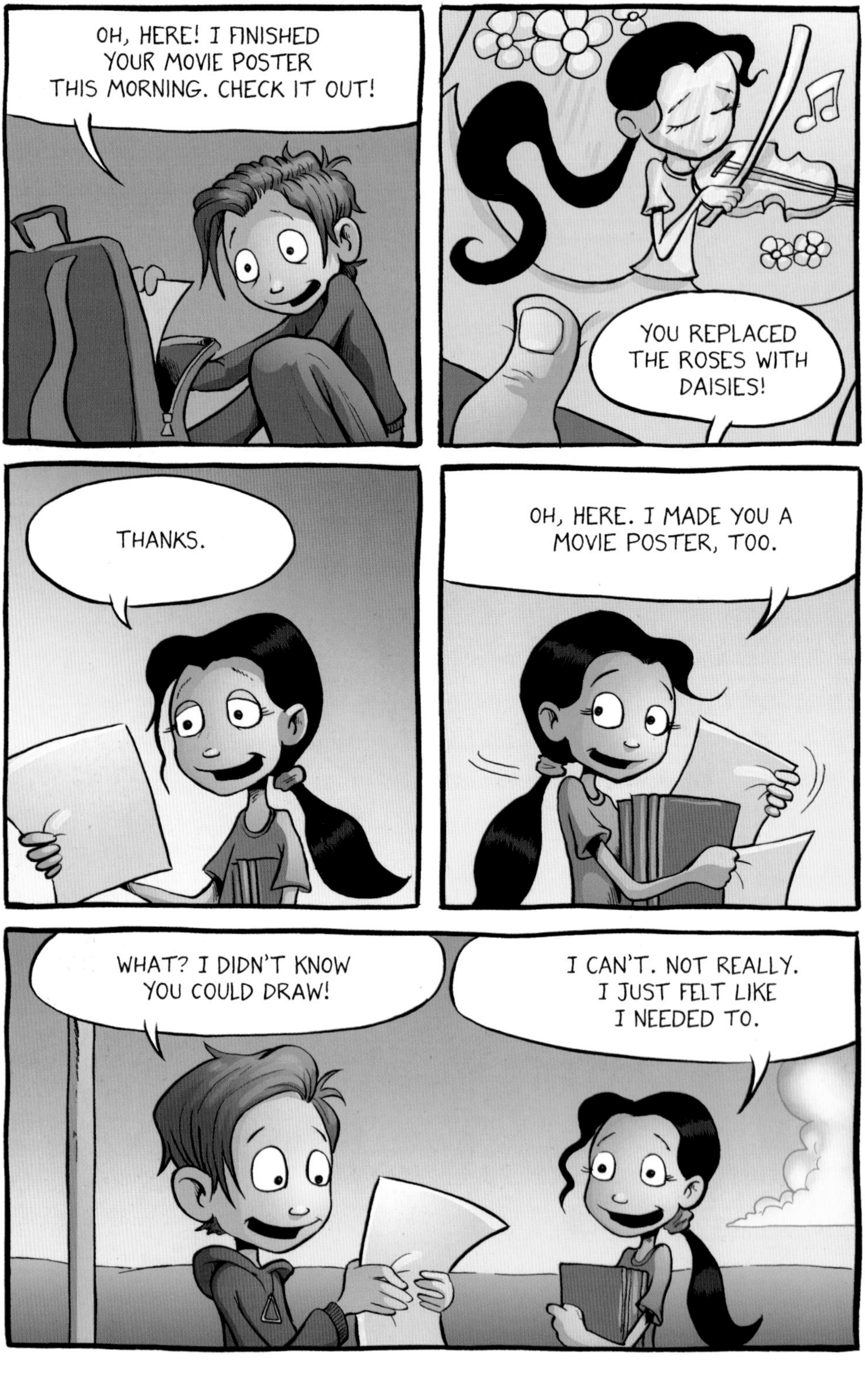
OH, HERE! I FINISHED YOUR MOVIE POSTER THIS MORNING. CHECK IT OUT!
YOU REPLACED THE ROSES WITH DAISIES!
THANKS.
OH, HERE. I MADE YOU A MOVIE POSTER, TOO.
WHAT? I DIDN'T KNOW YOU COULD DRAW!
I CAN'T. NOT REALLY. I JUST FELT LIKE I NEEDED TO.

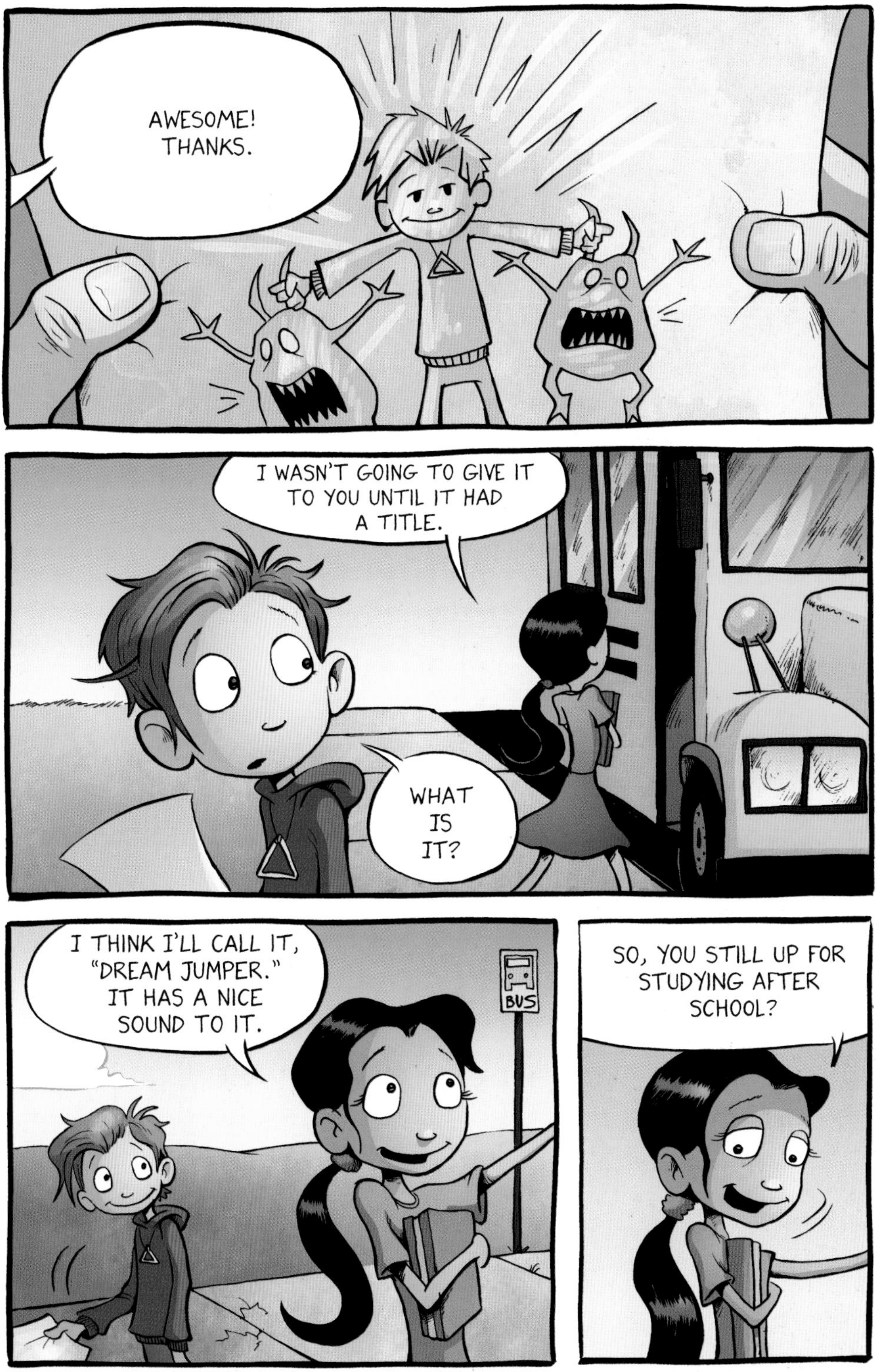
AWESOME! THANKS.
I WASN'T GOING TO GIVE IT TO YOU UNTIL IT HAD A TITLE.
WHAT IS IT?
I THINK I'LL CALL IT, "DREAM JUMPER." IT HAS A NICE SOUND TO IT.
BUS
SO, YOU STILL UP FOR STUDYING AFTER SCHOOL?

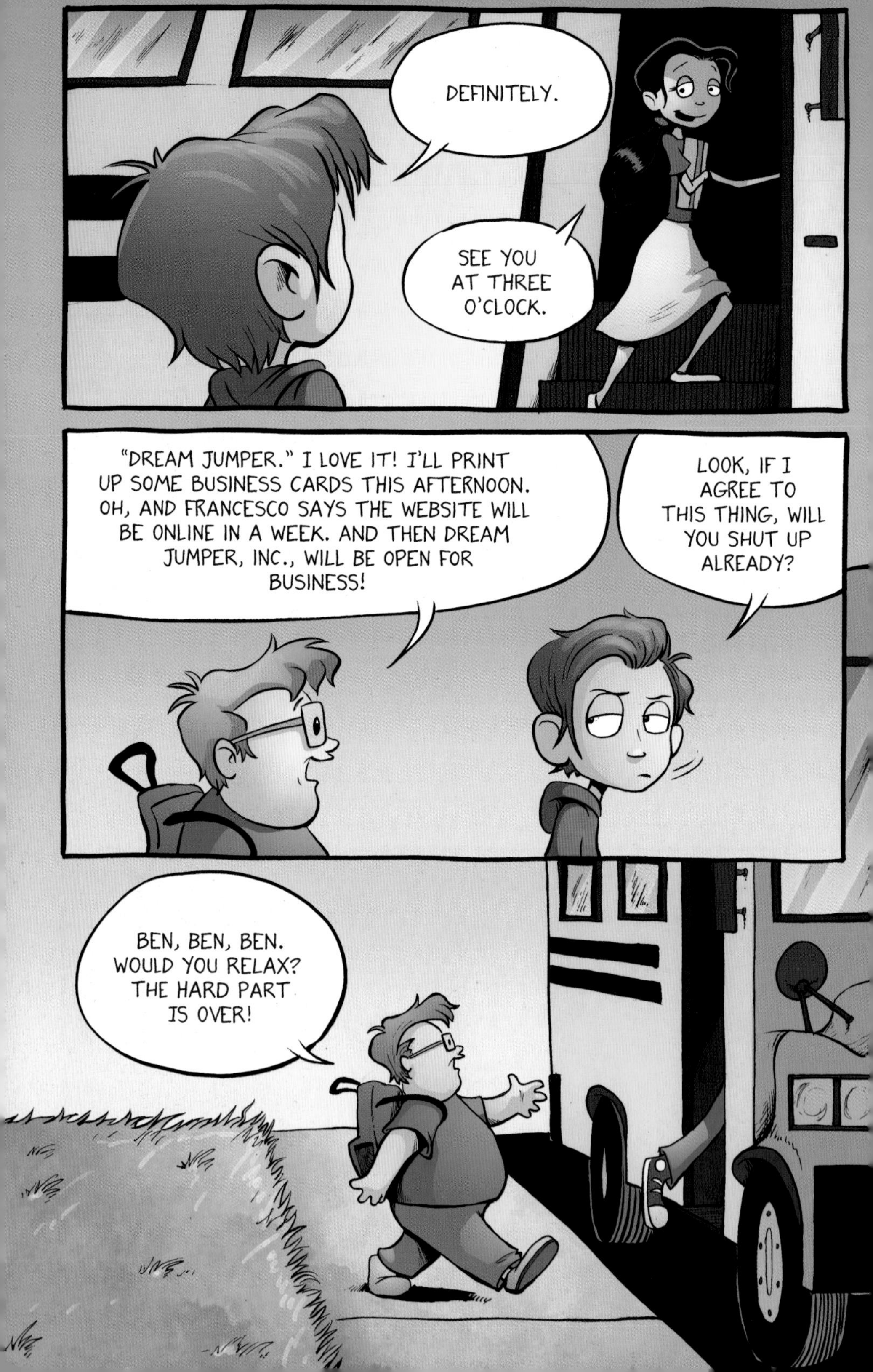
DEFINITELY.
SEE YOU AT THREE O'CLOCK.
"DREAM JUMPER." I LOVE IT! I'LL PRINT UP SOME BUSINESS CARDS THIS AFTERNOON. OH, AND FRANCESCO SAYS THE WEBSITE WILL BE ONLINE IN A WEEK. AND THEN DREAM JUMPER, INC., WILL BE OPEN FOR BUSINESS!
LOOK, IF I AGREE TO THIS THING, WILL YOU SHUT UP ALREADY?
BEN, BEN, BEN. WOULD YOU RELAX? THE HARD PART IS OVER!

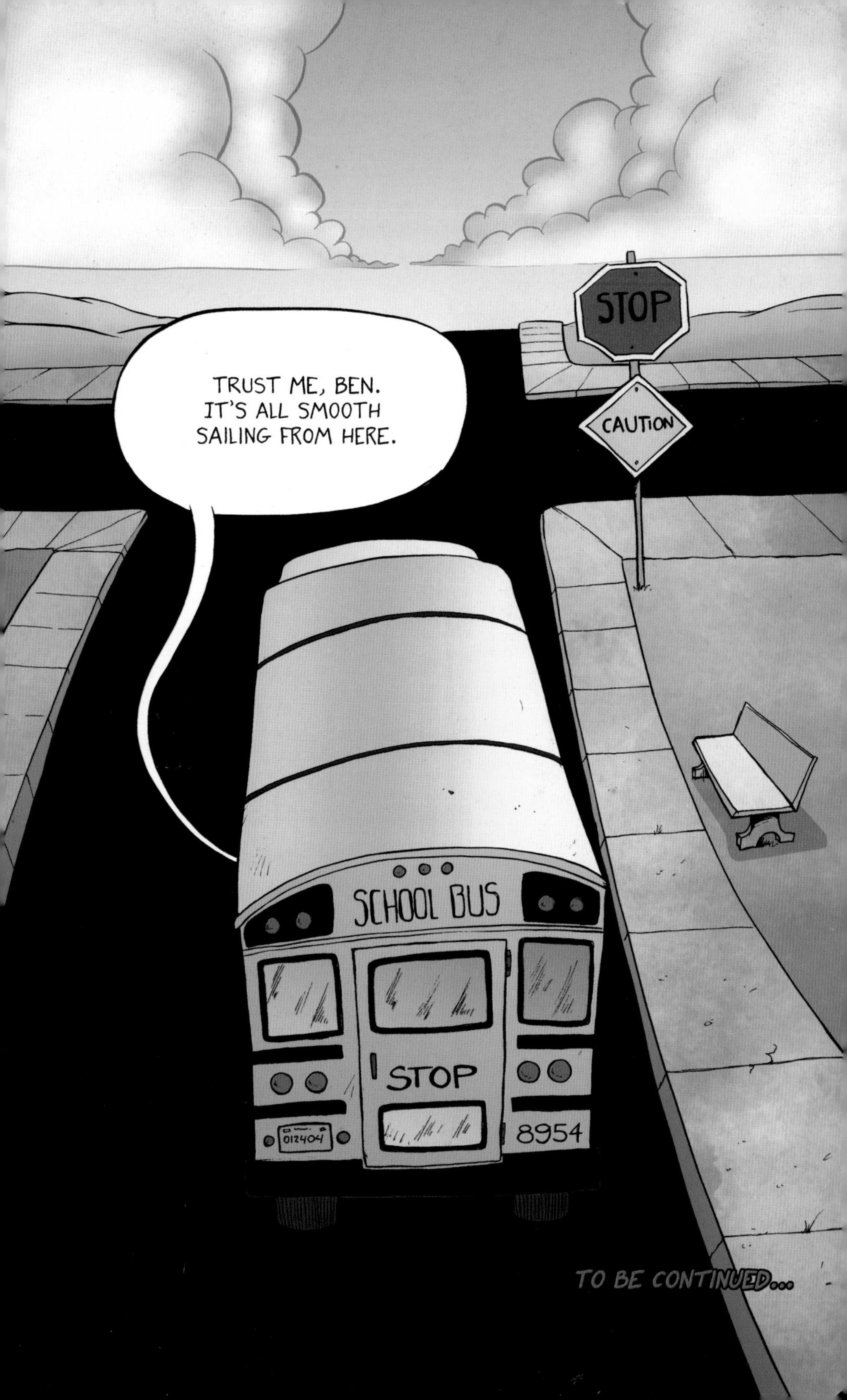
TRUST ME, BEN.
IT'S ALL SMOOTH
SAILING FROM HERE.
STOP
CAUTION
SCHOOL BUS
STOP
012404
8954
TO BE CONTINUED...

GREG GRUNBERG is best known for his acting roles in the award-winning series *Heroes*, *Alias*, and *Felicity*, and most recently in *Star Wars: The Force Awakens*. *Dream Jumper* is his first graphic novel and was inspired by dreams described by his son Ben. Greg lives in Los Angeles with his wife and three sons.

LUCAS TURNBLOOM is an award-winning cartoonist and illustrator who's best known for his comic strip *Imagine THIS*. He was a contributing artist for Dark Horse's Axe Cop graphic novel series. His work has also appeared in *USA Today* and on TIME.com. Lucas currently resides in San Diego with his wife and two sons.

GUY MAJOR has been a color artist since 1995 and has worked for Marvel and DC Comics. For Graphix, he was a colorist for the acclaimed graphic novel *Dogs of War* by Sheila Keenan, illustrated by Nathan Fox. Guy currently resides in Oakland, California, with his wife and Tae Kwon Do–loving daughter.